SECRETS AT THE AVIARY INN

MARYANN CLARKE

In memory of Darryl R. Stennnet
1944-1921
A warm, wise and funny friend, fellow writer, and possibly the very first fan of this book. (I think he had a crush on Sophie.) Thank you.

Secrets at the Aviary Inn

~

MaryAnn Clarke

Copyright © 2025 by Mary Ann F Clarke Scott

ALL RIGHTS RESERVED.

No part of this book may be reproduced in any form or by any electronic or mechanical means, including information storage and retrieval systems, without written permission from the publisher, except for the use of brief quotations in a book review.

Permission is not given to use any part of this text for training of AI LLM tools without express permission by the author.

This is a work of fiction. Names, characters, places and incidents are either a product of the author's imagination, or are used fictitiously, and any resemblance to persons living or dead, business establishments, events or locales, is entirely coincidental. MaryAnn Clarke Scott holds exclusive rights to this work.

Ebook ISBN: 978-1-988743-03-5
Print book ISBN: 978-0-9949507-9-6
Hardcover book ISBN: 978-1-988743-04-2

WANT TO CONNECT WITH ME?
www.maryannclarkescott.com
maryann@maryannclarkescott.com

All experience is an arch wherethrough gleams
that untravelled world whose margin fades
for ever and for ever when I move.

From *Ulysses* by

Alfred Lord Tennyson

CHAPTER 1

M *ay 21, 1997, York, England*

"Y ou're naive," they said. My parents, my big brother Matt, and Marc-Antoine too. But I wasn't as naive as all that. They saw something else in my nature. Idealism, maybe? I felt Marc-Antoine and I would part ways someday. Just not quite yet.

He may not be the perfect boyfriend, but I could always count on Marc-Antoine to teach me something—about life, about myself. He'd opened a lot of doors for me. Like this summer in England, even though he'd have preferred Paris over Yorkshire. Maybe what they called naiveté was more idealism, and stubbor-ness—the kind that led me here, determined to unlock the mystery of why my mother erased her entire childhood from our family story.

I watch the seduction unfold, at first content to observe Marc in action. The leggy blond Scandinavian thinks she's the aggres-sor, the way her hand punctuates her passionate words by patting and smacking and, occasionally, resting for annoyingly long moments on his hard thigh. He doesn't mind. She doesn't even notice his black-denim-clad knee pressing into her long, lean leg with enough pressure to indent her firm flesh.

From where I stand a few feet away in the noisy pub, I even detect a bulge in his jeans. He is aroused. But it's how he draws her in like a mesmerist, with his intense dark eyes locked on hers, his sensual mouth in a beard-shadowed face, his Gallic expressions, his exaggerated shrugs, emphatic hands, and his sharp, curious mind. The way he juts his chin forward and leans in when he listens, and his full sensual lips when he speaks. The way he loses himself in the moment.

My mouth twists in a bemused smile, and I wrap my arms around my midsection and silently wheeze with laughter. He has the same effect on me, I'm aware. I wish I had someone to share the joke with so I could laugh out loud.

But this isn't Marc-Antoine's story. It's mine. It's about how I'm drawn to people, curious about them, and involved in their stories. How they got to be the way they are. I guess you could say this is my weakness and my forte. I'm a writer, or truthfully, I'm going to be.

Marc-Antoine may not be the perfect boyfriend, but he is smart, he's exciting, and for now, he's mine. He's also my ticket to travel the world and experience life for myself, free from the stifling yoke of my family's well-meaning but overprotective control. Not that they approved of this trip at all. It's just over a week since I flew to London with Marc, and the bitterness of my departure still burns.

It isn't about sex with Marc. Not always, not exclusively. He's an architecture grad student. He's seduced by ideas, and by pretty things. Pictures and buildings and objects and girls. What I can never be sure of is whether it's the ideas they discuss so fervently that get him going, as he claims, or the close, personal presence of a stunningly beautiful Scandinavian practically touching his privates, and all that other stuff is for show.

Okay. This seduction is getting out of hand. He's really losing himself, and it's a bit nauseating. Watching Marc be Marc is fascinating, but I'm not interested in losing him. This sideshow is making me as green as the North Sea that brought the Vikings to England, and across the Atlantic to my home in Canada.

My facial muscles tighten. A heavy pressure sits on my chest and my throat wants to close, choking off any imagined words of protest, which would be futile, anyway.

Crossing my arms over my chest, I exhale and close my eyes. Don't overreact, Soph. He can't help himself.

"What's your name?" I flinch. One among the group of animated European architecture students that Marc has latched onto has broken away and is now leaning over me, barking in a strong German accent. He has too much unruly, thick brown hair and a hard, conceited face. His breath smells of sour hops and his German accent is quite hard and intimidating.

"Sophie."

"Zophie. Beautiful."

Who asked you? I suppose I should be civil, though I am so done with this scene. "And you are?"

"Ruff!" he barks in my face.

I flinch and draw back. "Pardon?"

"Ruff!"

I squeeze my eyes tight and open them, straining to hear through the music and voices and clinking glasses. There is no way I can infer a name from the coarse sound he just made. I shout back—a hint. "I'm sorry. I don't understand!"

He looks cross, his heavy brows hunkering down over dark eyes. His lips press together. "Vulf!" he shouts the word so the people around us turn and stare, questioning.

"O-oh." I nod finally. "I get it." I smile—a concession towards civility, but he squirms a little. Then he barks again, apologetically, "I go get another beer. You want something?"

I shake my head with a don't bother smile. "No. Thanks."

I'm relieved when he disappears into the crowd, and I turn my attention back to Marc and the Swedish blond, now leaning against his shoulder, her hand on his back. I follow the line of his rapt sight, right down her low top. Air rushes out of me, and I grit my teeth. Enough is enough.

"Marc, can we talk?"

Marc doesn't respond at first, and I have to jiggle his shoulder, elbowing myself between them. "Marc. We need to talk."

He looks up and graces me with that gorgeous, generous smile, slipping a hand around my hips. "Cherie! There you are. Are you 'aving a good time?"

I scowl and narrow my eyes. My head throbs from the relentless noise. How can he be so self-absorbed that he would even ask? I want to return to the hostel and get some sleep. "No. That's the point. I want to go."

His lips fall and he leans towards the blond, excusing himself with a mumbled apology, and rises. We slip through the crowd towards the back hall and press up against a wall, trying to find a bit of privacy. "What's the matter, cherie?" His voice is a seductive whisper, but I hear the note of irritation in it; I've interrupted his flow. He was in the zone.

"That girl's practically crawling inside your pants," I mumble, sulking, a burning sensation deep in my stomach. I don't know why I bother whining because this isn't the first time he's done this. Despite enjoying the past two years together, the forced proximity of traveling together, these past weeks has led to more bickering than intimacy. Yet, the way I see it, we're still in this together and owe each other something. Loyalty and consideration. I want him to care about my feelings. But we've had this conversation before, so I know what he's going to say next.

"Annika?" He exhales a gust of incredulous laughter, but his eyes dart towards the crowded room to my left, and he unconsciously shifts, adjusting his jeans. "No, no, you've got it wrong. We are jus' talking. She's brilliant, eh? We are deconstructing Deconstructionism." He laughs again at his own wit, but there is a hard glint in his dark eyes. "She 'as done a work term wit' Rem

Koolhaas, and Daniel Libeskind 'as taught at 'er school. She 'as some great story an' amazing idea!"

I twist my lips ruefully. Oh yeah, Marc, you're so cool. That's pretty much what I thought he'd say. Architectural theory apparently turns him on. My mouth is dry, my throat tight. Suddenly, I feel heavy, as though I'm trudging through quicksand. "I'm tired, Marc. I want to go back to our room. Tomorrow we're doing the Viking Museum, and I want to get up early."

He dispenses with the gloss of charm and his posture stiffens, his displeasure rising to the surface. He steps back and crosses his arms over his chest. "I can't go yet. D'is is what I love. You know dat, cherie. Dat museum can wait for another day. I don' care about dat."

"Well, I do! A lot. And it would be nice if, just once, you could be a little considerate of my wishes." I hear a quaver of nagging hysteria in my voice, and I swallow and grind the heels of my hands into my burning eye sockets. This little termagant is not going to get her own way tonight.

Marc rolls his shoulders and places his hands on my upper arms, dipping his head, tilting it to one side. His voice is soothing and seductive. "Come on, cherie. I make it up to you. 'Ow can I know dis opportunity come, eh?"

I twist out of his grasp, impatient with his diplomacy. "Do you have to jump on every bandwagon that rolls into town? Can't you and I just be our own show sometimes?"

His eyes glower and he shrugs. A huge shrug. A shrug with huge attitude and arrogance. "You want independence, eh? Isn't dat what you fight with your family about? Dat's why you come wit' me, no? But you 'ang on me like a leech. You can't do anything without me. I'm suffocating!"

I suck in a deep breath. My heart thumps, slow and hard, filling my chest, aching. The way he dismisses me and my conflict with my family hurts. He doesn't understand at all. I love my family. It's just that things at home got ... unbearably heavy. With Mom leaving Dad in some kind of angry menopausal funk, Dad moping like an abandoned dog missing her, Matt trying to soothe everyone from afar, telling me what to do and say, it all got to be too much. Really, I want everything to go back to the way it was, though I know that can't be. This trip is about more than escape … it's about figuring things out. Figuring me out. What's happening with my mother, and how her secretive past factors into this upheaval. Where I belong in all of it and how to go on.

I take a stiff step back. Ignoring my gathering tears, I press on. My words come out one at a time, barely squeezing through my tight throat. "I. Just. Want. To. Go. To. Bed."

A flash of remorse skips across his dark eyes like a pebble on the surface of a pond, then sinks. He shrugs again, less emphatically, but he can't slough off the resentment. "You better go back, den, 'cause I'm not done here. I'll see you later." Jerkily, he bends to plant a kiss on my cheek, and I shove him away, turning, my nostrils flaring and eyes burning.

Trying not to dwell on the fact that he has no qualms about sending me out onto the dark, foreign street alone, and what that says about him, I hitch my bag over my shoulder and push through the crowd, eager to leave before the hot tears erupt.

When I awaken the next morning, Marc-Antoine is not in the room. At first, I assume he's gotten up early, grabbed a coffee, and gone out to photograph some edifice in the morning light. But then I recall he stayed at the pub after me and would likely be tired and hung over.

Then last night floods back, all the details. My frustration. Our quarrel. His cruel words. I sit up and rub my sleepy eyes, swollen and hot from crying myself to sleep. Again. I should grow a thicker skin. Or fall in love with someone who's not a self-centred, moody artist. He's probably pissed with me for being so high maintenance.

My eyes snap to a torn sheet of paper from Marc's sketchbook lying on the floor near the door. I can see his dark, boxy lettering. My scalp tingling, I rise, shuffle over, and pick it up.

Cherie—
Don't worry about me. You want independence? You have a little taste. Do your own thing in York for a couple days. See some Vikings. I get a ride with Annika and Vulf. We don't bore you with our ARCHITECTURE stuff. I come back and take you to Stratford and Bath like you want.
X,
Marc-Antoine

Oh, Marc. What have you done?

I blink and look around, my breathing arrested. He came back? And left? His backpack is gone.

No, wait! What?

My heartbeat is suddenly fast and hard, whapping against my rib cage like a trapped bird. I crouch on my haunches and grab the backpack on the floor by the bed. The one without the green ribbon. This is *his* backpack!

I whip my head back and forth, scramble to search under the bed. My backpack is gone. I rip his open and search, yanking out T-shirts, boxers, his shaving kit, tossing everything onto the bed. In the bottom, a spare pair of black jeans, a cotton turtleneck. Nothing else. Marc, you idiot!

My legs wobble and I sink down to the floor. There's a roaring in my ears. He keeps his money and passport in his money belt. I keep mine in my backpack with me always—I set his down, my hands shaking, remembering the emergency cash Dad handed me the night before I left home, along with his words …

"I'm disappointed in you, Sophie, running off like this when Mom

needs you. I'm still hoping you'll come around by morning. But if you insist on going, well ... Take this." He pressed a blank envelope towards me. I could feel a thick wad of bills inside. "I don't want any harm to come to my little girl." He kissed my forehead and turned to go, then over his shoulder he said, "*Oh—don't mention it to your mother, eh?*"

Mom would've had a fit if she knew. She was hysterical that I dared go travelling without their permission. Worse, that I would dare to go poking around in York, where she was born, the place from which she'd fled as a young woman and never looked back. And worse yet, that I would leave with someone they despised.

Mom. We'd all been tiptoeing around on eggshells this year. She's been morose, cranky, critical, and then she had insisted on time away from Dad. He's been cowering like a kicked puppy and my heart hurts for him, camping out in Aunt Em's spare room, hoping things turn around. With Matt working in Ottawa and me in Toronto at university, there was no one home to intervene. Or help. Or anything. Though I don't know what any of us could have done about it. It just made me so sad and frustrated I couldn't stand it anymore.

I'm not sure I even care what they think of Marc-Antoine. Maybe they were right, after all. But I had to get away from it all.

My face and ears are hot, my throat tightening as tears build and overflow. There was something about Marc-Antoine they couldn't tolerate, and he was the subject of many, many arguments over the past two years. It burned that they didn't trust my judgment about men, or about anything else. They couldn't trust me to take care of myself.

But I trusted Marc. Sure, he can be selfish and impulsive. But he loves me. Once he realizes he has my passport and money, he'll hurry back. Won't he?

CHAPTER 2

The yellow-brick York police station on Acomb Road is a little dive of a place. Obviously, this isn't the primary station. I can see bars through the archway behind the beat-up front desk. It looks like they have just one cell, enough to contain the occasional delinquent or temporarily lost soul. My problem is not a lost soul, however, but a lost person. Marc-Antoine.

"Pardon me?" I say, squinting, as though this might improve my hearing.

This crazy Yorkshire dialect is giving me a migraine. I thought, with my mom growing up here, that I'd find it familiar and easy to understand. It's neither. Whatever my mom has, it's only a faint memory of the locals' speech.

A heavy-set grizzled cop leans back and props his booted feet on his desk, repeats some indecipherable gibberish. All aahs and oehs and ems. Like a guttural singsong.

My eyes slide over to the younger cop, with his traditional bobby hat and underbite, who's standing over a clipboard at the front counter. "Pardon?"

"He could come back any time. There's nowt we can do for a week," he translates.

I'll starve! "Yes, but maybe he … What if he can't come back?

He might have been mugged. It happens to tourists all the time." Who were those students he left with, anyway? I shake my head hopelessly. "If you don't look for him …"

The old cop glowers at me through his prickly brows, his nostrils flaring, impatient, and he shuffles his papers, muttering.

He reminds me of my great-uncle Adrian, so you can't get a word in edgewise. Except for his speech. My family, at least, I can understand. I answer with a blank stare at his assistant.

"'E says we can't file t' missing person's report since he's left you a note. But we've made a record of it. Go home, we'll contact you if we hear anything about yer boyfriend, lass," says the younger cop.

"But it's been over three days. He said he'd be back in a couple of days!" The note of hysteria builds in my voice. They're actually not going to help me. I don't believe it.

He shrugs. "Can you leave a number to call?"

"I'm at the youth hostel, the one on Water End. But I can't stay there long. I have no money. Marc-Antoine took all my stuff! I had hundreds of pounds, a train pass, airfare home. And a passport!"

"But ye won't report a theft," deadpans the bobby.

"Because it was an accident!" I'm sure it was. While Marc wasn't eager to linger in York while I did my research, I'm sure he'd never leave me ham strung without money on purpose.

The old cop grunts and rises from his desk, trudging his heft around the counter. He leans back with his arms across his brass-buttoned barrelled chest. "Aye, aye, an' so tha said. If Ah was tha fayther, lass—"

I grit my teeth, huffing with exasperation through my nose, and glare at him. "I'm not a child!"

He stops speaking and glares at my insubordination.

I blink and roll my swimming eyes up at the glaring fluorescent lights suspended from the ceiling of the Spartan police station and inhale deeply. I won't cry in front of them.

He's not totally unsympathetic. He pats a big heavy paw on

my shoulder, and it feels like I've been hit with a ham. "Tha must call up thy fayther and mam and get money fra ther an' get thissel doon t' 'igh Commission in Londontoon." He nods once, a punctuation mark.

Thank you very much! Clearly, he doesn't understand my predicament.

"I can't call my parents." I bite my lip. "I … uh, they're away right now. On a trip. I can't reach them," I extemporize. I won't call them for help. With everything they've been going through. Mom would go berserk. Not a chance.

He shakes his head, frowning and tugging on his long, twisting grey eyebrows. "It cap owt." He turns to the younger guy. "Am gan yam, Joe, lad. Shut t'wood in t'oil." He hooks his hat on his head and ambles down the back corridor.

"Aye, Chief. Good neet."

"What did he say?" I ask. I'm not sure he hasn't called me a rude name.

He turns back to me. "'E said 'e was goin' home and to lock up. Don't worrit, lass, summit'll come up. You'll see."

Back at the youth hostel two days later, I'm sweating between clammy sheets. Late May midday heat is building in my stuffy room—a co-ed room that Marc-Antoine and I checked into a week ago, and which I have now occupied, alone, for six days. It's idiotic to be lying in bed at noon under my circumstances, but I feel so heavy I can barely breathe. The air in the room is blue with emotion—anger, recrimination, guilt, worry, and fear.

Fighting the lethargy, I get up and dress, stepping over my discarded brown corduroys and sandals, marking the spot where I undressed last night, like the steps of a solitary dance lesson.

My eye catches the old black-and-white photo on the side table that I stole from Mom's drawer, and I pick it up. I suppose I can still investigate this while I wait for Marc to return. My secret quest. Marc doesn't know it's the main reason I wanted to come to York, my mother's birthplace. The only thing I know about her secret past. Two women, two kids, and an old building. In my gut I know it's the key … but to what?

I fondle the empty granola bar wrappers on the beat-up bedside table to make sure there are no worthy crumbs and slip the photo into my back pocket, along with my remaining cash— twenty pounds, seventy-some pence, at last count.

Reluctantly, I admit to myself it was no accident, and he's not coming back. I want to be bemused by Marc-Antoine's self-absorption, but all I feel is infuriated. How could he do this to me? How can he keep my backpack? He must realize by now he's left me in the lurch. He's a coward, a voice in my head insists. I've heard exactly nothing from the police.

I'll have to call Mom and Dad. No! I can't. If it weren't for Marc-Antoine, I would never have had the courage to defy them and come away on this trip to England on scant savings and borrowed money. To assert my so-called independence. I grit my teeth. Okay. Right.

Now Marc's gone, and I am truly alone.

My prepaid week at the youth hostel is almost up. I'll have to do something or perish, I decide, as I head downstairs to the hostel's canteen.

CHAPTER 3

Marmite! Again!
Euch!

Reluctantly, I help myself to a spongy square tile of white bread and a small plastic mystery packet with a yellow, red, and green peel-off label. I carry my plate and a cup of strong milky tea to one of the long aluminum and laminate tables almost fully occupied by other travellers. My scrape of metal chair legs on worn wooden flooring joins the chorus of skre-eeks, thumps, and murmuring voices that already echo through the hard cold room. I'm surrounded by international students, their heads bent over maps and guidebooks, planning their adventures, the way Marc-Antoine and I did a week ago.

I scrawl in my journal:

May 26, 1997, *York Youth Hostel*
Recipe for disgusting British breakfast:
One slice super-refined Wonder Bread
One thick smear smelly Marmite
Strong, bitter tea

. . .

I can't bring myself to eat it. I miss Mom's homemade multi-grain bread and strawberry jam. The sooner I can leave this godforsaken, inhospitable country, the happier I'll be.

Travelling to foreign lands isn't all it's cracked up to be. What, at first, seems exotic, romantic, and adventurous, with a modicum of familiarity, is merely discomfort, humiliation, inconvenience, and expense dressed up in the colours of a different flag.

I have to figure out how the heck to get home to Port Hope without money, ticket, or effing passport. By. My. Self.

"Oy. Ya gonna ayt that?"

I jerk my head up and meet the earnest gaze of an elfish raccoon with dark eyes and blue hair. Leaning back, I realize the girl is pointing to my uneaten breakfast, such as it is. "Probably not."

"Can I 'ave it?"

"Help yourself." I return to my journal.

"Whatcha writing?" She slides my plate closer to her and side-eyes my journal.

I sigh. Patience. She's just trying to be friendly. "My journal." I pull out a smile, stretch it, sit back. "You don't sound foreign."

"Oy'm not from Yorkshire!" She spreads the black goo.

I laugh obligingly. "Where's your home?"

"Souf-west. Bristol. I'm just looking round a bit before I got to work. I'm done schooling now."

"That's as far from Yorkshire as you can get in England."

"I guess that makes me a bit foreign, then, don't it? You American?"

I shake my head at the common assumption and set down my pen. Once you look past the hair and heavy eyeliner, she's nice. "Canadian."

"Oew." Now she's speaking through a mouthful of bread and Marmite, the black goo outlining her large, Chiclet-white front teeth. I blink at the image. "Where y'off to next, then?"

"Well. Nowhere anytime soon. I've lost my money and passport. I'm going to have to find some work here in York."

"Here, that's a problem, ain't it? Got anyfing lined up?"

I shake my head. I don't know where to begin. "I haven't got any papers. Nothing. Who will hire me?"

She chews and winks at me. Swallows. "There are ways."

The hairs on my arms lift. "What do you mean?

"I could hook you up wif someone who might help."

I hope she's not talking about something illegal. At least I mean not criminal. My mouth feels dry, and I take a big gulp of tea, scalding my tongue. I guess working as an alien is strictly illegal. But I'm desperate, and it would be only for a short time. "I need just enough cash to keep me going until my boyfriend resurfaces."

One of her pierced eyebrows lifts, but she doesn't ask. "I met some blokes t'other day in a used comic shop and internet café down in t'Shambles. They was talking." She nods. "Sounded like they knew what's what."

"What's what?"

"'Bout finding jobs what are"—she wiggles her facial features like Charlie Chaplin. All she's missing is a big moustache—"under t'table, so to speak." She provides enough details to find it.

Acutely aware of how far I've fallen, and how quickly, I thank her for the tip and head out, hoping I can find a way to survive that's not quite so sketchy.

M*ay 19, 1997, York*

I wish I were home. Or rather, back in Toronto, at university, with Kirstin and my other girlfriends. I never was great at being alone. I've always been drawn to people, but I've never considered it a weakness or insecurity until now.

Still, it's a relief I'm in England instead of Portugal or Latvia or God knows where. Then how would I find a job? In York, at least I speak the same language as the locals. Sort of. I'm almost getting used to the mélange of accents.

After walking south from the hostel to the historic walled city centre, I pass between the massive grey stone towers of Bootham Bar and stop, my heart thumping. The last time I walked here, only six days ago, Marc-Antoine was with me, spouting interesting historical facts from his architectural guidebook. At the top of High Petergate, a busker with a red goatee plays his sax under the bored stare of passing shoppers. The spires of the massive minster pull my eyes to where the narrow lane bends out of sight, but I know this street, or "gate," as they call them in York, continues all the way to King's Square.

At a blocky concrete and glass building on the corner, the landmark the girl at the hostel told me about, I pause. I wonder what Marc-Antoine would say about it. He would have loved it or hated it, that's for sure, and have a million erudite reasons why.

I turn down the lane and trudge onward, head down, mulling. I'm so not into the funky boutiques and antique clothing shops of the historic Shambles today. I'm searching for an internet café and used comic book shop called *Kapow! Kafe* and pondering my limited options.

My throat convulses suddenly, and unwanted tears well up, burning my tired eyes. I turn towards the display window of a clothing shop and blink, pretending to browse, but I can't stop the sob that escapes or my shaking shoulders.

How could he ditch me? After two years together? I believed he loved me as much as I loved him. Now I wonder if he cared for me at all.

Not that I wasn't warned. If I hadn't fought with my family, I'd have an easy way out of this predicament. Under normal conditions, I could call home collect and have money wired over. But things at home are anything but normal these days. The tension is so thick, a spoon could stand up in it. The way I left, with Mom and Dad recently separated, barely speaking to each other, never mind to me after our hurtful parting words, I'd rather die than go crawling back to their "I'm so disappointed in you" and "I told you so" commentary. Besides, I've already upset everyone enough. My condescending, bossy, and yes, all right, protective brother Matt would rip a strip off me.

No. I have to do this on my own. I have to prove to them that I can take care of myself. I'm so tired of people telling me what I should or can't do, as though I haven't got a brain in my head.

But God, I wish I could call Mom or Dad. Even Matt would be a comfort right now.

I catch a shadowy glimpse of a middle-aged sales lady through the glass; her height and grey-brown curly hair remind me of Mom. Suddenly, I need Mom's comforting arms around me so badly. What have I done? What a fool I am. I'm all alone here.

When I've blotted my tears and regained my dignity, I continue through the Shambles until I find the comic shop. A few geeky tatted and pierced guys hang around outside, smoking and talking, barely blinking as I approach. I slink into the cluttered interior and the elements fall into place. Small café tables are set up through the middle and against the windows. Cubicles, like in the library at the university, hug the walls with huge IBM computers in each one, rented by the minute, according to the posted signs. A coffee bar has a large shiny espresso machine and stacks of white porcelain cups.

To buy time, I stand at the counter and look around, eventually buying a cheap pasty. Then I see them, two guys sitting at a small table in the corner, talking animatedly. The one I'm looking for is the stocky one, with closely cut brownish hair and thick glasses. The other is small and nondescript. I sidle up.

Trying to catch his eye, I venture, "Simon? Simon Ware?"

They look up from the comic book they are jointly reading and frown at me. "Eh?"

I clear my throat. "Um. A … friend said I might find you here, and that you might be able to … um, help me out of a jam?"

Their eyes spark with interest, and I step a little closer, noticing his bad skin and a general stale odour of BO, cigarettes, and coffee. They just stare at me, so I continue.

"I'm not from here."

Blank stares. Obvious, I suppose.

"Right. So, I've been travelling and …" I chew my cheek a moment, trying to find the right words, then lower my voice. "And I've run into a bit of trouble. I need to make some quick cash so I can stay in York for a bit. While I wait for someone."

The stocky one sits up and squints at me. "Right. Sit down, then. I'm Simon." He doesn't bother introducing his friend.

I'm taken aback by his sudden friendliness. "Hi." I put out a hand. "I'm Sophie."

He gives my hand a brief, sweaty swipe. "What can ye do?"

My eyes widen and I shrug. "M-many things. I've got a BA." My eyes dart around. "I'm organized. Pretty handy." I'm at a loss. How can I respond when I don't know the calibre of jobs we're talking about? "I'm not too fussy at this point." God, they better not be pimps.

They eye me up, assess me, and exchange mumbled words that I barely catch. Presentable. Educated. Sales? Lovely rack. Waitress? Prissy, though. Bloody tall!

I press my lips together, waiting for some kind of verdict. What if this doesn't work? What if they can't help me? I feel my head getting hot, and an unpleasant mass congeals in my stomach.

"Bloody 'ell! Don't be starting with the waterworks, lass." They exchange concerned glances.

"I'm not," I gurgle.

"Shy, aye. We'll do something fer ye. Stop yer fretting."

"Nobody ever starved on Simon's watch, lass. Settle down," says the small one.

Simon works his fat lips a bit, chewing. "Well, yer best bet might be housekeeping. They don't ask so many questions. I think the Mayfair might be needing some help right quick."

My shoulders slump. Toilets and beds. Well. What can I expect? I sigh. "Is … is the Mayfair … a nice place?"

"Oy. Nice enough," Simon grumbles dismissively.

I get a jolt of nerves. We are actually talking about the same thing. "I lost my passport, right? You understand that I have no pap—"

"That's why yer here, lass. Obviously, ye wouldn't be talking to us if ye 'ad other options. I understand, ye're in a bad way."

Simon's sympathy increases my shame, and my efforts to fend off tears crumble as I long for Marc, or my parents, to swoop in and rescue me. My apparent lack of spine now that I have the independence I craved is humiliating. My lip trembles and my gaze darts around. I wish I could crawl under the table.

"Gaw. She be crying, Simon," whines the friend. They both cringe and glance at their laps, squirming. "There, there," Simon says and awkwardly pats my arm. They're just short of twisting their hankies, apparently so uncomfortable with my misery.

Suddenly defiant, I say, "I don't need your sympathy. I need a job!" I swipe at my dripping nose with the sleeve of my jacket, unsure whether embarrassment or despair is the greater cause of my tears.

They recoil at my short words and abrupt tone, and my chest tightens with instant remorse and worry that I've blown the deal. "I'm sorry. I didn't mean …," I stutter. "I'm in such a jam. My boyfriend left me and … and, I don't know why, but he took all my stuff. M-money, passport, everything!"

"It's always something," says Simon with a wise nod. "Life's like that."

Oh, to have such complacent confidence. They're so unworried. Unhurried. Maybe I've been too pampered. Too cloistered. I'm not tough enough for the world.

"Ye ask for Billy at the Mayfair. He'll take care of ye."

Humiliated, convinced I've outstayed my welcome, I thank them and hurry out the door, eager to escape their sympathetic stares.

From the comic café in the Shambles, I find the Mayfair hotel and my heart sinks into the cobbles underfoot. It's a skeevy dive. I can't even bring myself to cross the threshold. There are probably roaches under the beds. No way am I working there.

Disheartened, I pass on the Mayfair and seek out the official job centre to have a look around, skeptical they'll talk to me with no passport, work visa, or references. But I have to try every option.

It's not a very friendly place, cold and spare. An officious-looking matron in a lavender cardigan and large Lucite glasses sits behind a laminate desk and looks at me long and hard, making my skin tighten. Nevertheless, I mill about and scan the forms they require you to fill out, but clearly, there's nothing here for the likes of me. It's all too official.

The jobs I see posted on the boards are nothing to envy, anyway. In fact, they mostly suck. Except for office-type jobs at the university, the majority are in kitchens and cafés. A few housekeeping jobs, maybe at better establishments than the Mayfair, but I'm not convinced. Even those, I'm thinking, look appealing now. I'm so screwed.

"Is there something particular you're searching for, love?" the woman asks, and I turn. Her tone is gentler and kinder than I expected, and tears are again near the surface.

"Um. Something casual," I hedge. "I'm going back to school in September."

"Ah. I see." She rises and steps closer, and I get a whiff of talcum powder and lavender to match her outfit. "You're from away. Will you stay the whole summer?"

I bite my lip, considering. Would it be a big lie to say yes, if it meant survival? Who knows, anyway? "Maybe," I squeak.

"The university often has some clerical positions for a nice girl like you, with some skills," she probes, her eyes scanning the cards on the board.

"I … uh. I can type a little, answer phones. I'm very tidy and organized …" I'm stalling. "But … I have a problem."

She pauses, her clear gaze lifting to mine.

"I lost my passport."

She hums, clicks her tongue, and shakes her head, walking back to her desk. "I see."

I feel her dismissing me and in seconds, my throat closes up and tears well. Again.

As she sits and glances up at me, her chest filling as she prepares to speak, I start to blubber, spilling details about Marc-Antoine's sudden departure and the mixed-up bags. "And I have no money at all … or even a place to stay."

The tears are streaming down my face now and my nose is dripping. I rummage for a tissue or a paper napkin, anything, emptying my hoodie and pants pockets, dumping everything on her desk—stray receipts, coins, and hair ties.

"There, there, love." Calmly, she hands me a couple of tissues and I mop my face. "What's this, then?" She picks up the old photo of Mom's and studies it. I think she's trying to distract me from my woes.

"I don't really know. I found it in my mom's things. I'm pretty sure it's in York, though. She was born here. Right after the war."

"You don't say." She hums, studying the pic. "It's an oldie. Reminds me of when I was a girl. After the war. All the photographs looked like this, with the frilly edges." She runs a fingertip along the frayed scallops.

I pull myself together, tucking my odds and ends away in my pockets. She's still frowning at the old photo, one finger tapping the surface pensively.

"Do you recognize that building? I'm kind of looking for where my mom grew up."

"Hmm. Could be one of many terrace houses here. That style, those window details, looks late Georgian. Maybe somewhere up on the Mount?" Still pensive, she hums and hands it back to me, excusing herself while I blow my nose. I watch her step into a back office and make a phone call. She peers at me through the glass from time to time and I wonder if she's talking about me.

My suspicions are confirmed when she returns. "I might have something for you, love." She opens a drawer, rummages, and plucks out a dog-eared business card. "Ask for Ava. She'll help you out. I think this'll suit."

CHAPTER 4

Once outside in the bright sunlight, I walk briskly for one block and then stop, realizing I have no idea where to go. Peering at the card in my hand, I read:

The Aviary Inn on the Mount, 82 The Mount. Mrs. Ava Roxtoby, Proprietor.

A bubble of lightness forms in my chest, lifting, expanding. Hmm. Tourism industry again, hopefully a higher class than the Mayfair Hotel. What was I expecting? I'm desperate, but I'm no fool. I need food and shelter, pronto. This is an exciting opportunity.

I pull out my folded street map of York and scan for the Mount. Ah, there!

I head south, through the Shambles and past the Coppergate Shopping Centre where I notice a sign for the Jorvik Viking Centre Museum. That was to be the next stop on our tour of York. Setting my jaw, I promise myself I'll go there, anyway— with or without Marc-Antoine. Soon.

Under the canopy at the entrance, a bearded musician with straw-coloured dreadlocks tied back in a clump strums a guitar, reminding me of a more bohemian, earthier Marc-Antoine. Handsome despite all the hair. Leggy. My eyes well with tears again. I have a long way to go, but the busker's voice radiates warmth and comfort, and he draws me in. He turns towards me, and I'm struck by his piercing vivid green eyes. They seem to know everything about me. His brow darkens in a curious frown, as if he's trying to recognize me. Tearing my eyes away, I carry on.

I head across the bridge, stopping to catch my breath as I gaze along the winding River Ouse. The water meandering under the bridge is soothing and the air fresh. I'm tired already, and having barely eaten isn't helping. Remembering my pasty, I pull it out and take a bite. Fortified, I pass through Micklegate Bar, another of the medieval gates around this ancient city. Its twin grey stone towers, with their crenellated tops, rise above the passageway like hulking sentries, more shielding than sinister. Beyond the portal, the jarring contrast of a noisy six-lane thoroughfare, surrounded by the roar and oily stink of cars— Blossom Street. The modern city held at bay by the old wall.

The wide road climbs uphill. Within minutes, my thighs burn and I'm sweating in the summer sun. Great! I'll get to my job interview drenched and reeking like a logger.

I pause, hands on hips to air my pits while pretending to take in the view. Then I realize why they call it the Mount. I'm standing part way up a long axis with a spectacular panorama. As I spin around, Micklegate at the bottom of the hill, the entire city, its curved and jagged walls stretch out between the rooflines with their brick and terra-cotta chimney pots as far as I can see. The huge minster as well as the grey stone Clifford Tower on a mound of green to my right. The sparkling river meanders by like a sleeping silver serpent with its many bridges, and to the left, I see the ancient Roman Multangular Tower in a vast emerald-green park.

Everything is so beautiful and old and reminds me I've always wanted to live and work somewhere in Europe. England, or maybe Italy. For a while, anyway. Maybe rent a tiny attic garret and write my first novel. More than zipping around being a tourist. Maybe fate has taken a hand in my affairs. True, I'm registered for grad school in September, but a little life experience is essential for a writer. If not, what will I have to write about?

My mouth stretches in a more confident, optimistic smile as my mind begins to spin my current, unexpected circumstances into the beginning of a story. I imagine a character like myself, resourceful. I can do this. Working as a maid won't kill me. Who knows what interesting characters I'll meet, what stories they'll tell me? Maybe Marc-Antoine will come back with a thrilling explanation for leaving me alone. But whatever he does, I'll be able to say that I made the most of the experience. If I want my family to believe I can take care of myself, then that's exactly what I have to do.

At the top of Blossom Street where it turns into the Mount, I see it, and my heart lurches. A large grey stone house with pointed gables and fancy white bays and rows of chimney pots stands three stories tall with sloped peacock-blue awnings that read The Aviary Inn on the Mount. It looks like two terrace houses joined, and the house on the left is wrapped in vivid green ivy, with thick, creamy-white window frames and mullions with leaded glass panes peeking through. It looks like a fairy-tale castle, and I have to remind myself that old houses in England are, like, *really* old. Marc-Antoine would probably love it. Or maybe he would say it's kitsch and critique its details. I don't know and I don't care. I love it.

Somehow, this place, with rich historic details we don't have in the new world, embodies everything I lack but crave about my family's roots. A sense of history and belonging. All the stories that go along with that.

As I approach, some of the features start to feel familiar, and I recall the job centre lady said a lot of the old Georgian row houses were up here, on the Mount. Is that why she sent me here? I pull the old photo from my pocket and squint at it, shrugging. Only fragments of the building show in the background.

What if this is the one? Or one of its neighbours? That would be wild. I wonder how I could find out.

Taking a deep breath, I pull back my shoulders and stride up the steps to the elegant, pale blue entry door.

Inside, I stop to let my eyes adjust to the dim light and feel my heartbeat slow. It's silent as a church inside, with a sweet, musty smell, as if time stood still in here while the world marched on. Grand but shabby. Soothing but sad. It speaks to me as if it belongs to someone reluctant to let go of the past. Complex emotions suffuse me, swelling in my chest, heating my head, making me a little dizzy.

Under my feet, dark gold vines creep along a rich red carpet, threadbare in the centre. I step in and up two wide stairs, taking in my surroundings. The first thing I notice is a huge gilt frame on the opposite wall, around a shadowy, splotchy mirror. Beneath it, on a carved wood hall table, sits an ornate brass bird-cage, scratched and dented, as if it got hit by a bus. The cage is empty, with a taxidermy grouse mounted beside it on the table. A narrow red-runnered staircase leads up to the right, with a spindled baluster and balcony overlooking the lobby below.

"Can I help you, duck?"

I jump and spin towards the voice. This hushed and shadowy space seemed mine alone, but a young Black woman leans over a reception desk in an alcove to the left, watching me look around.

"Yes! Sorry. I was just ..." I wave an arm. "Is Mrs. Ava Roxtoby here? I've been sent over about a job?"

"Aow." She nods, as though she was expecting me. "Mmm-hmm. Moira's spot." Then she's gone and I wait. And wait. Catching my disheveled reflection in the sketchy mirror, I sniff my armpits and smooth back my frizzed hair. Maybe there's a ladies' toilet I could use to freshen up.

I spin around, taking in more of the entry hall. A dark, crackled oil painting of a couple of pheasants or some other wildfowl hangs in a carved wooden frame on the wall to one side. A large, less-than-fresh bouquet of creamy white tuberose and mums in a Grecian urn sits on a round table beside it, flanked by two mustard-coloured leather bucket chairs. The tuberoses still give off a powerful scent despite their faded, brown-edged petals. Far above me, the centre vault of a high-coved ceiling depicts faded clouds and more crackled birds in flight.

Even with the empty midday stillness, I can almost hear the echo of past guests, the din of many voices, the ghostly tread of busy footfalls. A blurry time-lapse film plays in my mind, complete with period costumes. A story starts to unfurl.

I wonder if she's ever coming back when an angular older woman strides into the entry lobby and peers at me. She has short, steel-grey hair dripping wet at the tips and she's wearing an old pink terry bathrobe. Is this one of the guests? She stops in front of me, eyes narrowed, and sticks out her hand.

"Ava Roxtoby. Excuse my attire, I was in the pool. Do we have an appointment I've forgotten?"

"Uh." I take her veined hand, and she grips mine with warmth as I look down at her bare bony feet in plastic slides. "No. Not at all. I'm sorry to disturb you," I say while she squeezes my hand in a friendly way. Oh. My name. *Jeez, Soph, don't be such a dweeb.* "Sophie Groenveld, ma'am. I came to inquire about employment? The lady at the job centre implied you might need help. Something about the desk?"

"Aah. Rose, yes." Mrs. Roxtoby presses her lips together and nods, her sparkling gaze studying my face carefully. "She sometimes sends me lost waifs and hard-luck cases."

Is that what I am? I can't speak for a moment, embarrassed by the truth of this statement. "I … um … I …"

Her knowing grey-blue eyes light up in a way that feels comforting and familiar. A wheezing series of coughs emerges from her thin chest, and I realize she's laughing. "Don't worry, dear. I'm teasing. But there's some truth in what I said. I can see it in your face."

I shake my head and shrug. "I only …"

"Come, sit with me in the lounge and we'll have a chat. Let's see what we can do for each other, shall we?"

~

I 've been saved!
Mrs. Roxtoby, the hotel owner, is so nice. She serves me tea and cookies—I mean, biscuits. I have to remember how to speak British English, I suppose. She orders the tea and a plump, red-faced woman she calls Cook brings it. Mrs. D-something. I've forgotten. Delbert? Delisle? Delicious?

I'm amazed. After a few probing questions about my background and situation, Mrs. Roxtoby offers me a casual job as a night desk clerk without any papers, seeming not worried at all about if I'm an addict or axe murderer. She seemed more curious about my hometown and family than my work experience. No toilets! Hurray! This is way better than I'd hoped for. Alone all night, I'll have time to dream and write my stories.

After Mrs. Roxtoby sends me off, the friendly Black girl I saw earlier leads me into the office area and speaks over her shoulder, her silky purplish-black bob swinging. I immediately like her.

"Are you sure I can't start tonight?" I ask. "I can, if you need …"

"We've go' a temp, right? Can't push her off now, can we?"

We squeeze into the tiny office and I take a good look at her. Zoë is her name, and she's as different from me as a girl can be. She's stunningly beautiful, with large almond-shaped amber eyes and sexy bee-stung lips, smooth deep brown skin, and a pointed chin.

"What you looking at?" Her accent is a little coarser than Mrs. Roxtoby's, but musical and tarty. I like it.

"You look exactly like Naomi Campbell," I say, stunned by the resemblance.

"Oh. That's right. Her short, fat twin sister, maybe," Zoë says, scorn twisting her beautiful face.

I wobble my head, grinning. "You're not fat. Those super-models are way too thin. You're gorgeous."

"You're my new bes' friend, you are," she says, pursing her full lips with suppressed mirth.

I stick out my hand, and she shakes it firmly. "Okay," I say. She's nice, and I could use a friend.

"I notice you didn't say 'You're not short, Zoë.' Not like you, eh? You're an Amazon, you are."

I make a face. "I'm not built like a supermodel either, though."

She laughs like a throaty song. Eh-heh-heh. "Bigger an' better. More to hold on to, my Ollie'd say."

Zoë shows me around the small office, quickly rattling off the locations of forms and office supplies, but I know I'll have to explore on my own later. Not only does she talk too fast, but the place is in total disarray. I'll have to tidy up a bit if I'm going to keep my sanity, but it's homey and comfortable. Perfect for me with Mom's B&B business under my belt.

"Right," she says. "By the time you start your shift at seven, there won't be many check-ins. An' probably no checkouts either." She shows me the procedure for checking in new guests, the big book, the cubbies with their big brass keys, and a list of emergency numbers and instructions. "Not sure what you're gonna do all night. It's boring enough during the afternoon."

I smile. "That's not a problem for me. I love to read and also write in my journal."

"Yeh? You're a writer? That's all right." She nods thought-fully. "Well, if you want to nod off for a spell after lockup at eleven, there's an old recliner in the back storeroom. No one'll bother. As long as you wake to the bell, obviously."

Right. Like I'd go to sleep on the job! "So, tell me about Mrs. Roxtoby. She seems nice," I say, hoping Zoë'll tell me more. During our interview, Mrs. Roxtoby was pleasant, watchful, but distant. Sort of perpetually distracted, although at one point when she looked into my eyes, nodded, and smiled, I felt a real connection, as though I'd been welcomed into a secret club. Like she knew all my secrets. I felt safe.

"Gaw. Oo knows? She's all right. A bit daft, really. Dunno. She keeps to herself pretty much. She swims every day and prattles on to her birds, right?"

"Birds?" I say, thinking about the dominant motif I've seen throughout the hotel. "You don't mean the pictures, and …" The foyer, the lounge, the pub, the corridors I've seen so far all have paintings of birds as well as taxidermy. Is she obsessed?

"Well, yeah." Zoë laughs her distinctive low-pitched eh-heh-heh. "That's been known to happen too. She is a bit of a strange bird herself. But no, she 'as actual live birds, in the garden. In her aviary. You can have a look about."

"Oh," I say. "I will." I check my watch. "Before I leave, maybe."

Zoë is staring at me. I lower my head and meet her eye warily. "What?"

"Jus' wonderin' what your story is, Miss Writer. I didn't hear what you told Mrs. R. But … well. She sure hired you in a flash. Bit of trouble?"

I nibble on my bottom lip, wondering how much to tell. I was honest with Mrs. Roxtoby. She was sympathetic, but then, I'd needed her sympathy. "Well, I've been travelling with my boyfriend, Marc-Antoine. He's an architecture student. And he wanted to go see some … buildings and, you know, museums up in, uh, Edinburgh and …" I try to remember the places Marc has mentioned. "I decided to stay in York for a while. But then he accidentally took my backpack, with my … um … stuff. So …"

She eyes me skeptically. "Why didn't you go with him?"

"I, uh, it would have been boring. Too much architecture." I tsk and shrug. "He sits and sketches for hours. Very … dull," I say, hoping she'll drop the subject.

"Yeh? So when's he coming back?"

"Not sure." I stare at her with a tight smile. "Meanwhile, I need some cash. I plan to explore York, see the Viking centre, Roman ruins, stuff like that."

"Sooo … you're interested in that old stuff, but not with Marc-Antoine. Have I got that right?"

"It's different," I say tersely, straightening a stack of promotional postcards that sit on the front desk showing a watercolour-tinted line drawing of the hotel's façade. They remind me of Marc's endless sketches. Zoë seems so nice, but something holds me back. Pride, I suppose.

Instead, I say, "You wouldn't understand." My chest aches with the need to confide my problems to someone. Anyone. It's not like me to keep my feelings inside, separate from others. I hate being so alone.

"No. Obviously," she says, raising her finely lined brows.

I've offended her. There's a thickness in my throat, and I swallow and swallow again, trying to clear the blockage, to no effect. It only feels like the lump has dropped to my belly. But it's a bit soon in our friendship for me to share my darkest secrets. "Can I have one of these for my collection? I'll send a note home to my folks. Explain that I'll be staying for a while." Put a positive spin on it. Lies, all of it. The momentary euphoria of my new job, my new friend, deflates like a parachute crumpling to the ground.

"Yeah, sure, duck. Well, come early tomorrow an' you can watch me do what I do for a bit. Get comfortable with it. Right?"

"Okay," I say, picking up a couple of postcards and heading for the lounge, intending to compare the drawing to my picture. "See you then."

CHAPTER 5

1 *0:08, March 8, 1945, Marylebone, London*

The moment Ava switched on the Hoover, Mother's ill-tempered voice cut through the whine of the electric motor.

"Ava! Stop that racket! You'll drive me mad."

Ava sighed and switched off the vacuum, stepping into the kitchen where her mother sat, lethargic, in her wool dressing gown, her elbows perched on the table, a cigarette burning in her limp hand. This house would never be cleaned. That's what was driving Ava crazy.

"You're overtired, Mum. It's too many nights in that damn Anderson shelter. You need to sleep in a proper bed."

Mother replied with a wan smile. "Language, dear. We'll go to Marylebone Station tonight to get some decent rest."

Ava shook her head. "You go. I can't sleep in a crowd."

Mother exhaled sharply, irritated. "I don't know how you do it. If I stay in the house, I lie awake all night, listening."

"There's no point listening for anything, Mum. You can't hear these ones coming. If it's coming for you, there's nothing to be done about it—"

"How reassuring."

"But you go ahead. You won't catch me sleeping underground with rats. I'd rather be blown to bits under the stars than die down there, buried alive in rubble and piles of bodies."

"Don't be macabre." Her voice was flat. Ava watched Mum turn her face away, inured to Ava's sarcasm, and take a languid sip of tea, her dull eyes staring out through the crisscross of tape on the kitchen windows to Harley Street.

Ava's eyes slid to the kitchen clock. It was nearly ten thirty.

"Stop fidgeting!" Her mother's gaze fixed on her again.

"I'm restless, Mum. I'm going to walk over to Smithfield Market and stand in the queue. I heard they got in a consignment of rabbits, and it would be nice to eat something besides sausages, wouldn't it?"

Her mother's laugh was bitter and humourless. "Take the pram. You might pass a coal dump."

Ava nodded.

She was only too glad to do the shopping. Mum was ground down with all the queuing, the waiting, the walking.

Mother's eyes narrowed in suspicion. Ava's stomach clenched. She tried to elude what was coming by turning to leave.

"Wait a moment. Are you sneaking off to meet that boy?"

"Who?" Ava stopped but didn't turn around, busying herself with coiling the idle Hoover's cord.

"Don't be coy with me, miss."

"Mum! I'm going shopping. I told you—"

"I know you're still seeing him, Ava, against my wishes. It won't do."

Ava turned back. "Why won't it do, Mum? Does it offend your outdated notions of class and position?"

Her mother glared. "Yes. It offends me. He's not good enough for you. I shouldn't have to tell you so, Ava."

"His father and Father are friends, Mum. I met him through Father at Oxford, for goodness' sake. He doesn't care!"

"Father and I have discussed this, Ava, and we are in agreement."

She knew Mum was lying. Father thought she was too young, yes, but he was attuned to the changes in the world. He admired Rupert's intelligence and confidence.

"His name might be Dean, Ava, but his father is only a clerk at the college. Your father is the dean! It doesn't compare. We expect so much better for you."

Ava responded through clenched teeth, her voice tight at her mother's disdain for the man she loved. "Mr. Dean is the registrar, Mother, not a clerk. I could never find a better man than Rupert. I don't care if his father's a lorry driver!"

Mother gritted her teeth, baring them ominously. "Well, you won't be seeing him again if I have anything to say about it."

Ava shrugged, heat building in her face.

"Go to your room."

"The rabbits!"

"We don't need a blasted rabbit." She glared. "Go!"

Ava scowled and stomped upstairs. She had to meet Rupert at eleven o'clock at Holborn Circus, but she'd never admit to her mother that the rabbits were a ruse. She stared at the clock, fuming and wringing her hands. She knew what she had to do. This was her life! She must see Rupert.

It was too damn difficult to set up these meetings. She stared, pensive, out her window at the Anderson shelter in the yard below, the grey hens in their pen scratching at the sod on its roof. Too far. But if she could sneak into the boys' room, she could probably scale down the big oak tree at the corner. Yes!

She changed into khaki trousers and sturdy walking shoes and tiptoed down the hall into her younger brothers' room, a place of dust and memories more still and poignant than elsewhere in the empty house. A wave of sadness washed over her.

Her two brothers had been at their aunt and uncle's in Yorkshire, far from the dangers of London, for most of the past five years. At eleven and thirteen, she hardly knew them now.

She had been part of the evacuation, too, and had stayed there, while her older cousin Eleanor had come to town to train and work as a nurse. Two years ago, Ava returned home. Now Eleanor was back in Yorkshire to marry her beau, that skinny, sour-faced young man whose father was in business up there with Uncle.

And Ava was here in London, sneaking out to meet Rupert.

She shoved open the bedroom casement window and peered out, a palm against her stomach. A bit of spring warmth carried on the air, smelling, even tasting like dust and coal smoke in the city. She reached across to grasp the branch nearest the window, gripping the rough bark, testing it for strength, and carefully edged herself out on the sill.

CHAPTER 6

M *ay 26, 1997, York*

I was so wracked with nerves when Mrs. Roxtoby interviewed me, I was a quivering, fluttering mess, unable to look around much, so now I wander through the lounge and pub, stopping to check out the weird and unbelievable collection of art, the worn upholstered armchairs and carpets with bare patches, old beat-up wooden tables and chairs. It's like a museum, only you can't fake threadbare and dust like this. It feels significant, but I don't know how or why.

There really are a lot of birds. More stuffed dead pheasants and dusty brown owls like gargoyles in a graveyard, dark oily pictures of little finches and sparrows and I don't know what. Waterbirds too, like ducks and gulls and things I've never seen before. I suppose English birds are not the same as Canadian ones, anyway. I wonder if it's some crazy obsession of Mrs. Roxtoby's. It seems a bit mad, a bit unnerving.

Two businessmen slouch over their beers, mumbling, as I stroll through the gloomy pub, nodding at the translucent wizened old man who polishes and polishes the surface of a small, panelled bar.

"Evenin'," he says as his rheumy eyes follow me. I shudder and then laugh at myself. I'm being ridiculous. It's my dark mood and the strangeness of this eccentric old country that makes everything seem like a Gothic mystery. Maybe this place will inspire a short ghost story.

"Evening," I mimic and continue by.

Out the other side, down a narrow hallway, I find myself in a dimly lit café, all incongruously light pine tables and pink chintz, with a lingering aroma of sausages and disinfectant. A barren buffet bar stretches across one end, and windows overlook the street on the other, with an eerie view of a streetlight through the bay windows. Glaring car headlights flare off the rippled panes as they pass, and I realize it's dusk, the summer sun setting later here than at home. The room is empty, the tables set with nesting pairs of salt-and-pepper shakers and cutlery rolled in rosy napkins, ready for the morning.

A glass-paned door entices me beyond the breakfast room into a greenhouse, and I wrinkle my nose. There is a damp odour of soil and rot. It's a wide hallway, but I can see the cloudless purpling sky beyond its sloped glass ceiling, murky with chalky streaks and condensation. Along the brown and gold leaf-patterned carpet, in a wide linear planter, is a jungle of tropical plants. Mostly, they're healthy, overgrown even, in a creepy way. I shudder. I file away ideas for a murder mystery instead of a ghost story.

The hallway, sparsly furnished with wicker chairs and small round tables, leads me past a series of bleak white numbered doors. These are hotel rooms, too, I suppose, but while old, this section is more seedy than historic.

The shush of my footfalls on the rug seems loud in the silence. I don't see a soul. One door is ajar, and try to steal a peek inside the room, but it's too dim to see.

Hee-agh!

I jump back, my heart racing. A ghostly, horsey face in the shadows stares back out at me, and abruptly the door slams shut. "Sorry. So sorry!" I plead to the door. That's all I need is to be caught spying on guests and I'll be out of a job before I begin.

At the end of the long greenhouse, a door takes me outside into a different kind of jungle. The overgrown garden still retains an air of English refinement, all shady and mossy. To my right, a wrought iron archway leads back towards the main building, but I turn left as peeps and cooing noises punctuate the twilight. Here is the infamous aviary.

It's a series of long, narrow wood-frame and wire-mesh cages maybe eight feet tall, with leafy trees and shrubbery growing inside. When I peer more closely, a couple of tiny birds flit from perch to perch and fluff their feathers, but I can't see them well. It's duskier in here.

Aqua-blue water, rippling over underwater lights hazy like searchlights in the fog, catches my eye, and I move past the bird-cages towards a kidney-shaped pool surrounded by more over-grown planting. To one side sit a small gazebo with a hot tub nestled in it, and a quaint little log cabin. A small low-roofed stone cottage forms the back wall to the garden, pots of boxwoods and nodding purple hollyhocks and frowsy clusters of yellow roses lined up along its wall, their soft scent rising to meet me. It's sweet and romantic back here. Mom would love this garden. Golden light glows behind the curtained windows. The door stands ajar, throwing a gash of yellow light across the paving stones.

"Hello, my lovelies." I hear a soft, musical voice coo behind me. "Trr … trrrrup." It's coming from the direction of the aviary. I'd better head out; it's getting late. I turn and tiptoe past the walkway that leads by the aviary, and sure enough, it's Mrs. Roxtoby, in her pink bathrobe, chattering at her doves and tossing lettuce and apples through a little hatchway. Do birds eat salad? I guess so. Weird lady.

I sneak away, wondering what her story is, and hurry back

into the hotel. I leave through the lobby and notice Zoë is gone. Another brown-haired girl reads in a pool of light behind the desk. The temp, I guess. An eerie glow lights the scene, like a van Gogh painting. A shiver dances over my skin. That'll be me this time tomorrow.

~

I'm too restless to sleep all day, despite knowing I'll have to stay up all night tonight. After yet another gross breakfast of Marmite and white bread at the youth hostel, I decide to treat myself to a visit to the Jorvik Viking Centre on my last free day.

It's the same walk as yesterday, but everything looks brighter now that I have prospects, as Dad would say. I enjoy the buskers' music and take time to peer into the shop windows on High Petergate. When I have a little money, I'll stop in and buy some of those super antique buttons. I love buttons.

Before King's Square, I detour again through the Shambles, soaking in the medieval atmosphere of the narrow meandering lanes and overhanging half-timber shops. I actually know my way around without my map now. Soon, I'm at the Coppergate Shopping Centre again. Yesterday's hot scruffy green-eyed musician isn't here. Instead, one of those mimes with bronze face paint and Elizabethan costume poses on a box, immobile. My heart sinks a little, but I don't know why. Maybe I wanted the musician to recognize the good news on my face.

Following the signs to the Viking Centre, I can't believe there's a line-up already, stretching along the arcaded redbrick wall to one side of the canopied entry. Granted, it's not the crack of dawn, but it's only late June. I take my place behind an obstreperous group of school children in forest green blazers and tartan ties, and wait.

I'm excited to view the reconstruction of medieval Jorvik. The fact that cities in Europe sit upon layers and layers of history fascinates me. First Roman, then Viking, then medieval, piled one on top of the other, the evidence waiting to be dug up. Our own modern cities are more likely to obliterate signs of the past. But the Viking stuff … I have a little Danish in my dad's family, so I'm particularly interested.

A wave of ruckus, snickers, and giggles passes through the school group and there's a commotion up ahead. Some guy has emerged from the entry door, and the hubbub is focused on him. The children break ranks and swarm him, squealing and laughing as he moves down the line, despite their teacher's admonishments to stay in place. A tall guy in Viking costume comes into view. Not the stereotypical horned helmet and sword that I associate with Vikings but rather a leather cap over unruly long dreadlocks, a scruffy beard, coarse wool tunic, leather apron and breeches, his leather boots encrusted with dried mud. The kids are all looking at something he holds, and I strain to make it out. Something in a Plexiglas box.

A murmur snakes through the crowd. Something about a turd?

"Have a look," the man says as he works his way down the line, his voice a melodic tenor, drawing me in. "Do you know what this is?" The children are way ahead of him, the broken telephone game speeding like lightning towards me.

"It's jus' a dirty rock."

"Naw, it's poo!" says one eager child.

"It is!" answers the Viking. "It's the Lloyds Bank Turd."

"Who's he?"

"Why'd you have his turd?"

"It's terribly old," he replies, grinning. "Who can tell me what it is?"

A hand shoots into the air. A young girl with frizzy pigtails like pom-poms jumps up and down. "Oh, oh, oh. Is it a coprolite?"

"Yes! Clever girl. It's genuine mineralized Viking excrement, found at Lloyds Bank at the Jorvik dig."

Way to go, Hermione.

"Ew!" offer several of her friends.

The Viking guy laughs and straightens up, and at last, I catch a glimpse of the object he's carrying. It does look like a dirty rock but also like a piece of shit. My disgust and bemusement must show on my face, because he turns, catches my eye, and laughs, and I'm stunned to recognize the familiar knowing green eyes twinkling back at me. My musician!

"Who's coming to the soil science workshop? Raise your hands." He turns towards the schoolchildren again, raising his voice. He's so sweet, so enthusiastic, trying to get the kids excited about their tour.

Another Viking emerges. He seems to be a warrior, wearing chain mail and a leather-and-metal helmet with a nose guard, and does indeed carry a scary poleaxe. "Rooaaarrrhhh!" He charges the gentle guitarist, purveyor of poo, and knocks him aside. "Bollocks! You'll come and learn abou' Viking weaponry and battle tactics wif me. Who wants to look at dirty old rocks?" he barks. The bully!

Musician Viking gives Warrior Viking an exasperated, quizzical glare and turns back to the students. "I'll see you kids inside."

"Bwah-ha-ha!" growls Warrior and shoves Musician once more, hard, and he goes flying against the bricks of the building with an "oomph" and a bone-shattering thwack that sounds like it hurt, sliding with a scraping noise down onto his backside, gripping his coprolite like the treasure it is.

"Watch it," he grumbles. "This is priceless." The children explode with laughter, assuming the antics are all part of the show.

But the musician's face tells me it wasn't in the script. Poor thing. I grab his arm and help him back to his feet. "Are you all right?" He gives off a rural aroma of clean dirt and fresh straw. Strange, but comforting.

His cheeks are flushed. He's pissed. "Yeah. Thanks. Competitive coworker," he mumbles. "We get evaluated on our workshop's popularity." He sighs and dusts off his backside, looking up, "American?"

I shake my head and smile. "Canadian."

"Ah, very nice." Grinning, he turns to leave, then doubles back. "Going in?"

I nod.

"See you, then." He disappears through the doorway.

We wait a few more minutes and the line moves as the children are ushered into the centre. I pay and enter, picking up a brochure and wandering inside while studying the floor plan. Up ahead, the musician is leading the schoolchildren down a corridor, already talking animatedly about what they'll see. I figure I might as well tag along.

It's dark, but the noisy children are easy to track. I hang back in the shadows, near enough to hear our guide's engaging presentation without being seen. He seems to know a lot about Viking life, leading us past reconstructions of the medieval village with thatched cottages, water wheels, and outdoor work areas where wax figures in costume are engaged in various trades and daily activities. Sounds are piped in, of Viking voices, animals braying, tools hammering, and the place smells … authentic? I detect some of that excrement, along with damp, woolly animals, food smells, smoke, fish and hops-y, mealy odours. It's rather disgusting, but I guess it's all part of the experience.

Other visitors meander past, listening for a bit and moving on. Musician describes the activities of the various people who lived in Jorvik a thousand years ago and how they came to live in England. His stories are amusing and animated, and the children love him. He's really good, yet somehow pitiable, aimless, lost. He's not really my type, but he seems nice, well-spoken, and knowledgeable, and he could be good-looking if he cleaned himself up. He seems too educated for such a goofy job, dressed in costume and acting the fool. But maybe he's a student paying his way.

At the end of the tour, he's taking questions from the children when Warrior returns and rudely interrupts, ushering the children away, apparently in search of archeological artifacts in an adjacent room. I go to follow them but hesitate. The sense of light-hearted fun is gone, and I'm not in the mood to listen to Warrior bark at the children about weapons and such. Maybe I'll return another time and study the artifacts on my own.

Turning back, I discover that Musician has vanished.

I've had enough. I'm interested in the interpretive material hanging on the walls, but I'm suddenly too tired. I'll grab a cheap pasty instead and head back to the hostel for a nap before my night shift.

CHAPTER 7

Later that evening, I watch Zoë and listen to her review check-in procedures and such for an hour. It's a snap. I can handle this job. After all, according to Zoë, I'll be alone while everyone else sleeps. She was right—only three new guests arrived between six thirty and seven fifteen, all of them single businesspeople. I perch on a stool and soak it all in. I like it here. It's still and hushed in the lobby so late at night, though a murmur of voices drifts from the pub.

Two women descend the stairs, padding softly on the plush red carpet, and head away from me, towards the dining room that I missed on my tour the other day. Curious, I slip off my stool and follow them to the doorway. On the opposite side of the lobby, the dining room is almost empty. Two singles sit at drab-draped tables as the women are seated by a young woman in a black skirt, blouse, and apron. Her thin blond hair is short and spiky. A large ladder mars her black stocking. Jeez! The place has a sleepy, shabby quality, and I don't wonder most of the guests choose to dine in town.

From what I've seen of the clientele, this place is second rate. But then, I guess I knew that from the weathered furnishings and threadbare carpets. It's a shame, though, with my North

American eyes, these aged features add to the hotel's charm. These could be turned into assets if the service were up to scratch.

"Ey up."

Startled, I turn around to find the old bartender hovering behind me, looking past my shoulder into the dining room. "Uh. Um."

"You 'ungry, darlin'?"

I step back to look into his eyes, which are pale, blue, and watery, with large purple pouches of loose skin under them, but sharp and friendly. Tufts of fine stark white hair poke down over his smooth forehead and large, fleshy ears, Einstein-like, giving him a peculiar boyish appearance, despite his advanced age. He must be eighty, or maybe only sixty-five. It's hard to tell. "I'm Sophie," I say, offering my hand. "I'm the new night desk clerk."

"I know that, darlin', I asked if you was 'ungry." He takes my hand in his gnarled, bony grip and pumps. His hand is stiff and as cold as ice. "I'm Edward, the caretaker. You can call me Teddy. Everybody else doos." He sounds a bit Irish. Different from the locals I've met.

"Oh. Aren't you the bartender?" I ask, taking his hand in both of mine and rubbing gently. "Your hands are freezing, Teddy."

"Aye. Indeed they are. Me circulation's not sa good anymore. I'm the bartender too, in the evenings," he adds. "And the gardener at week end." He smiles, his lips pulling into a broad thin line that's engaging, even though his teeth disappear and his chin juts out, reminding me of that old comedian Dad made me watch, Stan Laurel.

"Well, it's a pleasure to meet you, Teddy." I release his hand. "I guess we'll be seeing each other, then, if you work evenings. I'll be here all night."

"Aye. I know. Cook'll bring your tea when the guests are done theirs," he adds, smiling again and nodding.

"What? Really?" I say, surprised. They're going to serve me

snacks? Wow. That's … Bonus. I can save my Marmite sandwich for later. Or better yet, toss it. "That's so kind." I smile back at him, and at last he turns and shuffles away, his head still nodding over his hunched shoulders.

Later that night, after I've clumsily checked in a couple more guests (one family with two sleeping toddlers and a scholarly, middle-aged bald man with thick glasses, a visiting university professor), Cook appears with a tray bearing a covered dish and cutlery wrapped in a cloth napkin.

"Ah'm sorry Ah'm s'tardy, dearie," she clucks, distracted. "The drat dishwasher lad never shown up an' I had to do washin' up with my April. An' though I dote on 'er, she's no' much use." She punctuates this line by bugging out her eyes.

I stand, staring at Cook, open-mouthed. I haven't a clue how to respond. "Thank you?" I venture, eyeing the tray.

She lifts the lid on the plate to reveal pasta and sauce and crusty rolls with butter. "It's nowt much, but to tell the truth, I wouldna offer ye the roast beef tonight. 'Twas a tad dry, dearie. A tad dry. I'll use it for pies on the morrow."

"I'm sorry, Mrs. …" I've forgotten her name. "Deee …" I shake my head in apology.

"Delicata, dearie. Our Art, my 'usband … Arturo was Italian." She laughs soundlessly, her chins and bosom quivering, her heat-reddened face shining under the spotlight over the desk.

"Oh." I smile. "I was going to say Delicious. Mrs. Delicious. I thought it was something, you know. Tasty. Sorry."

She quivers again. "Call me Cook, dearie. That's my name here at the Aviary Inn."

"Is supper included? I was expecting tea and cookies, er, I mean, biscuits."

Her expression is blank. "Well, aye shy. You can't work all the neet wi'out a good tea in yer tummy, can ye?"

"Thank you," I repeat. I'm so hungry; I can't believe my good luck.

"Weell, goo ahead." She nods at the pasta, her chapped red

hands wrapped around her stained apron, though they can't quite reach the other side of her girth. "Don't let it starve, noo."

I fork a luscious nodule of pasta. It smells wonderful and I take a small bite. "Ooh. It is delicious!" I laugh.

Mrs. Delicata, who will always be Mrs. Delicious to me, jiggles along with me. "It's my homemade gnocchi. Better'n dreaded English food. Arturo's mamma taught me how t'cook when I was a new bride. Never serve't here, though." She scowls, her voice tapering off.

Why's that? I wonder. "If you're ever short of help in the kitchen again, let me know," I say. "I can help."

"Nooo. You've got your own work, dearie," she says. "An' me gran'daughter can learn to pull her weight. Tha's what Mrs. R. give 'er t'screw for, ain't it?"

"Screw?"

"Pay."

Ah. "April? She's your granddaughter?" How could that vacant-eyed, punkish waif be a relative of this rotund and warm-hearted woman?

"Aye," Cook mutters as she wanders back to the dining room. "Jes' let them there pots yonder. Teddy'll bring 'em to the kitchen afore 'e bahn yam."

Ban yam? I shake my head. Oh, right. 'Goes home,' I remember. After Cook has gone, I devour the incredible pasta but leave the rolls and butter for later, in case I'm hungry again. Better than Marmite.

I spend the rest of the quiet evening investigating the office, straightening piles and sorting forms. Reservations and accounts are managed in ledgers! It's so different from the way Mom runs her B and B business. My fingers itch to reorganize the whole place, but it's a little premature. Instead, I snoop and make plans.

Around eleven, Teddy materializes to lock the front door and then picks up my tray. "Ah. Tha's made up, lucky lass," he says.

"Yes," I reply. "Cook's pasta was fantastic!"

Teddy eyes my empty plate. "She's a fine baker too. Her

bread rolls are famous. But keep some goodies on hand, darlin', 'appen she brings you roas' beef or pork one night." He clucks his tongue and shakes his head. "The woman jus' can't make proper Yorkshire roast thee can eat."

I look at the tray as he lifts it and notice the two bread rolls are gone. "Did you ...?" But then, I'd better not say anything. He's welcome to them, the scrawny old thing. Maybe it'll improve his circulation.

I select a postcard from my collection, picked up at tourist shops.

May 27, 1997, Bath
Dear Mom, Dad, and Matt,

At last, I'm in the beautiful city of Bath with all its lovely Georgian buildings and Roman ruins. So exciting to visit the Jane Austen Museum too. Such an inspiration to an aspiring writer like me! Having a great time. I hope you can be happy for me.

Love,

Sophie

CHAPTER 8

I'm more than ready for a night off after a full week at my new job. It's exhausting staying up until five-thirty or six in the morning. After a couple of hours enjoying the solitude, writing stories and journal entries, I'm wishing for my bed. Tension crawls over and through me, and I'm a bit light-headed, even after sleeping past noon. My internal clock's screwed up. Around two in the afternoon, I wander through town and visit the Jorvik Viking Centre again. I want to explore those archeological finds.

Thank God I got paid this morning! Given my circumstances, Mrs. Roxtoby authorized a cash advance so I could pay for a few extra nights at the youth hostel. But I'm sick of being there. If it weren't for Mrs. Delicata's nightly suppers, I'd be in dire straits now. Though Teddy was right. I got pork roast, onions, and potatoes last night and, ugh! I'm glad I brought an apple. That's all I can say. The contrast between her Italian dishes and her English ones defies logic. I'm grateful for the free food, but it's no wonder the dining room is empty most nights.

Still no word from Marc-Antoine, though. Not a good sign. I won't feel guilty for sending that postcard home, telling Mom and Dad that I was in Bath, with no mention of Marc-Antoine, though it may bite me in the arse. They don't need to know that he left me. I didn't mention that I needed to get a job either. It's better this way.

I have so little money left, but I'm drawn into the antiques store where I browse the button display. Gosh, they're beautiful. Back home, I would have bought them in a minute to add to my homemade clothes or to personalize boring, plain separates. It would be foolish to spend my last few pounds on something so frivolous, though.

"Can I show you anything?" the clerk asks.

Buttons are sooo cool. "Could I see that tray?" I ask, pointing through the glass top. I fondle the smoothly carved ivory, horn, shiny discs of mother-of-pearl, and jagged frills of coral. "How much are these?" I gasp when she tells me. I could buy one, maybe. "Um. Can I see those?"

In the end, I buy a cheap set of four funky psychedelic plastic buttons from the '60s to cheer myself up—large flower-shaped ones with swirls of orange, brown, and pink. These would look great on the legs or pockets of my plain brown corduroys. With my bag gone, I have so few clothes, so it might be nice to deck them out a bit. Maybe I can find a scarf or some ribbon to match.

I pay to enter the Viking Centre and zip through the reconstructed village, stopping only occasionally to study an interesting garment or tool. In a separate room, a long, narrow hall filled with glass cases, I slow down and read and absorb. The carvings are fascinating, and I especially love the textiles. They have combs, and buttons too, made from wood or horn. I slide my hands over the cool, smooth glass tops, wishing I could touch the objects, but I know they're hermetically sealed in these cases. I'm amazed that any specimens have survived nearly a thousand years.

Something about the bog-like soil, similar to those places they find mummified remains, preserved leatherwork and wool, baskets, wood, and even foodstuff. Not to mention the excrement. Also stuff from the earthen floors of houses, things like seeds and grain, vegetable remains, and animal bones. It shows what people ate and what they wore. I can see now what Musician finds so fascinating about soil science and wish I could be a fly on the wall in one of his kids' workshops.

I'm both relieved and disappointed not to see him. Nor, thankfully, do I see the pushy Viking warrior. Time passes quickly and before I know it, it's five o'clock and the place is closing. Instead of going to work, I have the evening free. I guess I'll have to feed myself tonight, though.

I wander back towards the centre of town, on the lookout for a cheap fast-food joint.

"Hey. Hold up!" a voice shouts behind me.

I don't stop, because obviously the salutation isn't meant for lonesome me.

"Hey! Canadian!"

Hmm? Or maybe … I turn around, and sure enough, it's Musician Viking, loping towards me, his dusty dreadlocks bouncing, a weathered satchel flying from his shoulder. Huh. I wait for him. "Hi?"

"Hi. I saw you inside. I hoped I'd catch you. I just finished. But I had to change," he gasps out, breathless.

I nod. "Right," I say, scanning his clothes, which are perfectly twentieth century, though somehow rattier than his Viking tradesman getup. He's wearing a tattered crewneck sweater over a dingy grey T-shirt and faded, shredded jeans. His clothing, if you can call it that, hangs nicely on his tall, lean frame and broad shoulders, but he still looks shabby. I try not to stare at his long sandy dreadlocks, roughly tied back in a clump, as though he didn't bother with a mirror. His dull, matted hair gives me the heebie-jeebies and I wonder how he keeps it clean and free of lice. The familiar scent of straw and dirt remains.

An image flashes in my mind. I realize he looks pretty much how he did that first time I saw him, busking by the mall. "Where's your guitar?"

"What? How did you know I play?" He smiles, and his teeth are perfectly straight and white behind the screen of his wild and wiry brownish moustache and beard, which is twisted into tails at the ends, onto which he has threaded a couple of celadon beads. Nice touch, decorating the thatch. Ew. But the beads, oddly, bring out the clear, intelligent green of his eyes and somehow elevate the bohemian grunge look. At least he eats well and brushes his teeth.

"I saw you last week at the shopping centre. I recognized you."

"Ah," he says, falling in step beside me. He has long legs, but then so do I. It's not many men who I have to look up to.

"So. Would you like to get something to eat?"

I glance at him quizzically. "Um. We don't know each other." I make sure my tone is tart, but not too rude. I like this poor guy, so I don't want to damage him with my acerbic tongue.

He stops walking. "That can be remedied. I'm Nick." He puts out his long-fingered hand. "And you are …?"

"Sophie. Sophie Groenveld." His hand is soft, except for his calloused fingertips, which make my palm tingle as he hangs on while he talks.

"Green field, hey? What a coincidence. My name's Roodbaard."

I eye his ruddy brown beard. "Nooo." I scrunch up my nose, giving my head a tiny shake. That would be too weird.

He laughs and rolls his eyes. His nice, even teeth flash from behind his moustache. "No. Not really. Nick Savile." He releases my hand slowly, intensifying the tingles, and we continue walking. We've emerged from the enclosing Shambles into tall, narrow Petergate, and the towers of the minster loom up ahead in the fading light, violet shadows against sunlit grey stone walls.

"There. Now, Sophie, can I show you a great place to eat? It's not far."

I shrug. I was going to eat, anyway. It would be nice to have company. "As long as it's cheap. I got paid, but there's not much of it left after paying for my room at the hostel."

"The one up on Water End?"

"Yes."

"Well. I had planned to take you to Gillygate, anyway. Lots of great, cheap places to eat, and it's on your way home, by Bootham Bar."

He planned? I realize I've told a complete stranger where to find me. But somehow, Nick Savile, Viking musician, although he makes me prickle with alertness, doesn't frighten me. He has a refined, gentle way of speaking. The kind of English accent that us colonial girls swoon over. Very Fitzwilliam Darcy, except, of course, for the dreadlocks. "I won't be there for long. I've found a job, and I need to find something more permanent." Well. Not that permanent. I hope.

"I might be able to suggest something. A mate of mine recently left a boarding house across the Ouse, on Nunthorpe. It's nice, clean, and cheap."

"Thanks. That sounds perfect. I'd like to check it out. It's on the right side of town for my job too."

"Which is …"

"Um. Desk clerk. At a little hotel up on the Mount." As we pass the minster, I tilt my head back to absorb its immensity. That's another place I'd like to return. I never did climb the tower, and I'd love to sit and write in the Chapter House, with its fabulous vaulted ceiling.

"Really," he drawls. "And you travelled all the way from Canada to do … this?"

I purse my lips and narrow my eyes at him warily. He's

getting an awful lot of information out of me. "Noooo." I smile. "It's a short stopover. I'm touring."

He nods, and I can see by the light in his green eyes that he'd like to ask a dozen more questions, but he doesn't. "So. What kind of food? Italian? Indian?"

I realize we've turned into Gillygate, and pedestrian traffic has tripled. This really must be the place to eat. The lower profile streetscape is lined with narrow buildings, many of which sport wood-mullioned and bay windows that spill inviting gold light into the street. I ponder his question, remembering the dinners Mrs. Delicata has brought me the past four nights. Three of them were Italian. "I've had my fill of pasta lately. But I could really sink my teeth into a burger."

"I know a pub that serves terrific burgers and chips. And if you've room afterwards, their sticky toffee pudding is the best in town."

"Yeah. Okay. But I dunno about the pudding." I laugh.

Nick smiles and stares at me, and I'm about to ask what he's thinking when two guys approach us up the street.

One of them looks over and barks, "Tack!" in a nasal voice.

Nick looks up sharply, his smile vanishing. "Godfrey. Whooten," he murmurs as they sidle up.

The second of the two guys smirks, and it's not a nice thing. "I see you're still slumming, Tack." He sounds like he's got marbles in his mouth.

Muscles jump in Nick's jaw, and he still doesn't smile or respond. The two guys nod and walk on, and I can hear their muffled sniggering. He shoots a glare after them.

"Are you okay?" I ask. "Nick?"

He abruptly turns to me. "That wasn't what you think. It wasn't anything to do with you. Those bastards ..." The nostrils on his lean straight nose are flared and green fire flashes dangerously in his eyes.

I shake my head, a warning fluttering in my neck. Why

would such a little thing upset him so? Who were those guys? "I really didn't …," I say cautiously. "Are you—?"

"Never mind, then. Forget it." His pace picks up, and I match his agitated stride, biting my cheeks and keeping my gaze on the cobbles, listening to his harsh breathing, not sure I'm still comfortable with this suddenly intense, sullen stranger. Am I insane? He forces an apologetic smile. "I'm so sorry. They weren't exactly friends."

"Who's Tack? Didn't you say you were a Savile?"

"Tack's … no one. It's a nickname."

"So, tell me about yourself," I say. "Your family tailors or something?"

Nick's abrupt laughter sounds like a cough. "Are you referring to Savile Row?"

I nod, my smile sheepish.

"Distant relatives, perhaps. It's a common name. No …" He laughs, but it sounds faintly bitter. "No tailors in my family, I'm afraid. Not anymore. Though my grandmother did used to sew horse blankets."

"You don't sound like the locals. Are you from Yorkshire?"

"Aye. Ah'm a Yorkshireman." He shows a flash of white teeth in the dusk. He shrugs. "Nearby. South Yorkshire, around Halifax and Huddersfield."

I wait, but Nick offers no more. He's a couple of years older than me, I think, so I'm wondering what he's done with himself for the past few years.

"Do you … did you go to university?"

It's a few moments before Nick replies. I wonder if I've broached a sore subject. He certainly seems bright and educated, but maybe I'm wrong. He draws a breath. "I have two history degrees. And I started a D. Phil. in archeology and history," he says, hesitating, "but I dropped out."

"What?" Dare I ask? I have to know. "But why?"

He stares at me for a long minute, then huffs through his nose. "I felt like it, all right?"

"Seriously …" I laugh, teasing. "No, seriously! Why?"

He glares at me as if daring me to probe further.

Oooh-kay. Touchy subject. But I can't leave it alone. Why study history and then do nothing with it? "So, you're happy, like, being a Disney character and strumming your guitar on the street. Don't you have … I don't know, ambitions? Dreams?"

"Ha!" He stops walking and presses his lips into a thin line. I've really pissed him off now. He's going to change his mind about dinner. "Here it is." Totally dropping the subject, he turns towards a dull stone-fronted building with a brightly lit entryway and gestures for me to enter. I look up at the carved wooden sign.

The Lion and Lamb pub looks warm and inviting, and inside, its narrow passages and snug cubbies are darkly panelled and beamed in classic English pub style. The inviting main room with its scuffed, uneven floorboards has a log fire burning in a huge hearth. The room is warm, and besides a hint of fire smoke, I can smell the inviting aromas of beer and fried onions.

"There's a large beer garden on the patio, with a view of the minster, but it's quieter inside."

I hear the muffled clamour of many voices from the back passageway. We find a small table in a stone alcove and order drinks, chips, and burgers, which turn out to be huge, gooey, and scrumptious.

I'm surprised Nick wants to talk anymore after my probing questions, but he tells me a bit about his seven years at university.

"I read history and archeology," he tells me. He's an enigma, that's for sure. He seems well-bred, educated, smart. Yet his job's so dead end, and he seems so aimless.

When I venture again, "But why would you quit?" he avoids answering and talks about his job instead.

"I'm more than a tour guide, you know. I'm a docent, if you know what that means."

"I do."

"And I teach school groups. Which I like a lot." I remember his enthusiasm with the children. He obviously loves his subject. "Sometimes I help with the collection or the digs." His eyes light up with green sparks. "I would have done my thesis on Anglo-Scandinavian—" He stops abruptly and takes a pensive slug of his beer. He shrugs, as if anticipating my next question.

"Why don't you go back? You could run that place. Surely, it's not too …"

He interrupts me by singing lyrics from a song I've heard recently, by The Verve, one of my new favourite British bands.

"*'Happiness, more or less/It's just a change in me/Somethin' in my liberty. O-oh my, my…'*" He trails off, then takes another gulp of beer. He has a great voice. A few people look over surreptitiously, perhaps wondering if he's someone famous. It's that good. "*'I know just where I am.'*"

I smile. I like him.

"You should come and hear my band. We cover some new stuff, but we also play older R&B, punk. Some folk."

"Perhaps I will," I say. Obviously, the subject of his career is closed, but I study him closely, curious.

He hums the song again for a bit, an inscrutable expression on his face, then sings, "*'Well, I'm a lucky man/with fire in my hands.'*"

His music is sad and angsty, and I wonder who he is, really.

With a few questions, he gets me talking, too, about my English degree and my plans for grad school, and somehow, I end up telling him about Marc-Antoine, our relationship, and our big architectural tour. But again, I make Marc's departure sound like a planned thing and my missing things as an accident. Which it may well have been, I remind myself, though that still doesn't make sense. Marc could have no use for my clothes, my passport, or airline ticket. I refuse to think he even knew about my stash of cash.

Nick doesn't say anything, but his eyes narrow thoughtfully

as I tell my story. My stomach turns over with nerves. The check never comes, and I thank him for dinner.

Before we leave the pub, he writes down the address of the boarding house, and I plan to visit it tomorrow. Then, he insists on walking me back up Bootham to the hostel despite my assurances that I'm okay. As he waves and walks away humming, I think I'm pleased with my mysterious new Yorkshire friend, though he knows more about me than I do about him.

CHAPTER 9

May 31, 1997, Stratford-upon-Avon

Dear Mom, Dad, and Matt,
A change of plans! Marc was dying to go to Scotland, while I've arrived in Stratford-upon-Avon to visit Shakespeare's birthplace. This is a fabulous town with amazing medieval buildings, still in use today. I love it, although living in the Middle Ages, not so much.

It's fine, actually. I love wandering and exploring whatever interests me at my own pace. The solitude is lovely and gives me time to dream.

Love,
Sophie

CHAPTER 10

As I sit at the Aviary Inn's front desk, writing another postcard home, I'm hoping more details about my travels, though largely fabricated, will dispel any worry Mom or Dad might have about me. I've decided to tell a partial truth about Marc, in case he somehow goes home and they hear about it. I might have argued with them, but I don't need them freaking out and flying over to "save" me.

Incredibly, this old place has no computer. Not even internet connectivity. Why am I surprised? It seems to be lost in the Georgian age. Or Williams-ian, rather, as I've learned, the hotel was built during the brief reign of William IV, whoever he was. Or at least the 1950s when it became a hotel.

Cook has already fed me a supper of polenta and steamed veggies with garlic. It was delicious. I cup my hand over my mouth and check my breath. Whoo. Better keep my distance from guests. Cook seemed distracted tonight, grumbling about some crazy old biddy stealing something from the kitchen. I can't imagine she's talking about Mrs. Roxtoby, who I've not seen all week, by the way. It's quiet tonight otherwise.

That nice Canadian businessman stopped to chat again. He reminds me of my uncle Mark, Dad's older brother, red-faced, rotund, and friendly. He checked in a couple of days ago. Tonight, he said there's a Canadian consulate in Birmingham, if I want to apply for a replacement passport. It will be awhile yet before I have the money or the opportunity to—

"Holding up all right, Sophie, lass?" It's Teddy, finishing his last round before locking up. I glance at the old, yellowed clock on the wall. Eleven fifteen. Right on schedule.

"Hi, Teddy. Were you outside? How are your hands tonight?"

"Ah. Not bad, not bad." He stretches his face into its now familiar smile, his snowy tufted eyebrows unfurling like sea anemones. I can imagine him as a dapper young gentleman, his straight hair slicked back, his heathered brown cardigan replaced by a trim vest and tie. A mid-century James Van Der Beek.

"The weather's improving every day. Looks like we'll have a fine summer." He sets the tea tray on the front desk and pulls up a stool he keeps tucked around the corner. Sharing tea has quickly become our nightly routine. He locks up at eleven, finishes his final tour, and then makes a pot of tea in the kitchen, sharing it with me before he goes home for the night. The pleasant ritual breaks up the monotony of the long nights and I've already come to look forward to it.

He lifts a simple sandwich with a suspicious black line between the layers of bread. "Sarny?" he offers.

I shake my head. "No thanks. Ate dinner not long ago." I don't want to spoil Cook's wonderful meal with the foul taste of Marmite. "I'll have a biscuit."

After pouring tea for us both and taking a sip, I reach across the desk and take one of his gnarled and veined hands in mine and massage the crepey, translucent skin. "Cook was in a flap tonight about something. Someone stealing?"

He chuckles. "'Tis only Eleanor. Poor thing. Nowt to worry about. But Cook jes' don't countenance her. Never has. Never will."

I don't know who Eleanor is. Probably kitchen help I haven't met. Switching hands, I ask about Mrs. Roxtoby. "I haven't seen her around lately."

Speaking of poor things. Mrs. R. drifts around like a ghost, her eyes glazed over, lost in a dream. I don't know where her mind is, but she rarely speaks to anyone except on hotel business. And yet when she does speak, she seems to wake from a trance and is suddenly sharp-witted with a fierce energy. She's lonely and bored, maybe. I resolve to make an effort to talk to her next time I see her.

Teddy peers intently into my eyes. "By the by, is that your parents you're writing to?" He gestures at my postcard, thankfully face down.

"Yes." I focus on nibbling a biscuit, releasing the aroma of cinnamon, crunching the tiny sugar crystals between my teeth. I set it down and resume the massage.

"Are they going to send ye money to get home?"

"Nope." My gaze remains focused on Teddy's swollen knuckles. I don't want to get into the whole rift with my folks or how strongly Mom opposed my coming here. "How's that?" I release his hand with a pat and a tight smile.

"Mmm." His eyes level at my face. "Much better, thank you, lass." Teddy flexes his stiff fingers, and despite my efforts, his enlarged knuckles appear rigid and uncomfortable. I wish I could massage them in the afternoon when Teddy starts his workday. That's when his arthritis gives him the most trouble. By the time I arrive at seven thirty in the evening, he's past it.

"Weel. You'll be all right here at the Aviary till you figure it out, lass."

I hope so.

After Teddy leaves, I get to work fixing up the office. I save the busy work until Teddy's gone to make the lonely hours fly by. I've gradually reorganized drawers and office supplies. No one complained, so I guess they don't mind the improvements. Tonight, I plan to make new labels for the room key slots. I found a couple of unused stacking work trays in the dusty back storeroom and I'm going to label them too for check-in and -out slips, messages, faxes, mail, etc. That way, so many chaotic piles of paper won't clutter the worktops. I run my hand along the dents and gouges on the front desk. It could use a lick of varnish. Despite the dinged-up woodwork, it appears especially pitiful at the registration counter.

I'm already desperately anticipating my first proper pay cheque. The tiny advance I received to extend my stay at the hostel is nearly gone. Earlier today, I went to the boarding house on Nunthorpe Road and spoke to the landlady. She has a cheery vacant room. It includes breakfast and dinner, and it's perfect for me. She said it's being painted, so I can't move in until next Tuesday, even though it's after the first of June. Rent is week to week, and I'll finally have some privacy.

And it's so much closer to the Aviary Inn. Less than ten minutes hike up Scarcroft Road to Blossom Street and, boom, I'm here. I'll have to find Nick again and thank him for that. I'd never have found it on my own.

Best of all, it's just affordable enough that I'll be able to save a little money each week. In a few weeks, if I'm frugal, I can take the train to Birmingham or London for a new passport. Although, I rather like this job. My salary, though modest, is probably as good as I can expect for temporary work. The question is: How long before I save enough for a flight to Canada? If it ever comes to that.

I spend the wee hours pondering Marc-Antoine's whereabouts and scribbling unanswerable questions in my journal, along with truly frightening speculations that, hopefully, will turn out to be no more than fodder for future stories. I am utterly mortified. It is possible a perfectly good explanation exists. I mean, what use has he of my things? I'm sure he didn't know about the cash. However, I can't help but dwell on the fact that I have been accused of a certain naiveté. Marc-Antoine always says, "Sophie, don't be so gullible, eh?"

It's partly because Marc-Antoine knew me, and was always

looking out for me, that I find it so difficult to believe he would deliberately hurt me. Surely, I've missed something that would help it all make sense. Why did he leave me? Where did he go? And most important of all, is he coming back? Could it be that he was truly too selfish and impatient to allow me the time I needed to look into my mother's family here? I didn't envision being alone so far from home, yet here I am. A heavy weight presses on my ribs, making me feel small, especially alone in the middle of the night, and I brush away a few tears of self-pity.

I'm in the back storeroom, slicing coloured paper into strips for labels, when I hear a clanging crash echo across the foyer. I freeze, my heart thumping in my throat. I glance at the clock. It's close to four in the morning. Who could it be? No one else should be awake and about this late, now that Teddy is gone. For a moment, I stand still, listening, but all I can hear is the blood pounding in my ears. Probably a drying pan rattled down in the kitchen, right?

Glancing around, I grab a dusty black umbrella that's been forgotten in a corner of the storeroom, and brandishing it like a club, slowly, silently tiptoe out of the office and across the foyer towards the noise. A floorboard in the dining room creaks in the silence, and I stop again.

A shadow flickers across the wall up ahead, setting my pulse racing again. Oh, please, let it be my overactive imagination! Suddenly, a slight, robed figure dashes out of the kitchen doorway and streaks past me in a blur, like a blue phantom. What the heck?

"Hey!" Giving chase, which isn't difficult, I overtake the tiny intruder in seconds, darting towards the breakfast room to the other side of the front desk. I grab at an arm, brittle as a twig in my grasp. Whoever this burglar is, I'm twice her size, and my chest swells with indignation. "Who the hell are you? What are you doing crashing around at this hour?"

"Don't hit me!" a faint, creaky voice begs, raising a fragile, papery hand in self-defence.

"I'm not going to hit you," I say, outraged. I circle the little woman and bend to glare into a wide-eyed face, deeply creased and equine.

She looks like she's seen a ghost. "B-Ba-ba?" Her murky brown eyes pop from her head, her trembling hand still raised to ward me off. "B-babs! What are you doing here? It's me."

Babs? Who does she think I am?

Then I realize I have the umbrella raised over my head in a threatening gesture. I lower it slowly. "Don't run away." I release her as I comprehend I'm wrestling with an ancient, fragile grandmother in a pale blue nightdress. It's absurd to be manhandling her. "Who are you?"

Her smile falters as she peers closely at my face. "You aren't Babs?" she croaks.

"We-ell." I sigh. Or has this old woman lost her marbles? "No, I'm Sophie, the night desk clerk, and it's my business to know who's sneaking around the hotel at four a.m. Are you a guest?"

Her hooded eyes flit back and forth, as though weighing the merits of this suggestion, or planning her escape. Something niggles my memory.

"You wouldn't be Eleanor, by any chance, would you?"

I realize I've guessed correctly, even as her eyes narrow in suspicion.

"Cook had some complaints about you earlier," I answer her unasked question. "Do you live at the Aviary Inn?"

"Yes," she whimpers. "I only came to fetch a snack. The stingy old crow starves me and then guards her pantry like the Tower of London. It's not stealing!" she insists.

I gently lead her back towards the dining room. "So, you live here, and presumably eat here as well." I'm puzzling out the situation as we stroll back into the kitchen, wondering who she could be. I've never been in here before. The kitchen is a large addition at the back of the dining room, with a high metal ceiling. The equipment is old and out of date. The scent of disinfectant and old greasy stainless steel greets my nostrils.

"A little warm milk would help me sleep." Her grainy voice echoes in the hard space, sounding tinny.

In the kitchen, I help her warm a pan of milk. While we're waiting for it, I notice her watery eyes making greedy love to the mounds of baking Cook has left under Plexiglas domes awaiting the breakfast buffet in the morning. I'll bet anything that's what she's after.

"You know, my grandma used to tear bits of stale bread into her warm milk. She swore that put her right to sleep," I say as I pour the milk into a large mug, the aroma comforting and familiar, reminding me of home.

Pulling her eyes from the baking, Eleanor scowls at me. "One of those Danishes will make me sleep like a babe."

"Oh, I doubt it." I shake my head. "All that sugar and fat will give you indigestion at night. Keep you awake for sure." I shouldn't let her. Maybe she's diabetic or something.

She grunts, and the sound of machine gun fire erupts from her chest. One of those deathbed coughs old people always have ready.

I decide I'd better ask about Eleanor's diet in the morning and wonder who would best know. Probably Teddy. I suspect she's not supposed to eat this stuff, and that's why she resorts to midnight raids. I offer to carry her mug back to her room for her, and she lets me, leading the way with her shuffling gait down the tropical greenhouse corridor to one of the garden suites. She opens the last door without need of a key and turns towards me to retrieve the milk, a sly smile on her wrinkled face, and I appraise her features for anything familiar, but other than my common-as-dirt brown eyes, there's nothing.

Over her shoulder, I take note of the small kitchenette, where she could, and probably does keep milk, tea, and snacks. It is the same doorway that concealed the timid spy last week as I toured the hotel for the first time. I smile knowingly.

"Good night, Babs, dear." She sighs.

"Sophie." I smile. "Good night, Eleanor. Nice to meet you." Clearly, I'm playing a game of Clue, with only half the pieces. Mrs. White in the kitchen with the lead pipe? Only it's me, Sophie, clutching a bent old black umbrella as I head back to the front desk, shaking my head.

CHAPTER 11

1 *1:28, March 8, 1945, Holborn, London*

She lay face down in the field, her mouth full of mortar dust and ash, her eyelashes caked with dirt, slowly surfacing to an awareness of her surroundings. Time had stopped. She didn't know how long she lay there with no sound in her ears, only an echo, a quiet roaring, perhaps the sound of her own blood rushing, a distant thudding, maybe her own heartbeat.

She coughed, spit, and drew in a ragged breath, the acrid scent of smoke and taste of metal all too real.

Until that moment, for Ava, the war was a series of events and circumstances that were unfolding around her but had never deeply touched her. This was not surprising. She had been but ten when war broke out and had come of age among all the turmoil. Yes, it was inconvenient and uncomfortable—the evacuation, the rationing, the bomb shelters—a terrible tragedy for many, and she was not a heartless girl, but it was also an exciting adventure for the young who had not been hurt by it.

Her family was affluent, after all, and never suffered true

deprivation. They could still dine out at the Berkeley or the Savoy, even if the French sauces camouflaged the same sausage or SPAM they ate at home. Few bombs had fallen on the west side, none on the homes of her close friends. Her father had been too old to enlist, her brothers too young. And Rupert had been in training in Buckinghamshire.

She'd only begun to wonder and worry about his safety, though neither of them knew yet where he would be sent.

Her first sign something was amiss occurred two blocks from Holborn Circus: a sensation of pressure in her head, in her ears. Insufficient warning for action or knowledge before the ripping sound of the explosion tore through the air, a long, drawn-out rumble, like thunder, that went on and on and on, followed by the sonic boom she had heard, until now, only from a great distance. Yesterday, she'd heard another V-2 explosion in Deptford. All that way.

The ground had shuddered under her shoes and rattled the bones of her legs.

Carefully, she rolled over, her view of the sky framed by tall spires of purple pink, the early spring blooms of rose-bay willow herb in which she lay, a bright blue sky now obscured by billowing clouds of mushroom-coloured dust and choking black smoke, unfurling in slow motion, like a fist unclenching. Sensation and sentience gradually returned.

She pushed herself up, cringing as the pressure on her hands and elbows sent shooting pains up her arms. Clearing the dirt from her face and eyes, she flinched. Sharp objects were embedded in her skin. Her hands were cut, scraped, and dirty. Tenderly, she fingered her face, painfully extracting the larger shards of glass and a splinter of wood. Warm blood trickled down her cheek, and she pressed the back of her hand to the wounds.

Surveying the bombed-out basement where she lay, she saw the wrecked remains of a vegetable garden, rows of winter greens, kale and old cabbages grey with mortar dust, some uprooted and flung with clumps of black soil clinging to their roots. Rubble, broken glass, splintered boards, and dust were piled upon the garden.

She glanced up. She must have been thrown down from the street. Strange. She'd taken Gilbert Place to Theobald's Road on the way to admire the vibrant vegetables growing in the hollowed-out basements. The barnyard sounds of pigs and chickens dropped into the middle of town. She liked that.

Turning her head, she saw the jagged tops of brick basement walls above her, and her eyes focused on a familiar splash of blue fabric ahead. Her heart pounded against her rib cage.

Ava recognized the blue dress of the woman she'd passed on High Holborn Street moments before the explosion. They'd both been pushing prams, had paused, smiled and peered into each other's. The woman in the blue dress had a young infant bundled in hers, sleeping peacefully, and peering across, noted that Ava's was empty, but for a filthy, coal dust–streaked sack. She'd smiled and nodded, moving along. Not another young mother with whom to commiserate, only a young girl on a hunting expedition, or so it seemed.

Ava had brought the old pram with her, thinking that if she'd returned home with both a fresh rabbit and some coal from the dump, Mother might be more forgiving of her escape.

Pulling herself painfully to her feet, noting that one of her shoes was missing, Ava staggered towards the woman in the blue dress, lying cradled in a soft bed of willow herb, only her arm showing. She wasn't moving! Hurrying forward to help, Ava stopped. There was only the arm, still clutching her string bag, in a torn sleeve of the dress. No more.

Bile rose into Ava's throat, her stomach heaving, her pulse drumming frantically. Where was she? Where was her baby? She squeezed her eyes shut and tried to slow her frantic panting. Opening them, she searched for the woman and child, her stomach clenched in terror.

Beyond the thicket of blooming weeds, the woman's twisted

pram lay overturned in a fresh garden bed, among rows of young onions and small green potato plants that had sprouted once the early warm spell had arrived.

A broken, limp doll lay half out of the pram, its jumper dark with blood, caked with dirt. Oh, Lord! Ava turned and vomited into the purple herbs.

Sharp awareness surfaced, penetrating her fog of horror. She was nearly to Holborn Circus to meet Rupert. A quarter hour late, because of Mother. Hoping he would be waiting. But of course, he would wait.

Oh, Lord! The rocket had missed her!

She cast her eyes around, frantic, resting her hands to her middle. The vast cloud of black smoke billowed upward, only a block away, towards Smithfield Market.

So close. Yet she was alive! But where was Rupert?

She scrambled up a broken embankment, half dirt, half loose bricks that tumbled down behind her, heedless of the pain in her hands and arms. On the dusty, debris-cluttered street, she peered around at cars and trams frozen in place.

Casualties swarmed in every direction. Some, like herself, dusty and dazed, others screaming or moaning. Still others, helmeted and purposeful, the VFS and the police, running towards the cloud of smoke, barking commands.

Across Holborn Circus, she could see Wren's St. Andrew's Church, its nave hollowed out by the blitz years ago, and the bronze statue of Prince Albert still mounted on his steed, his hat tipped in salute, near the centre. Ava was to meet Rupert in front of St. Andrew's Tower. She scanned the wreckage for her own pram, but it had vanished.

She staggered, limping towards the church, stumbling over the rubble on the road, jostled by people careening in every direction. Her one shoe crunched over the shattered glass on the road, and she painfully set down her other stocking-clad foot, wincing, hoping to avoid more cuts.

She searched the yard, the street, the circus, but saw no sign of Rupert in the milling crowd. Had she been on time, perhaps she would already have been in the market, and Rupert too. And they'd both be dead. Hot tears welled up, and her chest squeezed in terror.

Rupert! Where are you?

Reaching Prince Albert's statue, she stood stunned, witnessing the chaos unfold around her, and shivered. She rubbed her arms, flinching when her hands skimmed over the raw skin on her elbows and wrists. Sirens wailed. Civil defence workers converged on the focal point of the explosion, shouting commands. Crashing glass, stone, and brick tumbled down in the explosion's aftershock, sending up new clouds of dust. A tramcar lurched to one side, its stunned and bleeding passengers staggering onto the road, holding on to each other, crying. The cacophony was muffled. Her ears must be damaged.

She stumbled on towards the church tower. "Rupert! Rupert!" Her voice croaked. Her throat and nose were parched and dry, and she could smell and taste the ash. She tripped and fell hard, her hands and knees landing painfully on the debris-littered sidewalk. Her trouser legs were torn, and she saw blood seeping from her cut knees into the woolen fabric and through her stocking.

Then she saw it. Behind a stalled Morris lorry, wooden barrels tumbling splintered from its box, a spider web with grey dust clinging to its golden strands. A filigree of fine lines converging on a familiar finial. An aerial? A birdcage! Rupert's dove cage, lying on its side.

She staggered towards it. Inside, two oval-shaped lumps coated in dust, clinging to seeping sticky moisture. Tiny, clawed feet, curled and rigid. She stared, recognizing the doves. Ares and Kythereia, trapped in the cage, stripped of feathers by the blast. She picked up the cage and turned around.

Rupert? Oh Rupert! His birds were here. He had to be here too!

CHAPTER 12

June 1, 1997, York

The next day, I come in a bit early, hoping to ask Zoë about my curious guest last night. I can't let go of the fact she mistook me for someone named Babs. An improbable thought intrudes. Babs is a nickname for Barbara, my mom's name—who I resemble more than a little—though she never went by it. Could Eleanor have known her? But that's too crazy. What are the odds I'd end up here? Is it only wishful thinking?

Zoë, however, is flipped out and hardly registers my questions.

"I dunno much. She's Mrs. R.'s older sister or cousin or something." She's tugging on her purplish-ebony hair, which is tied up in two spiky pigtails high on her head today. The hair, with its pink Lucite bobbles, seems styled to go with the short, flared skirt and striped over-the-knee socks, the pink platform high-tops, and the girly blouse, à la Spice Girls. "Been here forever, I guess."

They're related? My thoughts spin. I'll have to get the full scoop on Eleanor from Teddy. "What's bothering you, Zoë? You seem …" I shake my head. She seems wired, all tense and twitchy. "What's the matter?" I take her restless hand away from her hair before she yanks it apart, and I give it a squeeze. "Zoë?"

She sighs and heaves herself into a chair while I perch on an old wooden stool by the desk. "I am truly beggared."

I nod, waiting for the rest.

"My flatmate, Cora, moved out. Last night. No warning, no notice. Rent's due today, June first, and I can't afford it on me own!"

"How much?" Nausea roils in my gut, an omen of my own folly, even though I won't form the thought. Zoë tells me the rent, and it's cheap for a two-bedroom apartment, similar to what I would pay for my clean and cozy bed-sitter at the rooming house, but no meals. Still, I could afford the flat and food, with my free suppers here. I could afford it all if I wasn't trying to save money to get home.

"Your family can't help out? For a while?"

She rolls her eyes, laughing mirthlessly, and I remember the few details she's told me of her single mother, her four younger siblings, who live near Manchester, barely eking out a living.

The pressure on my chest makes it hard to breathe. "Where is it?" I'm looking for practical reasons not to do it, but a force propels me forward, out of control, like an invisible hand.

"Heslington, near Walmsgate. It's a funky area to the south, outside the wall near the uni." Zoë's staring at me now, her eyes questioning yet cloaked, though I can see the hope blooming there. She pulls her full bottom lip between her teeth. She won't ask. She's too proud.

I nod and fill my lungs. It's farther away from work, too, but it would be nice to share with a friend.Wouldn't it? "You know, I'm looking for a place to stay," I say, as though it's an obvious solution, and it doesn't cost me anguish. I shrug. "I can't promise long term. If Marc-Antoine comes back, who knows what he'll want to do next …" My words fade to a mumble.

Zoë's caramel eyes flood with tears. "Bloody hell, Sophie. Will you? It would give me time to find another flatmate." Yeah. Just long enough for me to lose my perfect room at the boarding house. Her tears of gratitude spill over and instantly wash my regrets away. "It'll be ever so much fun, you and me." She hugs and releases me.

"Yeah, it'll be great. I don't know why you didn't think of it immediately." I smile and mean it. I know I've done the right thing, and somehow, someway, it will all work out okay. Neither of us mentions the rooming house. She's embarrassed. I can't bear to. It's in the past now.

Zoë leaps out of the chair, suddenly energized, and sings, "'Come and sit beside us, we'll give you such a thrill,'" and dances around me, her hips gyrating and her arms pulsing in the air.

"Hey. I like that song. What is it?"

"'Rollercoaster.' B*Witched," she says. "That reminds me, sister. Do you want to trade MP3s for a bit?"

I nod. "Yeah. I'm really liking the British pop I've heard so far. Have you got any Backstreet Boys?"

"No, I—"

Raised voices coming from across the foyer interrupt her. Something's wrong. The few guests who do use the dining room tend to eat at this hour. "I'll go find out what's up." I jog through the entrance in time to see Eleanor pursue Cook into the kitchen, both their faces red as fire engines. I follow them in time to catch the tail end of their dispute.

"It's not fit to eat!" screeches Eleanor, her voice rising above the din of pots and dishes clattering. April and a guy I don't recognize work in the kitchen.

"I don't care. You've no call stirring up a commotion in front of guests. You're lucky to have a roof over your head, you crazy old bitch," Cook mumbles, under her breath, but we all hear it. April, Cook's granddaughter, looks up, elbow-deep in a sink full of dirty pans, her eyes wide and mouth an O of shock.

"Ava will sack you for that." Eleanor wags a bony finger in Cook's face.

"Ava will lock you in your room if you don't behave," Cook says between clenched teeth, her chins quivering.

I shush. "Ladies, please, keep it down." I step between them. "What's on the menu tonight?"

"Pig slop," hisses Eleanor. This seems unfair, given Cook's wonderful Italian fare.

"Heh. Watch yerself or that's what you'll be gettin' till the end of yer miserable days," growls Cook, wielding her wooden spoon.

I raise my eyebrows in both warning and question and move to look in the warming oven. Looks like some grey meat, the usual side dishes of potatoes and anemic, unappetizing vegetables. I can really sympathize with Eleanor but also realize it's not fair to criticize Cook. It's what she's expected to serve. "Is this what you're bringing me tonight, Mrs. D.?"

"'Course not, love. I've got a bit of fresh white fish an' nice juicy fennel. You'll love the way I do it up in a pan, you will."

"So. What if I traded my supper with Eleanor's? Unless you've got enough, that is. Maybe a bit of variety would ..." I shrug, appealing to her with my eyes.

Cook scowls. "She don't deserve no better, the shrew."

I purse my lips and give her a meaninful look.

"All right, all right, love. But Ah've no time to fix it now. Ye'll have to wait." She turns away, clanging pots and ladles as she resumes work. Apparently, we are dismissed.

"Humph." Eleanor turns and shuffles out of the kitchen and away to her room. She's wearing a pale lavender pantsuit and several chunky bracelets.

I let out a long breath and head back to relieve Zoë for my shift. She hugs me tightly before leaving. "You're a lifesaver, Sophie. Ta."

I sigh, recalling what I've done. We plan to meet up. "See you tomorrow."

At about eight thirty, Cook appears, carrying a tray with covered dishes stacked on it. "'Ere you go, love. But I will na deliver it to that mad old bat." She turns to leave.

"Thank you, Missus Delicious," I croon. "I'll return the favour somehow, I promise." I hear her belly-laughing down the hall to the kitchen. I'm about to unload my dinner so I can take the tray to Eleanor's room, but no sooner is Cook gone than Eleanor materializes from the shadows, as though she's been lurking. I wonder if she spies on me. She's probably hungry. "Come and sit with me, Eleanor. We'll see if the fish is better than the roast, hmm?"

I pull up a chair for her in the office, and she slides into it, her eyes darting left and right, as though she's never been invited in. We tuck into Cook's fish and fennel, the aroma intoxicating. It's another masterpiece—tender, mild, and sweet, and a smile spreads across my face as I watch Eleanor make the same discovery, amazement blooming on hers.

"Best kept secret at the Aviary Inn," I say.

"Hmm ha ha … stingy old cow. Been holding out on us, she has."

I laugh, forking up more yummy caramelized fennel and flaky fish. "I really don't think so. She can't cook traditional English fare, that's all."

Eleanor and I finish the meal, during which I egg her on as she tells me a few disjointed facts about herself. She has lived in the hotel since 1946 or maybe '50. She never married. She sounds half crazy, the way she talks, shooting off in all directions. She also says she stayed with the same man all her life. Maybe she has a bit of dementia, after all.

One thing she goes on and on about is her insomnia. She often can't sleep at night and sometimes goes on a walkabout, then sleeps the days away. She's a curious old thing, and I can't quite figure her out.

"Good night, Babbie, dear. It's so nice to have you back."

I shake my head. There it is again. I wonder who she thinks I am. Only when she's gone do I have time to remember my own new reality. Goodbye, perfect boarding house room with meals. Hello, two-bedroom, semi-furnished flat, sight unseen, with capricious roommate. I sure hope Zoë's flat is half as nice as that freshly painted room I'm passing up.

I scratch a few numbers on a pad of paper, calculating my new, revised savings plan. It's sooo depressing.

Unless Marc comes back and bails me out, I'm staying in York for a long, long time. Eventually, to get home, I may have to tell Mom and Dad what's gone down. My chest squeezes with anxiety, my breath strangled at the thought. I can see Matt's smug expression, hear my parents' kind, condescending reprimands. No, thank you.

Out of curiosity, when I leave in the early morning, the rising sun lighting the sky in a pale blue light, I fish my old photograph out of my journal and stand on the curb staring at details of the hotel, comparing them to the fragments that appear in the photo. I'm no architecture student, but if this is not the same building, it's darn near identical. At least now I'll have more time to investigate.

"What did you do about Eleanor?" I ask Cook when she brings me my supper at eight thirty the next evening.

She sets down the tray. "I gave her linguine pesto, jes' like yours. She ate at six. Therefore, yours is warmed up."

"I don't mind, you know. If it keeps the peace. I'm not fussy."

"Ye've a good heart, Sophie, love. But she'll find somethin' else to gripe about, mark my words." Cook heaves her bosom onto her plump folded arms on the edge of the desk. "An' you deserve a good meal, working all the night through."

"Your meals are always good, reheated or not. In fact, it's a crime that no one else knows." I twist the glistening pasta onto my fork and taste it. The aroma and flavour of creamy basil and garlic is gorgeous, and I revel in the perfect al dente texture as I chew and swallow. "You look a bit tired tonight."

"Aye. I'm peaky. Jes' gettin' old." She sighs heavily and shows no sign of leaving.

"Tell me about Eleanor. How did she come to live here?"

Cook grimaces. "She's been here since before I come. Mrs. Roxtoby's older cousin. They say it was 'ard for them all, after the war. Mrs. R. was raisin' her bubbies, and Eleanor, unmarried, came to help out with the daughter and never left." Cook rubs her sweaty forehead with the back of one chafed red hand. "When Mrs. R. lost everything, Eleanor stayed on. Mrs. R. would na kept on without her to lean on, I suppose. She will na kick her out now, even though she's touched in the 'ead." Cook taps her temple with a significant look.

I twist another mouthful around my fork and tuck it in, chewing. At her age, she could have a bit of Alzheimer's. I hope Mrs. Roxtoby is taking proper care of her. I swallow, licking the oily pesto from my lips. "I meant to ask. Is Eleanor diabetic or something? I wondered why she steals pastries."

"Hah." Cook barks. "She's as healthy as an ox, in body, if not in 'er 'ead. Nooo. She'd eat a dozen buns, and I'd have nothin' fer the guests next day. Done it before, she 'as."

I laugh, then sober. "You said Mrs. R. had children. Did something happen to them?"

"Aye. Lost 'em both. They was nearly grown, mind. But they're gone now. The poor boy, dead of drugs. An' the daughter, as good as. Everything fell apart after the boy died."

"Poor Mrs. R." I can't imagine what it would be like to lose one's children. Too tragic. "No wonder she's so melancholy. And her husband?"

Cook shakes her head, lips pressed together. "Gone too. An' left 'er with nothing but debt."

"He left her?" What a cad.

"Oh, no. Passed on too. But with one thing an' another, money's always been tight. She runs this place on a shoestring, minimal staff run off their feet, supplies on the cheap." Cook shakes her head. "Tha's half the trouble with the bloody dining room. Canna do everythin' myself, though I try. An' I canna turn a sow's ear into a silk purse, not without a bit o' magic."

Scraping the last of the delicious pesto sauce off my plate with a piece of bread, I think she does work magic on my suppers. She looks so tired. I never stopped to consider how many hours she works each day. And Teddy too. "You're very loyal and kind to work so hard for her."

"Well, love. She's a good woman. And I would na want to walk in her shoes."

"I could help," I say. "Maybe on one of my days off? Or I could slip an extra hour in before my shift, during dinner hour? Would that help?"

"Nonsense, love. You need your rest an' recreation. Get out and mingle with the other young folk. We'll manage all right, April and me."

CHAPTER 13

"Right. That's your room there." Zoë gestures into a vacant room, in which dust bunnies and scraps of paper hover listlessly. It's furnished only by a narrow bed and a tall dresser. The walls are pockmarked with nail holes and bits of tape and gobs of sticky stuff like a war zone. I realize I've been rigid with tension, afraid of what I've committed to sight unseen. With a resigned sigh, I toss my bags on the lumpy, stained striped mattress. Stay positive, Soph. It'll be fine.

"Cora 'n' me kept our groceries separate, since we were never here at the same time. So, maybe we can start out that way and see ..." Zoë's muffled voice drifts in from the other room. I follow it. I have to step over umpteen pairs of shoes and boots that are lined up, higgledy-piggledy along the hall. So many shoes! I eye her assorted plaid platform loafers and strappy sandals. I own one pair of Skechers Jammers that I have with me and a pair of Doc Martens that I reluctantly left at home. Why are hers all over the hall like a hurricane blew through?

"Um, Zoë ...?" I certainly can't start by criticizing. "You have so many shoes, girl!"

"Yeah. Bit of an obsession, really," she deadpans through a mouthful, flopping down onto an ugly chintz floral sofa with stuffing straining at the shredded armrests, a bag of chips under her arm. Having kicked off yet another pair of shoes, she lifts her now bare, tiny feet onto the crowded coffee table, gently nudging aside a few encrusted plates and stained mugs to make space on the stack of newspapers and magazines.

I tamp down the urge to spring over and pick up the mess. "I oughtn't really, but every time I get a pay cheque, it seems I fall in love again." She laughs, eh heh heh. I bend to pick up a few dishes to make room, and she waves me off. "Leave that. I'll get to 'em later. Sit down and settle in."

As if I can relax in a mess. I perch on the edge of an unmatched, boxy chair and steal a glance around the cluttered main room. It's clear "I'll get to it later" is Zoë's mantra, as there are dirty dishes and glasses and papers and clothing strewn everywhere. I sigh. "So," I say optimistically, tapping my foot. "Tell me your rules. I want to make sure I don't do anything, you know, to annoy you."

She looks blankly at me. "Rules?"

As I suspected. This is going to be harder than I imagined. "Well," I say, keeping my voice light. "Like, kitchen and bathroom cleaning schedules, who buys common stuff, cleaning supplies, toilet paper, and such?" I shrug and look at her hopefully. "Utilities?"

Her full lips turn inside out into a befuddled pout. "Aow. They jes' take care of themselves. Don' worry about it."

Hmm. I wonder if Cora took care of these things, though by the looks of the place, it's likely no one paid them much attention. I smile at her. Okay. One day at a time, Soph. "Well then. Let's celebrate by having a meal together." I'm thinking takeout, as I'm not ready to tackle the kitchen on my first day. "Is there a good Indian place nearby?"

"There's some leftover take-away curry in the fridge," Zoë says pensively. "From Saturday, I think." She's keeping track, anyway. That's a good thing. I shudder inwardly. Thankfully,

I've got the next two days off. I can clean house a little. "Or we can have Marmite sarnies."

"Erm, no thanks. Maybe fish and chips, then," I venture.

Zoë's brow furrows, and she wrinkles her nose. "Maybe Oliver will pop over. He might treat us."

I wonder how long I have to wait for supper if I depend upon Zoë's boyfriend. "You could call him and arrange to meet somewhere if he's free. Meanwhile, unless there's spare bedding, I'll have to go shopping."

Zoë's face lights and she jumps up. "Right. I know jes' the place. Nice and cheap. Come on, then."

We head out, and she takes me to none other than Coppergate Shopping Centre. There's a discount outlet store tucked away in there, and I find some inexpensive bedding in a funky green-and-brown retro polka dot pattern. Maybe change the colour of my room from ghastly piss yellow to a subtle taupe? Some green and white artwork maybe …

"Ollie finally called back," Zoë says as she joins me at the till, her tiny Motorola cell phone in hand. "Those won't go with the walls." She pokes at my purchase with a long nail.

"I had the notion to paint. If you don't mind," I tug at the cuff of my jacket. "What did he say?"

"He and his mate are already at the Frog an' Firkin. We'll jus' pop over."

The Frog and Firkin is one of a string of popular student pubs back along Micklegate, and only ten minutes later we're penetrating the smoky fug searching for Oliver, who I've only heard about, and his friend. I trail behind Zoë, my shopping bags in tow, as she squints and wends her way between the crowded tables, the din of many voices pulling my senses in every direction. She spots them, waves, and leads me over to a booth on the far wall.

"'Allo, sweetheart," croons a thin Black guy, grinning, his smooth skin as dark and cool as graphite, with a goatee-trimmed pointed chin, his red knit toque with ear flaps pulled down over his head, mirrored aviator glasses perched on his nose. He jumps up to give Zoë a wet, enthusiastic kiss and I can see the appeal. He's charming.

"Ollie! This is Sophie. My new flatmate." Zoë hugs him, bouncing. He's a smidge taller than her, but way shorter than me. I try not to react as I notice his vibrant yellow-and-blue plaid pants. He and Zoë clearly share the same fashion sense. My lumberjack shirt, cropped tee, and baggy joggers make me feel grotty next to their bodacious splendour. But then, I am from the colonies.

Oliver's eyes scan upward until they meet mine and then widen slightly. "Oy. Zoë said you was tall, but fuck." He has a musical lilt to his voice that might be slightly Caribbean. "'Ere's one for you, mate. Up with you, see who's taller." He chortles and his shoulders shake, and I feel my face fill with heat. Being "the tall one" gets old.

Oliver's friend extends his long limbs from the booth and straightens up. Now it's my turn to gawp as he towers over me, smirking. My mouth goes dry, and I lick my lips as he takes my hand and brings it to his, making my skin tingle and my stomach flutter. "Pleased to meet you, Sophie. My name's Elliot, Elliot Crowther." A blond Adonis. Smiling at me. He and Oliver are as mismatched as me and Zoë.

My face stretches into a grin as my eyes drink him in, from his long legs to his broad shoulders to his blond, preppy good looks, high above me. Me. Sophie the Amazon. Elliot must be six foot five! And he's not wearing plaid pants. "Hello, Elliot." I finally find my voice as we all shimmy back into the booth and I tuck my parcels underneath.

He keeps his bright blue eyes fixed on me and that same wide grin on his boyish, clean-shaven face. "You're not jus' tall, you're magnificent. Like a queen."

I grin back, and my breathing is quick and shallow in my chest, like a caged bird. Is this what love at first sight feels like? I'm being a bonehead.

"What'll you be drinkin' then, girls?" The sudden appearance of a server breaks the spell.

"Glass of ale, please," says Zoë.

"Oh. Do you have a white wine?" I ask.

After she's gone, we make small talk, and everyone decides what to eat. When the server returns with our drinks, I order fish and chips and peas. Elliot orders bangers and mash, saying he can't abide fish.

At my look, he explains, "That's all we ever ate at home."

Zoë and Oliver are so wrapped up in each other's bodies, I don't know how they manage to eat their suppers. It's distracting enough for me just sitting next to Elliot the stud, our thighs grazing ever so lightly, making me jumpy.

While we eat, Elliot tells me he's a student in the business school at the University of York. He also has a part-time job to pay his way. His family is from North Yorkshire, and he confesses shyly, they are rather proud of him. He leans his masculine mass close to me, and his warm, beery aroma wafts over me as he confides he's the first in his family to get a university education. "I'd like to have my own business someday. Not a common greengrocer, you know. Something respectable. Dunno what yet."

"Somewhere you can lord it over your workers and be a slacker, ay?" Oliver has stopped sucking on Zoë's neck long enough to catch a bit of our conversation.

"Shut up, you prat." Elliot gives Oliver a friendly shove on the head, sending his red cap askew as he keels over laughing, revealing an irresistible smile and a quirky crown of spiky twisted dreadlocks with undercut sides.

"Oh, I say. The match," says Elliot, snapping his fingers. "We've got tickets to the football match a week Monday, and my, uh, sister can't come, so would you like to come with us, Sophie?"

"Yeh. Sister. What bollocks, eh heh heh," chuckles Zoë. "But good idea, Elliot. It'd be proper mint if Sophie comes." They all look at me together.

I shrug. "I suppose, yes. I'd like that, thanks." Well then. That's settled. I smile shyly at Elliot, shrinking back, feeling small. Fingers of tension walk up my neck and scalp. Something's off. It's not really a date, though, is it? Only a football match. I suppose they mean soccer. What am I doing, flirting with a guy I only this minute met? Have I written off Marc-Antoine already? It's a sobering notion and dampens my mood and preoccupies me as we walk home.

It doesn't help that Zoë comes into my room later to help me make up the bed in my dusty, scarred yellow room, then stands and looks me in the eye and says, "Tell me the truth about Marc-Antoine. Did you split wif him or what?"

I sigh heavily and collapse on the bed, which feels better than it looks. Gazing at her despairingly, I confess, "I don't know what to tell you, Zoë. I woke up, and he was gone. I don't know what it means."

"The git!" She shakes her head in disbelief. "The bloody wanker. He buggered off?" She wraps her arms around me and my head suddenly flushes with heat as long-suppressed tears finally erupt.

I squeeze my eyes shut, but I can't stop my lips from curling and quivering. "I thought ..." My voice gurgles in my throat. "I ... he was ..." I can't seem to speak, the pressure on my chest too heavy. "I thought ..." I try again, but my words sputter.

She pulls away and touches her forehead to mine, wiping away my tears with the heels of her hands. "That's okay, duck. 'Ave a good cry. At least you've got a home now. You're safe wif me."

I meet Zoë's gentle golden-brown eyes and realize, despite the dust bunnies and holes in the walls, I need her as much as she needs me, and I am so glad to be with Zoë instead of in a freshly painted boarding house room all alone.

Zoë peers gravely at my face for a moment and then nods.

"Your brows could use a bit of tweezin' too, girl. Maybe we should have a spa day tomorrow. That'll cheer you."

I release a wet, snotty sob and choke out a little laugh. "You think?"

Teddy stands back assessing my work as I arrange the fresh sprigs of spring blossoms that he cut from the back garden. When I decided to freshen the bouquet in the foyer, which was past its prime, he offered to cut a few branches.

"Tha's loverly, lass, loverly."

I have to agree. He's brought a mixture of bright pink azaleas and soft lilacs, with showy peonies as a focal point. As I remove and replace one stem after another to get the composition perfect, their gorgeous, heady fragrance releases and I wonder for a brief moment how Mom's garden is coming along back home. She's so proud of it, but is she too melancholy this year? "There. Done." I wipe my damp hands on the back of my pants.

Teddy smiles. "An' these little 'uns are for yer desk." He grins and holds out a clump of nodding columbine.

"Aw, Teddy. These are beautiful." I take them, smiling down at the sweet little purple posy and clear my throat. "I've got a vase in the back too, collecting dust." I head into the office.

Teddy follows me with his stiff-legged gait and leans on the battered front desk. "I have me doubts it's dusty anymore, lass, the way you've been sprucing up the place. Mrs. Roxtoby won't recognize it when she gets home tomorrow."

I return with the small vase and pour my drinking water into it, popping in the small bunch of flowers in. Glancing coyly at him, I remember something. "You know, speaking of which, I've been thinking—"

Teddy's abrupt snort of laughter stops me mid-sentence. "What've ye got planned for us now, lass?" The expression on his face, his alarming white eyebrow tufts poised high on his creased forehead as though prepared to leap off, his thin-lipped mouth, wide open in a smile of anticipation, his pale pink tongue half out like a slab of bologna on display at the deli, makes me laugh.

"I'm not that bad."

"Anything but, lass. Ye're a surprise and a delight, that's what you are," he replies. "What've ye got in mind, then?"

I pucker my lips and smile slyly. "Well. I've noticed the woodwork is quite banged up …" Teddy's eyes widen in alarm. I hold up my palms. "And that's generally not a problem. But the front desk is even more chipped and dented and scratched. It's pretty small, so I figured one night I might, you know, freshen it up a little." I peer at him, expression open and questioning.

He's scowling. "Ye know varnish'll take too long t' dry. Tha's why I never get to it meself. We'd have to close the hotel to do any serious painting. Besides, there's jes' no money fer improvements, lass."

"I considered that. Yes, I did." I beam. I smooth my hand over the dented surface of the desk, lingering on the larger divots and scratches to make my point. "There's a product my Mom's used before … if I can find it at the paint store, it only reworks the existing varnish, and it would be dry to the touch by morning. It's a little bottle. I'll even pay for it."

"Tha' won't be necessary." He shakes his head. "Ye're a very persuasive young lady, ye know that? It ain't even my permission ye require. But as it's such a wee project, I don't see any harm …"

Yippee! I lean across the desk, attempting to throw my arms around his neck and kiss his sallow cheek, and knock papers flying. "Thank you, thank you, thank you. You'll see. It'll make such a difference."

"All right, lass, all right. Will ye look at the time? I'd better get on wi' me rounds so we can have our tea before the clock strikes twelve!" He scurries away, and I sit in the office hugging myself. My heart dances with delight at the thought of my plans. My mind is busy scheming a new restaurant concept, down to the décor and menus, when Teddy returns with the tea tray.

"That was quick," I say, leaning forward to absorb the aroma of tea and cookies.

"No more than usual," he says, setting it down. He runs his gnarled hands over the scarred surface of the desk and nods, his lips pressed together. "Ye've got a point, lass. I guess we're all blind to it. We've been at the inn so long."

As I pour our tea, I ask what I've been dying to know for some time. "Tell me about the Aviary Inn, Teddy. Tell me about Mrs. R. How did you come to be here? And Eleanor too. I feel like you're family, and there's all this history, but I don't know any of it."

"Aye. A lot of history. That's for sure, lass." He nods and stares into his teacup. "Me whole life, really, when ye look at it."

"You came as a young man, then?"

He nods and pulls up his stool, shifting back onto it with a sigh. "Aye. Not yet twenty. I was rather late, joining the war effort, because I was runnin' the farm. Me da had passed on. An' lucky, too, as I was never sent to the continent. Most danger I faced was right there in London, with the bombs a-fallin'."

"The blitz, you mean?" I ask, taking a gratifying sip of hot liquid. I remember so little from high school history classes.

"Well. No. The blitz come early on. An' then things settled down a bit. An' the children came back, many of them. But then, in '44, Fritz invented a new toy. The V-1. The buzz bomb." He shakes his head, slurping his tea.

"I remember a story about that. Some boys and a crater, or something ..." I'm so incredibly stupid. I was nodding off in social studies, and these people were living through it. It all seems awfully relevant now that I'm in England.

"Aye, well. There were many craters in London." He takes a long gulp, his loose neck moving. "But I came north after the war ended, in the spring of '46. Houses were all chopped up, on account of the housing shortage when all the men came home. Ava was no more than a girl, just married with a new babe. And a big house full of boarders, young men like meself, mostly. Rations went on for a long time afterwards. People don't realize that."

He picks up a biscuit between his gnarled fingers and holds it in the air.

"I remember it was her eighteenth birthday, and dear Lord, she was overwhelmed." Teddy shakes his head. "Eleanor was here too, helpin' out, and so was he. Mr. Roxtoby, I mean. He was a fair bit older than the rest of us. Thirty or so. Still young himself, but we thought of him as the old man. Acted like one. But he was never a serviceman. Somethin' wrong with his health. I never understood what … until later. After he was gone. It was 'is heart."

"Ah. That's why he died so young, then?"

"Aye. Not yet fifty." Teddy nods, his lips pressed together. "He had business interests after the war. But the women continued with boarders and babies. The little lad, James, came along in 1950. Eleanor went to work in London for a while before, as a nurse, you know—then Ava went there to have the baby with her and her mother's help. They came back together, the three of them. That's when I noticed—I still worked odd jobs elsewhere—I saw somethin' weren't right."

He bites into his biscuit, chewing thoughtfully.

"About what?" I glance around, but of course, there's no one astir after midnight. I can hear only a bit of wind stirring the trees outside.

"The whole setup. The marriage. They was under a lot of pressure, sure, but it ought to have been a joyful time. But there was a grimness to everythin'. Buried discontent."

"Grimness?" It all sounded awfully Brontë. I lean forward, elbows on the desk, and wet my lips, eager for the story. "What do you mean?"

"They didn't seem happy. And he and Eleanor were close.

Too close, I believed. Which made the women's relationship difficult, with all they had to do."

"What happened?"

"Well, to make a long story short, nothin'. It went on that way, the children growin' up, Mr. R. away a fair bit with his business, some manufacturin' plant in Leeds, I dunno. Maybe it weren't goin' so well, because they squeezed more boarders in here over the years. An' the women … well." Teddy shakes his head, scowling. "Ava doted on the lass, and Eleanor behaved as if little James was her own. Then there'd be a blow-up, an' Ava would keep James to herself, as if she was jealous, and that would leave Babbie to Eleanor's care. It was very odd." He takes a big bite of a biscuit, and it crumbles into his hand, so he has to scramble to shove the fragments into his mouth.

Babbie was Mrs. Roxtoby's daughter! I thought for a moment she could have been Eleanor's. "I guess, if Mr. Roxtoby was away so much, it was awkward for them. Did Eleanor have any boyfriends? Did she never marry?"

Teddy's eyes open wide. He brushes his two stiff, arthritic hands together to dust the crumbs from them, making a swooshing sound. "Ah. Very interestin' question. Well, I can't say, but no, she never had suitors. Never … but then 'e would come home, they would argue about somethin' or other, and Ava would sulk in 'er rooms, and Mr. R. an' Eleanor would carry on without 'er, 'ave their dinners and family outings with the children. 'Twas unseemly at times."

Wow. This sounds like a soap opera. I touch a finger to my mouth. "Do you suppose …?" I gape at Teddy, unblinking. "I mean, that would be so …"

Teddy leans back and makes a face and shrugs. "I can't say, lass. But it weren't a happy household. Mrs. R. was good to 'er, I'll say that, but then, it goes both ways, don't it?"

"How did it all end?" I break a corner off another sugar biscuit and nibble it.

"Well, somewhere about 1960, I remember Jamie was ten,

Babs was becoming a young woman already. She looked like you, y'know, so fresh an' pink an' roun', with dark wavy hair." Teddy pats my hand, gazing at my face, my hair, and I drop my gaze. "His nibs comes home and announces that he's bought the house next door, and plans to turn the 'ole thing into a hotel. Well, you can imagine. The women were already run off their feet."

"Did he stay home then?"

"Mmm. A bit more. Not enough. 'E hired me to help with the renovations. We 'ad to connect the two houses and convert rooms. Build the office and kitchen … Busy times. After a couple of years of that, he hired me on for maintenance and whatnot, same as now." He smiles and runs his gnarled hand over the dented surface of the desk again. "So long ago." He shakes his head. "Where did all the years go?"

"But Teddy. When did Mr. Roxtoby die? What happened then? And what about Eleanor?"

Teddy jolts out of his reverie, seemingly surprised by my presence, never mind my questions. He glances up at the wall clock. It's already quarter to one. "Will you look a' the time, lass? I'd better be off now. Good night." He pushes away from the desk and levers himself from his stool, hobbling off, his mind still in the past.

CHAPTER 14

June 8, 1997

Dear Mom, Dad, and Matt,

I've come to Coventry to see the cathedral that was bombed during the war and rebuilt by architecture students afterwards. Marc-Antoine always talked about it. It's so sad and beautiful, I can't explain it, but I stood there on the plaza and cried and cried and cried. It means so much to me to be able to experience England and a bit of history. I hope you can understand.

Love,

Sophie

CHAPTER 15

J *une 10, 1997, York*

"Hey! Canadian. I didn't expect to see you." Nick emerges from the Jorvik Centre after work, and he looks genuinely surprised to see me. Dare I think pleased?

"Dinner's on me tonight," I reply, holding up the plastic shopping bag I've packed with some food. At his slight scowl, a sudden idea occurs to me. Maybe he's horrified to see me again. "Unless you have, uh, plans or something?"

He scratches his scalp through his dreadlocks, which are loosely arrayed around his head tonight, reminding me how distasteful they are. Why does he have them? "Nooo. I don't have plans. But … what's in the bag?"

"Oh. I packed a picnic," I reply. "The weather's so warm I figured we could, I don't know, walk somewhere. Anywhere." I shrug, glancing away.

He nods and his moustache lifts on one side as he smiles in understanding. "Ahh." I wait while his eyes roam my face, and he blinks, searching for a solution. "I have an idea, actually.

Have you been to the Roman Multangular Tower? There are some cool shadows this time of day."

"Okay," I say. "Let's go."

Nick shrugs and leads the way. Instead of cutting through the Shambles, he leads me up Parliament Street past the fountain and the modern shops to a lovely open square with potted topiary shrubs.

My eyes pop at the view. "O-oh. Where are we?"

"St. Helen's Square. Used to be the churchyard, back when," Nick replies. He leads me across the square, at the end of which sits a striking, red-and-white Georgian building. I look at him, brow hiked, and he answers with, "The Mansion House, built in 1725. It's the mayor's residence."

We continue out of the square, and I note a sign showing we're now on Coney Street, which we take north to Museum Street. Marc-Antoine and I stopped to see the Multangular Tower, but only briefly at the end of a long and tiring day of walking. I can't recall enjoying it much. It seemed gloomy and grey.

Nick grabs my hand, holding tightly as we jog across the busy ring road, and I realize the enclosing city walls are notably absent here. Leaving the hubbub of the city behind, he leads me through a gate along a wide paved walk through undulating lawns. To the left and right, massive trees and shrubs cast long shadows across the grass and path, and a fair number of people stroll or sit on benches.

He releases my hand, and I realize how soft, dry, and warm it was. Reassuring. Comfortable. I rub my tingling fingers together. Confusing.

"You smell like dirt," I blurt.

His mouth quirks. "Well"—he sniffs in my direction—"you smell like lilacs, my lady."

I roll my eyes. "Seriously, but nice dirt. You smell like dry, dusty, clean dirt, and … and straw?"

He shrugs and peers at me. "Occupational hazard."

"The exhibits?" I ask, remembering the mock-ups of village life, the dirt floors.

"Yes. Partly. Also, we get dirty in the workshops, digging with the kids, and sometimes I help clean artifacts, which are dusty. And they're stored in straw."

"Aah." That explains it.

"I do actually bath every day," he adds, nonplussed.

I feel my face heat. "I'm sorry. I like it. It's … distinctive."

"So. Canadian. What's new? Are you getting settled in, then?"

I smile at his funny nickname for me. "Actually, that's one reason I looked for you. To thank you for the referral to that boarding house."

"Did it work out?"

I screw up my face. "Yes and no. I looked at it and loved it. I was all set to take the room, but then something happened."

"She didn't let it to someone else, did she?"

"No. No, I had to give it up." I explain about Zoë and the shared flat south of Walmsgate.

"Shame, that. It was rather good of you, under the circumstances." He gives me a knowing look, and I glance away, embarrassed.

"It'll be fun," I say.

He clears his throat. "You're living rather near me now. I'm over there, a bit southeast of you. I share with two of my bandmates."

"Really?" I say. "Are there three of you in the band?"

"No, four. But Arthur's married. They have a baby girl—Bea —and a flat in Eastfield." His mouth pulls in at the corners.

Wow. What a strange fact, one that suddenly makes Nick and his friends seem more mature and serious, though of course, I've never met them and they could be deadbeats. I study him closely, his profile crisp in the afternoon sun, his long straight nose leading up to fine, sandy eyebrows and a high, smooth forehead. Too bad about the hair and beard. He's handsome. He has good skin, fine and clear. And I do like his eyes.

"Look." He points ahead. "See what I mean about the shadows late in the day?" Nick leaves the path and strides away from me onto the well-manicured green carpet. I follow him towards the grey-gold mass of the Multangular Tower and adjoining wall I remember. Now, instead of gloomy, its stony mass looks warm and inviting.

Nick veers left and circumnavigates the tower until we arrive at an opening in its side, where the stones have collapsed or gone missing. The wall interior carves out a round, grassy room with a high band of archways set into the wall, each with a narrow niche in it. The walls capture the heat of the late afternoon sun, and I move forward, the warmth seeping into my skin. Below, set in a radial pattern on the grass like heavy spokes inside a wheel, are old, blackened, mossy boxes carved from stone.

"Hey! Are these what I think they are?" I move forward.

"Old Roman sarcophagi." He grins. "Do you have a problem having a picnic with ghosts?"

I look around, walking closer to one coffin, running my hand over the eroded carved patterns and Latin inscriptions, rough and jagged on my palm. "No. This is cool."

Nick chooses another one, in a swath of sunlight, and heaves himself onto it with a grunt. He pats a dense, mossy spot next to him. "Come on, then. What are we having for tea?"

I climb aboard and sit cross-legged on the moss, cool and soft as velvet, pulling my surprise out of the shopping bag. I grilled Italian vegetables according to Cook's directions and made a massive focaccia panino that she baked for me, cut into wedges. I've also brought salami and melon. "Not prosciutto, unfortunately, but maybe Cook will tell me where she shops one day." I've splurged on the cheapest bottle of Italian wine I could find. "I hope it's not rot gut. It's all I could afford."

Nick spreads his long-fingered hands out in a gesture of

amazement, grinning. "This is more than a picnic, Sophie." He laughs, a throaty tenor reminiscent of his singing voice. "This is a feast fit for a Roman legionnaire. It couldn't be more appropriate."

I'm pleased with my grilled veggies. They turned out well, tender and succulent, with a hint of balsamic vinegar and fresh basil. Cook taught me well. Even my bargain red is agreeably astringent with the focaccia.

Nick digs in, chewing appraisingly, and makes an approving face. A little juice from the sandwich dribbles onto his beard, and I hand him a serviette. He seems lighter today.

While we eat, I fill Nick in on both my new flat and my plans for it. He laughs at my anecdotes about Zoë's millions of shoes and the shabby furnishings. Then, when I tell him my plans for cleaning and painting, he cowers in mock horror.

"What?" I ask, blinking.

"I'd better never have you to my flat. You'd be appalled. We don't even have furniture, really. Just amps and wires and instruments." He sips his wine. "Well, we do have two tatty sofas."

I nod, laughing. "So, that's where you practice, then. Not at Arthur's house."

"No we have more room. In fact, we jam at odd hours whenever Arthur gets a break from the family. Bea isn't sleeping through the night yet." He chuckles through his nose softly.

The sinking sun has shifted, flashing like a laser beam over the tower parapet, and I squint against its glare.

"You have spectacular eyes."

"What?" I blink. "They're just boring hazel."

"Not just hazel." His gaze traces over mine. "They're more like clear gold with a crisp dark bronze ring, and little flecks of moss green, like ..." He glances up. "Like light filtered through tree branches and leaves, and you've got the most amazingly long dark lashes that sweep down at the corners. I'm entranced."

I lower said lashes and blush at the compliment. "Uh. Thanks." That's sweet, but I hope he doesn't get the wrong idea about me. I really like him, but he's not my type. Not my new type. Nothing like Elliot, with his towering, clean-cut preppy gorgeousness. Nick's a little rough-edged, even for my old, artsy type. Like Marc. Though these days I'm starting to place more value on character than appearance.

When Nick's eaten his fill, I pack up the food scraps, empty cups, and wine bottle.

The setting sun leaves us in part shadow, and I'm suddenly chilled. I shiver and rub my bare arms with my hands.

Nick offers me his tattered brown sweater. "Thanks." I pull it on over my head, inhaling the aroma of his warm, earthy musk.

"Shall we walk a bit?" Nick asks, hoisting my bag over his shoulder. I nod and we leave the shelter of the Multangular Tower. The sun is getting lower, and more shade than light fills the confined space, but outside, the park still sparkles with sunshine, and long shadows stretch across the trim lawns.

He leads me past the Yorkshire Museum and tells me all about the ruins of St. Mary's Abbey, which is stunning in the late-afternoon sun, and then we walk over to and around the Hospitium, back past the Observatory to the lodge. Nick is a fount of historical knowledge, and I'm reminded of his two history degrees and his aborted D. Phil.

"Tell me about work," Nick says when he's run out of historical facts to share. "How are you liking it on the Mount?"

I smile as I tell him, "I love it. It's funny, I took some crap job to survive, but I've come to love the place and all the people in it. I have this funny, eccentric family now." I fill Nick in on all the strange characters in my life: Mrs. Delicious and her contradictory cooking, her strained relationship with old Eleanor and all Eleanor's peculiar dotty ways, sweet Teddy and his long association with the hotel. I tell him I've been writing character studies to take home, so I remember the details for future writing projects.

"Teddy told me some strange things the other night," I confide in Nick. I relay Teddy's tale of the post-war years, with

Mr. and Mrs. Roxtoby, their two children, and cousin Eleanor cohabiting and sharing the work in a strangely intimate way. "Teddy said there was tension between them all and a sadness that pervaded the atmosphere. The word he used was grim."

"How terribly Gothic," exclaims Nick, grinning.

"He implied something. I don't know if I should say …"

"Hmm?" Nick's quirky half smile is all the invitation I need to go on.

"Well. Teddy didn't say so, exactly. But he hinted that maybe, maybe there was something going on between Mr. Roxtoby and Eleanor. You know, an affair."

"How scandalous." His green eyes scrunch at the corners, teasing.

I smile, distracted. I'm absorbed in this story. "I know. But seriously, I feel Mrs. Roxtoby's pain. She's such a sad, sad lady, living in a lonely bubble all by herself. She's lost her husband and both her children." I shake my head. What her life must have been like. "She's back from her trip to London, and I'm determined to make friends with her. She needs someone to talk to."

Nick pauses, turns towards me and slides one finger along my jaw, sending tingles over the back of my neck. "Sophie, love. I know you need to take care of everybody, but aren't you being presumptuous?"

I pull back, tensing, surprised by his words. "What do you mean?"

Having strolled back past the tower, Nick leads me under the beautiful vaults of St. Leonard Hospital, and I realize the light is quickly dimming. Time with Nick has been so easy, I've hardly noticed the hours passing.

He clears his throat, his gaze flicking to me warily. "What makes you think a mature woman like Mrs. Roxtoby wants a young girl for a confidante? I pity her, too, but she's survived her hard life without your help. You can't possibly know what she needs. Might she prefer to be left alone and in peace?"

I gasp, reeling as though I'd been slapped. Young girl! Not him too. I never expected him to be so callous. "Nick, I can't believe you. Where I come from, it's called kindness. Mrs. Roxtoby has done me a good turn, and obviously needs someone. She must be lonely. She has no one!" I can't give voice to my inklings, or my curiosity, about the strange parallels between Mrs. Roxtoby's life and the family story I'm trying to piece together. Not yet. I could be out to lunch, and I don't need more ridicule.

Nick's voice is abruptly more forceful, his firm jaw jutting forward. "Sophie! Really. Get some perspective. You imagine you've found yourself amid some Gothic tragedy. It's based upon nothing more substantial than gossip!"

My heart hammers in my ribcage, my shoulders pulling back in indignation. He doesn't understand. Wrapping my arms around my middle, my face tightening in a scowl, I dig in. "It's not gossip! I feel a connection to her. My heart is telling me to do something. How can I not listen?"

"It's simply not your place, Sophie. You're making assumptions, no? Leave the poor woman alone. Respect her privacy." He pronounces it with a soft British i, and it sounds so uptight and priggish, with his face creased in disapproval. His eyes flash green fire in the low-angled sunlight, and his narrow nostrils flare. Why is he being like this?

My head floods with heat, my ears and eyes burning, my teeth grinding. This again! How can he reprimand me for caring and trying to help? He's just like my critical parents, and Matt, and Marc, even, always patronizing and telling me my ideas are childish. Which they're not. I have my reasons. Good reasons.

I suddenly blurt, "Who are you to criticize me? Insufferable, opinionated stuffed shirt! You don't even know me!" I blink back the tears that blur my view of his judgmental face and avert my gaze, but turn back, immediately regretting my rude outburst. A part of me knows the flow of angry words stems from old wounds, and it's wrong to unload this resentment on Nick, but

I'm unable to stop myself from blurting, "You obviously don't care about anybody or anything but yourself." I turn away, my heart hammering wildly at my shocking attack, trying to catch my breath. That was childish, and now I feel as if I deserve his scorn. "I'm sorry. We'd better go. It's late."

"I'll walk you home," he says, calmer now, but stiff after my outburst, and we turn towards the park gate.

"That's unnecessary, thank you." I am choked, and my voice squeaks.

"Of course I will. I'm going that way." The perfect gentleman.

I feel horrid. I've ruined our evening with my emotional outburst.

We walk back through town towards Walmsgate in silence, the streets and squares now bare of pedestrians in the dusk. Nick makes no further attempt at conversation, but I sense his lingering annoyance in his rigid, aggressive stride. In the silence, I have ample time to reflect. My chest is tight, my feelings seriously bruised, and I regret the harshness of my words, but I refuse to contemplate the possibility of a hint of truth in his observations. He doesn't understand, that's all. Maybe if he knew about my mom, about the photograph and my suspicions, he'd see it differently. Perhaps from his perspective, I do look like a busy-body. I certaintly can't fault his thoughtful reaction when I compare it to Elliot's callous brush off. At least Nick means well.

After a while, I notice out of the corner of my eye that Nick is rummaging in his jeans pocket. He pulls out a spliff and then lights it, taking a long, intense drag, his eyes closed. I curl my nose as the sour, pungent odour of burning weed drifts over to me, invading my nostrils. I slide my eyes across at him. God! Is he a pothead? I should have known.

His eyebrows flatten and he wordlessly offers the joint to me, his breath held in, a thin snake of blue smoke curling up into the night air.

I shake my head abruptly. Chill, Sophie! I'm not a prude,

after all, I'm simply—I don't know—surprised. I temper my voice, and it comes out in a judgmental squeak. "No, thank you." It's no wonder his education and ambitions got derailed if he smokes a lot. He's lost his focus.

At last, we reach my flat on Wolseley Street off Wellington. "Well. I'm here." It's been fifteen minutes since we've spoken. Sickly spiders pull and crawl from my stomach to my throat and back. I stop and turn towards Nick, but I can't bring myself to look directly at him, my face tight. Why did I bother going to find him again? He's disagreeable and annoying.

"And I'm not a young girl!" I blurt, incongruously. "I'm a grown woman," I add, mumbling. My face flares. I've been pretty disagreeable too.

Nick's drooping eyes widen and burn into mine with a hint of sadness. "Believe me, Sophie. I'm quite aware of that." He lifts a hand, as though to touch my cheek again, but then he doesn't, sighs and it drops to his side.

From the corner of my eye, I see Nick's mouth pressed into a tight line. He's nibbling on his lower lip, his aristocratic nose still flared. "Look, Sophie … I didn't mean to speak out of turn. I'm sorry. We don't know each other at all well yet, but … well, I am sorry, but we had a lovely evening, and I felt I could speak my mind. I didn't mean to offend."

I notice he's not retracted his criticism, however. "It's fine," I snip, blinking slowly and avoiding his gaze, focusing instead on the celadon beads in his beard. But it's not fine, and I know I don't sound convincing.

"Well, thank you for bringing supper to share. I'm glad you came to find me." Nick sounds desolate, and a dreadful melancholy drapes over me like the falling night. Our wonderful time together has ended on a sour note. But perhaps it's for the best. He's not at all what I assumed. We obviously have contrary ideas and values. Not every new acquaintance is destined to be a good friend, after all. Though this conclusion sits heavy in my chest.

CHAPTER 16

"You have such flare, Babs, darling," exclaims Eleanor late one night, later that week. "That pink scarf is lovely in your dark hair."

"Thank you, Eleanor. You know I'm Sophie, though, right?" She has wandered out at about three in the morning, dressed in her usual pale blue dressing gown. Oddly, though, she's wearing dangly clip-on earrings with sparkly blue gems and a streak of orange lipstick approximating her thin, wrinkled lips. She seems to suffer her insomnia the worst at this hour, and maybe her memory loss as well.

As she's strolling in the direction of the kitchen, an innocent expression on her long, wrinkled face, I get up and follow. Best to keep an eye on her.

She grabs my hand and squeezes it tightly. "Of course, darling. Of course." She's pulling me along now, through the darkened dining room, her bony grip surprisingly strong. She's crushing my knuckles and when she releases me, I flex my hand. "I was quite the stylish dresser myself. As a young woman, I turned a few heads, yes, I did. I may not have been a conventionally pretty girl, but I knew how to dress." She fingers one earring.

We're in the kitchen now, and she flicks on the overhead lights. We both blink in the brightness, our eyes adjusting. "Oh, will you look at that!" She's eyeing the baking again, rubbing her thin, veined hands together with a papery shushing sound.

"Would you like a snack, Eleanor?" I ask. "Perhaps a pastry and a cup of tea? I'm sure Cook won't mind if we have one." Now that I've confirmed she's not diabetic, I can afford to be indulgent.

Her eyes light up, sparkling and dark. Her face is, upon further reflection, more ferret-like than equine. Her bony back is rounded into a hump, and her thin white hair is pulled back across her scalp. "Maybe a wee Marmite sarny?"

I grimace. "Uh. Not for me, thanks."

I serve us each a Danish from the tray under the Plexiglas dome, the sweet, sticky aroma of cinnamon and vanilla custard inviting as I lick my fingers. I put the kettle on the hob, and it hisses and hums immediately, as the water is still warm from my tea with Teddy. Eleanor sinks her long yellow teeth into her pastry with delight.

"William liked that about me," she says, and I frown, confused. Now what's she talking about? Her eyes are glazed, staring across the large kitchen, unseeing. Or seeing something I can't see. "He was quite smitten. I was always a lively girl. Vivacious!" She chuckles and takes another bite, talking while she chews. "But of course, it was mutual."

"Who was William? Your boyfriend?" I ask. I bite into my Danish, its flavour seductive, and I admire Cook's talents as a pastry chef.

She glares at me, her expression clearly saying she thinks I'm daft.

"My husband, silly girl."

"But I thought ..." And I stop. Maybe I am daft. Could she be referring to Mr. Roxtoby? I stay quiet, nibbling on my pastry. After making a pot of tea, I bring us each a mug, setting them down on the gleaming stainless steel countertop. I like mine stronger, with a bit of milk in it. The steam rising from it warms my nose. "How did you meet?"

"Ah." She nods. "Our families were acquainted. We both grew up in Yorkshire. My family has been in Leeds or York or hereabouts for generations."

"What about Mrs. Roxtoby? She's your cousin, right?"

"Yes. Aunt Margaret was Father's sister. Moved to London when she married. They would visit us, and we would stay with them in London when we went to town. We were as close as sisters." She chews and scowls thoughtfully. "It was her fault, really."

I inhale deeply and lean against the counter. It's challenging to keep up with this crazy old woman. "Mrs. Roxtoby's fault? For what?"

Eleanor looks up at me, scowling furiously. "What?"

"You said it was Mrs. Roxtoby's fault." My cup is empty, so I stand and refill it.

"No, no. Not Ava." She waves a gnarled, dismissive hand at me. "Your great-grandmother Margaret, of course. I never understood why Father agreed. I was his daughter. Ava didn't fancy William. She desperately wanted her young soldier back and cried and cried like her heart would break. But it didn't matter in the end, dear. They would have their propriety, and we would pay the price."

What soldier? Mrs. Roxtoby's soldier? I'm getting more and more confused.

She shakes her head dismissively. "Although I never had a proper home and family, did I? I suppose I should be bitter about that. But I had my darling little Jamie. William's boy. I loved them terribly." Her wrinkled face scrunches up, and her lip quivers.

This reinforces my belief that she's talking about Mr. Roxtoby. My head spins with disjointed facts. Or maybe the fragments of an old woman's long-held fantasies. Still, I'm curious. Trying to make sense of her story and what bearing it has on Mrs. R., I ask,

"Why did you stay with Mrs. Roxtoby after Mr. Roxtoby died? If you were resentful, I mean?"

Eleanor is perched on a kitchen stool, jaw hanging open, tears leaking out of her creased, baggy eyes, tea untouched in front of her, although she did manage to eat her entire Danish.

"What is it?"

"Poor little Jamie. My Jamie. Gone. He paid the price for all our sins." She's keening softly now, rocking back and forth, and I gently stroke her shoulder, her back, soothing circles with my hand on the velour of her robe, the angular bones of her shoulders and spine poking through like sticks. She's so thin and frail, like a little bird.

"He died too, I understand. Quite young?"

Her face contorts. "So young. So much anguish in a young boy."

"You stayed for him, then? For James?"

Eleanor blinks at me, a puzzled expression forming. "William and I stayed together always. I would never leave him. He was my husband." Her dark eyes open wide. "And she made Jamie suffer so."

"Mrs. Roxtoby?" I ask, shocked. "But he was her son."

Eleanor's orange-streaked lips twist. "Oh, yes. Of course he was. Hah!" Her bark of bitter laughter incites a coughing fit. I flinch and lean towards her, concerned. I think she's done for. "She pretended she loved him as much as her precious Barbara. But I always knew. She clung to Babbie like a drowning woman. It was disturbing. Pitiable."

My heart hammers in my rib cage at her words. Babbie is Barbara. "Why didn't she stop it?" I ponder aloud on my own tangent. If I understand what she's telling me, I would have kicked Eleanor out, no matter how helpful she'd been.

"A woman consumed by guilt, she was. She stole my husband, and she knew it." Eleanor delivers this well-rehearsed line with her chin raised and her shadowed eyes focused on some distant point. "She was obsessed with Rupert and his foolish birds," she says, sneering as an afterthought.

Rupert? Birds? Now who is she talking about? "Who was Rupert?" I venture.

"Her soldier!" Eleanor snaps at me, as if I'm a slow pupil.

"How could you stay?" How could they be so cruel to Mrs. R., to have an affair right under her roof, and in front of the children? But then maybe she never loved her husband at all. What a nightmare of a family! Could this be it?

Eleanor pushes herself up from her stool and shuffles away. "Because I loved him. And he loved me. We were inseparable, Ava and I. Devoted. There was no one left, in the end."

I massage my temples as she disappears through the darkened dining room. If I was confused before, our little chat certainly sealed the deal.

CHAPTER 17

J une 15, 1997, Nottingham

Dear Mom, Dad, and Matt,

I'm in Nottingham now, and I've been exploring the City of Caves carved into the sandstone under the streets.

This will arrive too late, but I wanted you to know I'm thinking of you on Father's Day, Dad. I hope it was a good one.

Love,

Sophie

CHAPTER 18

O*9:30, March 8, Whitehall, London*

"Lieutenant?"

"Yes, sir!"

"Follow me. A word with you."

The young officer trailed his superior down the corridor, puzzled. Had his orders come in? He'd been expecting them, now that he'd completed his radio operator and basic decryption training. That's why he'd arranged to meet with Ava. It was likely he wouldn't see her for a while. Maybe even until the end of the war, which, hopefully, would come sooner rather than later, despite the disappointment at Ardennes.

Could it be something else? News of his parents, back in Woodstock? He frowned. He'd already received bad news once, of a personal nature. While still at Oxford, the dean of his college had called him in to inform him that a doodlebug had killed his older sister, back in '41. His parents had been devastated. As had he. That's why he'd held back, though he'd been eager to sign up earlier. He couldn't do that to them, so soon after losing Barbara.

He followed Major Warren into his office and stood at attention.

"Lieutenant Dean."

"Sir!" He saluted.

"Stand at ease." The major, his long, lean face sober, stood and studied Rupert from under a hooded brow. Rupert, in turn, studied the golden crown stitched on the front of his brown hat on the large, steel desk between them. He kept his own tucked under his arm, where the trapped heat of perspiration built against the wool of his jacket.

Then the major's face cracked a bit. He was a stoic, but not a hard man, and well-liked by the men. "I've got good news for you, Lieutenant Dean. At least I trust you'll agree."

Rupert let out the breath he'd been holding. "Yes, sir." Then he dared to lift his eyes to meet the major's, his forehead taut.

In response to his unspoken question, the corners of the major's thin-lipped mouth bent upwards a little. "I can't tell you anything about your assignment, but know this. It's critical. We're entrusting you to replace a more senior officer who's suddenly taken ill. We need someone with your training promptly. Your exceptional performance at Hanslope and your availability have taken priority over your lack of field experience. You'll get specific orders once you're underway, and your partner will brief you when you get across the water. But you know what to expect." He paused, met Rupert's gaze and nodded. "It's a nocturnal existence. Lonely. You know that. But, with a little luck, it won't be for long."

Rupert could only nod his understanding, but he dropped his eyes, studying the cracked tan linoleum, a knot tightening in the pit of his stomach. His hands clenched into fists. Across the water! Where the hell were they sending him? Surely not France, not now!

"Once you get there, you should be safe enough, considering the times. It's a remote station. That's all I can tell you."

While Rupert sighed with relief, Major Warren reached

forward and slid a manila envelope across the cardboard blotter on his desk. "There's your train pass. You depart from Kings Cross at noon. Don't be late."

Noon! His heart kicked in protest. Ava would be waiting at Holborn Circus at eleven. He glanced at his watch. Half nine! He had to pack his gear and get to the station.

"Noon, sir? I can't be ready that soon!"

Major Warren's face hardened, and he glared from under the storm of his bushy grey brows, his lips pinched. One corner of his thin mouth twitched.

"We're holding transport for you. You must be on board immediately. They sail tonight. They are needed elsewhere. Pack your kit, Lieutenant."

Rupert nodded, swallowed, shifting his feet. Where were they sending him? North from Kings Cross. Tynemouth? He snatched the train ticket from the envelope and glanced at the typed words. Newcastle! He was right. He struggled to keep his voice steady and his breathing even, despite his agitation. "Yes, sir. Right away, sir."

He could never meet Ava at eleven. Somehow, he must get a message to her before he left. To say goodbye. He'd hoped she would take care of his doves while he was away.

"You'll be met at the train. Good luck, Lieutenant. Dismissed."

He saluted sharply and rushed away to pack his gear. Damn! He had to get word to Ava. What could he do?

CHAPTER 19

June 17, 1997, York, England

"Hurry up, hurry up! The match will begin before we find our seats," Oliver barks, flicking his long red striped scarf back over his shoulder. As usual, it clashes with his orange jeans, but he is wearing a silky jersey polo that is half red and half navy blue, apparently the colours of the home team. "Come on, Zoë love," he urges, even though Zoë cannot possibly navigate through the dense crowd any faster.

Zoë squeezes between jostling bodies to catch up with Oliver, her large bag bumping the people on either side of her. "Hold on, Ollie. I'm coming."

Standing beside Elliot, I'm unaccustomed to being small, and it makes me shrink back, letting him lead. My efforts to maintain some decorum in the increasingly boisterous environment seem futile. My gaze sweeps across the broad stadium, taking in the expanse of green Astroturf ringed by strips of ads that read Nestlé, Fitness First, and Bairstow Eves. The red seats in the stands are almost full, and the aisles swarm with people, filling the cavernous space with a loud hum like a hive of bees.

I know soccer—football—is a big deal in England, but I've never experienced energy like this. And apparently this isn't even one of the important games, at least by international standards, but don't tell the locals. I'm sure no one back home has ever heard of the York City Minstermen or the Bristol Rovers, whom they play tonight.

We are in the David Longhurst Stand, reserved for home team fans, under a broad overhanging roof. After a large party passes, Elliot guides me ahead, his big hand pressing lightly but warmly on my back, and we catch up with Zoë and Oliver, who are standing in the aisle peering at their tickets, searching for seat numbers. Elliot's being so gentlemanly, and I feel like a thirteen-year-old on my first date. Though I remind myself that we're not on a date, exactly, merely a football match with friends. Right?

Still, every time I look up at Elliot's tall, leonine form in a maroon jersey with a white Y-front that stretches across his broad chest, or catch his assertive, blue gaze, a burst of caged bird's wings beat in my stomach, and heat suffuses my limbs, my core. Is this just lust? Am I so ready to replace Marc-Antoine, with whom I've had an exclusive, intimate relationship for two years? What are my feelings for Marc-Antoine, anyway?

"Oy, Ollie. Let's sit over there," says Elliot, pointing to our left. "Better angle."

I look at a bank of several empty seats farther to our left and several rows down, closer to the action. "Isn't the seating reserved?" I whisper. "We're over here, aren't we?"

"Oh, yeah. But it doesn't matter. People don't come, often."

"But what if …?" How can this be true when the stadium is so full?

He either doesn't hear my protest or chooses not to. "Down here, Ollie! Here we go, Sophie." Elliot grabs my arm and pulls me down to the vacant seats while waving at the others. I look over my shoulder and see Oliver raise his eyebrows and shrug at Zoë and then follow us down to take their seats. Zoë sits next to me, in between the guys.

"Bloody 'ell. It's always a circus gettin' in and out." She sighs, wrestling her large bag down between her knees and pulling out a big blanket. The space is tight, and she elbows everyone around her.

"Right, I'll get the pints. All right, everyone?"

"Right," says Elliot, and we nod. I don't care for beer, but it's way too complicated to ask for anything else. Oliver disappears back into the throng.

Elliot's thigh brushes mine as he settles himself on the narrow bench and places his muscular arm along my back. An oppressive claustrophobia closes in on me, and I squirm a little, wishing I could breathe. I remember our earlier conversation on the long walk through the town centre to reach Bootham Crescent, the arena where the game is played.

While Oliver and Zoë were walking well behind us, I took a moment to make sure Elliot understood I wasn't going to be around long, and that we could be only friends. Elliot confided that this was fine with him, as he had recently been dumped by his girlfriend and was still bruised emotionally. His honesty and openness impressed me. A sure sign of maturity in a man. Who knows? By the time I learn what happened to Marc-Antoine, Elliot might be sufficiently recovered to … I mean, we might … I slam the door on that thought. These are not possibilities I'm ready to entertain, and I feel my face heating again. What's the point? I'm leaving soon, anyway.

Earlier in the evening, he and Oliver hadn't gotten very far trying to help me understand the game we're about to see. I turn to Elliot. "So, explain again, Elliot, about the league. You were saying about a pyramid?"

"Yeah. York City was promoted to Division Two after the match at Wembley in '93. First time in history. So far, this season, they did well before Christmas. They were in third place. But they've been slipping. Haven't won a single home game, though their performance has been better away."

"But where do they fit in the big picture again?" This is hard for me. Soccer doesn't have the status and public appeal at home that it does in England, or everywhere else in the world, I gather. There are layers and layers. I'm not convinced I care all that much.

"Right. York City's in League One, which is Division Two, so they're the third-ranking division in the pyramid, overall." Elliot animates his explanation with sweeping gestures. He's vibrating with excitement.

One, two, and three. No wonder I'm having a hard time understanding it all. I cast an imploring glance at Zoë, hoping she can translate.

She says, "The top division is the Premier league. But they didn't use to exist, so the one under them used to be first, but now it's second, and so on. So, Division Two is ranked third. And the top teams get moved up, and the bottom ones get demoted each year. York's never been higher than it is right now."

"Oh! So, that's good, then," I sum up. I've finally got a mental picture. "Do they play against those famous teams that I've heard so much about, like, I dunno, Manchester United or, what is it, Arsenal?"

Elliot cuts in. "Yeah. Early in the season, they do. But not during the playoffs, obviously."

I nod. "Obviously." Not.

Oliver returns with a cardboard tray and four plastic cups of ale, and wiggles in past a couple of people to hand them down to Zoë, who passes them down the row. I take a cold plastic cup, wrinkling my nose at its hoppy tang, taking a reluctant sip of the bitter ale.

Zoë shifts her bag and twists in her seat, then exclaims, "'Ang on. What's this?" She holds up what looks like a billfold. "Some bloke's dropped 'is wallet."

"Here, let me see it," says Elliot and reaches across me to snatch it out of Zoë's hand, opens it, and rifles through it. "Oy. There's over two hundred quid in here."

"I'll take it to the lost and found, then," Zoë says, reaching out her hand.

"No bother. I'll do it later, when I go for the next round," offers Elliot, and he slips the wallet into his jacket pocket.

I catch him giving Oliver a funny look over our heads, and I frown. "You will turn it in, won't you, Elliot? Someone will be looking for it," I say.

He tries to stretch out his long legs in the confined space of the bleachers, man-spreading and turning to face me, bumping thighs and knees, grinning and winking, rubbing a warm hand on my shoulder. "'Course, love. Don't you worry."

I notice a small cluster of people huddled in the aisle at the end of our row, examining their tickets and scowling in our direction. I turn to Elliot and put my hand on his sleeve. "Elliot, I wonder if …"

"Hey, Ollie, look. Tolson's come on. I heard he was out with an injury." The opposing players have come out on the field and are milling about, stretching, the Minstermen in trademark navy and red, the other guys in yellow and black.

I sigh. Maybe I really don't understand how things work around here. I don't know. I try to put the matter of our seats out of my mind.

"He's back, then, ain't he?" replies Oliver. "But I heard Greening's gone, and Stevenson."

"Do you think they'll do all right then, this season?" I ask, trying to stay in the conversation, though I can see it's a losing battle.

"Not if they keep sodding Little," spits Oliver.

"They've gotta sack him and soon or they'll be bumped to Conference, and see if they ever climb out of there again."

"Conference?"

Zoë turns to me and shakes her head, chuckling. "Little's the coach. Conference is the next league down. I'll draw a chart for you later. Watch the game. Ours are red and blue, like Ollie's jersey."

"Why aren't you wearing red and blue, too, Elliot?" I ask.

"Oy, this here's a vintage Minster jersey, it is. 'Twas my dad's, back in the old days. It's a collector's item." The match, which has begun, has captured his attention entirely now, and I won't be getting anymore conversation for the time being.

"Oh. Very handsome," I say, forcing a smile, though he doesn't see me, and then at Zoë, who grins back and rolls her expressive golden eyes.

I sigh, turning my attention to the playing field, determined to make sense of the chaotic movements of the players below, so I can at least know who's winning by the end of the game without being told.

Mrs. Roxtoby is back from London when I return to work a couple of nights later. I glimpse her around the dinner hour, nicely dressed in a skirt and jacket, greeting guests and chatting with regulars. At one point, I glimpse her walking with Eleanor into the lounge. She's cheerful and seems much revived by her brief holiday in town. I'm glad for her, but I also remember her solitude and melancholy before she left, and now seems a good time to get to know her. Before she sinks back into her ruminations about her lost family.

Nick's words of warning echo in my mind.

What makes you think a mature woman like Mrs. Roxtoby wants a young girl for a confidante? Might she prefer to be left alone and in peace?

I push them away. What does he know, anyway? He's so uptight, he wouldn't know a friend in need if he fell over one. After all I've learned, my heart bleeds for Mrs. Roxtoby. A fire in my belly tells me she needs me. And despite Eleanor's and Teddy's loyalty, I don't get the sense that Mrs. R. talks to them or anyone else about personal stuff. Nobody visits her, that I can see. Even Eleanor, who is purportedly so close, seems almost estranged, despite living together their entire lives. Despite Nick's warning, I have to do something.

Later in the evening, when things get quiet, but long before Teddy closes the bar and makes his final rounds, I see Mrs. R. again. I've got my journal open on the desk in front of me, scribbling my imaginary scenarios, in a halo of warm light from the spot overhead, and I watch her from the corner of my eye. She passes through the lobby, dressed in her signature pink house dress and bare feet, carrying a bowl of wilted lettuce and spinach, apple slices, and banana peels I suppose she got from the kitchen. I know where she's headed.

She stops in the middle of the lobby to gaze at the vacant golden birdcage, absently caressing a large stuffed pheasant mounted to a base on one side, her movement drawing my eye to the silken, tawny-grey feathers with their spots and crescents of black. I've seen the bland beige bird a hundred times, but only now do I register that its effective camouflage is achieved with an intricate feather pattern, its glassy, golden-brown eye arced with a delicate black line, seeming to gaze back at her in response.

"Well, that's better, isn't it, David? That'll do for a bit." She pronounces the bird's name like the Spanish or French version, Duh-veed. She seems unaware of my presence. What is it with these birds?

I recall Eleanor's puzzling words: She was obsessed with Rupert and his foolish birds. Rupert the soldier. Who was he? Not her husband, clearly. That's another mystery I need to solve. She turns and continues walking past me.

"Good evening, Mrs. Roxtoby." I smile warmly, inviting a response.

She looks up, and I study her features. "Oh, hello, dear. How are you managing, then?" Her feet hesitate in their stride on the worn vine-covered carpet as she blinks at me, but she doesn't stop.

"Did you enjoy your trip to London?" I persevere.

She offers me a broad smile. "Indeed, I did," she says. "Indeed, I did." Distracted, she carries on. She disappears into the service corridor behind the bar, where another door leads into the garden and patio. I know she lives alone in the small cottage at the back of the property, but to my knowledge, she eats her dinners in the restaurant. I imagine it seems too much trouble to cook dinner for one when food is available every day, but by the same token, Cook's appalling English menu can be no secret to her, and I don't understand why she doesn't change something. It is her hotel, after all.

I wonder where she lived when Mr. Roxtoby and the children were still with her, and if she cooked for them. She seems so far removed from a happy family life now, if indeed she ever had one.

Thoughts of Mrs. Roxtoby preoccupy me and fill my journal, and a little while later, I leave my desk and slip silently past the bar, where Teddy has nodded off, his smooth cheek folded over his gnarled fist, an unobtrusive fixture in the shadowy room. I smile, happy to have such a sweet, caring person to work with.

Out on the rear patio, I listen for sounds of water splashing, hearing nothing but silence. It's dark now, at ten thirty. Through the silhouetted trees and shrubs, I see the contour of the aviary roof against the otherworldly, blue-tinged light cast by the underwater pool lights, and beyond that, the glimmer of yellow light leaking from Mrs. Roxtoby's cottage windows. I creep forward, in case she's still in the pool, and I'm beside the aviary door when I see a shadowy figure moving inside and hear her voice.

"Trr. Trrr. How are you tonight, my lovelies?" she coos to her birds, holding the bowl of compost in her hand. I am in plain view and cannot sneak away unnoticed. She spins towards me suddenly, with a gasp of air.

"Oh! I'm sorry to disturb you, Mrs. Roxtoby."

She stares at me, blinking. "What are you doing …?"

"Um."

She looks a little freaked out.

"I needed a little cool air. Did you have your swim?"

She's alert then, as though I've jogged her from some faraway place. "Ah. Sophie. You resemble my daughter Barbara so much, sometimes it's truly alarming. Did I mention that?"

I draw in a halting breath, biting my lip. "Others have mentioned it, but I thought it might be … uh … a painful subject for you." My eyes slide sideways towards the doves in their cage.

"Oh, well. Yes, I imagine they would see it too. The resemblance is striking." Could it be? She doesn't directly address my hint at her loss, and I'm relieved. This is harder than I expected.

I nod, grasping for something to say. "I guess we're all made from a limited number of patterns."

She laughs, a rusty cough, like it hasn't been used much in recent years.

Warmth spreads over me and I smile. We're connecting for the first time since she hired me, weeks ago. But my courage falters as we each search for something more to say. She tucks her salad bowl under the arm of her pink robe, and I notice the wilted greens on the platform where the doves are perched, but that the banana peels and apple slices are still in the bowl.

"Who are the banana peels for?" I ask, hoping to extend the moment.

She glances down. "Ah. Not my doves." She doesn't answer my question.

"You keep them separate." I turn to ponder them again.

She frowns and turns with me to study them. "Yes. I've been having trouble with Kythereia." She points at one dove, a lovely buff colour with a whitish ring around her neck. "She's become territorial and aggressive. The male I first had, Ares I called him, fell ill and died. Years ago. The replacement I got turned out to be a female. They are difficult to sex, and I didn't realize it until I got three eggs."

"Three eggs?" I query.

"Yes. A female will lay only two. So, I knew the other one was also laying."

"And then?"

"Well. I got another male. That's when Kythereia attacked the other bird. She pummeled and pecked it to death."

"Cripes! I thought doves were docile."

"They are. Collared doves are normally very social and broody."

"So, then what happened?"

"I left her alone for quite a while. A few years. She seemed to calm down. Then I tried again, but she became aggressive again and I had to get rid of it." She croaks. "This new one, she completely ignores. I named him Hephaistos."

"That sounds like it's from Greek mythology?"

She nods and smiles. "Yes, Aphrodite—Kythereia—didn't care for her husband, the blacksmith. It seemed apropos."

I laugh. "Maybe she'll come around when she gets to know him," I say.

We stand side by side for several minutes, listening to the evening song of the small birds in the other enclosure above the soft low coo of her doves. She beckons for me to follow her through a mesh gate that swings closed behind me, and after she switches on a soft overhead light, I see that the larger aviary opens off a narrow, screened corridor, from which she can observe and feed her birds.

As we walk along, she pulls open shallow wooden drawers built into the frame of the side wall, examining the contents of small ceramic dishes. I peek over her shoulder and see seed mixtures, mealy stuff, and what looks like worms, or caterpillars, in the third dish.

"They eat meat," I observe.

"The softbills eat live insects, as well as meal and seed. My robins, song thrushes, pied waxwings, tits, and skylarks."

I squint inside, through the mesh, where live trees and shrubs grow, and can barely make out a few flutters of movement now and then as a bird stretches its wings or darts to a new perch. She points to a straight-sided plastic bin on the floor of the aviary, where I see more wormy things and jumping bugs awaiting slaughter. I cringe.

"Mealworms and crickets," she answers my implied question. "I also keep chaffinches, gold and green finches, yellowhammers, and siskins, who eat only seed and meal, and a little fruit."

As she moves down the aisle checking other drawers, I then notice the large cage is divided into three narrower bays, each with its own door, feeding drawer, watering tube, as well as an acrylic box of seed inside, and on the floor, shallow terra-cotta trays with water dripping from small irrigation hoses tucked in among the shrubbery.

Mrs. R. turns towards me. "I've been noting the changes you've made, Sophie," she says, her steel-grey eyes on mine. "I'm impressed. Few of my staff take much interest in the old place. You've really made your mark."

I pull my shoulders back and inhale deeply, a tingling sensation dancing over my shoulders and neck. "Oh." I blink, my mind a clean, clear blank. "Well, I, uh ... I come from a family of fixer-uppers, you know?"

"Really? Tell me." She leads the way out of the aviary, back towards the walkway to the pool.

"My mom and aunt own an antiques shop. So, I grew up with chairs and tables that needed wobbly legs reattached and wood refinished." I pause. I'm running at the mouth, but she's listening intently, so I'm happy to continue. "And even though my dad's a teacher, principal, actually, he caught the bug, and he and Mom have bought, renovated, and sold countless heritage houses in Port Hope." As an afterthought, I add, "My home ... where I'm from," in case she doesn't remember our initial interview.

"Port Hope," she murmurs, pensive. "You take after your mother, then?" Mrs. R.'s eyes sparkle with interest. She's gently teasing me, but I see approval too. And dare I think, genuine curiosity?

"'Fraid so. When I see problems, the solution just springs to mind. And I know how to do"—I wave my hand around in a circle—"things."

"Yes. Hmm. I imagine you see a lot of problems at the Aviary Inn …" She glances back at the main building, her eyebrows pinched together.

It's a leading question, and I take a tentative nibble at the bait. I roll my lips between my teeth and search her face. "I have a few ideas, yes. I … I think that … the potential of the place isn't fully realized. People are looking for something different. I'm certain you could improve your business …" I stop, uncertain. I've gone too far; I'm insulting her business acumen. "I … I mean … I think so, anyway. My mom and aunt run a couple of bed and breakfasts too, so I lived with—"

"I'm not offended, Sophie." She smiles. "The place has been neglected. We've fallen into a rather comfortable rut." She moves to walk past me. "I'd like to hear your ideas, but another time. I must get my sleep now."

I spin to keep my eyes on her as she walks by, and I see my opportunity slipping away. She pauses and turns back, grabs my arm. "Do you swim, dear?"

"Uh. Yes. I love to swim." My eyes dart to the pool behind her and back again, questioning.

"You are most welcome to use the pool, you know. Before or after your shift. It's not well used, and it's such pleasurable exercise."

My jaw drops in surprise. "Oh, yes. Thank you." At last, the invitation I've been waiting for, an opportunity to make myself available to her, somehow. Another chance to ask my questions. "I'll do that."

And I will, starting tomorrow.

When I get back to the front desk, I scowl in confusion. My journal is gone! I slap my hand down onto the desk, scowling as my pulse kicks up. I'm certain I left it right here a moment ago. I cast my eyes around the other cluttered surfaces, searching, my throat constricting. If it fell into the wrong hands, with all my most private thoughts and feelings laid bare ...

Oh! I sigh with relief. I see it on the side table by the door, closed. How peculiar. I seem to be catching a bit of dementia from Eleanor.

During the next week, Zoë and I spend our free time scrubbing, spackling, and sanding our bedroom walls to prepare for paint. When she leaves for her afternoon shift, I carry on, and without her knowledge touch up her rough work. Yes, I'm a bit of a perfectionist. Finally, we paint our rooms, mine taupe and hers butter cream. They look so lovely and fresh, at last our flat feels like a home instead of a flophouse.

Meanwhile, with Elliot's help, we dragged both our beds into the living room and are still sleeping there while the paint dries; we've eaten takeout all week, and it's been fun, like kids in a dorm or at camp. Though Oliver is in the doghouse, Elliot has stopped by our flat a couple of times to see our progress and share a pizza. He's been funny, warm, and attentive to me, and there's no denying he's hot. Tall, blond, and beefy. Mmm.

I've sent another postcard to Mom and Dad, the guilt over dissing them growing like a mutant mushroom. I hope mentioning new friends here in York eases their worry about not having Marc-Antoine watching over me.

The longer he stays away, apparently by choice, the farther my feelings for him drift from admiration to grief to resentment to I don't know … Not quite indifference. Not yet. A numb long-ing. I wonder if this is what withdrawal from an unhealthy addiction is like. He was my entire world for two years, my benchmark. I realize now how much I depended on him, how much I saw the world through his eyes. Without Marc, I don't know who I am anymore, and it scares me.

It's my night off, and I return to get ready for my date with Elliot after going out this afternoon to buy milk and muffins for our larder. I'm excited and apprehensive; it's our first solo date, and though an ambiguous shroud of melancholy about Marc-Antoine still hangs over me, not to mention the uncertainty over Elliot's girlfriend Joan, I can't help looking forward to spending time with Elliot, despite what Zoë said.

He seems grown up in a completely different way from Marc-Antoine. Responsible and mature, making Marc-Antoine seem a little pretentious now that I reflect on it. Maybe Mom and Dad had good reasons for disliking him. There is something rather appealing and trustworthy about an honest, wholesome, manly man.

As I turn my key in the lock and push the door ajar, I hear them. They sound like cattle, moaning, mewling, and grunting, punctuated by the squeak and rattle of Zoë's small bed-frame on the living room floor, and her high-pitched squeals of delight. Je-zuz! I swallow a shout and pull the door closed, mortified, and stand in the hallway, nonplussed. I guess this would be the hot make-up sex part. Now what do I do?

I haven't left myself much time to change, and sure enough, within ten minutes Elliot's polished loafers leap up the stairs two at a time with a tap tap tap on the wood, and when he sees me standing there, a puzzled expression appears on his large, open face. His short blond hair is styled into spikes with shiny gel, and he looks sexy and urbane in a dark blue shirt with no tie. "What's up, love?" he asks, taking my hand.

"We can't go in," I whisper, my face flushing hotly.

After I explain, Elliot cocks an ear at the door, says, "Oh, ho,

Ollie!" under his breath and, laughing, turns to me and pulls me towards him with his big, warm hands on my back. "I do believe I'm envious," he murmurs, and leans in, his blue eyes intense under heavy lids, and gives me an impulsive, hot kiss, his tongue slipping hungrily into my mouth.

His arousal presses against me, and it causes an unexpected shiver of heat to slide through me. I pull away. "Elliot!" I scold unconvincingly, confused.

"It's all right, love." He smiles. "It's quiet now." He bangs a fist on the door. "Oy! Ollie! We're coming in, so wrap it up an' make yourselves decent." He turns my key and enters without hesitation, laughing in his big booming voice, while I stand in the hall awkwardly. I hear the three of them talking and laughing and enter with trepidation.

"I'm so sorry, Sophie." Zoë giggles from behind the bathroom door, presumably throwing some clothes on. "That took longer than I expected." Oliver perches on the edge of the extremely rumpled bed wearing only baggy tartan pants and a sheepish grin. His spiky dreadlocks are exposed, for once, and his smooth bare chest glistens with sweat.

"So, you've been forgiven, have you?" I try to frown at Oliver, but I can't suppress a smile. I can see why Zoë has such a hard time resisting his boyish charm.

He at least has the grace to give a hangdog glance at the floor. "Yeah. I don't deserve her. She's an angel."

"Yes, she is," I say with narrowed eyes, my arms crossed.

An hour later, Elliot and I are seated at a small corner table in the Frog and Firkin, his usual pub. It's too brightly lit, and there's no privacy. Instead of music, we must raise our voices to be heard over the din of a rowdy, drunken crowd. And it smells of cigarettes, which I loathe, and greasy fried food. Stupidly, I expected a proper restaurant, at least. But I chide myself; he may not have the money for anyplace better. He's a student, after all.

I'm still recoiling from his swaggering possessiveness as we entered. Apparently still aroused from our encounter with Zoë and Oliver, he took the liberty to grab my butt and snog me again soon after we entered, which, of course, escaped no one's notice. It took three-quarters of an hour to make our way through the pub because he had to stop and effusively greet everyone he knew, introducing me and telling every soul that I was his "Canadian girl," his arm clamped around my waist or shoulders the entire time, as though he was afraid I might bolt, which, after half an hour, I was sorely tempted to do.

I picture a prize ham on display with a big fat red maple leaf stamped on it, and I'm still miffed as we wait for our meals. I grind my teeth and glare at the beads of condensation on a glass of ale that I've hardly touched, which he ordered without asking. He's made a big leap forward, considering it's our first proper date, and disappointment buzzes around and around in my head.

I've had plenty of time to absorb the details of the smoky pub, and I'm repulsed as my eye travels over the worn, grimy velour upholstery on the banquette, in dulled shades of puce and mustard, the sheen of stickiness on the dark wood posts and yellowed plaster walls. My nose curls at the lingering reek of stale ale, cold cigarette ash, and sweaty socks. It's a far cry from the charming pub Nick took me to on Gillygate, when I was a virtual stranger too. A long, slow sigh leaks out of me. He's hot, and I can hardly complain about being introduced to all his friends, but it was the way he did it that bothered me.

"Elliot, I appreciate meeting your mates, but I'm uncomfortable that you've given the impression we're an item. You know that can't be."

He grins and gives me yet another squeeze with his brawny arm. His head tips forward and butts my forehead gently, and he tries to kiss me again with a sexy growl, but I pull away. "Am I movin' too fast for you, love? Don't want to scare you away with my enthusiasm," he says, lowering his voice in a suggestive growl, his brows twitching. He takes a long pull on his pint, showing no remorse.

"I told you that my boyfriend—Marc-Antoine—will be back any day now."

He sets down his glass and closes his eyes for a moment, and I see him roll them back behind their lids. He takes a deep breath, as though it's going to take all the patience he has to address some daft girl. "Sweetheart." Oh, good start. "Look, love, I know you're still dealing with it, but it's plain to me loverboy is not comin' back."

My face and throat tighten. How dare he presume to make conclusions about my private, personal life, when he hardly knows me? Even if it's true, it was insensitive. "He's only gone on a bit of a tour—"

He gives me a smug look, shaking his head slightly. "I know he ditched you, Sophie, love. Oliver told me." He snorts. "I can't say I'm sorry. It means you're available for me, dunnit?" He grins, handsome and charming again.

My fingers fly to my lips, pressing. How can he think that? I stare at him, my nostrils flaring, but I can't decide who I'm more cross with. Possibly Zoë for sharing my secret with her stupid blabbermouth boyfriend. I set my teeth. "He'll be back. Whatever happened, he'll have a good explanation for it."

Elliot tsks. "He's a bloke! What do you expect?"

Hot tears burn my eyes, and I swipe at them, angry. "I expect him to behave like a human being! Anyway, it's my business, and until I decide I'm available, I'm not!"

Elliot makes a wry face. "You're here."

Sweat blooms on my scalp, itchy and hot. He has a point, but not one I'm prepared to deal with right now. "So are you! And it's come to my attention that you're not exactly single either." I know I'm not being rational. I didn't mean to broach the subject of his girlfriend. He stares at me, apparently unwilling to volunteer any information. "You lied to me when you said Joan had dumped you. It was the other way around, wasn't it?" Now I sound like a harpy, accusing him of infidelity, but I know my outrage is more on her behalf than my own. All these guys are pissing me off. Can none of them be trusted?

He's finally humbled, the edge gone from his swagger. His shoulders slump, and he looks hesitant, tonguing his teeth and reaching for my hand under the table. He rubs it with his large rough thumb while I glare at him, tight-lipped, waiting for an answer.

"You're right. But it's more complicated than that. Nobody really knows what goes on between us." In his discomfort, his Yorkshire accent grows stronger, and I realize he tries to adjust his speech a little the rest of the time. Elliot chews his cheek and fiddles with his pint, wiping away streaks in the condensation and slipping it back and forth on the wet surface of the battered wooden tabletop. He glances at me and away. "Joanie thinks she's too good for me. I don't know why she didn't split up this time, but it's probably because she enjoys abusing me, and figures I'll take it. And I did. I did for too long, Sophie, but I couldn't take it anymore." He meets my eye finally, and a surge of guilt swamps me, because I see earnestness and suffering in his clear blue eyes, and I believe him. I want to, anyway, despite Zoë's warning.

I take a sip of my beer and grimace at the bitter flavour. "Do you mind if I order a glass of wine, Elliot?"

"Eh? What's the matter with that?"

I sigh. "How long have you been together?"

"About five years, off and on. We've known each other for ages. She's always saying she can do better than me. I guess in that way, we're the same. We both want more, you know? Change our lives for the better. But I hope to go to school and build a business, and Joanie's answer is putting on airs and marrying above herself. I suppose. I dunno, really."

"So, she has dumped you before?"

"Yeah. Every time she sees somethin' better come along. An' then she comes crawlin' back when it don't work out. I'm gettin' pretty sick of it."

Maybe they deserve each other. I think of Zoë and Oliver, and how this same pattern repeats itself. What is it about people? Some keep shopping while they string some poor sucker on, and some cling to a love that, possibly, probably, isn't as right for them as they think it is. Out of fear. Like Marc-Antoine and me.

A great wave of self-pity washes over me. The entire game suddenly seems so stale. Love, mating. We've been sold a bill of goods. Maybe people don't ever really find that special someone to connect with, to fall in love with, despite all the hope inherent in mountains of romance books. It's all so pointless and, perhaps, hopeless. I think of Mom and Dad, at odds after decades of happy compatibility. If they can't work it out, no one can.

I'm reminded of that other sad, twisted love affair that unfolded years ago at the Aviary Inn. Mrs. Roxtoby, Eleanor, and the man they shared in an uncomfortable truce. And the mythical Rupert. How unsatisfying for both women. Maybe it was the knowledge that neither of them got their happy endings that held them together through the years. A mutual sympathy. What's worse, I wonder—never finding your true love, or finding and losing him?

"What you thinkin' about so hard, Sophie?"

I blink and realize I've been rubbing Elliot's hand and staring into space. I release it. Maybe because there's a lesson for us both buried somewhere in it, I tell him about Mrs. Roxtoby's unrequited love with a mysterious soldier, and how she married the wrong man who didn't love her, and how she lost both her children. I leave out, of course, my suspicions about who her daughter might be. "I can't believe so much misfortune can happen to one woman," I say, "and though she carries an air of melancholy with her all the time, I sense an inner strength in her—"

"You talkin' about the old lady at the hotel?" he interrupts.

"Well, not so old, really. Late sixties? Eleanor, her cousin, is more like seventy-five?"

"Why do you give a fuck? Wha' happened to them—it's so long ago. Their time's over. It's us who have our lives ahead that have problems to solve."

Yet another man telling me to mind my own damned business, but with an entirely different motive. This time, I won't lose my cool. I've had time to take Nick's caution to heart, and though I still think he was officious and exasperating, I've mellowed about his concerns. In the end, I have to trust my instincts with people. I sigh.

"It's the universal human problem," I say. "How we strive and hope, yet rarely get what we dream of."

He scowls at me, and I wonder if he's even listening.

"It doesn't seem fair, does it?" I say.

"Life is bloody unfair. Try growing up here, in bloody Yorkshire, on the wrong side of town. It's a life sentence." His voice is hard and bitter, and I wonder how difficult his own upbringing really was.

"You make it sound so hopeless. Surely that's not true anymore. Anything is possible if you—"

"Not anything." He shakes his head. "The toffs still keep to themselves and hold on to their privileges. The rest of us ordinary blokes have to work bloody hard to make a decent life."

"Well, I admire you, Elliot, for trying to change your circumstances."

His eyes glint with a sharp, blue light as he glances over at me. "I admire you, Sophie. You're bright and hopeful. You're comin' to be important to me, girl."

What? Already? Before I absorb what he's said, he leans towards me and presses his lips to mine. It's a tender kiss, but one without hesitation. The heat of his mouth engulfs mine, and his hand holds my arm in a sure and possessive grip that telegraphs his intentions as surely as a grope. Nevertheless, my body reacts to his sudden forceful ardour, and heat uncoils inside me, responding to him. Then I hear a chorus of whoops and cheers from the peanut gallery, and we separate, my cheeks hot, my gut twisting uncomfortably.

Perversely, my mind veers to the last time Marc-Antoine kissed me, warm, secure, and loved. Not the night we fought, but the night before. I can't be entirely wrong about that, can I? I gaze into the thickening atmosphere of the pub, no longer able to see the door on the other side of the room.

My hands slice with crisp precision through the calm, cool water, scattering shards of tungsten darkness across its silver surface. The underwater lights are off, as night is ending, the dark sky flooding with pale periwinkle like a watercolour wash bleeding from the tip of a paintbrush. I am alone except for the awakening birds.

I've become accustomed to the dawn light that rouses the birds to proclaim the day, the wild birds first, in the treetops, followed by Mrs. Roxtoby's pets who, though their garden aviary rests in deeper shadow, respond to their cousins' calls with abandon, singing harder and louder, not yet touched by the morning light and fueled by hope.

These are the longest days of the year, yet despite the light and the chorus of birdsong, I am the only soul up. Or so it seems, in the shadows of the Aviary Inn's garden. All week, since Mrs. R. issued the invitation, I've slipped into my new swimsuit at the end of my shift and slid into the dark, still pool at daybreak. Because of this trip, I've missed swimming in the Lake every day while at home this summer.

I adore it and have quickly become addicted to the peaceful interlude. The gritty-eyed, dusty fatigue of my long solitary night is stripped away, and I am revived and swim vigorous laps under the thin, translucent dome of the sky with an energy that belies my sleepless nights. Later, when I return home, I know I'll sleep a profound and peaceful sleep.

"Oh, to be young, and greet the morning after a sleepless night with such grace and aplomb."

I am towelling off on the pool deck and turn towards the voice. Mrs. R. stands in the shadows in her pink bathrobe. How long has she been watching me? "Good morning," I chirp. "It's beautiful, isn't it?" Life thrums in my veins, tingling on my skin.

"Yes, indeed," she replies. Her voice is cracked and stiff, the first few words of the day after a night of silence. "The kettle's ready for tea, if you'd like."

I stand dumbly, wondering that she's invited me inside her cottage. At last!

"Come, come. Don't worry about the water." She turns and walks through the open door of her cottage into the yellow light. "Or change first and then come," she offers over her shoulder. "Doesn't matter."

Deciding on the latter, I quickly change into dry clothes in the small log cabin that serves as a changing room and sauna for hotel guests and then follow her into her sanctuary before she changes her mind. To the best of my knowledge, no one comes here but her.

She is already setting a cozy-covered teapot down onto a small oak table and setting out proper china cups and saucers adorned with portraits of small birds, of course. "Are you sleepy, dear?"

"Not yet," I say, and tell her how well I've been sleeping since starting the morning swims.

She smiles knowingly and replies, "That's why I swim in the evening. At my age, sleep can be elusive."

"I love the birds," I say. "In the morning."

"Ahh." She smiles as she pours our tea. "Me too. Milk?"

"Um. Please. Have you had them long?"

She sips her tea, blinking into the middle distance. "Well. I've always loved birds, and it started with one or two, you know. Now I have many kinds. Like any hobby, it's grown."

"What kinds?"

"Ah." She gets up and brings back a large book, opening it to a page of colour plates, pointing as she names her species. "Finches of all sorts, chaffinches, song thrushes, blue and bearded tits, sparrows. I have a reed bunting. They come and go. I once had a pair of lovely blue dunnocks, but they didn't take to the aviary. And the collared doves, of course."

"They're native birds?"

"Mostly, though I can keep North American ones too."

"What about in winter? What happens?"

Mrs. Roxtoby sits quietly for a moment, then she says, "Most are bred in captivity. Sometimes it takes a year or two before they realize there is no need to migrate, and they settle down."

"Do they breed?"

"Sometimes." She nods with a wistful smile. "I have to make a special effort with their diet and help them build nests. The conditions have to be right."

I inhale. "Like people?" I remember my bitter reflections on the hopelessness of romantic relationships.

A rusty cough erupts from her throat, and she tosses her steely-grey head back, so I can see dark fillings and gold crowns that flash in the top of her mouth. "Well, now. I don't know about that. Have you had no word from your delinquent beau?"

I lean back, confused. For a second, my mind flashes to Nick, who I haven't heard from, and I wonder how Mrs. R. knows anything about him or our fight. He isn't a beau, anyway, even if he is delinquent, sort of. Then I realize how stupid this is. Of course she means Marc-Antoine. I shake my head. "Nothing."

She slides a small plate of buttered toast fingers smeared with a translucent layer of black towards me. "What do you think about that?"

I sigh. I think it looks like Marmite. "I'm running out of excuses for him."

She nods. "Sometimes things happen that are beyond our control."

"To be honest, I'm okay having some time alone to look around."

To be polite, I pick up a piece of toast and nibble it. It's actually quite pleasant, salty, and I wonder if there are ways to eat Marmite without gagging.

S lightly improved recipe for British snack:
One slice white bread, toasted and generously buttered, one side
Extremely thin veneer of Marmite

I take a sip of my tea and wait a beat. "Is that what happened to you, Mrs. Roxtoby, and your soldier?"

She stills, registering her shock, and I hold my breath, expecting to be shown the door for my insolence. "My loyal subjects have been gossiping, I see."

"Not really. I confess I've been rather nosy. But also, you know, sometimes Eleanor doesn't know what she's saying, so I'm sorry if I've invaded your privacy by asking, but, well ..." I shrug. "It sounds rather sad and romantic."

She chuckles, like pebbles rolling over in a creek bed, and smiles wistfully. "It was romantic, yes, and rather sad. They seem to go together."

"Not always," I protest. "At least, I hope not." I raise my eyes to hers. "You've never forgotten him?"

"Rupert?" Her head rocks back and forth as she peers into her teacup. "No. One never forgets one's first love."

"Would you tell me about him?"

Abruptly, she rises and leaves the room, returning a moment

later with a small, tarnished silver picture frame, handing it to me. Within is a tiny cracked sepia photograph of a young soldier in uniform. He has a nice jaw, a straight nose, and even with short dark hair slicked back under his jaunty cap, his ears don't stick out too much. He's handsome, similar to Matt in an old-fashioned way, and I nibble my cheek. He looks like he smiles easily, though he is serious in this grainy portrait.

She happily tells me about how they met—the attraction was instant and mutual—through her father, a dean at Oxford, where Rupert had enrolled to study law when the war began. He was so clever and articulate, once you got past his shyness, she said with a wistful smile. And then he had signed up, of course, although he'd never gone over. They'd met again when he'd been posted near London, training to be a radio operator, and they'd secretly met whenever they could. She'd been seventeen, he nineteen, and the war, the blitz, his imminent assignment, had lent urgency to their love, permitting them to take chances they would not have otherwise. When she'd discovered her pregnancy, she had hoped and expected them to marry before he was deployed. They were to meet, and she was to tell him about the baby.

I raise my eyebrows, surprised by this twist, and she lifts her chin in confirmation. "Oh, yes. That was no secret. Mother strongly disapproved of him and hoped to prevent our involvement, so she was rather distressed to find out how much too late she was. But that was after ..."

"What happened?"

"It was March 8, 1945. A V-2 bomb exploded on the Smithfield Market, near where we were to meet at Holborn Circus. I was late because of my mother. We'd argued. On the way there, the blast threw me. There was smoke and dust, chaos. I had only minor cuts and bruises, and the shock of it, but when I finally got nearer our meeting place, I found his cage in the dust and rubble. The doves were still inside, dead from the blast. But no Rupert, no message." A glazed expression comes over her eyes, as though the trauma of that day still lives within her.

While she speaks, she strokes the side of her cheek, and for the first time I notice a thin white line hidden among the creases.

As she speaks, I do mental math, wondering if my suspicion is plausible. "What happened to him? Did he leave the cage or …?" I realize it must be the same bronze cage that sits in the front lobby of the hotel, still bearing the scars of that day, exactly like Mrs. R.

"Just his doves at our meeting place. But I never found out why. I presumed he either died in the blast or was sent away, and then regretted our reckless, youthful affair, but either way, I never found him, never heard from him again."

"And then?" Something must have happened to him. If he'd looked for her, surely, he would have realized that the baby was his. Was it possible that baby was my mother? How can I figure this out?

She shakes her head. "It seemed like the rest of my life went flying out of control, huge pieces missing and ruined, like the debris from that massive V-bomb."

I'm desperate to learn more, but my eyelids are lead curtains, scratching like sandpaper over my tired eyes, my brain in a fog, my earlier energy worn off as my need to sleep encroaches. Mrs. Roxtoby sends me off. I walk home in a dream state, revisiting her story. More tragic and romantic than even I imagined.

CHAPTER 23

J *une 25, 1997, York, England*

S et among verdant lawns and blossoms in full summer
colour, the long incline up onto the city wall from Museum
Street beckons irresistibly on Thursday afternoon, on my
leisurely stroll through town. I'm relieved to have another night
off, a day for myself and my ruminations, as I've become increasingly preoccupied with Mrs. Roxtoby and her compelling, unfinished story.

Although I swam each morning, I did not receive another
invitation for tea. My frustration simmers over her misdirected
life, and more so its potential implications for my own family. I
need to know more. Perhaps this is simply a childish petulance
at the recognition that I can't have all that I want, any more than
Mrs. Roxtoby could have what she wanted. I'm rattling the bars
of my figurative cage in rebellion at this dawning realization.

Yesterday, Zoë and I celebrated our newly refurbished
bedrooms by shopping for some final decorating touches,
tidying up our now shabby-by-contrast living room (thank God

Zoë's finally made this discovery!), and while she was at work, I scrubbed our kitchen until it gleamed and cooked a nice supper. This morning, Oliver drove her to Manchester to visit her mum and little sisters and brothers for a couple of days. He can be a terrifically sweet guy and is on his best behaviour.

Ah, bliss! I have the day to myself before Elliot picks me up. I see us as a pathetic pair of cast-off lovers rather than a couple, despite the fact that, technically, Elliot has left the abusive Joanie, as she's called. He seems increasingly fond of me, and I do find him attractive, but I have a vague sense of biding my time, as though nothing can move forward until I find out what happened to Marc-Antoine.

Below me, York Minster looms brilliantly, warmly glowing stone and slate grey roofs and towers seeming closer than they really are on this vibrant summer day. The city is gorged with tourists, and I can see the line of bubble gum pink, red, and canary yellow buses parked, awaiting their charges from the cathedral. The tower spires of the minster pierce the overarching blue sky as cotton-wool clouds serenely scud by. On the other side of the wall, I see the entire park that contains St. Mary's Abbey and the Roman Multangular Tower stretch away from me between emerald-green globes of elms and oaks.

The sight of the Roman tower reminds me of my row with Nick. I haven't seen him in over three weeks, and I'm regretting the whole thing. It seems so petty now, and I wonder why either of us got so bent out of shape. I'm pretty sure I overreacted. I couldn't bear his criticism. We had such a terrific evening before the fight. He's gentlemanly and intelligent and warm. I enjoy his company a lot, and strangely, I miss him.

Perhaps it's this business with Mrs. Roxtoby. Despite Nick's disdain for my meddling, as he clearly sees it, at least he expressed sympathy for her. I'd like nothing better than to tell him what I now know, and suspect, in the next chapter of my so-called Gothic soap opera.

It's hot and I'm sticky with sweat from my long walk. I dab

my damp forehead with my sleeves, wishing I'd worn lighter clothing.

Crossing the Lendal Bridge with dragging feet, I stop at a gap in the battlements to look over the edge, watching a flock of waterbirds lift off the river, and look back towards the Roman tower one more time. A heavy weight hangs low in my belly, pulling my chin and my shoulders down. When I turn around, I practically crash into none other than Nick. He's carrying his guitar slung over his shoulder, trudging towards me, and we freeze and stare at each other.

"Canadian!" he exclaims. He hesitates, his green eyes searching mine intently; I guess he's looking for a clue. I have no desire to bite his head off again.

"Hi, Nick." I offer a tentative smile, and he lets out a breath and offers a wavering grin. I take in his stance, erect and wide-legged, like Peter Pan. I'd forgotten how tall he is, and how his long frame vibrates with latent energy.

"How have you been? You look great. Glowing," he adds, blinking at me, or perhaps it's at the glare of the afternoon sun slanting into his translucent jade eyes.

I feel my face flush even hotter than before. "I've been hiking around town for hours," I say. "It's a warm day." I pluck at my sticky shirt in illustration.

"I don't mean 'glowing' like a hot coal." His mouth pulls to one side in a crooked smile, bugging his eyes meaningfully, and I laugh, embarrassed but suddenly fizzing with happiness. "I mean fit, somehow healthier. You seem leaner too." His teeth flash. "You haven't been pining for me all these weeks, have you?"

I gasp. He's read my mind! Then I laugh, blushing, conscious of the fact that he, too, is aware of the time that's passed since our spat. I place a hand on my heaving chest, aware of my accelerating pulse. Trying for a sarcastic tone, I say, "Oh, yes! That's it. Haven't been able to eat or sleep." I give my head a little shake, then amend, "Actually, I've been swimming in the hotel pool."

"Oh, right?" Nick smiles and smiles, his straight white teeth glinting behind a screen of sandy brown whiskers. A moment passes in silence.

I gesture at his guitar. "Uh. You've been busking?"

He nods, his eyes searching my face.

"Look, Nick. I'm sorry. I overre—"

"I've been feeling dread—" Our words clash, and we both stop.

"I'm sorry—" we both attempt at once, and then we break into laughter.

"Where are you going? Shall we walk?" he asks, pointing towards Micklegate. I nod, and we move together along the wall. After a while, he says, "It was unkind of me to criticize you. I know you have only good intentions."

I shake my head, remembering Elliot's reaction to my story. "I'm sorry I said such horrible things to you. You reminded me so much of my family, always criticizing and condescending, I'm too sensitive. But I've thought about it a lot, and even though you raised good points, I still feel that I can help Mrs. Roxtoby somehow. She bailed me out, and I want to return the favour, you know?"

He nods and, shifting his guitar strap to the other side, hunches his shoulders and falls behind, placing a hand at the centre of my back, guiding me towards the ramparts so he can walk in my place along the edge that drops off sharply.

"It's not wrong to care about people, is it?"

"No, of course not—I understand how you feel. Have you learned any more?"

As we cross over Micklegate Bar and stroll towards Bishops-gate, I tell Nick about my après-swim teatime chat with Mrs. R. and all she confessed. "I swim every morning, hoping she'll be there, and invite me in, but ..." I shrug. "So far, nothing."

It's greener over here, with lovely trees marching along a grassy sward by the river's edge and inviting pathways that allow one down close to the shimmering water with its pleasure boats and waterbirds. My eye is drawn by a red and white motorboat skimming by, its motor a dull growl.

"I'm astonished. She's confided more than I … well …" He hesitates. I turn towards him. "Obviously, I was wrong. She sounds like a rather lonely woman who needs someone like you to listen to her."

"You mean she must be desperate or she wouldn't be talking to me?" I ask, smirking.

"Not at all." Nick shifts his guitar to his other shoulder and squints towards Clifford Tower. We climb down off the wall at Skeldergate Bridge and stroll along the tree-lined walk by the River Ouse, meandering towards Tower Street when he veers up onto the grassy hillock where the tower perches. Suddenly, he turns around and drops down onto the buttercup-speckled grass, pulling his guitar out of its case. He strums the strings absently, effortlessly, creating a haunting melody that seems familiar.

I sit down beside him and wait, plucking buttercups and twirling them between my fingers. Intrepid tourists trudge up the grand, steep staircase leading to the stone tower gate, invariably pausing halfway to gasp for air. We both watch them for a while. Nick is pensive, and yet on the verge of saying something more.

"I meant, rather, that you may have been right. Perhaps the other people around her are too familiar to confide in. Perhaps she's been putting on a good face for them for so many years, she's afraid to let her vulnerability show."

"Well, I hope so." After a moment, I add, "Everyone says I look like her daughter, the one who went to Canada." I wonder whether I can confide in him about my quest and suspicions about the identity of Mrs. Roxtoby's daughter. But it's so far-fetched, I need more facts, and it's so nice to reconnect with Nick. I don't want to push my luck.

"You've a kind heart, Sophie. Maybe you're just the ticket."

I lie back on the sun-warmed grass, resting my head on my

hand. "Losing one's children must be the hardest thing, especially for a mother. Heartbreaking, really."

Nick continues strumming, and for a moment, he's become so absorbed by his song, he isn't listening anymore. After humming a few bars under his breath, he blinks rapidly and frowns hard at his fingers working the frets of his guitar, his jaw tense. He's become somber and quiet, and I wait, wondering what he's thinking so hard about. He turns his face towards me, but only halfway. I can see his sharp profile, and I notice his lashes are wet. A stray teardrop hangs suspended on the side of his elegant nose. "A child's death is dreadfully hard on a mother, indeed," he finally says, "but perhaps it is as hard on the father."

"I suppose. But Mr. Roxtoby had died long before his son." I'm baffled by his intense reaction and wonder at such empathy in a young guy, so different from Elliot and his cold selfishness. I realize I know absolutely nothing about Nick Savile. Does he have firsthand experience of this kind of loss? He's a little older than me, but I'd be shocked to discover that he'd fathered a child.

To redirect the conversation, I say, "I wonder rather if it isn't as difficult, or more so, when a child rejects you. I can't help worrying over Mrs. R.'s estrangement with Barbara. What disagreement could be so serious as to drive a mother and daughter apart? Forever!"

Nick startles me by whirling on me abruptly and barking, "Perhaps she wanted the freedom to live her own life, away from the constraints and demands and emotional baggage of her family." His eyes are bleak and violent as the Atlantic under a furrowed brow.

I flinch at the vehemence of his statement, trying to relax my tight chest, calm my rapid breathing, but I nod, not wishing to dismiss his strongly held opinion. "But it was so soon after James died. They were grieving. They should have stayed close and helped each other through that time."

"What can we know of the workings of any family?" His

rancor spent, he seems to have closed the topic, and I see that, for some reason, his emotions are frayed, and he's defensive. He strums his guitar quietly, and I leave him alone for a few moments, listening to the gentle progression of chords, while I process my own memories of loss and bereavement.

"Ooooh, ooooh," he sings quietly, under his breath.

I can't imagine losing my parents or my brother. A wave of melancholy sweeps over me. The last time I saw them, I said such angry, rebellious things. *Stop telling me what to do! Why don't you trust me? I don't need you! I hate you all!* A tight fist of regret squeezes my heart. I miss them terribly, and I suppose they only want what's best for me. And it looks like they were right about Marc-Antoine. But that only makes my situation that much more humiliating. I can't tell them what's happened until I've sorted out my problems.

"There ain't no space and time/to keep our love alive ... We have existence and it's all we share ..." He hesitates and begins again.

"Tell me about your band," I ask. It's time to veer the topic to more cheerful matters. "What do you call yourselves?" I don't understand what moved him so, but I think he may be embarrassed.

"Bloodaxe," he says, with an exaggerated Yorkshire brogue.

"Delightful," I say with a hint of irony, I hope, smiling.

He laughs suddenly, tossing his head back, and repeats the chorus silently, his shoulders shaking. I'm transfixed by the long, strong line of his exposed neck beneath his beard, smooth and pale, as it disappears into the V of his T-shirt, and the cords of his back muscles through the thin fabric. His nose wrinkles and I'm charmed by his joyful laugh, part nerdy, part endearing.

"Erik Bloodaxe was the nickname of the last Viking king of York," he explains, laying his guitar down on the carpet of sunny buttercups. "It's a long story." He gives me a brief synopsis of the life and times of Erik Haraldsson, the oft violent and unpopular son of a Norwegian king, who fought first with his brothers, and later with the Irish, for supremacy in Yorkshire, finally dying a mysteriously violent death, possibly betrayed by his own benefactor.

While Nick speaks, his soft tenor weaves a deliciously dramatic tale, whispering history's secrets for me alone. His long-fingered tawny hands pull a braided bit of leather from the pocket of his frayed khaki cargo pants. He fiddles with it, flipping it over and over like worry beads. When he's not fidgeting, his hands sweep descriptive gestures to aid the narrative, and my eyes follow his movements, rapt. I listen and watch his expressive storytelling, drawn in by the details of his physical magnetism. Sunlight glints on the gold, and sometimes red, hairs on the back of his sinewy, tanned forearms. I study the signet ring on his right hand, trying to decipher the embossed golden image. It looks like a coat of arms, but it's old, worn gold, and his hands don't stop moving.

"Lovely story." I smile and pluck a few bits of dry grass from the shoulder of his greyish-green T-shirt, unable to resist the urge to touch him. The warm sun liberates his masculine musk, mingled with his usual aromas of dry straw, wool, and clay. My fingertips itch to touch him again. Nick has a way of bringing history to life, his own passion and enthusiasm infusing his anecdotes with emotion and humour. "You're a good teacher."

"Thank you." Small spots of pink appear high on his lean cheekbones, above the ragged edge of his beard. He changes the subject abruptly. "Anyway, we've been learning a few new songs, practicing quite a bit lately."

"Can I hear something?" I ask.

"Sure." He lifts his guitar and picks a series of eerie notes from its strings and then strums a couple bars and hums. "It starts with acoustic guitar, and then Art comes in with the drums, tah ta ta, and I switch to electric, so it doesn't sound quite the same," he explains, and then sings the popular Verve song they're working on.

"There ain't no space and time/to keep our love alive ... We have existence and it's all we share..."

He sings a chorus, and another verse, falters, and peters out. "So. I'm still learning it." He gives a sheepish smile. He can't realize how good he is, how wonderful his voice is to listen to. Hypnotic.

"How about you? Any news from your boyfriend?"

I sigh. "No." Nick listens, his face sympathetic, green eyes soft, nonjudgmental. Caught off guard, I confide more than perhaps I should. "He's the reason I argued with my family before I left home. They called him bohemian, vain, and arrogant. They didn't trust him." I laugh bitterly, remembering my burning resentment at their judgment. "Perhaps they were right, I don't know."

Nick's staring at me, a wry smile on his face. "Tell me what you liked best about him."

His response is so different from Elliot's. I'm taken aback. I recline on the lawn, casting my eyes up at the sky and at the crumbling stone top of the tower above us on the mound, and sigh. "I suppose … that he's artistic, he's erudite and knowledgeable. I loved his confidence. His sophistication." Pausing, I see something about my own motivation, like a shock of cold water.

He is everything that I wasn't and wished to be.

I glance over at Nick and back up to trace the outline of the clouds. "I guess, in retrospect, I was blinded by those things. Being with him made me feel more grown up. Maybe I chose not to see certain other, less attractive, things about him, because I wanted to belong in his circle. Be that cool." Chagrinned, I raise my gaze to Nick's, blinking, knowing that I've revealed something about myself.

"I think you're pretty cool." He gazes down at me intently, leaning over a little, and our proximity, or perhaps our honesty, feels intimate, as if he was about to bring his face to mine. My heart rate accelerates. My gaze wavers and I smile, feeling bashful.

"I suppose your family wouldn't approve of me either." He laughs, his eyes twinkling with impishness.

I squint at Nick's wild hair, scruffy clothes, and guitar, with a jaded eye, shaking my head. I didn't see him that way either. My natural instinct for people, my knack for seeing the real them, has always been my touchstone. Considering Nick's grunge, anti-establishment attire and rough grooming, somehow this doesn't give me a lot of confidence. I should choose my friends more carefully, think about where they're from, where they're going to, but ... His outside doesn't match his inside.

A clash of confusing feelings causes heat to rise to my cheeks. "I'm sure you're right," I agree, watching his long-fingered hands as they shred the petals from a buttercup. "They are rather traditional and conservative in their values." Backpedaling, I add, "Although liberal-minded, of course. Very tolerant and ... inclusive."

"You mean, typically Canadian?" he jokes.

"Oh, you think?" I grin and our eyes meet, dancing. "I confess, despite your ... dreads, which, to be honest, I'm not a fan of, I can see you're very intelligent, talented, and charming ... when you're not scolding." I grin, to make sure he knows I'm kidding. "But I do worry about you. I can see you have so much potential." Why he's working at a museum and playing guitar on the street still baffles me, despite his talents in both arenas. I'm trying to make my feelings about Nick fit with my impressions, but I only get a tight chest and a headache. It makes me inexplicably angry. I have difficulty accepting his lack of ambition and focus.

"You worry about me too, do you?" He's quiet a while, pensive, a hint of a smile lingering on his lips. Heaving himself up off the lawn, he paces, crushing grass and buttercups under his restless feet. He grabs his guitar case and lopes away down the slope. I follow, jogging to match his long strides. Dry grass sticks to the back of his misshapen T-shirt. A small tear over his lean shoulder blade reveals a patch of smooth skin. He stops at the bottom, on the sidewalk, and gazes wistfully across the Ouse.

"Things are not always as they appear, Canadian. Maybe you should learn to trust your instincts. Maybe you can see something beneath the surface that's even more real, like with your friend Mrs. Roxtoby."

"Like what?" I can't help myself. I brush some of the debris from his back, enjoying the feel of his sinewy buff muscles. We stroll along Tower Road towards Walmsgate.

Nick shrugs, looking at the ground, and I don't have a clue what we're talking about.

"I'm sorry if I was out of line, Nick. My dad's a teacher. Where I come from, dropping out of school is always a bad idea. Education opens doors, gives you options, you know? You're a smart guy. It seems to me that you, of all people, ought to know this." Whatever reason he had to quit, it's never too late to go back. "Why won't you re-enroll and finish your D. Phil? Surely, they won't object to your having taken a break. Lots of people do it. There will be a place for you when you're ready."

"Oh, there's a place for me, all right." His voice is strangely tinged with bile, and his beautiful wide mouth tightens in anger that punches me back in shock. He's usually so self-contained and serene. "I will always have a place waiting for me, no matter what I do. Therein lies the problem."

"How is that a problem?"

Nick turns to me suddenly, jabbing himself with his thumb. "Who am I, really? Does anyone care what I want?" His face is flushed, his brow furrowed, his eyes hard emerald shards as he speaks. I've asked myself the same questions.

"I don't know. What do you want, Nick?" I've not succeeded in keeping the exasperation and challenge from my voice. Instead of being offended, Nick seems further riled by my question.

"Liberty," he snaps. "Discovery," he says in a softer, uncertain tone. He spins around with his arms wide, palms facing the dome of blue sky. "Freedom to live as I choose. Obscurity, for fuck's sake!"

I pull away from his violent emotions, my heart in my throat. Strange answer. I bite back any further comment, waiting for the frisson of tension between us to cool a little. I let his words stand and we walk in silence for a while, towards Walmsgate on Hope Street, both of us heading home. I'm in no hurry to part ways, as I'm finally learning something meaningful about the enigmatic Nick. His kind of Englishman is like Spock, all the emotion tucked away under an unflappable facade. Except today, apparently. I remember his tears and his wrath. Well, maybe not quite totally unflappable.

As we approach Walmsgate Bar, the gateway to the university district, a tall, dark-haired guy stops suddenly, and trailed by a skinny, sandy-haired, thickly freckled companion, he approaches Nick. "I say, Savvy!" he exclaims.

Yikes! What timing. I brace for Nick's icy reaction.

This time, Nick's face lights up with genuine pleasure for a change in response to one of his well-heeled connections. "Stephen! Good God! What a surprise." They press their hands together and pump vigorously, then high-five and smack each other on the shoulders. Nick nods to Freckle Face, but their eyes are cold and they don't exchange greetings.

I hang back, trying not to eavesdrop, though I overhear every word, and gaze around at the buildings on Walmsgate. There is a lovely Tudor building, with mullioned bay windows on the brick bottom floor. In fact, there are many nice old brick buildings here, one with vivid, blue-painted windows and doors.

"How've you been getting on, bro? Any chance you'll be back come September?" Stephen asks in a quiet, confidential voice, leaning closer.

I glance over.

Nick's face falls and a muscle twitches in his jaw. "No plans at present." Wow, no wonder he's sensitive, if everyone he knows is constantly badgering him or judging him ill. I feel badly now for hounding him. I study the scowl on Freckle Face, who lingers a few yards away.

Stephen's eyes dart in my direction. He clears his throat.

Nick turns to me, gesturing me forward. "I'm sorry, Sophie. Meet my friend, Stephen Covington. Sophie Groenveld, Stephen."

Stephen offers his hand. "Pleasure to meet you, Sophie." I give him my hand, and he grasps it in a firm and gentle grasp. I observe his steady, assessing grey-eyed stare, smile, and glance at Nick for clues.

Nick coughs. "Well, I …"

Releasing my hand, Stephen Covington sobers and lowers his voice confidentially. "They ask about you, old chap. Don't know what to tell them."

Nick's face darkens. "What's there to tell? I'm the same as I ever was. I'm fine." His voice is tight and flat. So much for cheering him up.

Stephen places a consoling hand on Nick's shoulder, squeezing. "I know, old chap. I know." His throat sounds tight. He pauses, and his eyes dart to the left, and then to the ground. "It's hardest on your mum."

Nick's eyes close for a moment and his lips press into a thin white line. I can hear him breathing slowly and deliberately. Then he shakes it off and his face opens, though his green eyes remain shielded. "We're at the Priory tonight, if you've time. Or come up this weekend, Stephen. Bring Laura. We've got an unscheduled gig on Saturday night."

"I'll try, Savvy." His hand on Nick's shoulder clenches and then drops, and then he turns back to Freckle Face, nods, and they move away, but not before I hear the other growl, "Bloody arrogant fool. Thinks he's nobler than the rest of us. It's reverse snobbery, that's all."

I hear Stephen mutter before they stroll out of earshot, "Shut your cake hole, Devon."

"Wow." I peer closely at Nick.

He's breathing slowly, his jaw clenched.

A thousand questions clamour in my head, but I push them

all down. Nick gets curiouser and curiouser. Whatever it is that causes him so much pain, a lot of people seem to have a stake in it. "What 'unscheduled gig' is that?" I ask instead.

Nick's eyes slide over to me, and I catch a trace of his anguish. He looks back to the street as we continue walking through Walmsgate Bar, seemingly grateful that I don't ask uncomfortable questions. "We usually play Tuesday nights at the Priory, near Micklegate. The band they had booked in for Saturday cancelled last minute, so we're filling in. You should come. Or come tonight."

I say nothing for a few paces. After the sample of his singing this afternoon, I really would like to hear his band perform and meet more of his friends. But tonight, I'm seeing Elliot again, and it's just not right taking Elliot to hear Nick sing. At last, I say, "I'm sorry, I have plans tonight. And I work Saturday night, Nick. But I'll catch you next Tuesday for sure."

CHAPTER 24

June 28, 1997, #10 Wolseley Street, York

Dear Mom, Dad, and Matt,

I have so much to tell you. I haven't been traveling around quite as much as I've led you to believe. I've actually been staying in York for some time.

I have to confess I'm having doubts about Marc-Antoine, and we've parted ways for the time being.

I got a job at a little hotel, and I've made some wonderful friends. It feels like home. I'll write soon with all the details. I miss you both. (I even miss Matt.) You can write to me at my new friend Zoë's address above.

Love,
Sophie XOXOXO

CHAPTER 25

The overhead office light flickers and has done since my shift began at seven, making my temples and eyeballs throb in sympathy. I squint at the yellow wall clock, which seems to have stopped at five twenty-two a.m., just before I finished last night's shift. When things quiet down a bit, if they ever do, I will get the stepladder out, change the batteries, and reset the clock. A steady barrage of guests has kept me hopping all evening, and since the hotel is fully booked tonight, it doesn't show any signs of reprieve.

The reasons for my low mood circle and circle like vultures over carrion. Marc-Antoine's fate remains unresolved. I avoided details of Marc-Antoine's departure in my messages home. If something bad had happened to him, he might have tried to contact me there. Maybe I'll find out now that they can reach me.

And I'm feeling uncertain about Elliot's continued attentions; Nick's secret pain and peculiar friends make me uneasy; and I'm no closer to winning Mrs. Roxtoby's confidence or solving my perplexing situation. This morning's swim bore no fruit, and no one's seen Mrs. R. tonight. She must be out.

My chin quivers and my throat feels thick as I feel the vultures swoop closer, pressing down on my spirit. I'm at the

Aviary Inn under false pretenses; I don't belong here. I'm still utterly alone in a strange country. Attaching myself to these people and their problems is a way to make my own predicament seem less hopeless while I buy time. Probably imagining connections that don't exist in my fruitless quest to find … something intangible. More than ever, I wish I could go home and admit defeat, yet I'm no closer to having the means to do so. Nor have I accomplished what I came here to do. I wonder if I should be looking for other family connections, if I'm putting too much stake in this eerie coincidence I've stumbled onto here. I'm still not ready to confess the whole thing to Mom and Dad.

Another moisture-laden gust of wind blows through the lobby as someone wrestles their way through the entry door, the bell rattling, coat and umbrella flapping. I fill my lungs with the cool, fresh air, my head clearing. A moment later, my eyes fall on the unhappy dripping countenance of a forty-something woman in a drenched Burberry plaid raincoat. A droplet of water clings to the tip of her pointed nose, and a single black streak of mascara extends from her lower eyelash to her concave cheek, rather like a mime's face paint, suggesting a profound melancholy. She tugs at the sodden scarf she's tied around her frizzy hair and slumps in front of the desk as though all the fight has gone out of her.

"Good evening. Welcome to the Aviary Inn. Can I help you?"

"Well, I sure hope so."

She's American, apparently, and not very happy. "Do you have a reservation?"

"Yes, of course."

On top of regular summer tourists, two conventions are on this week, one at the University of York, and another in nearby Harrowgate, which is busting at the seams. As all our rooms are occupied, it doesn't bode well. Maybe she's joining someone.

"Your name, please?"

"Garroway. Linda Garroway." She leans on the welcome desk that I sanded and refinished during a couple of my shifts last week, dripping rainwater onto its shiny surface, which bead and refract the overhead spotlight like jewels.

I search through the reservation book but find no such name. Nervously, under her accusing glare, I rifle through the mess of scattered phone messages, some still attached to the little pink pad, others torn off and lying about in no apparent order. Who am I kidding? No order, apparent or otherwise, exists. Despite my constant efforts to tidy and organize the office, every time I return, the desk is a chaotic mess, papers randomly strewn everywhere, as though the place has been ransacked by thieves.

The troubles run deeper because no systems exist, no one oversees or sets standards. I'm not surprised that this woman's reservation has gone amiss, yet I persist in searching for it, because she's in such a bind. She will not likely find another room tonight, at less than three hundred quid, if at all.

Steam rises off her head and shoulders, and her jaw is set. "What's wrong?"

The lightning is invisible to me from my rear-facing cubbyhole behind the front desk, but a dull rumble of thunder ominously underscores her question. I can see the problem will be mine, but I have no solution. Despite my grandiose ideas, I'm still only a lowly desk clerk, no more able to pull a rabbit out of a hat than I am able to transform this sad, dilapidated hotel into a thriving business.

I swallow. "Well. Um. I don't seem to be able to locate a reservation in your name, Ms. … uh … Garroway." I pull my face into an apologetic grimace and shrug. "And unfortunately, we're completely full tonight."

"But I made a reservation. I've got …" Ms. Garroway plonks her rain-spattered red handbag on the desk and rummages through it, extracting a crinkled paper dinner napkin, and shoves it across the desk at me. "Look. I wrote down the confirmation number. You have to give me a room."

I dutifully regard the number scrawled in her beautiful hand on the napkin, which also bears pale splats of red wine, delicate rose-hued lip prints, and a brown smear of gravy.

I inhale shakily, realizing that my hands are trembling. I don't doubt she made the reservation. "I would, without hesitation, Ms. Garroway, give you a room. If we had any vacant." I wince helplessly. "But we don't."

I can see her gather herself up for battle, inflating somehow, growing in size and deepening in colour, and I shrink in expectation, wishing I could be anywhere else. "Now listen to me, you … you little—clerk!" she spits. "I've come from Washington, DC, for the conference at the university and there are twelve hundred delegates waiting to hear my presentation tomorrow morning on comparative constitutional law, religious tolerance, and racial equality, and if you think that I—"

"What's wrong here?"

I flinch, then let out the breath I held in a whoosh of air. "Mr. … uh …" I scramble to remember the name of the friendly, corpulent youngish American who checked in earlier. "Freiehauser! We don't seem to have a room for Ms. Garroway."

"Oh. No way. What a shame," he says in his odd, nasal twang. He turns to my angry guest and grabs her hand. "Ms. Garroway. I'm so thrilled to meet you. Jerry Freiehauser, Minnesota district attorney. I'm so looking forward to your talk tomorrow." He turns to me. "Listen, I have a spare bed in my room—" At Ms. Garroway's gasp and my raised brow, he stops mid-sentence and his meaty face floods with pink as he raises a hand. "I mean, I didn't mean … I wanted to suggest that … uh, my colleague might bunk with me, and you have his room, if that's all right with you, miss." He turns his flustered face back to me.

I exhale with relief and smile. "That would be fine, Mr. Freiehauser, if your friend agrees. Thank you for offering."

"I'll okay that with him. He's in the pub. Hold on a sec." He disappears.

Ms. Garroway and I stare mutely at each other for a few

minutes, each of us saying our own silent prayers. I tilt my head with a watery smile. I chew my cheek and twirl my pen, avoiding her glare. Then he's back, hopping from one foot to the other.

"It's fine. Go ahead. He'll move his stuff over and it's all yours!" He is beaming at a heaven-sent opportunity to do a good deed for an esteemed colleague, and I am every bit as relieved as the clammy Ms. Garroway. After we sort out the room swap and the key exchange, and I inform housekeeping, I check in Ms. Garroway. She is unable to resist an undeserved scold—"You're a very lucky girl, let me tell you!"—despite the successful outcome, which I endure with a tight smile and gritted teeth. She's the lucky one.

Another hour or so goes by with constant queries and complaints from the full house until at last, the place calms down. Even more frazzled than me, Cook bowls in with her tray and slams it down on the desk, setting the plates and cutlery sliding.

"I'm sorry to keep you waiting so long, poor dearie. What a night it's been! Run off me feet." She reaches up and pushes the pink paisley kerchief back on her shiny forehead with heat-scalded hands and heaves a sigh. "If you could but set eyes on the kitchen, what a state it's in! Not a spare moment to make anythin' special for ye, I'm afraid, dearie."

"Don't worry, Cook. I'm fine. Thank—" But she's scuttled back towards the kitchen, apron strings trailing, before I can complete my sentence. "You."

Though the wall clock still says five twenty-two, I know it's much later, so I can imagine how harassed Cook must be. She's usually conscientious about feeding me on schedule. Upon lifting the warming lid on my supper, not without trepidation, I am met with a monochromatic beige pile of dry meat, potatoes, and veggies. I dutifully cut and taste a few bites, but am not surprised to find the meat, possibly beef, overcooked, the gravy glutinous, mashed potatoes lumpy, carrots undercooked, and some pellets, shrivelled and grey, that may once have been peas. I force a few bites of the tough, flavourless stuff down to stave off starvation, but I can't make myself eat more and drop the lid back on it in distaste. My sympathy goes out to the hotel guests, and I am further discouraged about making any improvements to the Aviary Inn.

With a sigh, I listlessly turn to sort and tidy the chaotic office. I might as well be useful, though there seems to be little point. As if to highlight the futility of my efforts, I move the waste-basket and find, stuck to its underside, a pink phone message slip imprinted with crescent moons of coffee, reeking of tuna fish, and Linda Garroway's name and today's date scrawled in an illegible hand. I recognize it as belonging to Sean Smythe, the absent-minded sci-fi fanatic who relieves me at five each morning. I'm surprised he removed his bespectacled nose from his books long enough to pick up the phone.

This place! I'm so frustrated I'm not sure I can take it anymore. I really love Teddy and Cook and sympathize with Mrs. R., but they are all so damned eccentric and dysfunctional. I see myself letting go a high-pitched scream and throwing papers and pencils wildly around the stupid cluttered little office. Ripping that stupid old clock off the wall once and for all.

I'm panting and pushing the day's debris around the floor with an angry broom and muttering to myself when I hear the metallic sound of the warming lid lift off my uneaten dinner. Catching my breath, I whirl, expecting to be caught by Cook committing the ultimate sin—not eating—and come face-to-face with Mrs. Roxtoby herself, eyeing the remains of my dinner with curiosity.

She turns to me with a mix of chagrin and sympathy. "Oh, dear. Not hungry tonight, Sophie?"

Is she serious? Is she teasing me? I stand for a rather long moment with my jaw working before her lean face slowly cracks open in a smile.

"Tonight's was rather worse than usual, don't you agree?"

I smile wanly. "I … I don't often … I mean, usually she makes something special for me." I'm not sure if I'm betraying a secret, if Cook will get in trouble for her special efforts on my behalf. "I-it was, I couldn't …"

"Yes, her Italian cuisine is quite tasty, isn't it?" Mrs. R. sidles through the doorway and paces around the small office, poking at, lifting, and inspecting first a piece of paper and then the stapler, seemingly at random. She's frowning. I have to shift more than once as she makes her pensive rounds of the confined space.

I lean in the doorway, trying to stay out of her way, picking at the chipping paint on the jamb. She's never come into the office before. Is she angry with me? Am I in trouble?

Hot tears press to the surface. It's all too much. "If you know how good Cook's Italian food is, why do you let her serve that … that stuff to guests?" I blurt.

"Pish. Don't fret, Sophie, dear." Mrs. R. regards me a moment, head tilted, and then abruptly takes the tray and leaves the office in the direction of the dining room.

Oh. Great! I've offended her. Now she'll fire me. Or maybe she doesn't care. That explains everything.

About when I've decided that if Mrs. R. doesn't fire me for insubordination, and I'll have to quit out of humiliation, she returns with a plate of sandwiches and two glasses of milk. I gape, my brow dropped in astonishment.

"It's after ten. I sense you're suffering from low blood sugar, Sophie, dear. This will fix you up and then we can talk. Marmite, cucumber, and Fountain's Gold Yorkshire cheese," she says, as though this pronouncement will cheer me in and of itself. She picks up one triangle and hands it to me. It smells fresh and tangy. At my skeptical expression, she says, "Try it. You'll see what I mean."

•　•　•

British recipe for tasty midnight snack sandwich:
          Two slices of wheat bread
     Thin layer of Marmite
     Cucumbers sliced paper thin
     Thickly sliced Fountain's Gold Yorkshire cheese

Reluctantly, I accept it from her and take a small bite. I own I am hungry, but I actually like the combination of salty, creamy, and cool flavours and the crunch of cucumber. Marmite improves upon acquaintance, and in the right company, it seems. Mrs. R. eats a sandwich too, and we both sip our refreshing milk in companionable silence, creamy moustaches blooming on our lips, exchanging smiles.

A few minutes and a couple more sandwiches later, contentment suffuses me, and it's clear my tremulous mood was out of proportion to reality.

"So," says Mrs. R., licking her lips. "What do you propose I do about Cook's food? She's been a part of the Aviary Inn family for twenty-five years, Sophie. I can't let her go."

I laugh. "Why would you even consider that when she's such a fabulous cook?"

"Are you suggesting that we serve Italian cuisine at the restaurant?"

Mrs. R.'s incredulous expression tells me everything I need to know about her opinion on the subject. She sets her plate down with a clatter onto the desk.

"Well, why not?" I pick a few crumbs off my plate, sucking them off my finger.

"Well, I'll tell you why not. Because people expect good English fare when they visit the Aviary Inn. It's always been so."

I shake my head. "Who expects that? The hotel guests who had to choke down that dry meat tonight? Every one of them would have preferred Cook's homemade gnocchi ai funghi.

Everyone loves Italian food, and you've got an amazing untapped resource."

"Well …" Now it's her turn to shake her head. "Well."

"I have an idea," I say, perking up. "Since the hotel's full, you have a captive audience for a little market research. How about tomorrow we do a special Italian night?"

"Well …," she says again. "I suppose …"

"You'll see. It'll be great. I'll even come in early and help Cook, put up some signs. Then if you want to make the change permanent, all you need is a new menu and maybe a little advertising. Maybe rename the restaurant to give it a new image. You could draw in locals as well as tourists, not only guests at the hotel, but off the street."

Mrs. R.'s fear of change is evident in her shell-shocked expression, her quivering cheeks as her head oscillates back and forth in involuntary protest. I realize I've overwhelmed her with my enthusiasm. "Okay. One step at a time. It'll be fun. What's the worst thing that could happen?" I grab a sheet of the hotel's letterhead and pick up my pen, ready to sketch up menu ideas.

Her silence tells me she knows it couldn't be any worse. She has nothing to lose. We talk about the various dishes we've sampled: polenta, pastas, fish, and scallopini, and I can sense her excitement and optimism building.

After a while, a tentative plan in place, she looks at me and says, "I'm afraid to ask what other ideas for the hotel you've got swimming around in that head of yours, Sophie, but I feel compelled to now."

"Maybe you want to see how the restaurant thing turns out first." Smiling, I take our menu plan to the back and make two photocopies on the wheezing, clunking machine, one for Mrs. R. to look over and one for Cook.

A crackle of laughter rumbles up out of her. "Well, there's no harm in talking about it, is there?"

I laugh too, enjoying this warm camaraderie. We discuss minor fixups, not to change the character of the hotel but to highlight it and make it feel brighter, cheerier. I show her the mess of disorganized papers and suggest a computer, how useful it would be for keeping track of reservations, guests' registration, payroll, expenses, etc., citing the example of the irate Linda Garroway, explaining how the lack of orderly systems causes inefficiency and annoyance. Not to mention the opportunity for online bookings. I give her a brief synopsis of the system Mom started using a couple of years back.

"How lovely it is to have your young talent and energy at my hotel, Sophie," Mrs. R. says now. A sad smile illuminates her steely eyes, the creases at their corners accentuated as she considers me. She reaches out and fingers a curl of my hair. "You make it hard for me to ignore how much I've missed my daughter, although she is not a young woman any longer."

I look sharply away, surprised and disconcerted by her sudden intimate confession, now that it has come. Is she saying she knows we're connected? Or is my hopeful heart running away with itself?

"I miss my mom a lot too," I say, as if our adjacent pining could merge. "She's the one who inspires me. And taught me about hospitality, with her bed and breakfasts. The fluffy scones and lavender sachets. I've been curious about her English roots, which she's obviously sentimental about but won't discuss."

"Why does saying that fill your young eyes with sadness, dear?"

I shrug, hesitant to air my family's dirty laundry. But the intimacy of the moment, and all that she's shared, spur me onward. "My mom's not been herself this year. She's … I don't know, angry all the time. Critical. She and my dad separated earlier this year. I miss the way she used to be. The way we were all together."

Mrs. R. is silent, and after a moment I turn and meet her eye, my questions unspoken.

Frustratingly, she says only, "Hold on to your family, Sophie. No one will ever love you like they do." The amusement is gone from her eyes, leaving only sadness, and her voice is soft and hoarse.

Wondering if the returned Christmas packages from Regina were a dead end, I dare to ask, "Do you know where your daughter is now?"

Her lips purse like a limpet, and her speckled salt-and-pepper brows furrow. "Oh, yes. I do now. I know she moved to Canada and married, but not exactly where or to whom." She blinks and seems to see right into me, and I swallow, my heart pounding.

Is it possible she could bear so little resemblance to her daughter, yet share her intense grey eyes and straight brow? She continues. "I've heard through mutual acquaintances that she has children. But she won't have anything to do with me. She left after her brother died thirty years ago." Her eyes dart uncomfortably. "She blamed me, naturally."

"Maybe she's changed," I suggest, desperate. If we are talking about my mother, I'm overcome with resentment that she could be so rigid and unforgiving. No matter what circumstances she fled from in her youth, how could she sever ties with her own mother? I could never do that.

I really dare not push for more information, so I sit, silently empathizing and hope that she'll confide more in me, doodling pictograms in the margins of my journal. It takes a good few minutes of introspection, but at last her cloudy eyes come back into focus and see me sitting opposite her, waiting. I'm so out of my league. Though I want to know more, and to help her, I realize how profoundly underqualified I am to listen to her story, empathize with her grief. Or to consider brokering a reconciliation when I understand so little. For once, I fully feel the naiveté of my youth.

The breath she exhales carries the weight of her loss.

"You know, Sophie, when I was your age, I was already married with two little children. Back then, that's what young

girls dreamed of, but none of it was as I imagined it would be."
She sighs again.

"You had to marry Mr. Roxtoby?" I keep my eyes on my journal. "Because Rupert disappeared?"

She nods. "Yes. My parents saw to that. And I kno-ow …," she drags it out, "had my circumstances been less fortunate, and had I to fend for myself, that my life would have been much harder. But …"

"But maybe happier?" I venture, setting down my pen and turning to face her.

"Ah. Who can say? Now that they're all gone, I wish I had appreciated them more when I had them close, instead of resenting them and wishing things were different. Even poor William. Rupert was gone, and I was trapped. Young and broken-hearted, I dwelt on that one thing. And blamed everyone else. But now, I see that so much of what went wrong had to do with my inability to forget him. To accept that, however true our love was, it was not destined to be."

I hear decades of pain echo in her resignation, and my own pliable, more accessible tears well up. Marc-Antoine's unexplained disappearance thrusts itself into my mind. It's not the same—I'm not pregnant and seventeen, after all, nor desperately in love—and yet I feel some affinity with her sense of loss and abandonment, her alienation from her family. It's the not knowing that's worst. The wondering. Are you mourning lost love or innocence? Was that really love? And will you get another shot at it?

"But your husband, didn't he love you?"

Mrs. R. glances down with an intake of breath, pressing her lips into a line. "Maybe he would have, if I had let him. William was reserved and aloof with me, anyway, but he was a kind man. A gentle man. Of course he was. He married me in my predicament, didn't he? But I never let him get close. I blamed him as I blamed my parents for clipping my wings without considering his happiness or hopes." She flips one hand into the air, and her voice is self-mocking, censorious, not of them but of her youthful, perhaps unrealistic, self.

I ponder this reversal. How their efforts to protect her had made her feel caged and betrayed, and I wonder if I would have been any more complacent or grateful in her place, considering my present state of rebellion. At this moment, I regret the falling out with my family more than the loss of Marc, yet if not for any of that, I wouldn't be here.

A small group of guests return and file upstairs, and then Teddy emerges from the lounge to lock up the door. He saunters by and pauses just long enough to say, "Good evenin'" and pulls a face, raising curious eyebrows at me. I realize it must be closing in on eleven thirty. Mrs. R. and I have been talking for well over an hour!

Just as he disappears into the back, Eleanor emerges, and when she notes Ava's presense, stops and stares. "Go back to bed, Ellie," says Mrs. R. softly, and Eleanor pulls in her chin, blinks and complies, returning whence she came.

Mrs. R.'s sight turns inward again. She faces the desk and tap-tap-taps it absently with a rigid, bony finger, and I wonder if she remembers it's me, Sophie, she unburdens her heart to. Perhaps it's years since she's said these things aloud. Maybe she never has. This is what I wanted, isn't it?

Absently, she adds, "If we could have learned to love each other, maybe things would have gone differently with the children. And Eleanor, of course. What a muddle. I feel responsible for all of it."

"It wasn't your fault that Rupert disappeared. What else could you do, then?" My chest feels tight, and my eyes burn with sympathetic tears.

She shrugs. "I don't know. Perhaps nothing. I cried and cried until my mother despaired. I defied her and searched for him, refusing to believe he had died, but the army could tell me nothing, the police nothing." She pauses, her lids heavy and turned down at the corners. "Everyone was looking for someone in those days, and so many were lost. But finding him didn't matter anymore. By then, it was too late. I was married and my Barbara was on the way."

"I'm sorry, Mrs. Roxtoby. I'm so sorry." I reach for her hand and squeeze it. It's cold.

She rises stiffly from her chair, taking my hand in both of hers and rubbing it absently, as though it's me who needs comfort. "It doesn't matter anymore, Sophie. It's all in the past." She lifts her sharp gaze to mine. "But who knows what the future holds? Perhaps it will be brighter. I'd best get to bed now. I'm rather tired." She turns to the door, resting one thin wrist on the jamb.

"Mrs. R." I place my fingertips gently on her shoulder, and she turns back towards me. "Thank you for sharing your story with me. I wish there was something I could do."

"Perhaps you are already doing it, Sophie. These are the rambling regrets of a foolish old woman." Turning back to the door, she glides out and away into the darkened labyrinth of the hotel.

After she's gone, I replace the batteries in the wall clock, reviving its reassuring ti-ta-ti-tah rhythm and try to write in my journal until Teddy comes by with the tea tray. He asks a few leading questions: "Are ye all right, lass?" "Are ye feeling homesick?" But I don't feel like talking anymore, and he doesn't stay long.

For the remainder of the night, I sit quietly in a pool of warm light over the desk and ponder her words, her life, her sadness, feeling frustrated and helpless. She has done so much for me. Rescuing me, taking me under her wing, and now even indulging my wacky ideas for her hotel. But even if I can fix things up, it doesn't seem enough. I want to bring real happiness into her life. Somehow, I want to undo her tragic past and lighten her burden. But is it too late for that, or do I hold the key to do much more?

Besides, who am I? According to Nick, just a naive schoolgirl from Port Hope, Ontario. What can I do? Nothing.

But then I realize maybe that's not entirely true.

My chest floods in a wash of hope. Whether we're talking about my own mother, or some other woman named Barbara, born in York in 1946, maybe her anger has faded over the years. I sit up straighter, my pulse racing. Maybe, like Nick suggested, she was never angry, merely asserting her independence. Or feeling oppressed by the emotional turmoil at home. Maybe, like me, she regrets the rift between herself and her mother.

First, I have to find out if my suspicion about Mrs. Roxtoby's daughter is true. How can I do that without asking awkward, bald-faced questions?

Zoë said those returned packages were still in the back office somewhere. I wonder …

I head back there to rummage around, fuelled by a new optimism and sense of purpose. The office seems brighter, the warm glow of yellow light cheerier than a moment ago. It's euphoric. Maybe it's not too late for Rupert either. Mrs. R. may not have been able to find him in 1945, but no one confirmed that he was dead.

CHAPTER 26

1 *2:45, March 8, 1945, Holborn, London*

A man in a helmet and dull, dusty uniform led Ava gently towards a WVS lorry, handing her over to a woman in a neat olive-green jacket and cap with red piping, her golden curls in a hairnet.

"You're in shock, love. Just sit a minute." She settled Ava on a curb and handed her a tin cup of hot tea, then draped her in a heavy brown blanket. Ava didn't know she was shivering until at last, it subsided. She stood and handed the cup and blanket back to the WVS.

"What's that, then?" the woman asked her.

Ava looked down. She still carried Rupert's dented birdcage. She didn't reply. "Where's the Incident Inquiry Point?"

The woman squinted at her in concern. "In a public house, near the bomb site. Are you sure you're all right, love?"

"Yes, fine. Thanks for tea." Ava stumbled towards the remains of the market, limping, pushing down a tidal wave of anxiety, panic, grief. She had to find Rupert.

Ava moved deeper into the area crowded with curious onlookers, or people, like her, looking for someone in the wreckage. A fine litter of scraps, torn lumber, and bits of steel and concrete obscured Farringdon Road. The brutal remains of the market building were bound by the twisted skeleton of its once-beautiful ornate Victorian iron trusses jutting into the dusty atmosphere. She squinted up at a painted stone dragon that ineffectually guarded the corner of the market, surveying the scene of destruction below.

She tripped over broken trolley lines that hung down to the ground like cat-o'-nine-tails. Ava stepped around an overturned green Sunbeam-Talbot saloon car, then around a tram with smashed glass resting under dust and rubble. A steady stream of men in khaki coveralls disappeared into gaps in the wreckage and climbed out again, carrying limp bodies, like so many ants at an anthill. She could barely breathe.

After asking further directions, she located the Incident Inquiry Office, which had moved to Pearce's Restaurant in Charterhouse Street. She followed someone past cranes and a long line of ambulances standing by and stood in a long queue, feeling numb. Her cuts and bruises throbbed.

Finally, she was told that the first casualties were taken to St. Bartholomew's Hospital and immediately walked southward around Smithfield Park. Throngs of people crowded the gate. She had no sense of time passing, but her stomach twisted, hollow and tight with neglected hunger. She swooned from exhaustion before someone pushed a mug of tea in her face, and she drank it with relish, her parched throat welcoming the hot, fragrant liquid.

Scores of casualties lay, sat, and stood in long queues; over two hundred at St. Bart's alone. But Rupert was not there. She was told the hospital was full, and overflow casualties, the less serious cases, might be found at Great Ormond Street, the Homeopathic Hospital, University College, and finally the Royal Free. She found a shoe to replace her missing one, and somehow trudged to each hospital in succession, nearly five miles. Darkness fell, and she dragged her cut and aching feet onward, but could not stop until—until she knew. But she discovered no news of Rupert. Was it possible he'd escaped unharmed? Doubt gnawed at her gut, insistent, poisonous.

At last, resigned, terrified of what she might find, she begged a trolley conductor to let her ride for free and returned to Charterhouse and Farringdon, reluctantly locating the temporary morgue in a market on the corner.

"You can't come in 'ere. It's too late," said the warden guarding the door.

"I-I'm looking for someone," she replied, her voice hoarse, flat. "My … my brother's missing."

"Oh, yeah?" He sounded skeptical, but sympathetic. "Was 'e at the market this morning?"

"Yes. I was going to meet him."

"Let's see your identity card, miss."

"Em." She held out her empty hand, palm up, red with scratches. "I lost everything in the blast myself. I've been going round the hospitals all day."

The warden sighed and shook his head, scanning her dishevelled body up and down, taking in her mismatched shoes, squinting at her birdcage. "What's his name, then?"

She followed his gaze to the cage. "Ares?"

"Beg pardon?"

She gazed stupidly before she understood. "Oh! Rupert Dean. He's an army lieutenant."

"Ah." He allowed her to pass, his face grim, and led her to one side of the open space. Halos of yellow light glowed in the dim room. "We 'ave the enlisted men over here. Not many." He chewed his lip. "'Ow old? Can you describe him?"

She gazed around, stunned. The large open market was filled with canvas-covered mounds, some with paper tags. Hundreds of bodies. The odour was horrid, and her empty stomach heaved. She hesitated, cringing. "He's nineteen. M-medium height, I suppose. Dark, w-wavy hair."

"In uniform?"

"Yes. I expect so. Brown."

"Yes. I know, miss." He led her over to an area where half a dozen covered corpses lay separate from the others. Only one was tagged, and he passed by it. "This one's got red hair," he said, gesturing to the next. She shook her head. He pulled back the blanket from another, and she recoiled in shock and disgust. The soldier was rigid and grey, like a gruesome statue, and appeared a hundred years old under the cake of mortar dust and grime. His cadaverous mouth hung ajar, a crooked row of unfamiliar teeth exposed. She turned away, cringing, tears burning her eyes.

He showed her two more, peeling back the blankets carefully, showing her only enough of the faces for her to recognize.

She peered at him expectantly. "Are there more?"

His mouth set in a grim line, and he evaded her eye. "Bits and pieces. We try our best to put them together. Just a hand here," he said, exposing the lower part of an arm, a thick hand with a signet ring. She shook her head again.

Then hesitantly, he peeled back the blanket on another body on its side, enough to see the back of his head, his smooth white neck recently shorn by the barber, the delicate whorls of a young man's ear, a torn and burnt bit of uniform. The fine hair was encrusted with black, dried blood, dust, and grime, but it was dark and wavy. Like Rupert's. She stared at the ear, trying to dredge every detail from the memory of her kisses, but she could not be sure. She could smell the metallic iron tang of blood and charred flesh and soot. Air abandoned her lungs completely, and the room darkened around her. Her head buzzed and spun.

The warden's arm clamped around her shoulders, propping her up. "Easy now, miss."

"Are those lieutenant's stripes?" she asked, her voice wavering, pointing at the charred and torn remains of the epaulet on his shoulder.

"Not sure it's all there. Could be."

"Can I see his face?"

His head moved a fraction from side to side. "There's no face to see, miss."

"I don't know," she whispered. "I just don't know."

CHAPTER 27

July 1, 1997, York

Micklegate is a popular pub zone with students and other people our age, but even here it's quiet midweek. It feels weird to be out and have nobody celebrating Canada Day. Zoë and I enter the Priory, trading the relative peace of the dusky Tuesday evening streetscape for a much noisier and more crowded room, though as dark as outside.

"Blimey! So, this is where everyone comes, is it?"

"Hmm." I scan the crowded room.

The Priory is a proper nightclub, with a raised stage at one end, and a long, glossy wood and chrome bar along the length of the rectangular room. The ceiling is low, speckled with small recessed lights around the edges. Banged-up wooden tables and chairs cluster around the walls and are jammed with patrons, ranging wildly in age and class. There's a rumble of low voices.

I don't know what I expected. "It's very different from Elliot and Oliver's local," I murmur. No old men with caps pulled low over their scruffy faces huddle in greasy banquettes. I see spiked black and green hair and thin gray ponytails, studded leather, and floral polyester in the dim light.

The dance floor, a space near the stage where the dark finish is rubbed away from the wooden floorboards, is empty, and no music plays as we enter. From the elevated entry step, I peer towards the bodies radiant in the harsh stage lighting. At least the hovering fug of blue smoke meets my expectations.

"Relax, duck. What're you so worked up about?" Zoe grins, her golden eyes twinkling in the low lighting.

"Nothing," I reply, laughing and glancing away. "I'm just ..."

"Yeah, yeah." She smiles, shaking her head.

At last, I spot Nick, bending over some wires behind a large speaker to one side of the stage, a sliver of bare pale skin showing above the low belt on his skinny black jeans. I point, and Zoë and I make our way across the dark room. As we approach, Nick is standing up and slinging the strap of a peacock-blue acoustic guitar over his shoulder. He sees me, though, smiles, and sets it down again on its stand, hopping gracefully off the low stage to greet us.

"Hey, Canadian! You came." I'm relieved to see his look of genuine pleasure. I had my doubts. He smiles again and leans over to give me a soft peck on the cheek, which surprises me. He's usually so reserved. Maybe he's a little high, I think. He doesn't smell like weed or even dirt tonight. Actually, he smells nice, like soap, leather, and something citrusy. Seems strange to wear aftershave when he doesn't shave.

"Nick. This is Zoë. Zoë, meet Nick."

Zoë's eyes widen. "'Allo, Nick. I've heard a lot about you."

Nick smiles warmly and takes her hand in his, shocking her mouth open. "Not all bad, I hope. Pleased to make your acquaintance, Zoë."

"Likewise." She grins, but the assessing look remains in her amber eyes.

"You were about to play?" I ask. "Don't let us interrupt."

Nick puts a hand lightly on both our shoulders and steers us towards some reserved stools at the end of the bar. "Not at all. We haven't begun yet. Let me get you set up with drinks first."

"What'll it be, Nicky?" the bartender asks amiably.

"A half a Guinness for me, Tim, and something for my lady friends. What would you like, Zoë?"

"Glass of ale, thanks, guv," she replies, grinning, and I can see she's been totally won over.

"Same for you, Soph?"

"No beer for me, thanks," I say emphatically. "It goes straight to my bum, which is big enough."

Nick laughs, his bashful bleat soundless in the din. "I'm rather fond of your bum, actually," he says with mischief in his green eyes, and I feel my cheeks flush with heat. Tonight, in a different environment, he's animated and seems so much less weighed down. Like when he's working at the museum, as if he forgets himself and his worries when he's doing something he loves.

Zoë hoots loudly and I cluck my tongue. "A white wine spritzer, if you please," I say in a prim voice, hoping to deflect the conversation quickly away from my anatomy, grateful the low lighting hides my blush.

Our drinks appear before us moments later and we all have our first gratifying sips when Nick winks and nods coyly, takes his black-as-tar Guinness with him and steps up onto the stage. He takes another swig of his beer, sets it down on a big black speaker, and picks up his turquoise guitar, strumming it in an intimate, caressing way. Then he plugs in a pickup and adjusts the tuning and volume on his amp. Nick exchanges whispers with a shorter, stocky blond guy, who looks quite respectable, in contrast.

The house lights dim a little, while at the same moment a couple of soft spotlights intensify their glare on Nick and his mates, who strike a pose that's obviously premeditated, yet powerful. I recognize that ballsy Peter Pan stance, with slightly hunched shoulders and dropped head, and a current of sexual heat pulses through my veins. The bad boy persona that they convey is oddly stirring, a legion of rock-and-roll ghosts suggested by their posture. The song begins all at once, confidently, as though someone's dropped a loonie into a jukebox backstage.

Nick's sultry voice, familiar to me now but raunchier in the darkness, amplified and accompanied by electric guitars and keyboard, slides into the opening verse of Van Morrison's "Someone Like You." His voice is low, husky, and soft, deeper than usual, and has taken on a gravelly texture.

It's a brilliant rendition, but I'm jarred because the character and style of this old classic are so different from the edgier punk that I've sampled. The mixed audience is instantly appreciative; conversations ebb with a murmur of approval as ears perk, captured by the music. When the song is finished, a generous applause erupts. Pretty good, for a first number, so early in the evening.

Suddenly, the stage lights go black, and just as I'm figuring they've got an electrical problem, the clear, clean notes of the keyboard cut through the darkness. I recognize the tune, but I can't believe it's Nick whose warm tenor launches into Elton John's "We All Fall in Love Sometimes." How does he do that with his voice? Now the crowd is silent as they listen. It's not Sir Elton, but damn, it's good.

The next few numbers creep forwards a decade at a time. There's method to their madness. Now, it seems there's no difference, nothing to separate the varied members of the audience. Young and old alike, they're all into the sound, as am I. Turning to catch Zoë's eye, I smile as hers widen in delight. She leans towards me and pinches my arm.

"Ow!"

"They're brilliant!" she exclaims, laughing. I agree wholeheartedly. Somewhere mid-set, our drinks are replenished without a word. We applaud enthusiastically after each number, and at last, it seems the set is over. The dance floor empties and the hum of conversation fills the void. Nick turns to exchange words with his mates on stage, and then leaps lightly off and strolls towards us as a thin, recorded dance tune seeps into the void.

The same moment Nick arrives at the bar, two rail-thin pale blond socialites approach us.

They are both clad in scanty, silky tops and painted-on designer jeans, with their fine blond locks pinned back and up by sparkling jewels. More gold and jewels adorn their ears and slender fingers. "Oh, look, Abby. It's Tack. Remember us, darling?" says the first.

"Lucy," Nick says, his voice tight. I feel him tense beside me, like he did with those first guys we met on the street. "How could I forget?" He looks like he'd prefer to. When he looks at them, his eyes are hard as green agate and filled with something painful and angry. Reproach, maybe.

The second girl presses closer, leaning against Nick's denim-clad inner thigh, and I tear my eyes away from the familiar contact. The juxtaposition of these glossy girls with Nick's scruffy grunge is too weird, and bothers me almost more than Marc-Antoine's flirting, because it's so obviously unwelcome. "Nicky, love." She presses her cheek to his, kissing the air beside his ear.

"And Abigail, of course," Nick says, his eyes cold, his voice politely cool.

"Dance with me, love. I miss you, little one." She shimmies and pets his bearded cheek.

"Over the top, Abby. I have a dance partner, as you see." Nick places a proprietary hand on my arm, bringing mingled sensations of tension and a confusing, tingling thrill.

Abigail's tongue pokes lightly into her cheek as she casts an assessing glance over me. "Oh?" Her tone is a challenge.

"These are my friends, Sophie and Zoë." He gestures to Zoë on my other side. "Abigail and Lucy," Nick informs us, deadpan. Not his friends, by default.

"Call me Abby, please." She offers me her hand and a devilish smile, along with a bat of her long, false eyelashes. She doesn't spare a glance for Zoë.

"Hello," I say, trying to smile.

She nods and I hear her friend hiss "bog standard" into Abby's ear, whatever that means. "And where are you from? The West, I gather?" Abby says, her eyes assessing my clothing and undoubtedly Zoë's creative garb. As if we were sitting in a club in Mayfair.

"Sod off, sunshine," Zoë mutters, though she's being patently ignored.

"I'm from Canada," I offer.

"Canada!" Both women squeal. "How utterly charming," Abby adds, though it is plain to me she finds the fact simply quaint, and somehow reassuring, like a wee cloud that's passing quickly across the sun. She turns back to Nick. "Can't persuade you, Tack, love?"

Nick glares but doesn't deign to reply.

She leans in and pinches a handful of his beard, attempting to plant a kiss on his mouth. He turns his face to the side just in time, and it lands on his scruffy cheek. She grimaces. "Whenever will you remove that revolting disguise, love?" She pats his cheek and sneers.

"Sorry to disappoint you, ladies, but this is the real me, unplugged."

Two simultaneous peals of laughter rise above the din in the bar, and with a "Bollocks, Tack," they turn, giggling, and are swallowed by the crowd gathered on the dance floor.

"Gaw!" Zoë exclaims. "They was that stuck-up, the smarmy prat slags."

I offer a wry smile. "Whatever she said. What peculiar *friends* you have … Tack." I watch his face for a reaction.

His fine sandy brows tilt together and shadow his eyes, veiling their brightness. "Please don't call me that," he replies woodenly, turning his head away. "Don't give a toss, Zoë. They were in my brother's circle of so-called friends, never mine."

Were? He sits scowling while I study him and exchange a concerned, wide-eyed glance with Zoë.

Nick lifts his chin. "Well, Soph. Don't make a liar out of me. Let's have that dance now, shall we?" He offers his hand.

"But there's no mus…" Again, I catch a expectant expression on Zoë's face, which is so elastic she could convey a whole essay in one look, and I shrug a little.

"I'm going to the loo," she announces and prances away, singing, "'*Do you believe in life after luuurve …*'?"

One of the things that draws me to Nick is his confidence and easy bearing. Having evidently dismissed the deadly debutantes from his mind, he takes my hand and leads me across the dance floor nearer to the stage, as though he owns the place.

Turning to me, he smiles in his warm and soft way, and I instantly relax. Pausing, he catches the eye of the skinny ginger guitarist who remains on-stage and raises one hand, sending an encrypted signal: first two fingers, then four, and ends with a tight fist. Someone cuts the quiet taped music, and the short keyboard player and a dark, disheveled drummer slide into place.

I raise a questioning brow as the band begins to play, and I realize he's requested a slow instrumental version of Sting's "When We Dance." He opens his arms, smiling crookedly, and says, "Indulge me, Canadian."

Holy haberdashery, Batman! I step forward and he wraps his arms gently around me and sighs. "You're the only thing that makes any sense to me right now, Sophie," he says as he bends his bearded face to my hair and rocks me gently to the beat of his band's melodious rhythms.

I really like Nick, am drawn to his warmth, sincerity, and intelligence, quite aside from my visceral reactions to him, both postive and negative. He's certainly not what I *think* I'm looking for, neither like ambitious Elliot with his tall, blond, blue-eyed preppy good looks nor like sexy, dark, and intense Marc-Antoine, who is sophisticated, driven and artistic.

I can't get past my sense of Nick's indolence, underscored by his scruffy, shoddy appearance. Whatever's going on with him, I won't waste my energy trying to drag a lost soul, however poetic, along a reluctant path. I have my own dreams. And yet, he intrigues me and disturbs me somehow. With my eyes closed, it's the image of his sharp green eyes, his fine, smooth brow that I see, and the long, sensitive fingers of his capable hands, which hold me now, as subtly and surely as he holds his guitar.

I try to relax and enjoy the dance. Despite Elliot's persistence lately, I've managed to keep a friendly distance from him, claiming loyalty to Marc-Antoine. Even though it's only Nick, I haven't felt a man's hands on my body in such a long time, and the bit of heat we share is a delightful shock to my system. Too delightful. I can feel his lean, hard chest pressing against my tingling breasts, just close enough to tease.

As we sway to the music, the gentle friction of our clothes rubbing is worse than a passionate clutch, and I feel myself heating up, both between my legs and on my cheeks, and I work to keep my breathing even. His easy embrace is both reassuring and oddly exciting, which disorients me. There's chemistry at work here. I feel a shiver run through me as his hands gently caress my shoulders and back, though I'm sure he means nothing by it.

Nick releases a deep sigh and hums. I can feel the vibration of his voice through his sternum, tingling my skin, stirring my blood further. "You feel good, Sophie, so soft," he murmurs, fingering the end of my ponytail, tugging gently, and squeezing me a little tighter. "And smell so nice."

Then I feel his growing arousal press insistently against my belly and I shiver, stepping back, tittering uneasily. He raises his head and peers quizzically at me, loosening his hold with a quiet smile. I suppose he's embarrassed too. His voice is quiet and strangely distant when he says, "I'd better get ready for the next set." He turns away and steps up onto the stage, picks up his blue guitar, and glances back with a wistful smile.

Perching on the edge of a stool, he strums his guitar and croons, and within a couple of bars his band joins in, first the drums, then an electric bass, without the benefit of a coded hand signal, though the song remains a mystery to me. That is, until he sings the melancholy lyrics he sang last week at Clifford Tower, to "Space and Time" by the Verve.

There ain't no space and time/to keep our love alive,
We have existence and it's all we share,
There ain't no real truth/there ain't no real lies…

I'm astonished and moved by the emotion that creeps gradually out of his soul. He's more than mastered the song, his interpretation is beautiful. The room hushes as patrons stop to listen, mesmerized, although a couple of younger guys whistle in admiration at the new and popular song. His singing is more than a hobby, and Nick has more talent and depth than I ever knew.

Again, I am blindsided by this enigmatic and complex man who is quickly becoming someone special in this strange land.

CHAPTER 28

July 8, 1997, AOL, Kapow! Kafé, York

Dear Mom, Dad, and Matt,

Thanks for your letter. I'm replying by email from an internet café, to avoid the lag with snail mail. I'm having too much fun to be homesick, but I have been missing you, and it was nice to hear from you and hear what you've been doing this summer. I hope you and Auntie Bea can finish the painting on the Brooke Street house in time to list it before the weather turns. If it gets tight, Matt can come home for a few days. (You're not too important yet to roll up your sleeves and help, dude.) Give him something fun to do, like stripping the paint out of the joints in the balustrade. He'll love it! LOL

Thanks for trying to understand my need to do my thing. Despite your reservations, this trip has been a terrific experience.

But don't worry at all about me. I'm doing just fine. I have a great job and wonderful new friends here in York, and I'm definitely staying out the summer. I'll let you know if I need help to get home, but for now, everything is COOL.

All my love,

Sophie XOXOXO

CHAPTER 29

"Alan Stapleton? That's so weird," I exclaim, though no one is near me to hear it. I've found a familiar name on the list of reservations for next week, during another big conference at the uni. What are the odds this is the same guy who was a friend of my brother's a couple of years back? They were both involved in some environmental lobby group, or something, at the U of T. I only met him once, but Matt talked about him a lot back then. "Must be a coincidence," I mutter. "What would he be doing here?"

"Is that your homework, darling?"

My head jerks up and my heart thuds, its rapid pulse ebbing as quickly as it surged. It's only Eleanor. She's peering at me with her dark, suspicious eyes. I should know better than to be surprised when she sneaks up on me at three in the morning, but she scares the crap out of me every time. Sometimes she's quite lucid, but she's off-kilter tonight; I can tell by her state of attire.

Along with her ubiquitous pale blue dressing gown, she's wearing a bright fuchsia-pink turban, slightly askew. Wisps of her thin, white hair poke out over her large, soft ears as wrinkled as dried apples. Her badly painted, claw-like fingernails are a garish purple, like raw liver. It clashes with her headgear.

"The guest reservations for next week. How are you tonight? Trouble sleeping?" I set the register down on top of my open journal. Even though Eleanor often forgets things, she can be nosy, and I don't want her to notice Mrs. Roxtoby's name written over and over in my diary, to which I've been confiding all my worries, woes, and schemes—which do not include Nick's long silence.

No, they don't, I repeat the lie. As if I haven't been spiraling into storyland now that I know some of his tragic backstory. I know when to back off; he'll come to me when he's ready to talk about Saturday night. I feel so sorry for him, but I can't decide if his grief justifies his drunken wallowing, or if he's an emotional coward running from both his feelings and his responsibilities. What would I do if I lost my own brother? It's unthinkable.

Instead, I've been puzzling over Mrs. Roxtoby's case. Much as I'd like to find out more about her mysterious lost lover, Rupert the soldier, it seems sentimental and somewhat stupid to pursue something that happened fifty years ago. Even though his loss was the original source of her profound sadness, Mrs. Roxtoby appears to have confided all she's going to, and well … what else can I do?

I think it would be more fruitful and meaningful to focus on Barbara. That would be worthwhile. A reconciliation in that department would restore Mrs. R.'s her family. Some people might criticize my willingness to poke my nose into other's business, but I've always figured, if you can truly help someone—

"Ah. Well. Well. I'm all sixes and sevens tonight." Eleanor rubs her hands in an agitated manner back and forth over the shining desktop, nervously fingering the dents and scratches, now preserved under a glossy finish. I wish I could have stripped and sanded it properly.

I peer at Eleanor. Hmm. I stand up. "Are you hungry?"

She's staring off into space and doesn't reply. She could be in la-la land tonight, as the costume suggests, but one never knows. I try again.

"Do you want a snack from the kitchen?"

"Why don't you call me Aunt Eleanor anymore, Barbara, darling? Are you angry?"

When she calls me Barbara, I'm quite certain she's off her rocker. I won't make an issue of my identity. If Eleanor's going to take a trip down memory lane, maybe I can get something useful out of her about Barbara, about what happened to James that drove Barbara away forever.

When I move out from behind my desk and stroll towards the dining room, she follows listlessly, her slippers shuffling on the rug.

I smile at the notice taped to the door announcing the new Italian menu. The experimental Italian night was a wild success, reinforced by the continued popularity of these dishes. The menu change was a simple decision for Mrs. R. Cook has bustled smugly around her kitchen like the queen, not a grumble heard from her in two weeks. Cheerful red gingham dresses the tables now, an incremental step towards a complete reinvention of the restaurant. I'm brainstorming possible new names. Avia? Avante? By the fall, when the tourist traffic falls off, it should be well-enough established in the minds of locals to keep the restaurant busier through the low season than it's ever been.

I flick on a small light in the kitchen and put some milk on the stove to warm for Eleanor. Her shifting frame of reference doesn't seem to affect her appetite, and she's already ogling tomorrow morning's pastries.

"I knew some boys who came back from Italy," Eleanor says suddenly, pensively.

As I place her milk and a pastry down on the counter, she turns away.

"Come. I have something to show you."

Quickly, I pick up her snack and follow her shuffling form back through the darkened dining room over the golden vines of the red-carpeted lobby. As we pass, I glance at the old birdcage and glimpse myself in the shadowy mirror, and I have a strange vision of a young Barbara walking this same path, as though I'm looking through a window into another time. Eleanor's on a mission, her brightly capped long face jutting forward and her arms churning in determination, past my vacant desk with its halo of warm light, and through the breakfast room.

We enter the fern and spider-draped greenhouse corridor, and my nostrils fill with the damp, mildewed odour of soil and decaying plants. She shoves the door to her apartment open and disappears into the darkness while I hover on the threshold.

Her face pops back into view. "Come!"

Inside, I look around for somewhere to set down the dishes, absorbing the busy, cluttered space. It's a fair bit bigger than the typical hotel rooms inside the main building, the ones I've chanced to see, but it lacks any of the historical character of that part of the hotel. In fact, it looks exactly like what it is—a hastily and cheaply built, post-war addition, with low ceilings and windows too small and set too high on the wall to be pleasing. Eleanor's furnishings, too, lack the charm of the antiques that populate the main hotel, part of its attraction for me. I can hear my antique-dealer mother and aunt groaning in disgust. The mid-century knock-offs wear the weathered patina of long usage. Even the air is stuffy and cloying, redolent of perfumed talcum powder, peppermint, medications, and mothballs.

She has embroidered and crocheted doilies and runners on everything, and not an insignificant number of stuffed animals: dogs, cats, teddy bears. Curio cabinets display bric-a-brac. Ornately framed needlepoint and portraits cover every inch of wall space. I squint at a small gilt-edged frame beside the door, within which is displayed a needlepoint sampler on an ivory field, and the words: serenity, courage, wisdom, the tiny blue stitches perfectly uniform silken X's, row upon row. A spinster's life work.

A partially completed jigsaw puzzle paves the surface of a small dining table wedged into one corner, a chunky, dark-framed pair of reading glasses resting on top, answering my question as to what on earth Eleanor does all day.

She has forgotten her snack and is rummaging in a cupboard at the bottom of a cabinet, mumbling to herself. I set it down on her kitchenette counter once I've cleared enough space by stacking dirty cups and plates in the minuscule sink.

"Ah. Here we are," she exclaims at last and plops herself down onto her doily- and afghan-strewn love seat with a faded, paper-covered box on her lap and pulls off the lid. "Come, come, I'll show you," she adds, patting the seat beside her. I shrug and sit down after removing a stuffed beagle and her three pups. I thought Eleanor had forgotten my existence, but she seems purposeful.

The next thing I know, she's extracting envelopes, so worn with handling they are as soft and pliable as kid leather, stuffed with old photographs. Some of these end up in my lap, for lack of alternate space. Bundles of old letters are bound with petrified rubber bands. One has broken but stuck to the paper of the envelopes on the outside. The centre ones slide out, and I notice some of them addressed to Miss Eleanor Tremayne, and others to Mrs. Ava Roxtoby, the address typed on an old-fashioned typewriter with uneven letters.

"Oh, I say. Look, Babs, look!" Eleanor becomes more excited by the moment, flicking through stacks of odd-sized black-and-white photos with scalloped edges, very much like the one I carried from home. Peering over, I see assorted groupings of folks in post-war outfits, men in suits and hats, of course, women in tailored dresses, floral or plain, hems below the knee, their shoes still sturdy-heeled and blunt-toed. "There you are with little Jamie and William and Ava, dear. Look at your lovely curls."

I take the faded photograph from her and stare hard at it. A dapper, thin man stands in shirtsleeves and a tie, the brim of his hat casting a deep, crisp shadow over his face. An attractive s hort-haired brunette stands beside him, holding the hands of the two children. I study the woman and squinting little girl, trying to determine if they could be the same. Setting aside the post-war clothing, the girl resembles me a bit at that age, seven or so, although my hair was in pigtails, not a cap of Shirley Temple ringlets.

I point at the little boy. His hair is slicked down over his pate like a stroke of sandy paint. "Tell me what you remember about Jamie." His face, long and pointy like his father, is scrunched up tight against the glaring sunshine, his eyes slits. They are all posing in front of a large metal oil drum or perhaps a water tank.

Eleanor's intense expression softens. "My lovely boy." She hums off key. "So clever." She shakes her head. "They used to call him moody, because of the drugs, but they didn't understand him as I did."

I hand the photo back. "What about when he was older? Do you have any pictures?"

She hums and sets aside the whole bundle and dives into the depths of the box again. "But I told you I was looking for the Italian boys. The ones who came back ..." She pulls out another ribbon-tied bundle and tears it apart, flipping through the stack of photos, some of them sliding onto the sofa and the floor at her slippered feet. She doesn't seem to notice.

"Hah!" She passes a creased photograph to me. In it a young blonde nurse poses, a light cardigan draped over her stiff cotton uniform, standing with three young men in assorted bandages and states of undress. "That's Alastair, John, and Michael." She points, and I'm rather astonished at her memory. "They came to me after they all got shot up together on some secret mission near Napoli. They weren't even sure what they were doing there." She chuckles. I'm soaking up the complex map of their faces, joy, pain, fatigue, and hope, all wrapped up somehow. Eleanor's aquiline visage is unmistakable, her once dust-blond curls framing a laughing face. Though she has a long nose, and her teeth are too prominent, her chin too pointed to call pretty, her smile is easy, and she seems jolly. A fun girl.

"Aah. Look at Geoffrey." She hands me another picture of a beefy young man in a hospital bed, wearing a sleeveless undershirt, his biceps bulging, his leg in traction. A smiling Eleanor stands beside his bed, her arm loosely draped around his shoulders. "He was a lovely boy. We became quite fond of each other. I might have married him, but he was engaged to a girl down in Cornwall and was heading home, and I was engaged, too, then."

Her papery hands flutter over the pile. She passes me two or three more pictures of young men who were patients of hers. Everyone, including Eleanor, is always grinning. It's easy to understand why so many tired and frightened boys might have enjoyed her company and care.

"It must have hurt you very much when Mr. Roxtoby married Ava," I venture. "How old were you?"

She hesitates. "Oh. Just twenty-one." She sighs. "And even though I met so many nice boys at the hospital, there was none quite like my William. He was so quiet and dignified, not at all like me, though we were both from Yorkshire, you know. Oh, but I could make him laugh like no one else." Her hoarse chuckle is followed by an encore of violent hacking like cracking thunder, which causes the box to slide from her lap, tumbling its contents onto the floor.

I capture it, fumbling the flying photos, and try to pick up and assemble the strays when I notice a familiar face. I settle the box and reach for the photo, curious. It's the same soldier whose face I saw in the silver frame in Mrs. R.'s cottage. It's Rupert! It's Ava's Rupert, I'm sure of it.

"Hey! I've seen this before," I say. I wonder how it came to be in Eleanor's possession, when he was never a part of Mrs. R.'s home life.

Eleanor tries to grab it from me, and her eyes shift warily, but her voice is dismissive. "Oh, I don't know. I don't remember them all."

"Eleanor," I prod. "I recognize him." I meet her shifting, dark eyes, which she drops, and her face pulls into a contemplative frown, her lips puckering like the puce-coloured crepe curtains that block out the view of the garden behind her head.

"Oh, I suppose you'd be curious about him. It's only natural." Eleanor sniffs. "Don't be fooled by Ava's romantic notions. He never came back, did he? It was William who was there when you needed a father, not him. It's him who is due your love and loyalty, Barbara, darling."

"I am curious. I admit it." Never mind that I'm not who she thinks I am. I ignore the twist of guilt in my gut and tug gently on the photo, and she releases it so that I can get a closer look. Yup. Same wavy dark hair, prominent ears, straight patrician nose, and wide, full lips carrying the promise of a smile.

Eleanor rises and turns towards her bookshelf, takes down a larger framed photograph, this one of a slightly older, dour-faced man, his pale eyes staring out from below a protruding sandy brow, high and intelligent, if a little diffident. "You're the likeness of that Lieutenant Dean, sure enough, and my Jamie looked like his own father too. Quite an odd pair you two were." She pronounces it lef-tenant. Lieutenant Dean. Rupert Dean. A smile stretches my lips, and I feel my chest swell with hope.

I stand behind her, gazing at the beloved photo of William Roxtoby, the husband she never had, her lover, I presume. "I have to go back to work, Eleanor. Will you let me keep this for a while?"

She paws one hand at me half-heartedly. "Doesn't matter now."

As I slip out of her room, her pink-turbaned head remains bowed over the photo in her hands. "Don't forget your snack," I say as I turn and saunter back to the front desk, wondering about the role these photos play in the lingering love of old women for men long vanished from their lives. I realize, without a photo of Marc-Antoine to remind me, that the image of his once-familiar and well-loved face is fading into obscurity.

Climbing back onto my hard wooden stool behind the front desk, I'm stunned by Eleanor's inadvertent revelation. I never believed I'd find out more about Mrs. R.'s lost lover, Barbara's father, short of asking Mrs. R. to her face. And now I know his full name, and even his military rank during the war.

I lean the old grainy grey-tone photo up against the pillar behind the desk and stare at it for a while. These old portraits were always so aesthetically unfocused, rendering to every gawky young man a dreaminess reminiscent of movie stars, but Rupert Dean really was handsome, better than average. And I can't help but observe his features feel familiar, like you took bits of Mom, Matt, and me and mixed them up in a blender. Is it just wishful thinking? He'd be about seventy-one now, I calculate, nearly the same as Eleanor. He could, I suppose, still be alive. Reflecting on my dad's dad with his thinning hair and big ears, I wonder what Rupert might look like now.

Then, my pulse racing, an idea comes to me. I can hardly wait for my shift to end, and then hightail it to the internet café in town, my mind thrumming with possibilities.

CHAPTER 30

J uly 9, 1997, AOL, Kapow! Kafé, York
Hey, Matt,
This email is for your eyes only. Please. It's important. I need a small favour. Can you remember, or if not, then find out, the address of the house where Grandma and Grandpa Groenveld lived in Regina before Dad and Mom got married?

Also, weird coincidence. I'm working at an old hotel, and I think your old enviro friend Alan Stapleton is here for a conference!
X,
Soph

CHAPTER 31

J*uly 10, 1997, York*

"You again, miss?" says the dispassionate voice on the phone.

"Um. Yes, it is me, Sophie Groenveld. So sorry to bother you again, Mr. Updike." I hear him sigh heavily as I inhale hopefully. "I'm not trying to be a pest, but … last time I called, you asked if Mr. Dean is a relative. And, well, I said no, because … well, that's the point. It … it … it … I believe him to be my grandfather, maybe, possibly, but, but I have no proof, you see … it's complicated … That's why I need your help."

God, I'm a lousy liar!

"That's why I—"

"And you expect me to do what, exactly?"

"Well," I say, hearing the desperation in my voice, "there must be some way for a person to find a person, when one knows nothing about the person in question, except their name, and you know, possibly their profession, even if one doesn't exactly know if they are still alive—"

"Miss. Miss?" He interrupts my rambling, his voice imbued with a tone of profound forbearance, but I can tell his patience is wearing thin. It's the third time I've caused him grief in two days.

"Yes?"

"I really can't help you."

I stiffen. Bloody bureaucrats. Gatekeepers. "Can't? Or won't?"

"Can't. Even though you feel you might be a relation, though you can't prove the fact, and you only think he may have studied law after the war. We have rules. Laws, even. And even though I couldn't give you any information about him if he were here, our alumni and faculty database has no record of that name. Living. Or dead. Though there have been many Dean's through the years, none have been named Rupert. He has never been at Oxford in any capacity, never mind the Law Faculty. That is all I can tell you."

"Oh." Darn. "Really?" Especially considering, as I've learned, there are umpteen Rupert Deans in England. That fact is astonishing in itself.

"I'm sorry. Now, will you please stop calling?"

"Yes. Yes, thank you. Sorry."

After a long pause, he adds, "Have you tried vital statistics?"

"Huh?"

"To see if he, perhaps, has died."

"Oh, no." Good idea. Dreadfully final, but good. "Yes, thank you. I'll do that. Goodbye, Mr. Updike. Thank you." I hang up the phone and pace back and forth along the strip of open space between the sofa and the kitchen table. Zoë is at work. Not only am I wasting my time, but I'm wasting precious resources. I can't believe how much it costs to make a few phone calls in England! Unbelievable. I feel cooped up and restless in the summer heat, and my frustration isn't helping.

I should, I suppose, try vital stats. I really should, but I'm so tired of pestering people who can't help, or who aren't authorized to give me access to information, I can hardly summon the energy to look up the number. And what if this time I am successful?

My efforts to track Lieutenant Rupert Dean through Veterans UK were the most frustrating, because that is the one thing I actually know he did. But, of course, they won't give me access to his file unless I can prove I'm next of kin, or unless he has been dead for twenty-five years and I can prove it, which I can't do, or that he was born over 116 years ago, which isn't true. It was a complete dead end. It's no wonder people, like Mrs. Roxtoby, couldn't find lost loved ones after the war. They are so secretive, so protective.

The screech and twitter of circling birds draws my attention out the open window of our flat. July is well underway. The air is sultry, still, and dusty as the long days of summer trudge onwards. An aroma, sweet and cloying, wafts upwards, some flowers, or possibly spilt ice cream, but it's underlain by the dense, stomach-curdling odour of sun-baked dog shit, probably on the pavement outside.

I should be at home in Port Hope, in a hammock by the lake reading a good, thick novel. Marc-Antoine and I were scheduled to fly home on August seventeenth. A few weeks of summer at home before a new semester of grad school would be lovely. My first. Even if I never saw Marc again, and I'm beginning to believe I don't care, I sure would like to have my passport and airline ticket back. I can't believe it's two months since he disappeared. What an arsehole.

The sounds of a squabble drift up from the street two stories below, and I sidle to the window to spy on my neighbours. It's Mrs. Leech's Pomeranian complaining loudly about the territorial incursion made by Raymond's rather larger floppy-eared bloodhound, Trevor, and Trevor's terse, grumbling disgust with the yappy, annoying little fluff ball, aptly named Bubbles. Mrs.

Leech is the landlady, and so she invariably gets after Raymond, a balding, middle-aged bachelor as droopy and lethargic as his dog, about Trevor's smelly habits and his intimidation of Bubbles in particular. It's a familiar scenario, occurring several times a week. Lucky me, I'm always home in the afternoon to witness it.

Now I smell Raymond's pipe smoke, mingling with the other aromas of summer, smoking being his silent, stoic response to Mrs. Leech's recriminations. I see his eyes roll heavenward, and he sees me peeking out the third-storey window and clamps down on the stem of his pipe with a wink and a stifled smile.

I have to get out of here.

Outside, both dogs and their owners are gone. I turn in the direction of the uni, to the southeast. I've never visited Elliot on campus, even though we've been out there for a movie at the student union building.

I see little point trying to get anything out of vital statistics. I don't know enough about Rupert Dean, and I haven't any right to be looking. My attempts to find the living Mr. Dean have been equally frustrating. The library, of course, has British Telecom directories of everyone in the country. And, of course, there are hundreds of Rupert Deans and R. Deans listed. Hopeless!

But maybe, with a little inside help, I can find something out. I trudge along Heslington Road through the arid, seedy edge of town, through some unkempt green space towards the campus, where the scenery includes fewer cars and more trees. Between the buildings I see gravel walks slicing through expansive lawns leading down to the large central lake, and I feel the water-cooled atmosphere wash over my face, several degrees cooler than the dry urban environment.

University Road is off to the left, but I recognize some land-marks, such as the kind-of-triangular concert hall, and I cut straight through to the Market Square. The campus is sparsely populated midsummer, but some students mill about, many lounging on open green lawns or cycling around purposefully.

At the information centre, I'm told that I walked right past the management and law school on my way in, so I double back in search of the Sally Baldwin Buildings, which turns out to be a modest quadrangle of stone and brick blocks, neither modern nor ancient.

Inside, it's cool and quiet. The building is deserted, the reception desk unattended. I wait a few minutes, studying the lipstick-stained straw sticking out of a cola by the phone, and listen to the surrounding emptiness. The space hums with the steady stream of refrigerated air rushing from an overhead grill, the idle purr of the quiescent photocopier resting by a wall, and the distant drone of a floor polisher. At the far end of an extremely long corridor, a tall janitor in a full blue coverall oscillating a floor buffer over the already gleaming linoleum appears like a tiny blue shimmering splotch in the distance. Finally, a young woman emerges from a doorway with an armload of files and returns to her post. She's pretty in a soft, doll-like way. She seems surprised to see me.

"Hallo!" she says in possibly the strongest Yorkshire accent I've heard yet. "Can I help you?"

"Yes. Hi there. I'm looking for a friend. A student named Elliot Crowther."

She squints at me for a long moment, looking me up and down suspiciously. "Oh, yeah. A student, is he?" Her eyes dart down the corridor for a moment. "Well, there's not many about right now, but I'll look him up for you, will I?"

"Please." I wait while she wakes her sleeping IBM computer screen and clicks and scrolls. Clicks and scrolls, her broad, smooth face frowning in concentration. Her mouth works, as though she's chewing on a sour lemon drop.

"I'm sorry. Ah can't seem to find him." When she looks up and sees my expression, she adds, "But maybe I'm missing somethin'. Jest hold on. I'll 'ave a chat with the director. Your chap Elliot may be doing summer research, or somethin'." She smiles and strides away.

Again, I stand and wait, watching her swish down the highly polished linoleum of the long corridor to the far end, her hips swaying in a vermilion sundress splashed with yellow daisies, its flirty little hem jouncing. It seems to take an eternity for her to get to the end and disappear. I gaze at a poster on the wall promoting a summer exchange program to Brussels, remembering the three romantic days I spent with Marc-Antoine, not so long ago, gazing up at those same Art Nouveau buildings. One pushpin has gone missing, and the top corner curls back like a forlorn page waiting to be turned.

It seems like another ten minutes before she reemerges and begins the long trek back. She stops by the janitor, and he turns towards her, pushing back his cap as they exchange mumbled words. His laugh is a rumble, a strangely familiar sound, and he pulls her towards him for a stolen kiss. I can see his tongue thrusting greedily, and then I hear her tinkling laughter echo off the smooth walls. The corridor is so long it feels as though time and space are distorted, like a desert mirage, and their mirror images, orange and blue, upside down, undulate on the glossy floor.

I flinch when she finally speaks to me.

"I'm so sorry. The director says we 'ave no student by that name."

I'm puzzled. "He told me he was in management school, but also taking some law courses. Maybe I got them mixed up?"

She lifts her chin. "Well. The two schools share administration, as well as the building, so he'd show up either way."

"Hmm." I ponder a moment. Could I have misunderstood Elliot so completely? "Well, thank you for your trouble." I chew my lip. "Goodbye."

"Goodbye, miss. I'm so sorry you couldn't find your friend." She smirks, and her gaze darts again for a split second down the hall. I frown, looking closely into her twinkling brown eyes.

I offer a lukewarm smile and nod, turning to leave the building, strangely self-conscious of my own wavering reflection in the shining linoleum.

Then an odd idea strikes me, and I turn around and peer intently at the janitor down the hall. The chill conditioned air afflicts me suddenly like the flu, my bare skin shrinking and tightening in a rash of gooseflesh.

"Miss?"

Striding past the receptionist down the corridor, I call out, "Elliot?" He doesn't react, his head bent over his work, cap pulled low over his eyes. The machine is louder the closer I get, but not that loud. "Elliot!" I bark, and finally he looks up, and the self-conscious expression on his face tells me more than I wanted to know.

We stare at each other for a few awkward moments. I want him to tell me that this is his summer job, that he's earning extra money for his tuition or whatever, but I don't need to. I can see the answer on his crumpled, crimson face.

"We need to talk," I say.

He nods minutely, his jaw working. His gaze flicks up the corridor towards the girl.

"I'll wait outside."

I sit on the lawn, in the sun, for about half an hour, my chilled skin gradually warming, until Elliot finally emerges. He has shed his blue coveralls and now looks more like himself in a preppy white polo and neatly pressed khaki shorts, loafers with no socks. Well, he sure knows how to play the part. Business school! Bah!

He falls in beside me as I rise from the lawn, and we strike off towards the lake by unspoken consent. He avoids eye contact. He doesn't lean down to kiss me. He doesn't toss his heavy arm around my shoulders like he usually does.

In the distance, Central Hall looms over the end of the huge lake like a UFO landed. We head towards it and stroll onto the bridge. I'll be damned if I know what to say.

Finally, Elliot stops mid-span and turns to me. "I never meant to mess you about, Sophie."

"But you did. You lied to me."

We walk along in silence while he processes that.

"I know you must think I'm a plonker, but you need to understand why I did it."

I raise my eyes to his, cool and level, letting him know that I'm listening, and it better be good. "Do I?"

"I thought you'd never find out."

A snort of laughter escapes me. "Lies are like that, usually."

"I mean, I figured you'd go home to Canada, and it wouldn't matter in the long run, because I do actually mean to go to uni. Someday. I have to put some dosh away before I can do it. And … if we stayed in touch … eventually, I'd catch up with my lies." His voice falls. "Not the other way round."

"You don't owe me anything, but there's no need to be a poser. Why not tell the truth? You're not some school kid, Elliot."

"I only wanted you to like me. A man's gotta have something. An' since I've no money, I had to have a good reason for it."

"Why did you think I'd care?"

His face falls, and for a moment he resembles a sad little boy. "Don't you?"

"I did like you, Elliot. I mean, I do. But that doesn't mean—" I shake my head. "Anyway, that's not what I meant."

"I was tryin' to impress you a bit. You can hardly blame a bloke for that. As soon as I met you, I liked you, Sophie. Wanted you to like me too." He reaches for my hand, but I leave it limp, and it slides out of his grip.

"So, you lied. Do you have so little faith in yourself or in me that you didn't think I'd like you for yourself, without … I don't know, without credentials? Did you think I would diss you if you weren't educated?"

He bristles, squaring his broad shoulders. "Yeh. I did."

"What does that say about me?"

"It's not you. You can't help it. That's the way it is." His strong square jaw juts stubbornly.

"Not where I come from."

"Bollocks! Don't try to make Canada sound like some classless paradise. That's bullshit. It's the same everywhere."

"And you speak from vast experience!" I can't help the sarcastic tone. He's pissing me off with his righteous self-pity. "Anyway, I wasn't talking about Canada. I meant … my world."

"Well, I wouldn't have had much chance to travel the world, would I, if I can't even afford an education!"

I'm fuming now, my breathing fast and shallow. "Look. Elliot." I twist my lips a moment, trying to find the right words, but my mind's in a steaming muddle. "In my opinion, if you really care one iota for me, or for anyone else … I'm not saying life's perfect, but you're not the only one with challenges. It's how a man deals with them that says more about his character. Honesty and integrity count for more, in my books, than a few letters after your name. Maybe your life wouldn't be so damn difficult if you didn't carry around such a big chip on your shoulder."

"Aye," he says. "That's what they always say," and strides off across the bridge.

I stand there in silence. I don't care to pursue Elliot or the discussion any further. I'm remembering Nick's inebriated caution. That Crowther twat ish tro-trouble … that Crowther bloke isn't what he says. He knows. Nick must've known! And he tried to warn me, when nobody else did. Not even Zoë. Although, to give Zoë her due, maybe she didn't know about Elliot's lies. She's always so busy snogging with Oliver she never listens to our conversations. I frown. It's possible, I suppose. In any case, Zoë holds no illusions about Elliot and never encouraged me.

Then I remember why I came, what I came to ask Elliot about in the first place.

"Elliot! Wait!" I race to catch up with him.

His pace has slowed, as though he's afraid of what I'll say. I put my hand on his arm, and he stops and turns towards me. His face is stern, frowning, but he doesn't meet my eye. Rather, he glares intently at the ground between us, his shoulders hunched, his shoe sliding noisily on the fine pea gravel of the path.

"I almost forgot. The reason I came looking for you." I pause and catch my breath.

His brow creases, as though this hasn't occurred to him. "Why did you?"

"It's Mrs. Roxtoby, my boss at the hotel?"

"Are you still on about that?"

I fill my lungs. It wouldn't take much for me to walk away from him forever, and never look back. "Yes, I'm still on about that. I'm trying to help her. I want to find her lover, that soldier who disappeared in 1945. Remember I told you?"

His lips press into a thin line, and a muscle jumps in his jaw. His eyes flicker upwards, and he blinks slowly.

I shake my head. "You know what? Never mind, Elliot. Forget about it!" I spin and take a stride away from him.

"Sophie, wait." He grabs my elbow.

I stop and slowly turn to face him.

Elliot releases my arm and drops his head, shoving a meaty hand through his pale hair, leaving it standing in messy, parallel peaked rows, like a field of wheat after the harvest. "What do you 'spect me to do?"

"I was hoping you had access to some …" I shrug. "Some directories or registers. To look him up. I think he might've been a lawyer, and your … school …" I flick my eyes back towards the Sally Baldwin Buildings. The words hang in the air between us. "Maybe someone there knows him? Or maybe the library?" I shrug again. "I don't know. Don't you have access to information? Or friends at the uni? I'm getting nowhere on my own. Too much confidentiality and stuff."

His mouth works for a moment. "Well, I have some perks as a staff member. Library access. I can ask around, I suppose."

"His name's Rupert Dean, and he was born in 1924 or '25." I offer a tentative half-smile. "Thanks."

He dimples and nods, and I turn and walk away.

CHAPTER 32

"Do you like this colour?" asks Zoë, waving a small bottle of nail polish back and forth in front of my nose.

"Hold still, I can't see it," I reply, laughing. She stops and I assess the offering. "Nope, too pretty-pink for summer. I'd rather—"

"Yeh, it's a bit twee. How 'bout this?" She thrusts another one towards me. I squint. It's a coppery rust, like summer coneflowers, that suits me better. "Yup. I like that." Funny, there was a time when I wouldn't wear anything but pale blush polish. I guess I'm feeling a bit more adventurous these days.

"Right, then, feet up here on the newsprint." She pats the prepared surface on the sofa between us with a rustle of paper and I comply. We can't get too far apart, as we've each got one ear bud of her MP3 player in an ear, listening to Madonna's new album. After twisting tissues and weaving them between my toes, she sets to work painting my toenails. "It's called Venetian Carnavale," she says.

"Mmm," I say, my mouth full of sweet sticky bun, the aroma of cinnamon stronger and more insistent than the intermittent odour of nail polish, drugging me into a happy complaisance.

We've got the afternoon free and are hanging out at home together. Both the guys we usually spend Sundays with are in the doghouse, so we've made ourselves unavailable. Yes, Ollie's transgressed again, though this time it's just his compulsive flirting. I realize it's probably Elliot who's the bad influence.

Besides, next week we're expecting a mad busy week at work, with another huge conference coming up, and I promised to work a ton of extra hours to help out. I need to enjoy my downtime when it comes.

Zoë jumps up off the sofa as though someone hit the eject button, her ear bud tugging mine as it pops out, and then she hobbles to the kitchen on her heels, her toes splayed like a chimpanzee, since I painted her nails first and they're still soft.

"I'll put the kettle on." She does so and hobbles back. "We should've run down to the offie. I wish we had some plonk. Now we're stuck with Chelsea buns and clementines. I wonder if we've got any Marmite?" She plugs herself back in. Madonna is in the middle of "Ray of Light."

"Hmm. I'm content." I watch her stroke Venetian Carnavale meticulously onto my toenails one by one, and I suck sticky bun residue from the gaps in my teeth.

"I'd as rather drown my sorrows," she says in reply, pulling a sad face. She's been regaling me with the latest trials and tribulations of life and love with Oliver.

"Why don't you confront him if you suspect something?"

"He'll only deny it. Bat his eyelashes at me. What's the use?"

"Then break up with him once and for all. Why should you take it?" I've got no patience for lying men these days.

"You don't understand. I love him!" Her face twists in anguish.

I roll my eyes. We've had this stupid debate a thousand times. "So get over it. There are plenty of others out there. You might even find another one just as selfish and cruel as Oliver." I smile. "Odds are ..."

Zoë's smile is tolerant and amused, her amber eyes twinkling with mischief. "You'll know when it happens to you. When Ollie kisses me, when 'e 'olds me, when 'e makes the most delicious love to me, none of it matters. I know 'e's the one. We're gettin' married someday."

I'm appalled. "It's not about good sex, Zoë! You can't choose your life's companion based on skill in bed."

"It's not only skill, duck, it's … it's chemistry. You know it deep inside somewhere. It's real."

"Chemistry! You're talking about your G-spot," I say, and she laughs. "Besides, Oliver's a schmuck. Look who his bestie is."

"Well. Nobody said life was perfect." She sighs. "You 'ate men, is all." She sulks. She's heard all about Elliot's latest. "You're just having a run of bad luck, duck."

Bad luck duck, that's me. "I do. They're useless," I say with emphasis. "Not one can be trusted."

A sudden muffled clanking noise drifts up the stairs from the entry hall through the open door.

"Did you hear that?"

"Probably Raymond, taking out his trash." I perk up. "Or maybe the mail?"

"Do you care?"

"Might be something from my folks. Do you mind?"

Having finished one coat, she sets down the little bottle and limps out our door. I can hear her thumping awkwardly down the stairs on her heels.

While she's gone, I gaze at my glimmering metallic toes and contemplate the fickleness of men. I'm feeling as low as Zoë does in her tempestuous love affair with Oliver, who toggles between utter devotion and wanderlust, literally, on a near bi-weekly basis. I can set my clock by his infidelities, and I can almost—almost—sympathize with Zoë's blasé attitude and tendency to let some of them blow by without incident. He doesn't seem to take any of his flirts as seriously as he does his long-term romance with Zoë. Although why she doesn't tire of him alto-gether, I don't understand.

I wonder if there's anything to what she said about chemistry and try in vain to remember what it felt like to be with Marc-Antoine. Charm or good looks alone don't cut it, Oliver's best friend Elliot being a case in point. What a pair.

I'm still furious with Elliot for lying to me, though, really, what do I care? We don't even have a relationship, never mind any commitment or expectation. And yet I feel awfully bummed out that he bothered to spend all that time with me, and imply that I was somebody important to him, and base it all on lies. It's so cheap. I feel slightly sickened, and filled with remorse, like you do after binge eating a giant bag of cheesy nacho chips.

That, combined with that bastard Marc-Antoine, and then there's Nick, who has not tried to contact me in two weeks, since I inadvertently discovered his big secret and embarrassed him. Some friend. Everyone's worried about appearances. It makes me question my ability to judge character.

A muted thud interrupts my musings, followed by the whisper of a papery landslide.

"Fuck!"

Zoë crashes in through the door and tosses a mess of mail into my lap. "I've gone and buggered three bloody nails! Sod it!"

I laugh. "I'll do them over. Come here."

She stomps into the kitchen to make the tea, and while she's banging around, I sort through the pile of flyers, bills, and letters. A Canadian postmark and familiar handwriting catch my eye and I zero in on it, astonished but curious. A letter from home.

"Oh. My. God!" I exclaim as I tear it open. "My mother wrote a long letter to me!"

"Is that odd?" Zoë sets down a teapot and two mugs next to our snacks.

I wave it in the air and then peer intently at it. "It's not normal," is my belated reply. Though Mom's familiar handwriting addresses the envelope, the thick letter inside is typed. Hardly anybody writes letters anymore, but I suddenly recall that Mom used to write to friends using an old typewriter. She always said her hand could never keep up with her thoughts. And I suppose she emails them now. But it raises my suspicions further. Why did Eleanor have typed letters in her possession addressed to Mrs. Roxtoby? Who were they from?

Zoë sits quietly, removing her damaged nail polish, releasing a wave of acetone into the air, leaving me to read the letter dated almost a week ago.

J*uly 9*

Sophie dearest,

Thank you for your email. I'm so glad you're safe. I must admit my feelings are a little bruised that I'm receiving your news second hand through your brother.

(W*ell. I did send postcards home until the last one. Even if they were fake.)*

I *would email, or phone, if you'd share your info with me, but you leave me little choice. I'm writing this so I can speak my mind in privacy. I don't need your father and brother getting involved in this.*

"H*old still," says Zoë. "I'll do your second coat."

I do, my eyes skipping ahead, and continue reading, my pulse racing. My mom is finally talking about her past.

•   •   •

ow that I know you're in York and have somehow managed to set yourself up for a longer stay, I know exactly what you're up to. And I'm not pleased about it.

But you already know this. When you declared your intention to go travelling with that boyfriend of yours, I had my suspicions, but now I know I was right. It was your intention all along to poke around in my family history. I don't know if you've dug anything up, but perhaps by now you have.

So, reluctantly, I'm going to share some details that, if it were up to me, I'd rather leave buried in the past. But you seem to have forced my hand.

The estrangement with my mother goes back almost thirty years. I had good reasons. At first, of course, I was young and angry, and several years passed during which I went on with my life and didn't try to contact her, and she didn't know my whereabouts. It was the sixties and seventies. That's when I first travelled to Canada and soon after met your dad.

I feel remorse now, for as a mother of two young adults, I can well imagine how painful my departure was to her, notwithstanding our differences. However, back in about 1971, after Matt was born, I deeply regretted cutting all ties to my family. For Matt. And for you, Sophie.

I made several attempts to contact her, to no avail. In every case, my calls were rebuffed, my letters repeatedly unanswered. I tried for years, and then I'd had enough.

"*O*h, no! That can't be true!" I gasp.

"What? What is it?" asks Zoë, frowning, the little paintbrush frozen mid-air above my foot.

I mumble, shake my head, and continue reading.

*M*y mother was always opinionated and intractable, but I thought, I hoped, enough time had passed to heal our respective wounds. It seems I was wrong, and for her, pride and righteousness *played a stronger role. I'm sorry for it, but I have reconciled myself to it. She may have had her own regrets, but for me, it's too late. There is no hope of reconciliation. Now, even if she was willing, I am not.*

I'm sorry to disappoint you, Sophie. You're a caring and romantic soul, and I love that about you. But in this case, I'm afraid, there can be no happy ending. So please, my darling. Trust me when I tell you that you're setting yourself up for disappointment and heartbreak. I don't want that for you, and it will do me no good to get dragged through all this again after putting it behind me.

I've enclosed some travellers' cheques and a voucher for a flight home. I beg you, Sophie, please, please, let it go. Come home.

With all my love,

Mom

"No, no, no," I moan, dropping the letter and my forehead to my palms. Why is she so stubborn? How can she do this to me?

"What the devil …?" Zoë takes the letter from my limp hand and scans the bottom half. Then she looks up at me quizzically. "Are you in trouble with your mom now?"

"Oh, don't say it. I still don't even know if Mrs. Roxtoby is my grandmother. I could be way off. And everyone warned me I didn't know Mrs. Roxtoby, and how could I interfere in her business, anyhow? But the two ends of this story sound like they fit together, don't they? And if there's a chance …" I grind the heels of my hands into my eye sockets, pushing back tears of disappointment. "It's that I really, truly felt I could help. How can a mother and daughter sever all ties forever? It doesn't make sense."

"Well," mutters Zoë. "There's not a helluva lot more you can do about it. Does that mean you'll be leaving?" Her big golden eyes crease at the idea.

I shake my head sadly, pondering my options.

"Poor you, love. But I supposed you was going to hit a wall, eventually. This entire project of yours is a bit daft, ain't it?" She peels an orange and shoves it towards me. "Here. Eat this. It'll make you feel better."

I groan and flop back onto the sofa cushions with an arm thrown over my face. I just don't know. I need to know what happened! How can I give up now?

"Gaw! Look it! Now you've gone and mucked up a nail!"

CHAPTER 33

"Your key, sir, room 201," Zoë says to a couple of ageless Japanese businessmen in suits a week later. "We got a very grand Italian menu tonight in the restaurant. It's famous!"

They nod earnestly and move off with their bags. They didn't speak a word, I noticed.

"Were they jest bein' polite? Or maybe they don't speak English?" Zoë says.

"They'd have to, to attend an English language conference, wouldn't they?" I ask. "Unless they have interpreters …"

"Takesumi and …" She consults her register. "Kinekawa. Gaw, they must speak English. Maybe just very shy?" Zoë exclaims.

"Maybe they thought you were daft. Left them speechless," I tease.

She smacks me on the shoulder. "Don't wind me up. I'm shattered. Been here since noon!"

It's Wednesday and the huge summer environmental conference at the uni begins tomorrow, so all the speakers and delegates checked in today, from all over the world. It's the big one we've all been anticipating, and we're fully booked for the week, along with every other hotel in town. Guests are shoehorned into every bed. Zoë and I are each working an extra two hours a day so we can staff the desk side by side from five to nine in the evening, when it's busiest.

I've checked in three parties in a row and stand tense and ready, awaiting the next onslaught. The lobby is full of people milling around, and I don't know if they've been registered. Some of them I don't recognize.

"If I don't head to the loo soon, I'll piss in me pants and embarrass you, I guarantee it," Zoë hisses. She's wearing her Baby Spice pigtails and striped tights tonight, with tall platform biker boots. If I were easily embarrassed, it would be much too late.

"Okay, well, there's a lull right now, so make it quick before the next wave comes through," I say. She doesn't need to be told twice and slips out. We don't dare leave the desk unattended with so many people around. We could even use a third person to float through the lobby answering people's questions, of which there is an endless flood. But, of course, we don't have any more help. Even the disobliging Sean Smythe, who works the morning shift, is relieving me an hour earlier than usual, so I don't drop dead from exhaustion. I'm feeling it already. My back and feet throb with a dull ache. Even though being busy makes the hours fly by, dealing with a constant stream of customers wears me down.

No sooner does Zoë disappear down the back hall when a young man approaches the desk. He's short and slender and nice-looking in a delicate way, but his cotton blazer is rumpled and his shiny dark hair is kinked up on one side, like he fell asleep on the train.

"The name is St-Stapleton? I've a reservation for the week," he says in a rather high voice, pulling a creased paper out of his pocket and smoothing it down on the desk with his fine-boned, pink-skinned hands. His nails are chewed down to the quick, and he's nibbled the skin away on the side of his thumbs. He sounds like a Yankee or Canuck. I feel like I've seen his bland, youthful face somewhere before, then I remember. Something about his stutter is familiar.

"Oh, oh! I know you. Did you just arrive in town?" I greet him.

He squints strangely at me. "Uh. I flew into Edinburgh from T-toronto, and then took the train down to York. I was p-picked up at the train and taken out to the uni, as they call it, to register and meet the organizers first, before they dropped me off." He smiles hesitantly. "You're n-n-not a Brit!"

"No. A fellow Canadian." Alan Stapleton. I smile and scan the list for his name and slide the registration forms across the desk.

"Professor Alan Stapleton. University of Toronto?" I squint at the name tag hanging in the plastic sleeve around his neck. "You know my brother."

"Really? Who's that?" His voice squeaks.

"Matt Groenveld?"

"Matt. Of course! You're …" He hesitates.

"Sophie. I graduated last year. BA English."

"You don't look old enough to be a grad." His face flushes bright red the moment he utters these words. "I'm so sorry. I suppose that's not a c-compliment to someone so young."

"I'm twenty-two." I laugh. He's so flustered and awkward I can't imagine him teaching at university. Next to him, I feel like the Amazon people are always calling me. I could squash him. "Never mind. You don't look old enough to be a professor." In fact, he hardly looks old enough to shave.

"T-touché." He laughs and seems to relax a little. "Assistant p-professor, anyway. I only got my PhD last month. I'm p-presenting my dissertation at the c-conference, on the effects of c-climate change on migratory patterns of nesting birds in the Northern Hemisphere. I … I worked through my degrees rather q-quickly." He hesitates. "I'm only t-twenty-six." His face reddens yet again.

A year younger than Matt. How is such a timid guy going to present anything to the conference?

I whistle appreciatively. "Wow. A child prodigy!"

That drives even more colour into his face. "Well, nice to meet you," he says, chuckling.

"Nice to see you, Professor," I say, presenting my hand, which he presses lightly and drops quickly. "We actually met once, at a rally on campus, but you probably don't—"

"Yes, yes, I remember now. P-p-please call me Alan." He blushes again. His stutter seems to disappear when he relaxes. "What's Matt up to these days? I haven't heard from him in ages."

"He's in Ottawa, working as a parliamentary assistant."

He nods. "That seems like the perfect place for Matt."

I agree, and our eyes meet with a warm smile, sharing a private joke about my officious and bureaucratic brother. "Let's get you checked in so you can rest a bit before dinner. You look bagged. You've got to try the Italian menu at the restaurant. It's to die for." Maybe Cook can put some meat on him before his big event.

He grins and we finish up as Zoë returns, and several other guests crowd around the desk. I hand him his long brass key, and he makes an amused face at it like most North Americans do.

"Enjoy your stay, Alan. And good luck with your presentation."

"Thanks!" He rolls his eyes, smiling, and walks away.

CHAPTER 34

1 *6:35, March 9, 1945, the North Sea*

Lt. Dean awoke sweating from a fitful slumber on a hard metal bunk with a thin clammy mattress in his cramped quarters on the Varangian, a V-class submarine bound for a secret and remote radio outpost on the island of Öland, Sweden. This was a brief detour on its regular reconnaissance run, after stopping for supplies and fuel at Tynemouth. Soon after he'd come aboard, they had dived, sliding silently under the dark water, concealed by the night.

His stomach rocked and rolled with the unfamiliar craft and from the sour air he shared with the thirty-odd crew. Although the Varangian had been flushed out and taken on fresh supplies at Tynemouth, the cumulative odours of spoiled food, fuel oil, musty clothing, bilge water, and sewage overwhelmed his system.

A familiar and welcome face popped in through the open doorway like a jack-in-the-box. "Hello, Rupert. Welcome aboard." He wore the ubiquitous woolly white jumper and short beard he'd seen on several crew members.

Rupert sat up, startled. "Chris! You're here, are you?" Christopher Mansfield had been at Hanslope before Rupert, and their training had overlapped by eight months or so. He hadn't seen Chris for over a year. A welcome distraction. He pushed aside thoughts of Ava and their failed rendezvous that had tortured his sleep.

Chris nodded, grinning. "Indeed. Jolly good to see you again. How're you doing?"

Rupert groaned. "The foul air isn't much to my liking," replied Rupert wryly.

"Foul? It's fresh as a daisy!" said Chris. "It'll be about four days to Öland. Wait and see how it smells then, when the food's gone off."

"You mean it hasn't?"

Chris laughed. "No, we'll have the best of dinners tonight. Fresh sausages and bread. Bread!" He laughed again, giddy. "It's all downhill from here. Probably Train Smash and toast for brekky before we dive."

"I can hardly wait." Rupert sat up, running his hands through his damp matted hair, smoothing it down and reaching for his cap with a smile.

"Care for a tour of the radio room?"

"I would, indeed." Rupert leapt up from his bunk to follow his friend down a series of constricted, steel corridors, through several sealed ports and up a spindly iron staircase until they finally entered a long, narrow, hot and stuffy room filled with the familiar equipment of their trade: radio switchboards, a tangle of headsets, lights, wires, and knobs, with a row of J-38 straight keys on the workbench. Two operators sat at the desk, headphones on, as they entered. The sound of clicks and beeps filled the sour-smelling air.

"Hello, mates," said Chris. "Meet my chum Rupert, from Hanslope. He's the replacement for ol' Roger, over on Öland."

"'Allo, mate," said one. The other raised a hand in friendly salute and carried on his transcription.

After watching for a few minutes, Rupert absorbing every detail of his first real-life submarine radio room, they headed back towards Rupert's quarters.

"So, this fellow Roger. What happened to him?" Rupert asked, curious.

"Ate something off, I suppose. Probably them damn herring. Got a terrible stomach-ache. Then a fever. The strangest thing. But he was incapacitated, so he had to be taken to hospital. It was a scramble to find someone to come on such short notice. They need two men there to keep an ear on things around the clock. You'll get the night shift, I expect."

Rupert nodded. "The major implied as much."

"We've got permission from C-byrån, the Swedish intelligence, to man a station on Öland. To intercept encoded messages coming into the airspace between Germany and Norway."

"What are they looking for? The major was very tight-lipped."

"He would be. Watching for Enigma and Chaffinch, especially. We can't decode, of course, but it helps if you can recognize them. That's top priority. The Swedes are intercepting Jerry's transmissions on the landlines. Loads of activity up this way," he said. "Plans to liberate Denmark and Norway, of course."

"Is that it?"

"Well, aside from Operation Rädda Danmark, it's those damned V-2s, aye? Top brass have got their knickers in a knot. Even though the launch sites in The Hague will be dismantled as soon as our boys move into Holland, and that will be soon. We've got to make sure they aren't building smarter rockets that can be launched from Germany or Finland. Got to stop those damned rockets. Once we have, our work is done. The whole damn war will be over soon, anyway."

"Let's hope so."

"Were you posted elsewhere?"

"No. Cooling my heels in London, awaiting a posting."

"In the city? Blimey, with all those girls, were you? Tough going."

"Well …," Rupert said, his heart heavy. "I had eyes for only one."

They'd reached Rupert's room, and Chris leaned on the doorjamb and turned, allowing Rupert to enter. "You've got it bad, sounds like."

"Hmm."

"What's her name, then?"

Rupert hesitated. "Ava," he said, lying back on his bunk.

"Well, don't mope too much. You'll have a bit of an adventure and be home before long." He grinned. "You'll be a far sight safer on Öland than you were in London, anyway. Another V-2 fell on the city yesterday. Just past eleven hundred hours. It hit the Smithfield Market bang on. One of the worst yet, they say. Sad. Lots of women and children shopping, aye? Difficult to identify them. The entire building collapsed into the goods yard of the North Eastern Railway below. What a mess. Still trying to piece what's left of the bodies together."

Rupert's stomach roiled. "I heard it on my way out. I didn't know what or where it …"

Chris hesitated, frowning. "Where's your girl live?"

"Marylebone, but …" He couldn't speak of it. It might not be so.

"Oh, aye? She's all right, then. Not so close."

The muscles in Rupert's face clenched, his teeth biting down on the bile that rose up his gullet. A hard fist of grief socked him in the gut and left him breathless. Dear God, Ava! Please, please let her be safe. He drew in his lips, as if to contain the sudden quake of fear that ran through him like ice water. He raked a hand through his damp, dark hair and rolled towards the metal wall, trying to keep his tears under control.

Chris went silent for a moment. "Looking a bit green around

the gills, Rupert. Better not be sick or you'll set off a chain reaction we'd as soon avoid. You think it smells bad now?" He smacked the metal wall in farewell. "Sleep it off. We won't eat until we surface to charge the battery, well after dark, and after the chores are done." He laughed and disappeared through the door.

CHAPTER 35

I'm not sure who got the worse deal: Zoë for having to manage the mad rush after a long shift, or me for having to help with it and then hang around afterwards and stay awake for hours and hours with nothing much to do. I've never been so tempted to curl up in that cracked Naugahyde recliner in the storeroom to catch a few Zs. I've not yet succumbed, but it's awfully tempting.

After we dealt with the bulk of the check-ins, Zoë went home and I tidied up and sorted through the paperwork, checking over all the registration forms, visa chits, and whatnot. A few stragglers checked in later, but not many, and the full house means there are more random inquiries from guests.

Mrs. R. was bustling around being gracious but obviously wore herself out and disappeared about nine, presumably to sleep. I'm quite jealous, imagining her snoozing in her cottage while I sit in the office, figuratively propping my eyelids open with toothpicks. A huge yawn stretches my jaw open wide with a full-body shudder.

Fortunately, I was too busy earlier to think much about the upsetting letter from Mom last week, and her seemingly hopeless relationship with her mother, who may or may not be Mrs. Roxtoby. A shiver races up my neck and down my spine at the mere prospect of Mrs. R. being my grandmother. I haven't gotten a reply from Matt to my address query, and I wonder why. Is he punishing me?

It still doesn't sit well. If my intuition is good for anything at all, the situation could be resolvable. I can't give up on people that easily.

The restaurant was so popular and busy tonight that my dinner was a shocking hodge-podge of somewhat sorry-looking pasta, meat, and grilled vegetables. There wasn't much left over, and I'm grateful to get it at all. I didn't even see Cook. She sent her granddaughter April with my tray about ten p.m., by which time I was starving.

Even Teddy looked frazzled. As if he wasn't busy enough with the bar, and it was hopping tonight, a preponderance of burnt-out light bulbs, blown fuses, ill-running toilets, and other complaints kept him tottering upstairs and downstairs all night. His complexion looked grey with fatigue when he finally left at midnight.

"Hi, Sophie."

I glance up. It's Alan Stapleton, dressed way down, in sweatpants and a T-shirt, with mussed hair. He looks even younger, if that's possible. I peek up at the old wall clock. It's three a.m. "Alan! Do you know what time it is?"

He grimaces. "Unfortunately, yes. I couldn't sleep."

"Jet lag?" I ask.

"I suppose. And anxiety. I'm not sure if the anxiety is feeding off the jet lag or vice versa."

"You look eaten up. Are you worried about your presentation?"

His smile is wry. "T-t-terrified."

"When is it?"

"Not until Saturday afternoon, thank goodness," he says.

"Are you nervous in front of crowds?"

"Not exactly. I've sufficient experience, or one would sup-p-pose I do. Besides my d-dissertation, I used to head a student environmental p-party and ran for office. Made p-plenty of speeches at rallies and stuff around c-c-campus—"

"I remember your face," I interrupt. "On the posters."

He nods, grinning. "Yes. I was p-pretty active a c-couple of years ago."

"So …" I shake my head in question. "What are you afraid of? This audience is bound to be more forgiving than a bunch of disinterested students. And they did already give you your doctorate, didn't they?"

"I know. But it's a gathering of all the t-top environmentalists and naturalists in the world. All the greats. My m-mmmm-entors and idols." He's pensive for a moment, chewing on his thumb. "You know how it is. Suddenly all my c-c-clever ideas seem trite. My p-profound observations appear obvious." He shrugs. "My dire warnings, p-p-presumptuous."

"Is it long? Do you need to … rehearse, or something?"

He guffaws. "God no! That would be foolish. Anyway. I know it well enough." He shakes his head.

"All right," I say. He seems about to withdraw. I guess it's the middle-of-the-night jitters.

"M-mmm-maybe …?" he says, his expression hesitant.

I raise my brow and smile.

"Would you review my lecture notes? Just …" He waggles his head uncertainly. "T-tell me if you think it's engaging?"

I laugh. "I'd love to, Alan. I'm sure I'll be very impressed. Especially since I know absolutely nothing about the impact of climate change on the …," I falter.

"The migratory p-patterns of nesting birds in the Northern

Hemisphere." He laughs. It's a nice, friendly sound, so easy compared to his tortured speech.

I make a sudden connection. "Hey. Is that why you're here? At the Aviary Inn, I mean?"

He laughs again. "Absolutely. This place is a legend. I had to see it for myself. And it's worth the extra hike to the university. It's incredible. There are no fewer than four gorgeous little oil p-paintings of sparrows and t-t-tits in my room alone." He raises a finger. "Not to mention the ceramic figurine on the dresser, and the stencilled motif in the bathroom. It's like visiting my grand-mother, if she was as c-c-crazy about birds as I am." He chuckles. "The p-pillows are embroidered with p-p-peacocks," he adds in an awed tone, sketching their fan-shaped tails in the air.

"Have you seen the taxidermy in the bar?" I inquire.

"No. Sounds great." He heads for the stairs. "I'll get the p-p-paper now. I know I won't want to get up early, and I don't suppose you'll be here when I do."

When he returns a few minutes later and hands me his paper, he chews on his thumb a moment and then says, "Any chance you can read it by Friday? Is two days sufficient? You could meet me in the bar to give me your impressions?"

I nod. "I'll come an hour before work. At six, okay?"

"Okay. Good night, Sophie. I feel so much better already."

CHAPTER 36

Teddy has too much time on his hands. On Friday, when I arrive at the bar a little after five, he looks at me funny and says nothing, bringing me a glass of apple juice and saying, "Evenin', lass," and "How are you doin' tonight?"

But soon, I suppose, he can see that I'm agitated and so he's been asking searching questions from time to time about whether I've called my parents yet, and what I'm waiting for, all of which I deflect. He's been eyeing me like he thinks I'm a lunatic.

The bar is not as full tonight as it's been all week, so I presume there is some function at the uni that's a part of the conference, drawing people away. I resume my seat in the bar for the umpteenth time after jumping up nervously to check the old wall clock behind the front desk. It's five fifty.

"What are you staring at?" I mutter at the barn owl perched on a pedestal near my table.

I can hardly wait for Alan to show up. I came early for our meeting, hoping to run into him, but he's not here yet and I'm vibrating with excitement. I read Alan's paper yesterday afternoon when I got up and found it surprisingly engrossing. It was so interesting, in fact, that I brought it to work to continue reading it last night. The more I read, the more shocked I became about the relationship between human behavior and the disruption of these long-established migratory patterns.

Anyway, I really got into it, but the most exciting part was when I flipped through the references section to see what other books I might read on the subject, and I came upon the name Dr. Rupert Dean of Cambridge University and nearly fell off my stool, my heart was pounding so hard. I was stunned. I don't know where Alan was last night, but he slipped past my notice, and I've been dying to talk to him all day.

"I guarantee it, lass, not more than five minutes have passed since the last time you looked." Teddy is standing over me with his polishing cloth, working a highball glass up to a gleam and peering at me suspiciously.

I feel my face flushing hot and I smile at him.

"What in the dickens has got ye all worked up? Who're ye waitin' on, anyway?"

"I'm waiting for Alan Stapleton, that Canadian environmentalist who checked in on Wednesday."

Teddy screws up his face. "Another new beau? Ain't ye got enough complications in yer life, lass?"

"No, no, no, no." I leap out of my chair and hug him impulsively. "Oh, Teddy. I can't tell you anything, but it's so exciting. I can hardly wait to talk to him—"

"Who, me?" comes Alan's soft voice from behind me, and I spin around.

"Alan!" I throw my arms around him as well and hug him tightly, then catch Teddy's gimbaled eye over his shoulder, instantly release him, and back away. Alan's eyes are wide. I am acting like a lunatic. Probably it's not even the same Rupert Dean. But, oh! My gut tells me it is. The birds! The birds!

"Gosh, I hope this means you liked my p-paper and you're not anxious to warn me off and send me home before I humiliate myself t-t-tomorrow." He laughs, his cheeks flaming.

I laugh along with him. "Alan, I'd like to introduce you to

Teddy, the caretaker and bartender at the Aviary Inn. Teddy, this is Alan Stapleton, from Toronto. He's presenting his paper tomorrow at the conference and asked me to look it over for him."

"T-T-Teddy." Alan extends his hand.

"Well, well. That is exciting," says Teddy dryly, looking from me to Alan as they shake hands, and back to me again, his pale eyes widened comically and an intentionally dense grin on his face. "What will you be drinkin', lad?"

"A glass of lager, p-please."

Teddy's bushy white brows huddle together, and he nods solemnly and moves off behind the bar.

He silently slides a glass a beer in front of Alan and moves away, although I feel him loitering close by, his big ears primed like a woodland animal.

Alan scowls skeptically at his glass and takes a tentative sip. He has rather long, fine eyebrows for such a delicate man, and when he frowns, the hairs rotate outward like the hackles of a scared cat.

I nod and grin at him, then sip my juice, trying to stay calm, but I'm jiggling on the edge of my chair.

"Well?" he finally asks, his face a torture of anticipation.

"Oh, Alan, I don't know what to say. I'm so excited. I loved your paper, and I learned so much, and I want to talk to you about it, but I have to ask you about something else!"

"What is it?"

I realize how unfair I'm being to Alan, who is nervous about his presentation tomorrow and has asked for my help, but I can't help it. I draw in a great, deep breath. "It's about a name I found in your bibliography. Rupert Dean." I lean forward, eager to capture his response, to glean instantly how well he knows him.

"Dr. Rupert Dean?" His voice seems too loud, suddenly, and I glance around, afraid I'll see Mrs. R. or Eleanor lurking in the shadows, but they've been scarce since the hotel's been so crowded.

"Shhh!" I speak in a low whisper. "I'm searching for someone named Rupert Dean, who—I never realized it before, but who may have something to do with birds. I gather from his titles that he's an expert."

Alan's reply is agreeably whispered, conspiratorial. "Dr. Dean was one of the all-t-time great British ornithologists. His early work was a great inspiration to me, and his books and p-papers have been important in laying the groundwork for my research. Even though they're q-q-quite out of date now. He p-p-published mostly from the fifties through the eighties."

Was? I frown. "Please tell me he's not dead."

"I-I don't know. I assumed he w-w-was." Alan mirrors my expression and leans in. "Why are we whispering?"

"Ooh!" I moan and cover my face with my hands, tears suddenly forcing their way out of my eyes. Please, no. Don't let him be dead. Not now. I was going to make up some story about looking for a long-lost friend of my grandfather's, as a favour, but I can't lie. I look up desperately and hiss, "I can't talk about it here." I realize I'm about to say things that even Teddy shouldn't overhear.

Alan sits back, puzzled. "Do you want to, uh, go up t-to my room to t-t-talk privately?" The tips of his ears suddenly flame red.

I chew my lip. "Okay. I'll make it quick."

"What about our drinks?" he asks.

"Leave them." I glance at Teddy, who's glaring at me formidably as Alan and I stand up. I point a finger at Teddy. "We'll be right back. Five minutes." His snowy brows shoot up like scared rabbits.

Upstairs in his room, Alan says, "You'd better hurry. I got the impression T-Teddy was going to c-come after us with a c-c-crowbar." He's chewing his thumb again.

"Okay. It's like this." And I relate to Alan the entire history of Mrs. Roxtoby and her long-lost lover, and as brief a history of her tragic post-war family tale as I can manage. I talk so fast my words trip over each other, ending with my theory that Dr. Dean might be my grandfather. My pounding heart does a tumble and sinks like a stone. "Or … might have been," I add sadly. "If he's dead."

He looks quite stunned. "Holy c-c-c-crap!"

I sigh and slump slightly. "I have been accused of meddling, if that's what you mean."

He raises both hands in protest. "Far be it from me to suggest—"

"I tried everything to locate him. But I thought he was in law. Do you really think Dr. Dean is deceased?"

"I don't know. I'm sorry. I think his last p-published article was dated about '88."

I silently calculate. "Seems about the right age. I know my Rupert Dean would be about seventy-one or -two. Well past retirement age. But …"

Alan smiles and shrugs, his brows lifting hopefully. "I couldn't be in a better p-position to find out for you. The c-conference is c-crawling with ornithologists and other natural-ists. I'll make a few inquiries tomorrow after my p-p-presenta-tion. If I'm not laughed off the p-podium first!"

I offer him a wry smile. "Maybe you'd better ask around before you present," I tease.

"Th-thanks a lot!" He smiles hopefully. "What did you think? Really."

"It seems important. To me, at any rate." I frown. "It's like those frogs, you know, where there are these early warning signs that people aren't paying attention to."

"Exactly!" He smiles.

"I found it far more interesting than I expected to find a scientific paper about golden plovers, wood thrushes, house wrens, and Canada geese and their migration and nesting patterns."

He nods sadly. "The birds are fairly adaptable, but global warming, deforestation, and development are changing climate zones so rapidly that they cannot keep up, and it's really screwing up their ability to reproduce."

"I see that. It makes me want to … to do something!"

He nods and smiles and chews. "You didn't find it …" He shrugs. "Dry? Or a bit too, um, p-p-preachy, maybe?"

I ponder his question seriously for a moment, blinking at the charming peacocks embroidered on his bed with their bright blue-green tail feathers. Remembering his description, I glance around at the various small paintings of birds. They are mostly dull browns and greens and match the overall green and beige décor. A funky fifties lamp base shaped like a teardrop matches the peacock's blue. I realize I've not been in many of the infamous guest rooms. Each one really is unique.

"Shall we go back to the pub?" he asks.

As we descend the stairs, I finally answer him.

"You know, no. It wasn't dry, because if I found it engaging and understandable, I think anyone could, and as for preachy." I shake my head. "No. More like shocking. But you tell me, what have the other presentations been like? Isn't that the norm among environmentalists?"

He laughs, retrieving his beer.

My eyes dart to Teddy. But he's behind the bar, polishing glasses and blinking innocently as though he weren't burning with curiosity. I shake my head.

"I suppose that's what p-people assume. But no, it's balanced. There are lobbyists, sure, but some are very c-c-conservative. Government reps are there. Academics. Not everyone's on a soapbox." He gnaws, pressing his cuticle against his teeth as though his life depends on it, his forehead puckered.

I nod. "So, you don't want to be labeled a radical straight out of the starting gate, is that it?"

He releases a puff of laughter through his nose and rolls his eyes. "Yes, I guess that's fair."

"Well then, don't worry. Your facts speak for themselves, and you've been careful to make only balanced, quite reasonable arguments."

He nods and sips his beer. "Thanks. Thank you for reading it. That makes me feel much more c-c-comfortable about t-tomorrow."

Glancing up, I catch Teddy's glowering eyes, incongruous in his funny, folded-up face. I jump up to look at the clock behind the front desk. Eek!

"Goodness, look at the time! I have to work, Alan." A wave of exhaustion rolls over me, making my head spin and my legs wobbly. What a week! I'm not looking forward to staying awake for the next ten hours. "Good luck. I'll talk to you Sunday, okay?" I give his hand a squeeze of encouragement.

He rises and smiles. "Thanks again." Lowering his voice, he adds, "And yeah, I'll ask around about your professor."

Lifelike wax mannequins of families and tradesmen in period costume posed in activities of daily life animate the Jorvik Viking Centre exhibits where I meander in the near darkness. They carve combs, tan hides, slaughter wax chickens, and crouch around (electric) cooking fires. The light is gloomy, as though it's late evening, the horizon a soft apricot-toned painted scene behind the diorama, the only light from fake firelight glowing and reflecting off the faces of the people and flashing off their glass eyes, the palette reds, browns, and black. Long shadows distort everything. The humid air is alive with piped-in rural smells and the sounds of a community of people settling down for the night—murmuring voices, the soft braying of livestock, the muffled cry of a child and the cooing response of its mother, and Teddy's voice?

"There you go, poor lass." The sweet aroma of sugar biscuits and the perfume of Earl Grey tea, warm steam condensing on my nose hairs.

"Hmm?" My eyes flutter open, clock the tea tray, and drift closed again. "Thanks."

Faintly strummed music fills the air. It's all so realistic, it's creepy. Following the music, I move towards a group gathered by a campfire, where a lissome musician perches on a boulder, his green-stockinged knees and long, leather-clad shins nestling a stringed instrument, like a large mandolin or lute. I'm drawn to him and seem to drift even nearer without moving my feet. He bears an uncanny resemblance to Nick, with his tangled, sandy hair and beard and elegant hands on which a gold signet ring glints in the firelight.

I recognize his warm, earthy smell. As I approach, he lifts his head, and his familiar, compelling green eyes, brilliant as chlorophyll, peer at my face from beneath the brim of his soft suede cap. He smiles enigmatically in recognition. It is Nick!

I smile back. I'm pulled closer, and his face is suddenly next to mine, his mouth moving towards my own, still smiling. I close my eyes and lift my face in expectation of his kiss.

"Hey, Canadian." I hear his soft voice.

I open my bleary eyes and try to focus on the hairy face leaning in towards me across the desk.

"Nick?" What? Where am I? My heavy eyelids fall closed again, preferring the dreamscape.

"Sophie. It's me." He jostles my arm. My eyes fly open. His green eyes twinkle and his mouth quirks.

I jerk fully awake. It really is Nick! I wasn't dreaming. Er ... Yes, I was. I feel my face flush hot at the memory of his not-quite-kiss. What was I ...? God, I'm confused. Then I realize I've been caught napping on the job. It's about eleven p.m. Things got quiet after dinner. I must have dozed off. I've been sleeping on my hands, the spotlight warming the top of my head, so he's not very far away. I sit up straight, blinking.

"What are you doing here?" Stupid question.

"I came to find you, obviously. I haven't seen you since ... for quite a while. Are you ..." He shrugs. "All right?"

"Oh … uh, yeah. I'm, I'm fine." I scrunch my eyes tightly and rub them, trying to clear the fog and stifle a yawn. "We've been so busy all week with the conference at the uni. I guess I'm over-tired. How are you?"

He hesitates and shrugs one shoulder a tiny bit.

I realize I haven't seen him since that night at his flat, when he was the disoriented one. I meet his eyes, so he knows it's okay with me, that I'm not judging him. "Are you okay?"

Two spots of colour appear on his cheeks, and his gaze drops to his shoes. "I'm fine. I didn't know when I'd see you. I owe you an apology … I wasn't at all a good host when you dropped by. I'm sorry you chose that particular night. I, ah, don't remember much."

Hesitantly, he lifts his wary eyes to mine.

I gaze at him and feel a slight smile pull at my lips. My middle fills with a warm, molten flow of pleasure. I'm glad to see him, I realize. I'm not angry with him. My arms itch to give him a big hug.

"I was feeling rather low about family stuff and had overindulged. I know Art …" His voice breaks and he clears his throat. His slender hand comes up and tugs at the dread-locks by his ear. "I'm sorry to keep such … important … infor-mation from you. It's only that, it's rather personal and difficult, and I was barely feeling that we'd gotten to know each other sufficiently to confide such a thing without seeming maudlin."

I love the way he talks. Mawd-lin. It's like being inside a lovely BBC drama, soothing and exciting at the same time. "It's okay, Savvy. I understand."

His eyebrows lift and curl, perplexed, hopeful, maybe relieved.

"I feel …" My throat aches. I shake my head sadly. "I feel so awful for you. You've been through so much and I …" I glance away.

He coughs and turns it into a tentative laugh. "I have to

confess, I knew what you'd say to me about healing the rift with my parents, and I wasn't sure I was up for the scold."

I meet his eyes, and there is mutual understanding and amusement in equal measure. We share a companionable chuckle. Despite his secrets, I never feel as though Nick is pulling any punches. We just naturally get each other.

"It's been weeks. What have you been doing?"

I shrug. "Working. Hanging out with Zoë."

He tips his head to the side in question. His smile is provoking.

"Okay, I've had a few irons in the fire." I tsk and glance about, my cheeks tingling. He knows me so well. "I've actually been gathering facts, busy trying to mend fences." I lower my voice and glance around for eavesdroppers.

"Any luck?" He's mocking me, but it doesn't matter. His tone is gentle and affectionate.

I tongue my teeth coyly and nod. "Something I didn't tell you before. I actually came here— to York —with the intention of finding my mom's family. Mom wrote me a letter and is pissed that I'm poking around in her past. Even though I'm not sure there's a connection to …" I wave a hand around us. "This place. She claims she tried to reconcile years ago, and her mother would have none of it."

Nick juts his jaw and his eyes widen at this new information. "So that's why you've been so nosy. But why this place? What led you here?"

I grimace. "I could be way off, but …" I pull the old photo out of my journal and show him. "I don't know, but I think this might be my mom with her family." I point at the building behind the group, where a small sign only reads ROOMS TO LET. "But it could be, couldn't it?"

He looks skeptical, so I tell him more. About the things Eleanor has let slip, Mrs. R.'s history, and the returned packages. I show him the army portrait of Lieutenant Dean.

"This could be my grandfather."

He pulls his mouth into a tight line and his brow pulls down in a sympathetic frown. He doesn't seem at all surprised at my failure, and the improbability of it all hits home.

"It's disappointing."

He nods. "Very sad, indeed."

"And I've been searching for Mrs. Roxtoby's old beau, without much success so far. But the really amazing news … hot off the press," I say.

"Ye-es?"

I tell him how hard I tried to find Rupert Dean, unsuccessfully, and how, through the strangest of coincidences, Alan Stapleton happened to come to the Aviary Inn and happens to know of Professor Dean the ornithologist through his research.

"An ornithologist?" He screws up his brow, impressed. "I suppose the sleuth of Baker Street would have anticipated as much." He spins a finger around at the lobby.

I squint at him. "Perhaps." I wait for my rebuke, but it doesn't come.

"Well. Congratulations, Sophie. You persevered and look what's come of it."

"Nothing's come of it. Alan's presenting his paper tomorrow and then he's going to ask around. I just pray …" I shrug.

"Good luck. I hope you find him. For your sake, if not for Mrs. Roxtoby's."

I peer at him a while, trying to discern if he's teasing or serious, and decide maybe a bit of both, but I detect no sign of sarcasm or ridicule.

"Thanks."

"Hey! The reason I came round, other than to apologize, I mean, was to tell you that we've got another gig Wednesday night. Any chance? It would be awfully nice if you—"

"I'd like that, Nick." I really would. "I'll talk to Zoë. And I have to talk to Mrs. R. See if she'll agree to get a temp and let me off because of my extra hours."

"Excellent! Well … I hope you can."

I nod. "Me too."

I sense him trying to withdraw, but tangible tendrils of affection, regret, and attraction are strung between us. "I'd better push off, then."

Disappointment weighs heavy in my chest. I pull my lip between my teeth, and his eyes follow. Without my say-so, my own curious gaze is drawn to his mouth in turn. Heat suffuses my face, my neck, my chest, and lower. Oh, my. Maybe I should offer him tea or something, but I can imagine what Teddy would say ... What, another beau? I sigh. "The Priory, right?"

"Yes." He backs up, turns, and moves away. "I'll see you Wednesday night, then."

"I'm glad you stopped by," I blurt, reluctant to let him go.

His smile is warm and wry, and he holds my gaze with his knowing green eyes until he rounds the corner towards the door.

I frown, puzzled, and place three fingertips to my lips, remembering the almost-kiss of my dream.

CHAPTER 37

"Ollie, you wanker!" exclaims Zoë. We're in our usual seats at the end of the bar in the Priory on Wednesday night.

"Oof!" I grunt as she elbows me in the ribs, and a sharp pain radiates through my middle. What? She shoots me a look before turning back to Oliver, who's just strutted in, grinning sheepishly. She's trying for outrage, but she can't disguise her secret delight. Hopeless!

It's a poor match for my mortification upon seeing who Oliver brought with him. Elliot!

He shows the good sense not to smile at all, his expression sheepish. "'Allo, Sophie." He tries to kiss my cheek, but I turn my head away.

"What are you doing here?"

"Didn't expect to see me, oy? Oliver found out from some bloke at the Frog an' Firkin that saw you girls 'ere tonight." I can smell ale on his breath, and his eyes are glassy.

I draw back and peer at him, pulling a tight, reluctant smile. It seems so wrong to see him here, where we came to see Nick and the guys play. Elliot and I haven't seen each other since that day at the uni.

"I was desperate to see you, and … well, we weren't sure when we might get a chance." His smile falters.

With good reason.

Zoë accepts Oliver's enthusiastic embrace and wet, hungry kisses with satisfaction, despite her pretence of indignation. It's a lost cause. To ensure himself of a favourable acceptance, Oliver is content to grovel and wait on Zoë, fetching drinks, petting her, and hamming it up. It's a fine art with him. I wonder how I will sleep later with all the noise. Humph.

I'm not pleased to see Elliot again, especially here. I was relaxed and ready to enjoy my evening, but now I feel myself tense up, irritated.

Elliot's attempts to smile fail him, and he sidles up close and drops his head. "I …" He hesitates. "I'm sorry for hoodwinkin' you, Sophie. I'm 'opin' you've forgiven me."

"I'm still considering it." I scowl. "I'm so disappointed. I took you at your word, but I don't know …" If I can trust you. I give my head a shake.

"Gor, Sophie. I'm sorry. You know why I did it," he whines.

I nod. "That doesn't excuse lying, Elliot, and stringing me along."

He glowers at the bar for a minute or two and turns to accept a glass of ale from Oliver. "Thanks, mate. You all right for drinks, then?" he addresses me.

"Yes, fine." I sip my cool, dry cider and ponder a moment, watching the band and listening to Nick singing, my mind wandering. My mood is spoiled, and I'm twitchy with impatience. I don't want to spend the evening playing cat and mouse with Elliot. I was looking forward to catching up with Nick at intermission. Now … it's bound to be awkward. I know they know each other, but I don't get the impression they're on great terms.

"Did you have any luck with Rupert Dean?" Since I have a new lead on Lieutenant Dean, it's not as important, but I'm testing Elliot.

"Who?"

"Elliot! You know, the old guy who—"

"Oh, yeh. I know … eh, well …" He takes a swig of his ale and drags his tongue slowly over his foamy lips.

This doesn't bode well. But then, I didn't have great expectations. I raise my brows in mock amazement and smile. I'm enjoying watching him squirm.

"Well, actually, you see, it's only that I didn't get far along with it yet. I thought I'd find something concrete before—"

I feel a tightening sensation crawl up my arms. "Have you even looked?"

"Hasn't been much opportunity yet. Maybe the library is—"

"Just forget it." I turn away in disdain and notice Zoë and Oliver in earnest conversation, for a change. At least they're talking. Maybe my coaching and questioning has provoked Zoë into resisting his smooth excuses.

"I hope she lays down the law this time," I say.

"Heh?" Elliot glances at them over his shoulder and smiles. "They're all right."

"They won't ever be all right until he learns fidelity. Zoë won't put up with it forever."

He shrugs, his upper lip curling. "She has so far."

"But she shouldn't!" I insist. "He totally takes her for granted."

"Nay, he don't! He's good to 'er. They've been steady for years."

"You call that steady? He's off making out or worse with another girl every … couple of weeks!"

"He always comes back." Elliot blinks his eyes slowly. "An' he probably always will, from what I can tell."

"Probably! What kind of commitment is that?"

"Commitment?" He gives an exaggerated shudder. "What's commitment got to do with it?" He laughs without humour.

"But she has a right to know he's faithful. Or he shouldn't keep her dangling. It's not fair."

"It's not the same thing at all. A man's got to look around, keep 'is options open. If he spends too long with one bird, he'll get leg-shackled before he knows it."

A man's got a right to be a jerk. "What a load of horseshit, Elliot. A relationship takes two, and it takes work. Commitment is important or a couple can't move forward."

"Bah!"

"You can't be serious."

"I am serious." He sits up straighter. He's not usually so attentive to anything, except football. "Procreation an' all that. It's survival of the fittest. It's everyone's responsibility to keep looking. Only natural."

I gape at him open-mouthed and feel a sneer curl my lip. "Is that what you're doing?"

He shrugs. "You're doing it, too, aren't you?"

"I'm not! I've always been monogamous. You know I've told you since we met that I'm still obligated to Marc-Antoine. That I can't move on until—"

"Bollocks, Sophie! That's what you say, but it hasn't stopped you from dating two other blokes, that I'm aware of, anyway."

"What?"

He hooks his thumb towards Nick on-stage. "I know 'bout yon shaggy artiste, you know."

"Nick and I are not dating!" I protest. "We're only friends. And neither are we, you know that!"

Elliot puffs air out through loose lips and bugs his eyes out at me.

What an ass! I squeak in outrage and turn my back on him, gritting my teeth. He obliges me by turning his back and talking to Oliver and Zoë. A moment later, as Nick comes to the end of a song, he catches my eye. His gaze slides over to Elliot and open a little wider, then his brows lift in question.

What's up?

I shrug and scowl and roll my eyes in answer.

He offers an exaggerated pout. Poor Sophie. He lifts one

finger and slices himself across the throat. One more number and I'll take a break, he mouths.

I smile and nod. Then he breaks into Van Morrison's "Brown-Eyed Girl" and watches me while he sings. It makes me feel warm and tingly, like he's singing it especially for me. Foolish girl. I push Elliot's accusations from my mind.

Five minutes later, the house lights come up a bit and Nick strolls over. "Hey, Canadian. Did Mrs. R. get a temp?"

"No. I couldn't bring myself to ask, but I did persuade Sean Smythe to trade shifts with me. Had to buy him off with a promise to send him a limited edition, autographed copy of Robert Sawyer's novel Golden Fleece when I get back to Canada."

He laughs. "How much will that set you back?"

"Fifty bucks US!"

"I'm honoured!" He laughs. "Most people would not pay that much to hear me sing."

"I bet that's not true. You're so good."

Nick casts his eyes down. "Thanks."

Tim, the bartender, brings Nick his half glass of Guinness. He takes a grateful slug and leans against the bar, on the other side of me from Elliot, glances at him over my shoulder, and cocks a sardonic brow.

I close my eyes, shake my head. "They just showed up," I mouth.

He quirks his lips into a funny, Kermit-like smile and nods in understanding. Then he goes serious and tenses.

I follow his eyes over my shoulder, where Elliot's sticking his face near mine. "Oh, 'allo, Tack," Elliot sneers. "Taking a break, are we?"

I don't like his tone. "Elliot. I gather you know Nick Savile?" I say.

Elliot smirks.

"We've met, yes," says Nick dryly.

I haven't told Nick all the details of Elliot's lies, but I can sense that he's always known that Elliot is a schmuck. My back is still half-turned to Elliot, and Nick meets my eyes and reads everything, widening his eyes with a wink.

"So, Crowther, your opinion on the World Cup Finals? Did you see Owen's goal in the second round?" asks Nick. "Spectacular!"

Elliot takes the bait. "Yeh, but they were off. Beckham's antics didn't 'elp. He might've overcome the draw."

"Doubt it. Anyway, Simeone bounced back all right, until the Argentines got a piece of him."

Christ! More bloody soccer talk!

Elliot grunts. "Croatia had it, after the quarters, the way Šuker was playing. Have to respect that kind of consistency in a striker."

"Mm-hmm. But Zidane prevailed in the end," says Nick, drawing a long sip from his beer. "With those awesome headers from the corner."

I'm rather surprised Nick's up on football at all, with his academic leanings. But I suppose it's not optional in England. I'm grateful for the diversion, anyway.

"Bloody good thing his suspension didn't come any later ..."

Their conversation fades into the hum of voices in the pub, along with my interest, and my eyes scan the crowded pub, people-watching. Then, I see him.

Marc-Antoine!

A sudden ice-cold wind flutters through my core. I slide off my stool but can't move, can't decide which direction to jump, forwards or backwards. Fight or flight. Part of me wants to shatter, the other, crawl under a table.

By the door, entering with a group of people, standing and looking around for seats. My heart lodges in my throat, pounding like a drum, and I stare, squint, blink, and stare. I must be mistaken. It's some guy who looks like him. Then his head turns towards me, and our eyes meet. He freezes, the expression on his face one of ... horror?

"Excuse me," I mumble and shuffle forwards, my knees loose, one hand pushing off the bar to steady myself. I feel both Nick and Elliot's heads turn in question as I move away.

"All right, Sophie?" asks Nick, but I don't look back.

I see the shock on Marc-Antoine's face, his eyes wide, his mouth slack, his neat dark brows furrowed. He freezes, and his friends collide with him, jostling him, and he stumbles. A tentative half-smile pulls at the corners of his mouth.

Am I imagining things? "Marc-Antoine?" No, it's really him. I stride towards him, my heart pounding in my throat with astonishment, and fury, my fists clenching at my sides. Once I'm standing in front of him, despite my confusion, my hands come to his chest and shove. Hard. He stumbles backwards, astonished. Something I hadn't planned to do, yet all my worry and frustration and resentment surfaces in one huge spasm of anger, even while a part of my mind recoils, confused. I wind up to push again.

Ever quick on his feet, he grabs me by the arms and holds me back, scowling.

"Sophie? Is dat you? What the fuck are you doing 'ere still?"

What? I sway on my heels, my heart contracting to a small hard stone, my stomach sinking to my shoes. The last shard of my faith that he never meant to leave me clatters to the floor. "Who did you expect to find when you returned to York, Marc?" My mouth twists bitterly. "Where did you suppose I'd be, after you took my money and passport with you? Conveniently gone back to Canada, out of your hair?"

He shrugs, evasive, his dark eyes darting sideways.

"Where the hell have you been?" I bring my hands to my hips, my arms akimbo, demanding.

"I'm stunned, bébé! I did not know what 'appen to you." Belatedly, he tries to wrap his arms around me, but this time I shove him away, and after a moment he murmurs, under his breath, "I miss you so much." He plants a kiss on my lips, and it feels odd. Oddly foreign. Too soft and cool. "You won't believe what I've been t'rough!"

Suddenly, I'm seething with long pent-up fury, humiliation, and pain. A torrent of heat floods through my body, filling my head to bursting, burning my ears. What he's been through?

My vision floods with red; my hands curl into fists. I can't stop myself. I slam his chest and slap and claw at his face. "You?" I roar, my voice rising into a screech. "You selfish bastard! What have you got to say for yourself? How could you do this to me?"

Marc's hands rise, deflecting my blows, swatting my hands away. His lips curl in disgust and disbelief.

Then, suddenly, a strong pair of arms closes gently but firmly around me, holding down my flailing hands. I flex against the sudden confinement, but he's not letting go. Hot breath on my ear, whispering, "Easy, Sophie, love." It's Nick. My frantic breathing slows, and I shudder, tears stinging my eyelids.

Elliot appears beside us. "You might want to think twice about pawing my bird," he growls. "What 'ave you done to 'er?"

I moan. "Elliot! For God's sake! Don't!"

"Don't what?" Marc's puffed up and squaring his shoulders.

I've got to stop him, so I step forward out of the safe circle of Nick's arms. "Marc, this is my … friend, Elliot Crowther. El-li-ot, this is Marc-Antoine." I lift my brows in Elliot's direction, trying to get him to understand.

"Aye, it's 'im, is it?" he says, but he's had too much to drink. And he's Elliot. He shows no sign of calming down. In fact, if anything, he's puffed up, his shoulders forward, his fists curled.

Marc-Antoine sneers. "Who is dis, Sophie? Your new lover?"

I'm speechless. They're both acting like buffoons.

Elliot suddenly gives Marc a rough shove on the shoulder. "Maybe I am, yeah. What would you have to say about it, ya git?"

I gasp. "Elliot!"

Then, in the split second before Marc-Antoine can react, Nick steps calmly between Elliot and me, placing a hand on Elliot's arm. "Crowther," he says, his voice a low rumbling threat. "This is no business of—"

But he's too late.

While I blink in amazement, Elliot turns to him. "Sod off, Tack, it ain't none of yours either—" He shakes off Nick's hand, while Marc-Antoine laughs unpleasantly and says, "What, another one? I been away only a few week, Sophie! 'Aven't miss me much, 'ave you?"

How dare he?

Elliot, next to me, is bristling like an angry bear and glaring at Marc-Antoine. "Hold on a minute. I asked you a question!" He advances, his fists clenched.

Marc responds by twisting his dark brows with an air of condescension, and sneering.

Elliot leaps on him with macho fury. He body slams Marc with his huge chest, knocking him into a group of guys sitting beside us. They push back, holding him up, mumbling and cursing. "Watch out, mate!"

I flinch, sucking in a breath. Nick's warm hands return to my arms, calming, holding me still.

Marc's face darkens in anger as he scrambles upright. "Back off, you gorilla!" He rushes Elliot, shoving him hard in the chest.

Elliot's arms swing wildly as he loses his balance and topples onto another table, this time, knocking the table over and its drinks to the floor in a violent crash, sending patrons scrambling in outrage. A crescendo of squeals and murmured complaints drowns out both music and conversation. Chair legs groan and thud on the wooden floor as other patrons jostle to shift out of the way of the melee.

"Elliot!" I scream, rushing forward.

Nick pulls me out of the way. Oliver appears and reaches down to hoist Elliot up off the floor, but once on his feet, Elliot shoves Ollie out of his way and advances once more on Marc-Antoine, who's foolishly sniggering at Elliot's tumble. My heart races wildly. Suddenly, his enormous height and muscular girth take on new meaning. He eclipses Marc, like the sun obliterating the moon. He'll crush him!

A nanosecond later, Marc is on the floor, blood gushing from his elegant nose. I hardly saw the blur of Elliot's fist as it sailed by. Marc moans in pain, holding his hands to his face, blood dripping down his wrist and chin, red stains spattering onto his white T-shirt.

Oh my God! I tear myself from Nick's grip to drop to Marc-Antoine's side. "Marc! Marc!" The sharp iron tang of his blood assaults my senses, mingled with cigarette smoke and spilled beer, and a bottom note of Marc's familiar warm musk.

Zoë appears by his other side, throwing me a wide-eyed look, her hands full of tissues that she shoves at him. "Are you all right, duck?"

"Who de 'ell are you?" he replies through his fingers, taking the tissues from her as she presses them against his face.

I whirl on Elliot. "Look what you've done, you brute! Stop this!"

A number of bar patrons have discreetly dispersed or left.

Elliot's jaw juts and he says through clenched teeth, "I'm only helping—" And then his face contorts in sudden pain. "What the fu—Ow!"

"Don't get your knickers in a knot, you plonker," Nick says, "You're not helping Sophie with your larking." It doesn't look like he could, but he seems to have a persuasive grip on Elliot's arm. "It's time you headed home, Crowther." He quietly shoves Elliot in the direction of the door, while Oliver hovers, his loyalties divided.

With his free hand, Nick straightens chairs at a recently vacated table near us. "Sophie's been fretting over Marc-Antoine's welfare for three months. We're going to sit down and have a nice, civilized chat so Marc-Antoine can explain himself. Your diplomatic assistance is definitely not required."

Elliot stands firm, sulking, while Nick turns to face us.

As Zoë and I haul Marc-Antoine to his feet, Nick says, "Introduce me to your friend, Sophie?" He suddenly seems taller and more grown-up than either Marc-Antoine or Elliot.

I inhale, grasping for an iota of calm. "Marc-Antoine Charpentier, this is Nick—"

"Tack, eh?" interrupts Marc, his dark eyes narrowing at Nick.

"No, actually." Nick smiles. "The name's Savile. Nick Savile." He offers his hand, ignoring the blood that smears it. Marc-Antoine can't avoid accepting it and they squeeze briefly and warily, taking each other's measure.

"If you're not leavin', I'm not leavin'." It's Elliot, standing like an oak tree behind Nick. "I've got as much right to be 'ere as anyone."

CHAPTER 38

A few minutes later, after a bunch of jockeying, we're all seated around the table, Marc-Antoine's nose is cleaned up, and he holds a wad of fresh tissues to it. Nick sits to my left, and Zoë grips my right hand under the table in support. The table and floor have been mopped of spilt beer and smashed glass, leaving a trace of strong cleaning solution mingled in the fetid air.

Nick nods towards Marc-Antoine and says, "Well. We're all dying to hear what you have to say."

Marc's thin dark brows pinch. "What is it you mean?"

Nick glances at me, his eyes wide, and traces a long finger along the arc of his eyebrow in disbelief.

Marc smirks. "It's interesting, you have an army of admirers come to defend you from de wicked boyfriend. Which one is your true champion, Sophie, the beefcake who doesn't want you to talk to me, or the 'ippie who does?"

Very funny! "They both have only my best interests at heart," I reply, narrowing my eyes. "That's what friends are for, isn't it?"

Marc-Antoine lifts his shoulders and smiles enigmatically, and I marvel that he dares to imply anything about my conduct after what he's done to me.

This feels more like an inquisition than a conversation, but I shrug. Having my friends around me gives me courage and resolve. "I'm entitled to an explanation, Marc. You vanished! It's been two and a half months!"

He seems surprised that I'm speaking to him in a tone that, while not quite aggressive, is certainly more assertive than he was used to.

After an empty beat, he laughs, darting a glance at Elliot, perched ominously to his left. "Mon Dieu! Sophie. You do not t'ink I abandon you on purpose, do you, chouette?"

I glare at him, my lips pressed together, and raise one brow.

"Bollocks!" Zoë gasps in disbelief, echoing my own sentiments.

"Nice try, ye prat," offers Oliver, rolling his eyes. "D'ye think she's completely gormless?"

I chuckle softly, leaning back, crossing my arms. "Oh, you mean it was an accident? How curious. I'm even more interested to hear what happened to you now than I was before." I feel oddly detached. I'm content to watch him squirm and see what creative excuses he can come up with on the spot, under the cool and curious gazes of my protective friends. I'm rather surprised he hasn't already worked something out, but obviously he really didn't expect to bump into me.

"Cherie, were you freaked out?" Marc-Antoine stretches a hand forward and drops it on the table. He can't reach me. I blink at him. "I plan to come back right away … I leave you de note, before t'ings go sideways wit' me."

Instead of feeling comforted however, I'm uneasy. A chill caresses my arms and neck, and I rub them. A brick of tension presses on my chest, making my throat tighten. His once-sexy, whining, nasal Quebecois French accent is strangely unfamiliar to my ears after three months immersed in Yorkshire.

"I try to contact you, Sophie, but by the time I figure me out, I could not find you."

I glare at him, unable to utter a reply.

He offers a Gallic shrug. "See, it was only that I met someone who was 'ead straight to Glasgow, this night. You remember. I 'ad no time to tell you, run in only and grab my t'ings and 'op in the car. It was easy so, I was going to get a ride there and back in a few days, and it would cost nothing!"

"Glasgow?" repeats Nick.

Marc glances at him. "Sophie know 'ow much I want to see Macintosh work, and visit de Glasgow School of Art there. Always I talk about it." His dark eyes plead with me, but I'm not so keen to be won over. I feel myself pulling a cocoon of detachment around me, my vision blurring, everything slowing down like I'm watching the scene unfold through a gauzy curtain.

It's true he talked about going to Glasgow, and I had been complaining that I was getting road weary and wanted to stay in one place for longer than a couple of days. In fact, it was probably that exact difference of opinion about our travel plans that made me so sensitive to his chatting up the Swedish girl at the pub. She was, as I recall, an architecture student. That's why he claimed he was so into her, but convenient as his explanation is, I don't buy it. Clearly, it was the pale blond hair and long slender legs. Now I don't know whether to believe him.

"Was it really so difficult to talk to me? I thought you were dead!"

"What is it you accusing me, Sophie?"

I shake my head. "I don't know, Marc. You could've at least let me know you were going instead of sneaking out in the night!"

"Bloody good point," says Elliot.

"I leave you a note!" Marc squirms, eyeing Elliot the Bear nervously. He's shifts uncomfortably under the weight of eight pairs of eyes boring into him, judging.

"I'd love to hear all about your adventures in Glasgow," I say through clenched teeth, my face tight. I'm trying to keep an open mind, despite my initial, granted confusing, mix of relief and fury at seeing him after almost three agonizing months.

A waitress interrupts with a tray of the drinks we all abandoned on the bar, setting them down in front of us one by one. She looks at Marc. Nick says, "A glass of ale for my guest. It's on me."

She gives him a meaningful look. "Gordy was wantin' t'know if you was goin' to play agin tonight, Nick. Ye are bein' paid, an all."

He nods. "I'd better excuse myself. You'll be all right for a bit, Sophie?" he asks, his warm hands squeezing my shoulder. I nod, lifting my gaze to meet his, and he disappears, back towards the stage, where Art and the others have been hovering, at a loss. The sound of their instruments tuning fills the room moments later.

The waitress returns and drops off Marc's draft, and he takes a gulp. With Nick gone, Marc-Antoine shifts his chair closer to mine, leaning closer. "But oui, I 'ad adventures, truly, Sophie," he says. "You 'ave no h'idea what I been t'rough."

CHAPTER 39

"Try me," I offer, by way of encouragement. I lean my chin on my hand and cast a penetrating gaze at his face, a little frown of concern on my brow. Is this what you expect to see, Marc? God, I'm being such a bitch. Maybe something terrible prevented him from coming back? Should I be happy and relieved to see him, or utterly outraged and hurt?

The band starts up again, Nick's mellow voice singing, *"'Woke up another day, the pain won't go away, I am growing in peculiar ways ...'"* provides a disconcerting backdrop to my conversation with Marc-Antoine. I feel a spasm of tension run through me, and a dull throbbing in my temples. I turn away and take a sip of cider, but the taste has gone sour in my mouth.

Marc's voice drops to an intimate whisper, soothing me. "I know what you're t'inking, cherie. That I ditched you. But no, it is not true!" He peers intently at me, leaning closer, his arm snaking around me, and I can smell his warm cologne, the familiar scent of his body, and part of me wants to believe him. His poor elegant nose is swollen and red. Wouldn't it be wonderful? Wouldn't it be romantic if he really did have such disastrous bad luck, and had to fight tooth and nail to make his way back to me, because of his love and devotion, his concern for my well-being, his commitment to our future together? Yeah, right. My romantic storytelling brain has run amok.

I can feel the comfort of Zoë hovering to my right, listening, my hand in hers. Keeping me strong.

I know it's a fantasy, but Marc must see something hopeful in my gaze, because he suddenly lifts one hand to my chin, and kisses me, at first tentatively, and then surely, taking possession. My breath catches uncertainly. His kiss is familiar, and unwillingly, my body responds. How dare he?

I lean away, self-conscious, and dart a glance towards the others, who look away conspicuously. Elliot, however, makes a low, grumbling noise and can't stop himself from glancing back. Zoe squeezes my hand.

Marc's eyes, as dark as dark chocolate, meltingly seductive, fringed by long, downward-sweeping lashes, do their thing to my insides. A coiling like a snake, tense, hot, excited. I feel it happening, yet a part of me remains detached, assessing, unsure.

Zoë, at least, is impressed. "Aow. That's sweet." To me in an aside, she whispers, "He is hot, Sophie."

"Too smarmy by half," says Oliver, tossing a glance at Elliot.

"Quit pissin' around and talk," says Elliot in disgust. "We're not here for a show."

My gaze flicks back to Marc-Antoine.

Long wavy strands escape his thick sable-coloured ponytail, and fall across his forehead. He tosses his head, rakes a fine, artistic hand through the offending locks, and they fall back down. His movements seem both painfully familiar and strangely rehearsed. I wonder, as I've never wondered before, whether he practices them in the mirror, even. My limbs feel as heavy as concrete.

It's suddenly obvious to me how shallow and insincere he is. I was so naive to think that we were in love. The fact is, I was swayed by his charm and worldly sophistication. And me ...? Me? I was easy.

Then he does a little thing, another mannerism I recognize.

It's a way he holds his shoulders, back and in towards his ears. Both his hands come up, ready to gesticulate, to sell his line. Saliva works its way into the corners of his mouth, and he casts his not-quite-focused gaze not into my eyes, but more, I think cynically, towards his audience in its entirety, and I cringe inwardly. He's like a stage actor who's hit his stride, found the zone where everything comes together for him. He's utterly self-absorbed.

I'm oddly immune. It's a thing that, in my awareness of it, disarms the performance.

"Sometime, an opportunity come along, you 'ave to take advantage, eh? You know 'ow desperately I want to go to Glasgow. It is a Mecca for us, the School of Art."

He means architecture students. I know this, because indeed he has spoken of Mackintosh's work and the Glasgow School of Art many times.

"So, when Annika say she is leaving that night, driving there ..." Marc-Antoine's affected shrug is classic. "She offer to take me and another guy from the pub, he's an architecture student from Germany, an' I rise to de occasion, eh? 'Ow can I say no? What could I do?"

Aha. At last, the tall Swedish blond makes her entrance. "Wake me up and talk to me?" I insist, slapping the table with my hand. My palm stings, and the violence feels right somehow.

Marc swags his head back and forth like a cornered bear, as though this suggestion is nothing short of preposterous but somehow threatening. "Sophie, chouette! In the middle of the night, I could not disturb you. I tiptoe in and take de bag and leave de note. I expect to call you in the morning, certainly, when we get somewhere. It was jus' a lark!"

Oliver shakes his head. "A brilliant cock-up, mate."

This explanation does not seem unlikely, in the moment, however selfish and irresponsible. Despite myself, I'm falling under the sway of his passionate delivery, and feel myself nodding for him to continue. In retrospect, this diversion does not seem very different from any number of other adventures he's gone on. Only I was busy with school and friends and tolerated it. Foolishly.

Now he's shaking his head sadly. "That's when everyt'ing went to 'ell in a 'andbasket." He takes a dramatic swig of his beer, wiping his mouth with the back of his hand.

"You went with that girl? The blond art student?"

He rises to the scent of my culpability, his eyes bugging out, his hands lifted. "But, yes! Exactly! I didn't suspect a t'ing. Not yet!"

"You jes' went t'get yer oats, ye tosser."

Marc pauses to glare at Elliot, and I wait, silently complicit in his personal drama.

"The car, she run out of gas, nowhere near a city. 'Ow stupide! By the time we deal wit' that problem, drive the rest of the way to Glasgow, it's lunch time. We are exhausted. We find a 'otel, as cheap as possible, but they spend all their cash on the gas, the car, so I 'lend' them the mo-nee." He rocks his head back and forth. His dramatic eyes foreshadow the coming scandal.

"Them?" I repeat.

"Exactement." He nods. "Annika, and de other guy who come wit' us, 'is name was Wolf. Can you believe it? Vuff! Vuff!" He barks like a dog.

Oh, do I get it. Everyone shakes their heads, baffled only by the fact that he's so obviously enjoying telling his tale of woe. The attention it garners him.

"What the fuck you goin' on about now?"

"Bloody hell, get t' the point, you wanker."

"Donc, the next day, we go to see the School of Art. I try to find a pay phone to call you, but I don't 'ave much chance."

"It's not that 'ard, mate," says Oliver.

I'm trying to recall where I was then. Frantically running around York, checking in with the local police, thinking Marc-Antoine was mugged or dead. No messages awaited me at the youth hostel.

He continues. "The next day, same t'ing. Wolf 'as plan to 'ike all 'round the city like a maniac, looking at important edifice like the Hill House by Mackintosh, an' galleries wit' works by Macdonald, Macdonald an' McNair, an' Jessie M. King and Archibal' Knox. There was so much to see!"

"Who?" asks Zoë, losing the thread.

"Architects," I explain, sipping my cider.

I have no difficulty believing that Marc and his friends were carried away in an ecstasy of artistic appreciation. Despite my mounting cynicism, there is no denying Marc-Antoine's true passion for his art. His blood gets a-boiling over little things, like the proportions of a stained glass window or the detailed engraving on a spoon. I guess it's not unlike the passion I feel for a classic piece of literature by Joyce or Austen. But, still.

What's lacking is my credence in his attempts to contact me and put me out of my misery. Did he even give me a second thought during his entire exploit? He's knowingly, and cleverly, couching his desertion of me in a cloak of saintly architectural rapture. Nevertheless, I allow him to take my hand in his and squeeze it expressively.

"Of course, I 'ave an amazing time with Annika, who is so smart, Sophie, you 'ave no idea. About this stuff, she know everyt'ing."

I'm sure that was precisely the characteristic he admired most about her. Her long, white-blond hair and tall, willowy figure flash in my mind.

Perhaps in response to the skeptical expression on my face, Elliot says, "Bit o' fluff, aye?"

Marc's lips tighten for a moment, huffing. He's not holding his audience as enthralled as he'd like. "Then we decide to go to Edinburgh also. It seem so close, we can't resist. Wolf decide to come too. I call the yout' 'ostel in York a couple times to tell you where I am, but they are not so frien'ly. At last, they tell me you are not anymore there. Then, I think, fuck! Where did you go? Now what do I do? I feel so bad! I'm t'inking you are probably getting pretty worried about me by now, an' meanwhile, I'm paying for the meals, the gas, the tickets because Annika an' Wolf both say they're trying to get money wired soon."

I clearly see where he's heading and I can't believe how stupid he was, but I say nothing, just shake my head slowly, close my eyes. I'm also picturing him discovering the envelope of cash in the bottom of my backpack and spending it on his new friends.

"After a couple weeks or so of this—there is a lot to see in Edinburgh, eh?—I wake up an' they are bot' gone. Pffft! They left my pack, but the stuffs are gone."

"Oh my Lord! You poor sod," says Zoë.

"That experience sounds strangely familiar." Remembering my nest egg suddenly, I ask, "What stuff?" Marc never knew it was there! Maybe he hadn't found it and spent it.

He ignores me. "I 'ave no more money. They left me a note saying, 'T'anks for the lovely tour of Scotland. An' for the t'ousand dollar bonus. 'Ave a nice life. Annika & Wolf.'"

My stomach falls, and I squeeze my eyes shut. Damn!

Marc-Antoine shakes his head, his dark eyes glazing over with unshed tears. Despite my conviction that he's playing me, I feel for him, his humiliation. He deluded himself into thinking he might have something going on with Annika if he stuck it out. More fool he. Maybe she actually slept with him, maybe not. I'm sure he won't be telling me that part.

"Ha!" The more Marc suffers, the more Elliot enjoys his story.

"What thousand dollars?" Zoë asks nobody in particular, and I jab her in the ribs with my elbow.

"Poetic justice," says Oliver.

Marc's slender nostrils flare and he snuffs in frustration. "I don' know what they talking about. So that's when I realize they were a couple, an' they were working me." He smacks himself on the head with the heel of his hand. "What a patsy!"

Yes! A real sucker! His gullibility makes me look wily. He got scammed. I could say he deserved it. I could call him the naive one. But it's me who lost everything, and it seems he's had his comedown already. I turn to Zoë. "That would be my emergency funds from Dad."

Zoë's jaw drops. "Fuck! They took it?"

"Didn't you wonder for one minute how I was getting on, Marc?"

His brow puckers slightly, then clears.

"Non, chouette! You are so clever. I figure you would be h'okay for a time."

"No, no," moans Zoë, dropping her head onto the table with a thud. "That won't do at all."

"You prat!" Oliver sneers. "You deserve what you got, if you ask me."

"Aye. Ah'll second that."

"Without my passport, Marc-Antoine? With no money?" I glare at him, daring him to deny he took them.

"Mon Dieu! That was complete accident."

I roll my eyes.

Elliot makes a rude noise.

I turn to him. "What are you snorting about? Aren't you the one who said this is normal behaviour for guys?"

He lowers his eyes, grumbling under his breath.

Nick returns, standing for a moment in his Peter Pan pose, his arms crossed, trying to catch up with the conversation.

"H'aren't you always talking about 'ow independent and competent you are, an' nobody give you a chance to prove it? That is exactly what you fight wit' your parents about."

That's partly true, at least. I never did tell him how much they hated him. "That doesn't excuse what you did to me."

Nick pulls up an empty chair and straddles it backwards, leaning in, once again separating Marc-Antoine from me. His eyes meet mine, assessing my emotional state, and I try to convey the confused, exasperated, helpless way I feel. His tiny smile is warm and reassuring, and he takes my hand and rubs it with his thumb, resting it on his thigh.

"Don't change the subject, you wanker," says Zoë.

Marc adopts a pensive demeanour. "I did try to call again, when I get stranded. I 'ope maybe you could help me some'ow, but it was too late to find you by then. I think ..." He shrugs and thrusts out his lower lip. "Maybe you fly 'ome? Maybe you call your mom and dad for money? I don't know."

Arrogant bastard! Not even a flicker of concern for my well-being. It's all me, me, me! He has some nerve to suggest I'm the capable, independent one, then assume I called home to get bailed out by the parents I fought with over this precise subject. The inherent contradiction doesn't seem to bother him. And while the plausibility of his story is moderately high—he's a clever fellow, after all—it still doesn't have the ring of truth to it. Or not the complete truth. Something's missing—oh, right! Empathy!

He leans across Nick and clasps my shoulders in his hands, bringing his forehead near to mine. "You can jus' imagine 'ow 'appy I am to find you 'ere!"

Nick clears his throat, and our eyes meet.

"I'll bet," I retort. "Bail you out," I mumble. I wonder who he conned to get back here.

"That's right! We can go 'ome together, cherie. We can go early. Right now, even. I am ready."

Where does he suppose I'll get the money for two flights home? I shake my head in disbelief. "I want my backpack. Do you have it?"

He waves a dismissive hand. "It's at the 'ostel." He frowns slightly. "Where are you staying?"

"I have a flat." I gesture to Zoë, beside me. I catch her eye, and she smiles in acknowledgment. I read a question on her face, and I give her a tiny reassuring smile, lift my brows, and tilt my head. She nods. "Zoë's my roommate." She leans in close to Oliver and whispers in his ear.

"No kidding!"

"No kidding."

He leans back and shifts his weight, as though he's ready to get up.

"Not a chance, mate," says Nick, deadpan, placing a staying hand on Marc's shoulder. Marc sits up and squares his shoulders, frowning.

"I'm tired, Marc. I'm going now."

He grabs for my hand. "Bien sur. I walk you 'ome."

"No. I'll go home with Zoë and Oliver. I have a double shift tomorrow and I really need to get to sleep."

"Work?" Marc-Antoine scowls. "When can I see you? We should talk, eh? Make some plan …"

I sigh. I suppose he thinks I'll gladly fly home with him too. Bewildered as I am, I leave it open-ended, implicit. I can't handle any more tonight. No decisions. I need to be alone and think. The noise of the pub, and the circular, pointless discussion are suddenly too much for me. My head feels light and foggy.

I chew my lip, my gaze drilling through the tabletop, unsure what to say. "Maybe Saturday morning, not too early, though. Say, ten thirty." I wave him away, muttering. "I have to go." I stand and shift towards the door, waiting for Zoë and Oliver. Elliot stands up and moves towards me, uncertain of his standing. I glare at him. I suppose I won't object to his walking home with us, but that's where it will end. I'm so tired of lies.

Zoë pulls a pen out of her bag and drags a square Boddington's Pub Ale paper coaster towards her, jotting her cell phone number on its yellow border. "Call tomorrow late afternoon and I'll give you directions."

Marc slips the coaster into his jeans pocket with a frown.

Zoë and Oliver stand and join me by the door. I wobble and lean into Zoë, and she holds my arm.

"Just a sec," I say, moving closer to Nick who's sidling back towards the stage for his last set.

I move to intercept him, putting a hand on his arm, and he stops, turns uncertainly to face me, a question in his eyes.

"Thank you," I say and place my hands on his shoulders,

stretch onto my toes, and kiss him gently on his smooth cheek, above the scruffy top of his beard. Then I cover the spot with four fingers. "And I'm so sorry for all this."

He gawks at me, then composes himself and says, "Are you all right, then?"

A tiny smile. "I will be."

CHAPTER 40

J*uly 31, 1997, York*

I groan softly. Being up so early in the morning is excruciating. My eyes burn and my bones ache with fatigue. Even if I'd had more than four hours' sleep last night, after three months of graveyard this shift would have been gruelling. I don't know how Sean does it. But then he probably has no social life to speak of and goes to bed at eight every night. That would fit. Of course, he left me a scrawled note with all the particulars of how to order the special edition book I promised him. Couldn't let that go. I definitely have to get some sleep before I return for my usual night shift.

Without a doubt, Sunday mornings are usually quieter, but the conference winding down has brought an exodus of guests draped in swag. I've been kept hopping checking out guests, calling taxis, and answering unfamiliar questions about train schedules and routes, as they prepare to drive home or shuttle to airports in various cities. The lobby is chock-a-block with piles of luggage. A constant hum of voices fills the lobby as well as the clatter and crash, along with the aroma of coffee and bacon from the breakfast room down the hall. People walk to and fro and jog up and down the stairs. My usual shift is a piece of cake. It feels like I've been here a hundred hours already. The big clock reads ten twenty.

I wonder how Alan's presentation went. I haven't seen him yet.

I've been so caught up in my own affairs, so to speak, God, what a debacle! Marc-Antoine never once backed down from his position—

Oh my God! My heart hammers in panic as I rush to the resident register. Alan wouldn't have checked out yesterday afternoon after his presentation, would he? I'd have seen him this morning if he'd—oh, thank God. Still here. Bill unpaid. Whew. I settle back onto my stool to wait.

During my few idle moments, I write in my journal, but in such a state of agitation, I've ended by doodling and glowering at the random jagged shapes flowing from my pen. I wonder if Marc's always been so cocky and glib, and if I was always so naive, as I was accused of being. In retrospect, he was always laughing and teasing me, saying how gullible I was. He liked that about me. Didn't he? I was a convenient patsy. I spent two years of my life believing I was in love with a guy who didn't even take me seriously. My head is buzzing, my chest tight, as tears well up yet again.

It's unlikely he was faithful to me during that time. Contrasting my situation to Zoë's, I look stupid by comparison. At least she's putting up with Oliver's follies with her eyes wide open. I write Oliver's Follies in my journal. It has a nice ring to it. Maybe I'll write a book about arrogant young men and their lies and infidelities. I've got enough experience under my belt to pull it off. Ha! I sound like such an embittered old crow.

"What's got you scowling so, Sophie?"

"Oh, Alan!" I perk up. "Did you sleep late? I've been waiting for you." His damp hair is neatly combed and his cheeks have a pink glow, freshly shaved. He smells like soap and clean cotton.

"I'll b-bet."

"Well, how did it go?" I lean in. "Tell me everything."

"You don't want to know everything." He smiles.

"You seem relaxed. Was it well received?" His stutter is all but gone.

"Indeed, it was." He grins. "I got my first good night's sleep in a while." His eyes narrow crookedly, assessing. "You, however, have aged t-t-ten years since Friday night. What happened to you?"

"Oh," I groan. "I traded shifts so I could go out to see my friend's band last night, and … I told you about my boyfriend disappearing back in May? Well, he showed up! Back from Glasgow."

"Oh ho!" Alan exclaims, jerking his head back. "A late-night reunion, then."

"No, no, not like that." I shake my head and make a face at him. "There was an ugly scene. And we talked. But …"

"T-t-trouble in paradise?"

"I'm going to see him again tomorrow morning, but … I don't think I'll be going home with him." As I say the words, I know they're true.

"Oh. I'm sorry."

"It's okay. It's for the best. It wasn't what I thought it was, you know?"

He nods, ponders, then grins. "Well, maybe what I have to t-tell you will cheer you up a bit."

I sit up and grimace, my eyes wide. "What? Did you find something out?"

He nods. "Even better than that."

I squeal and jump up and down. I can't believe it. "Tell me!"

Teddy strides by carrying a bucket and a long pole and glares at us. I'm not sure if it's Alan he disapproves of or if he's jealous that I've got a new friend. Maybe he thinks Alan's going to whisk me back to Canada.

"Well, not only did I find out that he's retired, P-professor Emeritus from Cambridge University and all that, but—"

A man sidles up next to Alan and pushes his credit card towards me, the expression on his face suggesting that I deal with his urgent needs before I chat with my friend. I apologize to Alan with my eyes and deal with the guest before I can come back.

"Go on!"

"So. He's alive." Alan raises a finger and grins widely. "He's still in t-t-touch with a few of his old cronies, though he doesn't t-t-travel anymore. I was introduced to one—a Dr. Davison, we had a couple drinks last night—and he's given me a handwritten p-p-personal note of introduction, along with his address, and said he'd call ahead to warn P-professor Dean that I'm coming for a visit within the next day or two!"

"Oh my God! That's … that's amazing!" I press my hands to my cheeks. I'm so excited. "Are you going to go? What am I saying? Of course you're going! When do you fly home to Canada?"

"Calm down. Yes, of course, I'm going. I wouldn't p-pass up this opportunity for the world, even if it meant p-postponing my flight. But thankfully I don't fly home from Heathrow until Thursday, so as long as I leave t-tomorrow, I can fit it in. And get this …" He does a little jig, and I laugh. "He lives near Windermere, in the Lake District, which I wanted to see, anyway!"

"Oh, me too!" I cry, but then I realize I'm not the one who's going and deflate.

"Wait! Before you get too long in the face. I haven't told you the best part. Dr. Davison is going to mention that I might be bringing a friend with me, someone else who really wants to meet the professor."

I'm astonished. "Alan! You told him about me?"

"Not too much. I made up a little story, said your grandfather was an old friend and asked you to look him up while you were in England."

I laugh. How ironic. "So, he'll be expecting me too?"

"Yup. Can you get away? I mean, I assumed …"

"I will. I'll ask Mrs. R. right away. Oh, Alan, thank you so much!" My chest expands with the pressure of my excitement.

"Now we have to figure out how to get there. Do you know about the buses or trains?"

I shake my head. "I've given so many brochures and train timetables out over the last week I have none left. Most people were heading either south or north, though. And I don't remember anything about buses at all."

"I've got some time to kill. I'll stroll down to the tourist info office and inquire." He turns to go. "Hey. I realized you're not usually working in the morning. How will I reach you?"

"I'm working my regular shift tonight," I grimace. "If I'm still awake. I'll be back at seven."

"I'll stop by then. We can make plans. Good luck getting the time off." He lifts his crossed fingers, and I grin. He really has cheered me up.

After Zoë relieves me at noon, I manage to have a nap. Soon after I get back to the Aviary in the evening for my regular shift, groggy and lethargic, Mrs. R. comes by the front desk carrying a small, rectangular box, draped with a dark cloth, and sets it down on the shiny wood desk with a smile. I'm exhausted from the long week, the late night, and the early morning. Worst of all, I'm stunned at Marc-Antoine's return and all the confusing events of last night at the Priory. I definitely have to see him to retrieve my satchel. He implied he wants to return home together as planned. How can I believe him? I don't know. My eyes well with tears of frustration and fatigue.

I really need a break.

Mrs. R. stops and peers keenly at me, setting her little package on the gleaming desk.

"Are you feeling well, Sophie?" she asks.

I sniff. "It's been a long week, Mrs. R." A muffled cooing emerges from under the cover. "What's that?" I croak.

"Aah. My new male dove. The supplier called and said he had a new shipment, so I'm giving her one more chance."

I smile weakly. She's a hopeless romantic. "I hope it works this time." This is my chance to ask her. No sense putting it off. "Actually, Mrs. R. I'm more than tired. Marc-Antoine showed up last night, at last."

Her steely eyebrows tilt, and she inclines her head. I study her face, as ever, scanning for familiar features and mannerisms. Something in her eyes and nose, maybe.

"I'm okay. But I could really use a little personal time. I was wondering …" I hesitate. It's not even close to the whole truth, but it's not unjustified all the same.

"Of course. Take a few extra days to rest and sort yourself out." Her perceptive eyes narrow and study me for a moment. "You are coming back, Sophie, aren't you? You won't just—"

Oh! "Yes, ma'am. I wouldn't leave without giving you proper notice. And I have no immediate plans, despite …" I shake my head. She has no idea. "You know."

She nods in understanding. "Why don't you call Rose at the employment agency and make the arrangements for a temp yourself."

"I'll do that. Thank you." I was going to tell her about my trip to the Lakes with Alan Stapleton, but it's not necessary now. She obviously assumes I'll be spending the time with Marc-Antoine. Maybe after I've been away from everything for a few days, I'll have some perspective on that situation. Right now … I just feel numb.

CHAPTER 41

I stopped in at the employment centre before work today to arrange for a temp, motivated to see and speak with Rose in person. I knew I wouldn't have the courage to ask her outright about the photo, and her referral, but I thought, given all I now know, and suspect, I might get a read on her. This can't have been a random, lucky alignment of stars. Sadly, she wasn't there, and I took care of my business with another, younger woman and came to work none the wiser.

Last night, Alan stopped by again, and we decided to leave tomorrow if arrangements could be made. I was too exhausted to figure much out, so he agreed to gather information about transportation routes and schedules and come by tonight so we can sort out a plan. But I do have the time off, so that's a start.

"So, they really don't do intercity buses, like we have," he rambles, leaning on the desk with both elbows stretched out across a road map of northern England, which covers the desk entirely. "It's all p-p-private c-coaches and such, and the really f-f-frustrating thing is, it's only about a t-t-two-and-a-half-hour drive by car, but how c-c-could we do that? I really c-can't deal with driving on the wrong side of the road, and you c-c-can't afford to rent one. And what do we do once we get to Windermere? Dr. Dean isn't in the middle of town." He sighs and sucks his teeth, tracing a finger along the yellow highlighter that marks the more direct route from York to Windermere, frustratingly beyond our reach.

I was writing in my journal when Alan came in after dinner, and now I'm absently doodling in the margins, listening to his account of his research. I can hardly breathe for fear that he's going to say we can't do the trip at all. I certainly can't do it without him. But I can't think of a solution either. I should have known the whole "personal introduction to Dr. Dean" was too good to be true.

"Anyway, it's not ideal, but the t-t-train seems to be our only viable option. But I mean … five and three-quarter hours' t-t-travel and four station t-t-t-transfers to get such a little distance! Pooh." He jabs the map with an affronted forefinger and then transfers it to his mouth for a good chew. "It's easier t-t-to go t-t-ten t-t-times the distance in Canada."

"It's not cheap either." My meagre savings can barely stretch that far.

"Never mind the wasted time," adds Alan.

"I sure hope I can get my train pass back from Marc-Antoine in the morning." If he hasn't already sold it to someone.

"There you are, bro!" Chills race up my spine. The disturbingly familiar male voice suddenly interrupts us from the front door. The foyer is mostly empty now, the last stragglers from the conference having gone.

Alan's head jerks up, and the wide smile splitting his face tells me all I need to know, just before my brother materializes in front of me. The two friends greet each other, laughing and arm slapping while I stare at them, my jaw slack and my pulse accelerating.

"What. Are. You. Doing here?"

At first, he doesn't seem to hear or see me. Then he does, and flinches, stepping back from Alan. "Oh! You're literally right here!"

I frown, bewildered, and shoot a glance at Alan.

He is suitably embarrassed, his ears gone rosy. "I … I was j-j-just about to mention to you …?"

"That you brought my brother here?" My voice rises an octave. "To York? To my work?"

He registers that I'm less than thrilled, his mouth working. Then, blinking rapidly, finally he mutters, "I t-t-thought it'd be a nice s-s-surprise for you?" He's as confused by my distinct lack of pleasure as I am at the whole situation.

I turn my stony gaze to my brother and wait.

Matt has the decency to look guilty. "Alan emailed me, after meeting you, to reconnect." He shrugs. "I might have conned him into telling me where to find you."

"C-c-conned me?" Alan scowls at his friend.

"Sorry, bro," Matt says, chucking him on the shoulder. "Mother's orders. Maybe you don't know, but this one's been AWOL all summer."

Alan's eyes swivel to me, but I ignore him.

"I'm an adult, Matthew Groenveld. You can't do this."

Matt shrugs again, with a cocky one-sided grin. "Do what? Come by to see that my baby sister's all right?"

I'm starting to see red. I won't accept his condescension or interference. I won't. "Did Mom send you? Did you tell her where I am?"

He doesn't have to answer. I can see it on his face. Great.

Alan fidgets and mumbles, "I'll just … leave you t-t-two alone and … p-p-op back later." He skedaddles up the red-carpeted staircase like a Canada goose in the fall.

"Well?"

Matt pulls a thick envelope from his shoulder bag and sets it on the desk. "So, you're working here? How long?"

Curious, I open the envelope and pull out an airline ticket home and a wad of traveller's cheques to supplement what Mom already sent. The air rushes out of me, my shoulders slumping. I'm half annoyed, half relieved. "A couple of months."

"Wow. All those postcards?"

"Bogus," I say, having no further need to lie. "I just needed time on my own to work stuff out."

"And? Have you?"

Have I? I glare at him, but my wrath disintegrates in the face of my big brother's honest, caring expression. He's not here to beat me up about all this. It's my turn to shrug. "I'm making headway," I say.

I ask Matt if he rented a car and he says no, he came straight here and plans to leave immediately. "Are you coming home with me?"

Slowly, my head oscillates side to side. As easy at that would be, to pack up and fly off with Matt, leave all of this behind. I know I can't. "No. I have people here I'm obligated to. Things I'm in the middle of that I have to see through."

"How can you get so embroiled so quickly? You always did have a knack for getting twisted up in people's business."

I stiffen. This gets my back up. "You know? I'm kind of tired of everybody else telling me what I should think and do." My voice sounds brittle in my ears. Too much resentment is stockpiled. I take a deep breath, calming myself. I'm okay. "One. I needed to get away from the tension at home. You were in Ottawa, you didn't know. Two, I wanted to travel with Marc, and see some of the world, and I did that." I'm lifting fingers to emphasize my points, and Matt's eyes widen slightly, unaccustomed to my assertiveness. "Three, I had an agenda coming to York, yes." I pull the old photo out of my journal and slide it across the desk towards Matt. "Mom suspected, I guess. She wrote me a letter. But I don't think she knows I took this from her drawer."

He studies it. I'm sure he's seen it before. Though Mom never exactly pulled out her box of childhood photos to show them off, we'd seen them. He purses his lips. "Is that ... this place in the background? Do you suppose the little girl is Mom?"

"I think so." Then I remember. "Hey! You never told me if you checked on the address. In Regina?"

He looks up. "Oh. Yeah, sorry. Totally forgot. I asked Dad, and he said it is. Their old address. Why?"

My heart clenches, thumping wildly. It's true. For a moment I can't speak; I'm just absorbing and processing the reality. Despite all the evidence, I really thought there was a chance I was just dreaming. But it's true. Mrs. Roxtoby is my ... our grandmother. And Rupert Dean is our grandfather. Even if they don't know it.

"What was Mom's maiden name?" I hold my breath.

"Uh. Jones, I think? Why?"

"Could it be Glynn-Jones by any chance?"

His bottom lip curls out as he ponders. "That rings a bell. Maybe she dropped the first part."

I gasp. That proves it.

"What's the matter? Why is that important?" Matt asks.

I swallow, looking at him. "Just a sec." I dash to the store-room and grab a couple of the packages from the far shelf. Setting them on the desk, I wait for Matt to register their significance.

He spins one around, studying the address. "Yeah, that's it." He twists his face, confused. "So?"

"Why do you think it's here?" I poke one package with my finger. When he thrusts out his lower lip, not getting it, I go on. "These packages were sent to this address, addressed to Mom ..."

"Barbara Glynn-Jones Roxtoby," he muses, frowning, then meets my gaze. "Mom?"

"The person who sent these packages, only to have them sent back, is named Ava Roxtoby, and she's the owner of this inn, and my employer." I wait.

Matt's eyes dart back and forth, searching for meaning in my words. He's not quite getting it.

"Our grandmother," I whisper, eyes wide. I point at the old

photo again, at the shorter, darker of the two women standing behind the children, in front of what I now know is the inn.

"What? How can you ...?" He shakes his head. "That's so random."

"I had a lot of clues, but the address and name clinched it. I found her. This"—I lift both hands, palm up—"is where Mom grew up. Right here. The people here knew her. They've even mistaken me for her."

His lip is curled, jaw slack, taking it all in. "Whoa. So that's why Mom's so pissed at you. I mean, she's gonna be even more pissed when she realizes what you've done."

"That's your takeaway? That's all you've got to say?"

"I don't know, Soph. Mom left. I'm sure she had good reasons."

I huff. "She may have, then. But people change. And furthermore, there's so much more to the story."

"I suppose you've been digging it all up."

I tsk. "Yes, I have. I was drawn to Mrs. R. from the beginning. First of all, she was so kind to me. She gave me this job, no questions asked."

"Does she know?" he asks suddenly.

"I don't know. I don't think so?" The idea takes root in my mind. Does she? Did she suspect from the beginning? Our conversations play back in my head. "But Matt, there's more."

I fill him in briefly about the wartime disaster that tore our grandparents apart, the complicated and painful family situation that resulted, and then finally, I say, "And with Alan's help, I've located Professor Dean. That's what we're doing, planning our trip there to meet him."

Matt pushes back from the desk with both hands. "Aw, now you've gone too far, Soph. You can't mess with people's lives like that."

"This is a good thing, Matt! Don't you want to know your own grandfather? You look like him, you know?" I extract the old army photo of Lieutenant Dean from my journal and show him. Watching his face, I can tell it makes an impact. We've both grown up with this big void about Mom's side of the family. He frowns, chewing his lip.

"I'm curious, of course. But … oh, sis, this could go so badly. People could be hurt."

I nod. "I know. I'm taking it slow. I haven't spoken to Mrs. R. yet. And I … I want to meet him before I tell her I've found him." I nod. "Just in case …" I shrug. Who knows? Maybe he's married. Maybe he disappeared from her life because he wanted to. Maybe he's awful. I don't know.

Matt covers his mouth with his hand, thinking. "I won't alienate Mom over this, no matter what else is at stake," he finally says. "If she has a clue what you're up to, she'll probably need me at home. But … you go, girl." He shakes his head, a small smile playing on his lips. "I guess this means you won't be flying home with me?"

I shake my head, amazed at his concession, his reluctant admiration. Our gazes lock, and I see it. My face splits in a gleeful grin. I'm doing this. For all of us.

CHAPTER 42

Matt and I sit in the lounge for a few minutes, talking, and I ignore Teddy's curious gaze, laughing to myself. I fill Matt in about Marc-Antoine and everything I've been doing since I left home. He updates me on the Mom-and-Dad situation. Then I thank him for bringing the ticket and money, which takes so much pressure off me, it's unbelievable, and we hug. Before he heads out, he asks me to pass a message to Alan, to meet up later for a drink. I suggest the Priory as a meeting place, and he agrees.

Once back at my desk, I ring Alan's room to call him back downstairs. A few minutes later, he appears, chagrinned. "I'm so sorry, Sophie."

"I'm not mad at you, Alan," I say to his wooden face. "You didn't know."

He breathes an audible sigh of relief and slumps against the desk. "Where's Matt gone?"

I tell him about the meeting place and time. Because I'll be at home waiting for Marc-Antoine to show up in the morning, we agree to meet up at the train station at noon. Before then, he'll book us a cheap place to stay in Windermere.

"Where are you two off to, then?"

Alan and I both look up, startled to be interrupted again.

"Savvy!" I say, glancing at the clock. It's ten to ten.

"Hey, Canadian." His smile is warm, sending a zing of fizzy tingles dancing over my skin.

"You can't call me that today," I say, smiling back, my face heating.

"Why ever not?"

"Because you're outnumbered, Englishman," I reply, laughing. "Nick, I'd like to introduce Alan Stapleton. Alan, Nick Savile, a friend of mine."

The two guys shake hands.

"Sophie's told me about your work, Alan."

Alan nods. I can see him processing the disconnect between Nick's posh speech and gracious manners, and his grunge, anti-establishment appearance. Nick has the advantage as I did tell him about Alan, whereas Alan has no idea who Nick is. I grin.

"Th-th-th-thanks," Alan stutters, blushing a little.

"What brings you here so late?" I ask Nick. "Not jamming tonight?"

He seems disconcerted, glancing fleetingly at Alan, who shows no sign of leaving. "Oh." He shakes his head and shrugs. "I wondered how you made out after Wednesday evening's brouhaha." He peers at me, conveying with his intense green eyes the things he doesn't feel he can say in front of Alan. "I was unoccupied this evening. I wanted to know that you were …" He shrugs again. "All right."

"I'm fine, as you can see," I reply graciously, crinkling my eyes at him. It's sweet that he came all this way to check on me.

"I was concerned you might have … gone away … already," he says, eyeing the map laid out on the desk, but he doesn't repeat his question about where we're going.

I see what he's thinking, but he'll have to wait to find out what happens with Marc-Antoine. I tell him how Alan found the professor through a colleague at the conference and got the introduction and permission to visit him.

"So … we're going to Windermere," I announce, with a trace of false optimism. "Or we're trying to go to Windermere. It turns out it's not that easy."

"Windermere? It couldn't be simpler," says Nick. "It's not far at all." He leans his elbows on the map next to Alan.

"If you have a car," Alan says despondently.

"Well, how else would you do it?" Nick asks, wrinkling his nose.

Alan explains again about the ridiculously circuitous train route, heading south to Leeds and then across and up through Manchester before going north to the Lakes.

Nick frowns and tilts his head while he's listening, watching Alan's finger trace the alternate routes on his map.

"Well, you can't go by train. That would be preposterous."

"We don't seem to have any other option," I say, meeting his sympathetic gaze. "We can't pass up this opportunity to meet the professor. Neither of us can."

Nick chews his lip silently, studying the map, as though it's a foreign country and not his own familiar backyard.

"Have you planned what you'll say to him, when you meet him?" Nick asks, thoughtful as ever.

I suppose he's tempted to scold me for being an interfering busybody again. He's as surprised as anyone that I found Rupert Dean and would dare to go meet him in person. But he doesn't yet know what I've discovered.

I waver. "Of course. I've thought a lot about it. But I have to play it by ear. I can't tell him anything before I meet him. Then I'll have to take it one step at a time. And I can't interfere with Alan's visit either. It'll have to wait until after."

"Hmm. Yes, I see," mumbles Nick, distracted. His eyes seem unfocused. I wonder if he's really interested in the agenda or if he's preoccupied with whether I should be doing this at all.

"It's okay, Nick," I say. "I'm going to take it very slowly. But … I found out something important earlier tonight. My brother came, and I learned some—"

"Pardon?" His eyes crease and he blinks at me, as though he isn't even listening. He's still worrying his lip.

"Excuse me a moment," says Alan, glancing at Nick and then meeting my eye with concern. "I have to use the washroom. I'll be back in a bit."

Nick looks up absently and nods.

After Alan goes upstairs, I turn back to Nick. "I know what you're thinking, Nick."

He's frowning. "No. I don't think you do."

"I understand that your sense of propriety and privacy is a little different from mine. But this is important. And Nick. I found out from my brother that Dr. Dean really is my grandfather. I have to trust my own—"

"You do. You do." He nods, pensive. Has he heard a word I said? "Sophie. I have to say, before Alan comes back, about Marc-Antoine—I know this has to be your own decision, and really, it's none of my business and I shouldn't say anything, but, Wednesday night, I—"

"Nick Savile!" I grin. "Are you meddling in my private affairs?"

He looks sheepish. "'Fraid so. I can't help myself."

I shake my head and smile.

"You can't go back to him, Sophie. It's your decision, and I respect that, but you've got to keep your own best interests in mind." He can't keep a straight face, and his cheeks flare hotly. "I can't believe I'm saying this, but my advice to you, Sophie Groenveld, is to say goodbye to that smarmy narcissistic creep." He drops his gaze, laughing, then meets my gaze, earnest. "Send him packing back to Canada, or to his Swedish squeeze, or wherever, but don't you dare go off with him. Please."

"Nick. You darling. You do care," I tease, but my chest swells and my heart flutters wildly.

He loses his smile. "Of course I care, Canadian."

I peer at him seriously for a moment. "I made arrangements to meet him tomorrow morning. To talk."

He chews his cheek a long moment. "I have a motor, you know."

I frown. "A motor ... what?"

He looks at me funny. "It's an old Range Rover."

I squint and stare. Huh?

"It's a junker, but it runs fine, and there's room for three and luggage."

"What are you saying?"

He scratches his head and his eyes dart around. "I've been planning on going ... Rather, I have some personal things I've been meaning to take care of, anyway. It's a little out of my way, but nothing serious. I could drop you two off in Windermere and pick you up a couple of days later."

"What? Drive us?"

Nick licks his lips, and his gaze is earnest to the point of heartbreaking. I don't know what moves me more, his offering to facilitate this trip, knowing how important it is to me, and despite his own misgivings, or the fact that I have a good idea what his personal business might be.

My eyes well with tears, and I pull my lips between my teeth to stop them quivering. I nod, trying to get a grip. My voice comes out in a hoarse whisper. "You won't regret it, Nick. It's the right thing to do."

He exhales noisily through flared nostrils and nods.

"Mrs. R. said to me, no one will ever love you like your family." I reach for his hands and give them a squeeze, and he nods. "Nick," I whisper. "Listen to this. I'm now ninety percent certain that Mrs. Roxtoby is my grandmother and Dr. Dean is my grandfather. I didn't mention my suspicions before, but I've been gathering evidence."

"What?" Nick's expression morphs from turmoil to shock in a flash. Before I can elaborate, Alan jogs down the staircase, and I shoot Nick an apologetic glance and mouth, Later.

"Oh, I'm sorry—" Alan says when he sees us.

"It's okay!" I drop Nick's hands and gaze and turn to Alan,

relieved that the tension is broken. "Alan, you'll never guess! Nick has offered to drive us to Windermere!" My enthusiastic tone sounds forced to my own ears, despite my genuine happiness. It's too much, and I'd rather be alone so I can have a good cry about … everything.

"Well, that's … damn nice of you, Nick. I hope it's not an inc-c-convenience."

Nick coughs to clear his throat. "Not at all, Alan." His voice creaks a little and he coughs again. "It's on my way, and I'd planned to go, anyway. It's no trouble." His smile is tight, and our gazes meet for a fleeting, reassuring moment.

"Okay, then," Alan rubs his hands together. "When can we leave?"

Nick glances at me. "When will you be ready?"

I peer at Alan. "I know we have to go tomorrow, and I've cleared the time off, but … would it be okay if we delayed our departure until afternoon?" I peek at Nick, tipping my head back and forth. "I, uh, have to meet with Marc before we go." I grimace.

Alan shrugs, and Nick says briskly, avoiding my eye, "That'll leave us plenty of time. We can even stop for tea in Harrowgate if you like, and perhaps have a look at the castle at Skipton en route."

"But Nick, how far will you have to drive afterwards?" I ask. "Don't you live south—?"

He waves my concern aside with a sweep of his hand. "It's nothing. I'm quite used to the roads. And it's not dark until after nine. Perhaps we can have supper at Kirkby-Lonsdale and avoid the tourist traps in Windermere." He smiles gamely. "Oh! Do you have a place to stay?"

Alan pushes a few brochures on top of the map, fanning them out. "I found these bed and breakfasts at the t-tourist office."

Nick glances through them quickly and lifts one up. "Call this one first to make a reservation, or perhaps this one. It's peak season, they'll be busy. Shall I pick you up at your flat at noon, Sophie?"

I nod.

"All right. We'll swing by here fifteen minutes later, Alan. I'd better push off; I have some things to take care of before we go. Canadian." He shoots me a look that tells me he expects the full story tomorrow, and I smile and nod.

We wish him good night and I watch him leave, wondering if he's regretting his offer, and if he really will go home to see his parents while Alan and I visit Professor Dean. I mean … my grandfather. My stomach feels queasy. Poor Nick! I don't know which of us has the harder mission.

"Awfully nice guy," says Alan as he heads out to meet Matt.

"Yes," I say. "He is, isn't he?"

CHAPTER 43

Much later, I'm alone again in the middle of the night with my thoughts. What an eventful day it's been. I can hardly believe that I've seen Alan, my brother, and Nick tonight.

My journal has grown fat, stuffed with artifacts. Unused postcards, travel brochures, receipts, and the two old photos, along with my own sketches and musings. I've even jotted outlines and openings for several short stories inspired by all the things that have been happening.

I pull out Mom's smoothly folded letter and turn it over and over in my hands, holding it under the desk's spotlight. The linen-textured white stationery from one of our bed and breakfasts—Scarborough Faire B&B—with the little ink drawing of a Victorian house in one corner. That I drew. The sentimental name now makes sense in a way it never did. Though she typed the body of the letter, the salutations are hand written. I trace a finger over Mom's fine, even, slanting hand in her favourite blue fountain pen. A faint scent of mint and oranges reminds me of home.

It would be nothing less than heartbreaking to find Rupert Dean, inform him he has a daughter he didn't know about, and then have to say, "But unfortunately, she's estranged—hasn't spoken to her mother in thirty years. Sorry." What will he say? How will Mom react when I tell her I've found the true father she never knew?

I've read and re-read Mom's letter, scouring the lines, searching for a clue about why her interpretation of her mother doesn't mesh with my impression of Mrs. R. But it's too vague.

Mrs. R. is so, so melancholy. It's more than a mood that comes and goes, it's her constant companion, as though she moves through life without purpose or joy. Teddy even said that once in a while, it gets so bad she has to escape. And yet I wonder why she doesn't sell the hotel and really go away, make a new life for herself somewhere else, somewhere without all the painful memories. It's as if she's waiting. Waiting for them to come back. Her ghosts.

Since Nick left, Alan went out to meet up with Matt and staggered to bed a few hours later, and Teddy locked up and went home. I've been brooding about family rifts and reconciliations, my own, not least of all.

I've begun drafting a letter to Mom and Dad, basically confessing all, thanking them for sending a new ticket home and the money. Even though they sicced my big brother on me. After all, I owe them something of an apology. And reassurances not to worry, that I'll be home by early September, in time to get ready for the new semester at university, but that I want to stay as long as possible. Even if Marc-Antoine lost or sold my passport, and I have to go to Birmingham for a replacement.

All of which got me thinking about Mom's rift with Mrs. R. again, living in Canada under the mistaken belief that her mother doesn't want to see her or her children. Misunderstandings. Mistaken judgments. False first impressions. Crossed wires. I sigh heavily. So much of our lives seems to depend upon momentary mistakes and judgments, you'd think we'd learn a lesson by it and try to be more forgiving and open-minded. But it doesn't seem to make much difference.

I vow to be the exception. I've learned my lesson. Human

beings are so frail. Even in Elliot's case, I've come to the conclusion that though he was wrong to fabricate an identity to impress me, he didn't really mean any harm. He's insecure and wanted me to like him. How human is that?

"What's that, Sophie dear? Another letter from home?"

I jerk by reflex and slide my own half-finished letter over Mom's, covering it. I glower at Eleanor, in her diminutive form, peering at me over the desk. Her wispy white hair is in curlers, wrapped in a blue chiffon scarf. It matches her robe. She obviously knows who I am tonight.

"You frightened me, Eleanor. Again!" I gust with laughter. She doesn't do it on purpose, but she's so light and slides around silently on her slippered feet.

"What are you hiding?" She's scowling suspiciously at my hands, which hold down the two letters, attempting rather unsuccessfully to look casual.

"Nothing!" I reply gaily. "I was writing to my parents. I'll be heading home at the start of September. I'm enrolled in university for the fall term, grad school." My nerves make me babble.

"Mm." She sucks in her hollow cheeks and nods, but her beady dark eyes burn a hole through my fingers, her curiosity is so intense. Then she casts her gaze around the desk, and settles on the envelope that contained Mom's letter, which I've forgotten about. Eleanor's face goes momentarily lax, and her eyes widen in a look of alarm.

"What's this?" Her hand darts out.

Oh shit! I slap my hand onto the envelope as she makes a grab for it, but she's seen it now.

"Is that mine? Did you take that from my room?" Her voice is sharp.

"Of course not!" I slide it under my pile of paper, although my efforts to be nonchalant are ludicrous. "I wouldn't go into your room, Eleanor."

"Why not? You've got the key."

"It's private. I wouldn't do that. Besides, it's a letter to me."

She saw something to raise her interest. Why did she think it was hers? Does she recognize Mom's handwriting? From long ago? Or … hmm.

"I suppose you're wondering where I got this letter from."

Her brows knit and she sets her stubborn jaw.

I stare into Eleanor's eyes. "Do you have letters that look like this one? Are they from Barbara? Is that your secret?"

She purses her wrinkled lips and raises her chin high. "That's none of your business," she squeaks.

I peer at her. It might be my business. "Does Ava know you have them?"

Her face is pinched, and two uneven spots of colour appear on her sallow cheeks. As her eyes dart around, I can see her mind working away at excuses.

Another more sinister notion occurs to me. It's crazy, but I can't shake it off. "Or is it even worse than that?" I ask, frowning at her. "That day you were showing me old wartime photos. Telling me about Mr. Roxtoby and the children. Those letters I saw in your box were addressed to Mrs. Roxtoby." I remember now. At the time, I was so intrigued by the photos, I hardly thought about them. Is it possible that the letters addressed to Mrs. R. I saw in Eleanor's box were stolen before Ava received them?

Eleanor gasps but says nothing. She stares at me, her sparse wiry white eyebrows prickling over her wary dark eyes.

I'm right! I shift on my stool and wait to see what Eleanor will say.

She, too, waits, saying nothing, rubbing a veined hand in little circles over the glossy surface of the desk.

Eleanor's tight face is crumpling, little twitches and vibrations appearing, like a small earthquake tremor under the surface, though she's trying to maintain her composure. I wait it out. I feel a confession coming.

Her dark eyes shine with moisture, and her nostrils flare and her lips pinch with the effort of controlling her emotions.

I sigh, suddenly feeling the weight of responsibility for all my meddling, squeezing my heart. Who am I to be policing the crimes this old woman committed who knows how many years ago? I reach for her old, bony hand and clasp it in mine. "I don't want to hurt you, Eleanor. But it's dawned on me that maybe this terrible, useless, sad separation between Mrs. R. and Barbara has had a little help along the way. Am I mistaken?"

Eleanor's thin lips press together tightly with a wobble, and she shakes her head from side to side. "It was wrong. A … a desperate act. I … I was so …" She stops, blinking rapidly, her face crumpled.

"This has gone on long enough. I won't say anything to Mrs. R., but you might do something to help now, if you feel remorse."

Eleanor's eyes drop, hooded now under the heavy wrinkled folds of her eyelids. "Ava would never forgive me," she whispers in her hoarse, cracked voice, and lifts her eyes to mine. Her tears overflow at last, clinging to her sparse lashes, clumping them together in wet spikes.

"She's forgiven you for sleeping with her husband. Why not this too?"

Eleanor's eyes flare open, and her mouth gapes, so that I can see a few gaps in her teeth. Her tongue is pale and furry. "That wasn't it at all! How can you accuse me of such a thing?"

Her shock and outrage seem genuine, and immediately I regret my intemperate accusation. I was certain. "I'm sorry. From the things you've said, I was under the impression that you and Mr. Roxtoby, you know … over the years, I thought that perhaps Mr. Roxtoby …"

Her head shakes again, and she frowns deeply. "William was never unfaithful. He was too good, too honourable a man." Her deeply crevassed mouth turns down even further as she ponders this fact. "You don't understand anything about it. We were close. He trusted me, shared his feelings with me. It hurt him. He didn't like the situation at all, it's true, but we had an under-

standing. All of us. And Ava is my friend, too, despite our difficulties. She's family!"

"Not such a good friend that you wouldn't keep her only
remaining child from her. What can you have gained by stealing
Barbara's letters?"

"She left so soon after Jamie's death. I wasn't myself in my
grief. At the time I believed, if I couldn't have Jamie, it was only
fair that Ava wouldn't have Barbara either. When she tried to
contact Ava a few years later, I lashed out in jealousy. And once
I'd begun, I … I didn't know how to stop. Then, even now, I'm
too ashamed, too afraid of Ava's ire." She's waving her stiff,
arthritic hands around, and they are trembling.

I knead my tired eyes with my fingers, pondering the facts,
my options, nibbling my lip.

"Eleanor." She is standing, hunched, looking smaller and
frailer than ever before. "How would you like to phone
Barbara?" I hesitate.

Eleanor's gaze lifts skeptically, a hint of terror in her eyes.
"You know where she is?"

I nod. "I do." Dare I? Mom did reach out, and I was about to
tell her everything in a letter, anyway. Maybe it's time. Besides, it
would mean so much to her to learn that Ava had tried to reach
out. It would help her more than Eleanor, probably.

I wish I could read the content of the letters in Eleanor's
possession. What if they're filled with vitriol? I could make
everything worse. Should I tell Eleanor that Barbara is my mom?

"You mean, tell Barbara?" Eleanor's dark little eyes dart over
to the desk phone beside me. Her voice is a tiny, timid thing.
"You can do that?"

I nod again. "If you think you're able to."

We stare at each other for quite a while. She's lucid tonight,
her gaze sharp. I'm imagining she's wishing, as I am, and probably more so, that this whole thing would go away. That it had
never happened and didn't really scream to be fixed. My

stomach roils like curdled milk at the thought of Mom learning this fact.

Eleanor finally nods, her whole body rocking forwards and backwards, forwards and backwards, as she turns away. "You are right, of course. I give you leave," she whispers.

So easy to fix. And it will cost me nothing. But will I be making things worse?

The black desk phone glares at me, and I glare back. I glance at the old yellow clock on the wall and calculate the time difference between York and Port Hope. In the silence, I can hear its relentless ti-ta-ti-tah. Five hours. So, it's now … just about four-thirty in the afternoon. Mom should be home, doing books or resting. Seems like a good enough time to call.

I take a deep breath and pick up the phone with trembling hands as Eleanor looks on, wary. I don't suppose I should really be making a long-distance, overseas call from work, but then, I'm working for Mrs. Roxtoby, aren't I? Anyway, I rationalize, I can always pay the bill myself if this blows up in my face.

I'm listening to that weird series of clicks and buzzes and that hollow sound like a wind tunnel that precedes an overseas connection. After about five rings, there's a click, and I shove the handset at Eleanor. She takes it, reluctantly, placing it to her ear, and listens.

With sagging shoulders, more relief than disappointment, I think, the phone slips down and Eleanor gives it back to me.

"Just a message," she mutters. "Some bed and breakfast."

She's not in.

I take Eleanor's hand and say, "Well. Maybe another time. But I really think you should tell Ava. It would make you both feel better." I return the phone to its cradle.

But before Eleanor shuffles back to her suite, she turns to me and says, "She sounds just the same."

CHAPTER 44

O 1:50, *March 9, 1945, Marylebone, London*

A policeman drove her home. She carried the dented birdcage around to the back garden, found the spade, dug a hole, and buried the charred remains of Ares and Kythereia.

Stunned, lethargic, she entered the parlour, where a single yellow light glowed, and music squawked faintly from the radio.

"Ava? Is that you?" Mother rose from her favourite brocade wing chair, rushing towards her and gasped.

"Who else would it be?"

"You snuck out and went there." Her voice was accusatory, but her hands cupped Ava's damaged face, plucked at her torn clothes, releasing a puff of dust that settled to the carpet. "You're hurt!"

"No. I'm not."

"You look … like an old woman." She flutters her hands about.

How ironic. She felt like one.

Mother resumed her seat by the radio. "I've been scared to death since I heard about the rocket. How close were you?"

Ava swallowed, and in a flat, toneless voice, replied, "Not close enough."

Mother gave the battered cage in her hand a sharp look, and her face hardened. "You defied me. You saw that boy."

Ava glared, feeling as cold and dead as the doves. "No. I didn't see him."

Mother's lips tightened, and her chin lifted.

Ava smiled grimly and said, "Don't look so smug, Mother. He's dead. And I'm pregnant."

"Dear Lord!"

CHAPTER 45

A *ugust 1, 1997, York*

The Naugahyde recliner in the storeroom is calling my name: So-phie. Soooo-phie! And the old yellow wall clock whispers its soothing beat, ti-ta-ti-ta-ti-tah. Teddy's come and gone. I'm barely going to make it to four o'clock, when Sean is due to relieve me; I'm so, so tired—exhausted and emotionally frazzled.

But it's a matter of principle with me that I won't curl up and go to sleep while I'm being paid to do a job. That's all I need is Sean Smythe coming in to find me snoring away. My eyes betray me and creep to the doorway, through which I can see the edge of one worn chair arm; the cracked chocolate brown vinyl suddenly looks like the softest, most comfortable surface on earth. I shuffle closer. The old chair is tucked into one dusty corner with an unobstructed view of the office supplies on the shelf and the broom that leans beside it. Looks lovely.

The stack of returned packages tucked into the back of the

shelf seem to call to me. Frowning, I pick one up. I now know they were meant for my family.

I sit down at the desk and carefully peel the brittle tape from one of the packages. Inside are small gifts suitable for a family of four, lovely but kind of sad and generic. Books, a pretty cashmere scarf in greens and blues, and a puzzle—a snowy scene of birds in the woods, of course, some stale British candies gone sticky in their wrappers. There's a traditional Christmas card with a handwritten note, tentative but heartfelt. I can feel the love and longing in her careful words. The fact that Mrs. R. knows so little about her daughter's life fills me with sadness, and all the emotional turmoil of the week catches up with me, the tears spilling over, my chest convulsing with sobs. I don't know if I'm heartsick or homesick. Both, I guess.

I sigh deeply, blowing frustration out through my puffed cheeks, and rub my eyes hard. Pulling my tired bones off my stool, which is the hair-shirt I've been using to stay awake, I shuffle towards the kitchen to make a fresh pot of strong black tea. While I wait for the kettle to boil, my mind wanders to Alan and our coming trip to Windermere, barely giving Marc-Antoine's impending visit later this morning a passing thought. I'm excited and apprehensive, trying to fit the pieces together, imagining what I will say to Dr. Dean, how I will break the news and gauge his reaction. What he'll be like.

Curiously, I'm even more excited about the fact that Nick will be driving us all the way there. It's more than the knowledge that it'll take hours of useless train travel off our itinerary, for which I'm grateful. It feels somehow like a personal, intimate gesture, a special treat. I know he's doing it for me, and I'm touched. I didn't even know he had a car.

The kettle's jarring whistle wakes me from a standing dream. I groan. It's past two thirty. An hour and a half to go. I make my pot of tea and carry it back to the office, just in time to hear the telephone ringing. Brrrriiing! Christ! How long has it been ringing? I race back to the desk and crash the teapot down with a wobbling thud in my haste, sloshing scalding hot tea over my hand, and swear as I dive for the phone.

"Hello!" I practically shout, waving my burning hand to cool it down. "The Aviary Inn," I amend, calmer. While it's rare, it's not unheard of for prospective hotel guests to call in the wee hours. Usually from abroad.

"Sophie?"

My breath catches, my heart leaping into my throat. Oh, God! "Mom! Hi."

"Yes. Is this a good time? Can you talk?"

I look around me. "Um, yes. It's three thirty in the morning. Not too many people around," I say with a hint of sarcasm.

She laughs. "Good. I'm glad. You tried to call?"

"Yeah, yeah. Earlier. We didn't leave a message, though."

There's a pause. "Who's we?"

Oh, shit. My voice is a whisper, as though the force of its full volume might extinguish this moment, like a candle flame. She's putting the pieces together. "Um. Eleanor?"

She hums. "I thought so. There was a recorded message, actually. I caught a few words."

Oh my God. What did she hear?

"So," she says. "I'm curious, naturally. Eleanor's still at the inn? You know her."

"Uh, what time is it there?" My exhausted brain can't even do the math again. And I'm stalling. Matt must have told her where I am.

"Eight thirty."

"Ah."

"Are you sleepy?"

"No, I'm fine," I lie. But then I realize I'm wide awake now, adrenaline racing through my body. "I'm used to this shift."

"How did you come to be working there?" she asks. Part of me realizes she's stalling too, trying to make me comfortable so I'll tell her what the hell is going on, but I'm a wreck, my mind buzzing.

"Long story," I say. When silence meets me on the empty, hollow-sounding, under-sea line, I'm prompted to give her some details. With nothing more than sympathetic noises, she manages to get pretty much my whole story out of me.

I pour myself a cup of tea and gently blow on its steaming hot surface. It's a long time since Mom and I had a good talk like this. Her familiar soft lilt sounds different to me now. She lost most of her accent long ago, but now I discern the familiar rhythms of the Yorkshire accent in what remains.

"I remember what it was like to be a young woman travelling and living alone. It seems not so long ago I was in your shoes."

"When you left York," I venture. My entire life, I've been waiting for her confidences. I hold my breath, hopeful.

She hums in agreement. "I stayed in London for a few years, travelled a bit, and ended up over here."

The fact that she never returned hovers, unsaid.

"I still wonder about that lady at the employment office. Rose, her name is."

"Hmm. Maybe. Sounds vaguely familiar." Her voice is gentle, reflective.

Perhaps she recognized Mrs. R. in the photo. The building too, probably, despite what she said. The implications of this barely touch my feeble consciousness.

Mom hums, and I hear her sip her evening tea and shuffle papers on her desk. Then, "Does my mother know who you are?"

"I don't know. She hasn't said anything to suggest she does. But she's been really nice to me. I like her. I'd like to know her better."

"Sweetheart … I … I'm worried. I understand your feelings, but I'm unsure she'll welcome the news, or you, if she finds out who you are. I don't want you to get hurt."

"But Mom. This is what I came for. And I'm so close now, and … involved."

"I know how idealistic you are, but I rather think you should leave well enough alone. I can't think this will end well. But at least I know you're safe, and you have your ticket home."

"Yes, thanks for that. But even if I lost this job, I wouldn't leave right away. I've made new friends here." I hesitate. "And Mom, I just know Mrs. R. would be happy to have her family back. I know it in my gut."

She sighs, long and deep.

"In your letter, you were adamant there was no hope of reconciliation. But Mom, I learned something important."

"Something to do with Eleanor?" she deduces.

"Yes. It turns out your mom never received those letters you wrote. I've seen them. They're unopened." My voice fades. I wait through a prolonged pause. My tea is finally cool enough to take a cautious sip. And I wait, my stomach tense, the skin on my arms and neck tingling with dread. "I thought you'd want to know."

Finally, she says, "I was angry for a long time, Sophie. Now it seems, looking back, that I was angry at everyone, everything. Rebellious." She laughs, a higher, brighter version of her own mother's dry bark. "It was the times, too, I suppose. They flamed our generations' discontent."

I make a noncommittal grunting sound, hoping she'll continue.

"Once Matt was born, and I guess while I was pregnant with you, I … well, I guess my anger faded. I imagined what the whole thing must've been like from her point of view. From a mother's perspective."

I settle down into the old desk chair and recline, no longer in need of a backless stool to stay awake.

She tells me how she wished she could have offered us a grandmother, some roots, and how deeply wounded she was when her courageous attempts to reconcile with her mother resulted in a cold shoulder.

"I was hurt, and angry all over again, but I kept trying for several years. For your sakes." She falters.

"It was Eleanor," I blurt, before I lose my nerve. "She stole them."

"I gathered that."

"She's terribly sorry, but it was so long ago, she's buried it behind a wall of fear. She's so afraid of what your mom will say. She's never had another home or family. And she's old now, confused sometimes, and frail."

"Poor Eleanor. That doesn't even sound like her. She was like a second mother to us. In a completely different way than Mum was. Fun, irreverent, and tough. And she brought out the best in my father."

I swallow thickly. Telling Mom about her real father right now would be over the top.

"She was apparently overwrought when James died, from what she's said. Somehow in her grief your leaving seemed fair game to her. She'd always envied your mother, because she had everything, but ironically, they both lost everything in the end, didn't they?"

Mom is silent for a long time.

"I'm not judging her," I deflect. "In fact, lately, I've had reason to empathize with the most questionable behaviour. People do the stupidest, meanest, and most self-damaging things when they are hurting."

Mom grunts softly. "Those are wise words from someone so young."

"I guess what I'm saying is, these days I'm inclined to give anyone a second chance."

"Your own parents, for example?"

I laugh, relieved at the diversion. "Yes, definitely you. I am sorry, Mom, for all the fighting. I was pretty upset about you and Dad."

"Does that all-encompassing forgiveness include your boyfriend?"

A woof of cynical laughter erupts out of me, from somewhere deep. "Boy, you sure know how to ask the hard questions."

She laughs. "I gather that's a hard one."

I draw a breath. "He came back, grovelling, you know, full of smooth excuses. I'm meeting with him later in the morning, actually. And to tell you the truth, I have no idea what I'll do, or say, or feel."

"Well, that means you're keeping an open mind, sweetheart. That's all anyone can promise to do, isn't it?"

"Hmm. I guess." I pause. "What about you and your mom? What will you do now?" My teacup is empty, and I refill it. I realize we've been on the phone for over forty-five minutes. This is going to cost a small fortune.

"I've always regretted falling out with my mother, of course. But it isn't merely a matter of the missing letters. That's a significant thing, and no mistake, but we still have our differences. The reason I left in the first instance ..."

"Something to do with James's death?"

"James's death, James's life. Yes. We had strong opinions about that."

"But that's a thirty-year-old dispute! Surely your perspectives have changed over the years."

"Did you discover anything about him?"

"No. I daren't ask anyone," I reply.

"Under the circumstances, perhaps you should know. It's my opinion, and the passing years have only strengthened my view, that my brother was bipolar, though he was never diagnosed."

"Bipolar? Are you serious? I thought he'd died of a drug overdose!"

"He did. But our fight was about why. Mother was so overwhelmed with guilt. She was convinced she'd somehow driven him to it, driven him away. That his death was a suicide."

"And you didn't agree?" I'm perched on the edge of my chair now. I can't quite believe she's telling me all this; it's like she's been waiting decades to talk to someone about it, and the floodgates have opened.

"No. I knew of his drug use, of course, and kept it secret. She never forgave me for that either. I was quite sure the overdose was purely accidental, even if he did self-destruct, in his way. If he was trying to escape anything, it was himself. Mom would never accept that there was something more fundamentally wrong with him. She believed his mood swings, his poor performance at school, his erratic behaviour, even his drug abuse, had something to do with her and our dysfunctional family life. I couldn't stand her self-pity."

"Was the situation that bad?"

"It was weird, in retrospect. There's no question. But we kids weren't party to the difficulties our parents suffered. And we never questioned the way things were. It was normal. You know, kids measure everything in terms of themselves. If a parent misbehaves, you imagine it's because of you. You have no perspective on their lives, the choices they made, or didn't make."

"Did you understand what was going on?" I query, trepidatious. I don't want to add to Mom's pain by revealing more than she already knows.

"I assume you have some insight into it," she says, and my worries fade. She must know. A moment passes while she ponders the past. "You know, their marriage was no worse than so many others. They were there, they loved us, they didn't abuse us. We had a home, clothes, and food, and we had Eleanor to boot, and she loved us too. There were good times and bad times. What they were to each other, well ... who knew? I never thought about it until I grew up. They didn't win any awards as role models, but we were basically okay."

"So ... it wasn't bad enough to explain James's problems."

"No, not at all."

"Did you understand about your mom? And ... and your father?" I realize neither she nor I have made explicit reference to her birth father, and for a moment I fear she doesn't know about him.

"Yes and no. It was never spoken of, my real dad, I mean,

though somehow it was no secret either. I'm not sure how that worked. It wasn't relevant. But Mom made a big deal out of it later, when we were fighting. She told me all about him, eventually. She came to believe it was her feelings for him that had caused … everything. She felt so guilty."

I can imagine her shrug. "Maybe she was at least partly right," I say. "I can't help feeling she never stopped loving him." I remember the way she brought out that framed picture of Rupert Dean to show me, from her bedroom, so tenderly.

Mom continues. "It's irrelevant. He died before I was born. In the war. It's easy to love a ghost. They're not there to demonstrate all their human frailty. It's natural to idealize them."

"But what if he hadn't died?" My stomach is in knots. I know I can't tell her that I found her father. Not before her mom knows. Not before I'm a hundred percent sure. But I wish I could give her something.

"Well, if he didn't, Mother never knew it. It wouldn't have changed anything. She was always so tied up in knots, second-guessing everything she did, all her motives and all her mistakes. She got to thinking she hadn't brought James and I up … the same. She worried that she never loved him as much, enough, and that somehow, he knew. That's the thing that seemed so crazy to me. I couldn't convince her she wasn't personally responsible for his death. That it wouldn't have mattered what she did. It made me so furious."

"I feel sorry for her. That's how I got started with all this, Mom. I really like her. I want to know her better."

Mom sighs heavily. I can hear little puffs of air from her nose. Then she sniffs, and I realize she's crying.

Tears spring to my eyes, my throat burning, my ribs squeezing tight. Now what do I do? Once again, I'm out of my depth. I feel so sorry for her, too, and guilty for forcing open a subject she'd no doubt closed the lid on years ago. "I'm sorry, Mom," I whisper.

When she speaks again, her voice is pinched in her throat

and watery sounding. "Father and Eleanor didn't help. They were critical of her treatment of James. Oh, not in any blatant way, but subtly, subversively. Maybe they suffered her emotional absence and transferred it all to James. They accused her of being too lenient and too strict by turns. Of spoiling me too. It's no wonder she doubted herself."

During the long pause that follows, I sit quietly. I sense she's not finished, and there's nothing meaningful that I can add. My own tears have ebbed away, leaving a tight ache in my chest, the skin of my cheeks taut. I listen to the rhythm of my own breathing.

"I should have defended her, not added my criticism to the heap."

"I'm sure she'd love to hear you say that now. Because everyone is gone, except for Eleanor, she hasn't been able to move on. Or maybe … and this is a weird feeling I have, maybe she refuses to let go. It seems like she has unfinished business and won't allow herself to live."

"Oh, Mother," Mom groans, and I can feel her regret, her pity, her sadness.

I wait for a long moment, steeling my nerve. I want so badly for these two women to make amends. My voice, when it comes, would fit snugly in a thimble.

"Will you call her?"

Mom barks, skeptical. "I'm glad you told me, but what would she say if I called out of the blue?"

"She'd be overjoyed!"

"I'm not so sure. I don't think I …"

"Even if you never reconcile with your mom, I deserve to know my grandmother." This sounds so selfish the moment it leaves my lips, but maybe, maybe it will motivate Mom.

"I'd still rather you came home, Sophie. Leave well enough alone. There's so much potential hurt here."

She's afraid. I want to help. "Do you want …"

She knows what I'm offering. "You seem to be on good terms with her. Maybe you could … somehow test the waters?"

"I could. I'm leaving town tomorrow for a few days with friends, but when I get back, I'll speak with her. Drop a hint. I don't know …"

"You'll find a way, sweetheart. I trust you."

After we say goodbye, I'm numb with all that's happened. I can't possibly know how Mrs. R. will react, and in that regard I'm grateful that I have the few days of my trip to Windermere to prepare.

The magnitude of what I may have done is rather awe-inspiring, but also terrifying. Maybe when I get back, I'll know even more. I sink down gratefully into the soft, worn recliner, going over the details of my conversation with Mom, imagining how I will explain it all to Mrs. R. Now that the anxiety of talking to Mom is over, my utter exhaustion returns like a tsunami. I can hear the clock, ti-ta-ti-ta-ti-tah. My tired eyes drift closed.

The next thing I know, I'm jerking awake with my heart racing wildly, flopped over in the Naugahyde recliner, gaping into the smug, smirking face of Sean Smythe bending over me.

"Good morning, sunshine!"

Bollocks!

CHAPTER 46

I sleep like the dead, and when I do wake up, it's to Zoë yelling from the living room.

"Sophie! Ain't your bloke coming over this morning?" She appears in my bedroom doorway as I drag myself upright. "Didn't you want me out of 'ere by ten?"

"What timezit?" I croak.

"Crikey, you look like shit."

"Thanks a bunch. The time?" I feel so groggy.

"Just ten. I'm off to meet Ollie at the jewelers. We're buyin' an engagement ring!"

"Crap!" I leap out of bed and race for the bathroom. I've barely got enough time to shower and dress before Marc-Antoine arrives. Her words finally sink in. "Where are you going?"

I hear her laugh, eh heh heh. "You heard me. Ollie got a promotion and a transfer to London. We're gettin' married." There is a beat of silence, while she waits for me to comprehend. I'm not sure I can absorb these new facts right now and stare at her with my mouth ajar.. "Right, then. We'll see you when you get back from your jaunt."

"Thanks, Zoë. Bye, sweetie!" I jump into the shower, which

hasn't quite warmed up yet. "Aahh! Cold! Cold!" Well, I'll be damned. A promotion, a transfer, and an engagement. What did I miss last night while I was wrapped up in my own problems?

Ten minutes later I'm towelling off. My swimming at the hotel pool and hoofing all over York has slimmed me down since the spring. I see my brows draw together in the mirror. Marc-Antoine didn't show any sign that he thought I looked sexy when he saw me Wednesday night. In fact, I don't believe he was happy to see me at all.

The self-centered scum!

A turbulent spasm of nausea curls inside me. As I'm drying my hair, an image of Meg Ryan in that movie French Kiss pops into my head, and how she wore that pretty blue dress to win back her deadbeat fiancé, and in the end, she didn't want him. The revenge was sweet. I can't decide what to wear, because I can't decide what I want.

Despite myself, I'm doing that thing girls do, and it bugs me. First the denim skirt and a yellow tank top, then the white blouse and two different pairs of pants get tossed on the bed in frustration, rejected. He doesn't even deserve to look at me, the turd! I'll be practical. I decide on the khaki shorts, so I'll be ready for the drive to Windermere afterwards, and because they flatter my new slimmer hips. Not that I care what he thinks. Argh! I'm annoying myself. Then I yank on a stretchy green U of T T-shirt with a scoop neck. Hmmm. I realize it shows off a little more cleavage than is appropriate for a morning meeting with one's deadbeat boyfriend, whom one is possibly—probably—going to cut loose. Humph!

Maybe he'll feel genuine remorse if he gets a good long look at the girls. Let him sweat.

I lean towards the mirror. No time for make-up. I pinch my cheeks and nibble on my lips to bring out some colour, like Grandma Groenveld taught me. I tilt my head, assessing the results. The shirt accents the green flecks in my hazel eyes and complements the auburn highlights in my dark hair. It's longer now than it was in May, and I wonder if I should wear it loose. I fluff it and turn my head this way and that. No. I tie it back into a simple low ponytail with a few loose curls.

I'm nuts. What a hypocrite!

Then I realize it's ten thirty and I'm out of time, so this has to do. I race around the flat tidying, which of course never occurred to Zoë before she left, while I chew on a bit of stale cake to suppress the loud complaints of my empty stomach. I fill the kettle. I'll offer him a cup of tea, at least. That would be civilized.

Glancing at the kitchen clock, I realize it's past ten thirty. He's late! Maybe he's not even going to show up, the deceitful creep.

I'm bursting with an irritated, riled-up feeling through my whole body, and I unclench my teeth. This must be fight or flight. I wish this whole situation with Marc-Antoine would go away so I wouldn't have to deal with it at all, and I could get on with my life.

Then I stand up straight and let that realization wash over me like a flood of clear sparkling light. That's exactly what I wish. That Marc would just go away. Hunh.

Then I think back to my conversation with Mom last night.

These days I'm inclined to give anyone a second chance.

Well, that means you're keeping an open mind, Sophie. That's all anyone can promise to do, isn't it?

I guess I owe Marc-Antoine that much, at least.

The sound of snarling dogs draws me to the open window that overlooks the front of our building. I lean out, and sure enough, it's Bubbles and Trevor kicking up a fuss. Our neighbour Raymond stands there, leaning back on Trevor's leash, holding him just out of Bubbles's reach, but allowing him his voice. It seems to stand in for all the things he'd like to say to Mrs. Leech but for whatever reason won't. Or so I imagine. Mrs. Leech has no such reservations, regaling Raymond with her opinions about his dog and their respective habits while he stoically listens and puffs away on his pipe. I chuckle silently.

"Good morning, Mrs. Leech. Hi, Raymond. Lovely day," I holler, hoping to break the momentum of her rant.

"Oh, 'allo, Sophie, love. How's tha doin'?" Mrs. Leech responds, all sweetness and light, as though she wasn't lambasting her other tenant.

"Fine, thanks. I'm expecting a guest any moment. Can you send him up if you see him?"

"Aye. Will do," she sings.

I smile and wave at Raymond once Mrs. Leech turns away and notice one corner of his mouth crook upwards around the pipe clenched between his teeth. A small cloud puffs from his pipe into the warm summer air, like a smoke signal offering peace.

Then, out of the corner of my eye, I recognize Marc-Antoine approaching a few buildings away. I draw back inside the window and watch him strut up the street. He's wearing dark sunglasses, his habitual skinny black jeans, and Doc Martens. I notice his exposed white T-shirt, because of the heat, I suppose, or else he would still be wearing a black V-neck sweater over it, which he wears three seasons out of four, like a uniform of designer cool. Suddenly, it seems rather contrived to wear only one thing all the time. Ridiculous in the summer weather.

Slung over his shoulder, he carries a leather jacket I've never seen before and two backpacks. I'm relieved to see, one is weathered, black, identical to the one he left with me at the hostel, except for the green ribbon tied around the side loop, marking it as mine. It occurs to me that he would have had to know he had taken mine within moments of sneaking out of our dark room. His cred plummets.

A few minutes later, he's prowling around my flat looking at things while I put the kettle on for tea. I busy myself with the tray in the kitchen, so I can watch him surreptitiously. He hasn't changed. He's still attractive and sexy, no question, but his looks and manners seem phony and pretentious, instead of captivating.

"So, you live here 'ow long?" he finally says, peeking into my green and taupe bedroom. His French Canadian accent still comes as a shock after so long in England.

"Since about a week after you left," I reply.

"How come you decide to settle down like this?" he asks.

I stare at him, incredulous. "I had to do something. You know exactly what it's like to be in a foreign country with no papers. No money."

He shrugs expressively. "You had no money?"

"I had less than twenty pounds!" My vitriol surprises me. I'd worked through it, but now that he's facing me, I realize I'm still furious. "Marc! You took my bag. My wallet and passport were in there. My train pass and airplane ticket. Didn't you look? Don't you realize what you did to me? I'm lucky I got a job." I march towards him and grab my bag, ripping open the zip and pulling things out and tossing them onto the coffee table. Except everything isn't where it should be. There's my passport zipped in the inside pocket, but no wallet. A hairbrush, a pair of socks.

"It was an accident, Sophie. I do not mean to take your things."

"Whatever!" The whistling kettle interrupts, and I stride to the kitchen, fill the teapot, and carry the tray back before I reply.

"But you left. And you did take them. And you still haven't apologized or acknowledged the shit I've had to deal with. Where's my wallet?" I shove my arm in my backpack again and feel around, dumping a few items of clothing out on the sofa in my search.

"I tell to you I am sorry."

"No, actually. You didn't. All you talked about on Wednesday night were your own troubles. Yourself. That's all you talked about. That's all you ever talk about."

He slumps down onto the tattered sofa with a heavy sigh. "You are so h'angry with me, cherie. You do not mean what you say. I understand."

I scowl at him. "I know what I mean. I can see clearly now for the first time in two years. I've been such an idiot." My fists clench at my sides and I have a strong desire to hit something. Maybe Marc.

"Non, chouette. Je t'aime." He drops his head between his hands, clutching his hair.

Two years of his smooth words echo in my mind, each address, each lecture, each endearment floats like flies in amber. He's so self-centred, so manipulative. Maybe that is what my parents saw and objected to so strongly. I always thought it was his artistic bohemian ways, but now I see it's not that. It's his character, his values … Perhaps at one time, he was good for me, and I loved him. He opened my eyes, taught me to see the world a different way. But whatever it was, I realize I've grown—and Marc-Antoine hasn't.

I flop down on the chair opposite him and irritably splash the tea into mugs, handing one over to him and sitting back with my own. My movements are jerky with anger. I take a deep breath to calm my voice. "No, you don't. That's horseshit. You loved that I was in love with you. You loved having someone worship you and listen to you preach, someone to make you feel like an intellectual god. Someone who would put up with you wandering off with all your cool designer friends and wait dutifully for you to come back." I shake my head. "Not this time, Marc-Antoine."

He sits upright. "Sophie, ma chere, you are cruel to me." Tears gather on his dark lashes. Marc-Antoine's unshaven face is deeply shadowed with his heavy shadowed beard. With his dark waves and aristocratic nose, he looks the perfect spurned lover. Handsome. Dramatic. It's a good act.

I shake my head in scorn. "What happened? Did Annika break your heart?"

His face parodies indignation.

I narrow my eyes to slits and give him a wry smile. "Do you really believe I'm that stupid?" I'm surprised how detached and cool and strong I feel about this. He really has no power over me anymore.

"You are not stupid. I come back for you!"

It occurs to me suddenly that he has all his things with him. Why bring a leather jacket and his full backpack along for a chat? He better not be planning to stay at my flat!

I point at his bag accusingly, my eyes darting over to his face. "You are not staying here. I'm going out of town for a few days. And even if I weren't, you're not welcome." I pour a little milk into my teacup and take a big gulp, licking my lips.

He tries to disguise it, but I can see he's disappointed, and more than a little worried. Then he screws up his face. "When you start putting milk in your tea?"

I scowl again. "Don't you have any money saved?"

His left eyebrow twitches involuntarily, and although he tries to peer intently at me with his dark eyes, his gaze shifts away and blinks.

I get a sinking feeling. I turn my backpack inside out, dumping all its remaining contents in a heap on the floor. My old toothbrush, a few toiletries. A notebook and pen. No wallet or tickets.

"Did she steal my wallet? My train and air tickets?"

"Erm ..." He leans back, absently plucking at the stuffing poking out of the sofa's arm.

"Marc? Did she clean us both out? Or did you sell my stuff to get by?"

He winces, deflated, his fine dark brows curling into pitiful puppy-dog brackets. His lips curl into a sneer. "Actually, her boyfriend, he take everything."

I close my eyes a moment and exhale. I'm sure the clever Annika had nothing to do with it.

"How did you get back to York? Where have you been staying?"

He looks chagrinned. "I hitch a ride with a guy, and he lend me a few bucks."

Crap! "So, you're flat broke. And our tickets? Gone?"

He nods.

"And you expect me to bail you out?"

"No! I come back to you so we can go home together."

"How?"

"I call my brother. He is wire the money to me in a few days."

I gaze at my passport on the coffee table, and realize I am free to go home, at last. But then I think of Mrs. R., Professor Dean—my actual grandparents!—my friends Zoë, Alan, and Nick. "I can't go yet. I have commitments." As if I would go with him, anyway.

"What? Your job?" He shrugs. "Just quit."

I shake my head. "No. I couldn't do that to Mrs. R. And I have friends here. I have things to do before I go home."

"I wait for you." He seems determined. He takes a sip of tea, makes a face, and puts the mug down.

"No—"

A knock rattles my door. I pause, rise, and walk towards it, opening it. It's Mrs. Leech, her face pinched with worry. "Was that other one the right one? 'Cause there's another lad come to see you and Ah thought 'appen I made a mistake afore."

"No. Thank you, Mrs. Leech. You didn't make a mistake. I'm expecting him too, it's okay."

She nods and frowns, dubious.

I glance at the clock. It's five to twelve. "This one is leaving now, Mrs. Leech," I say to put her mind at ease, in case she is imagining some sordid ménage, or perhaps worse, a profitable sideline. I glare at Marc-Antoine, in case he didn't get the hint. To Mrs. Leech, I explain, "That's Nick downstairs. I'm heading out of town for a few days, but Zoë'll be home."

Mrs. Leech purses her lips and heads back down the stairs to her own apartment, leaving the door ajar.

I go to the open window and wave down at Nick, who's leaning on an old beat-up brown Range Rover. He waves back, grinning. He's wearing plaid shorts, a baggy greenish-grey T-shirt, and aviator sunglasses. My eyes follow his long, lean legs down to worn loafers with no socks, and I laugh. He's not trying to impress anyone. I feel an irrepressible urge to get going.

I sigh and turn back to Marc-Antoine. "I have to go. Do you need money to tide you over for a few days?"

He responds with a Gallic shrug of massive proportions. His mouth works but he doesn't seem able to speak.

I grab my empty backpack and walk to my room to pack quickly for Windermere. Fortunately, all my nicest clothes are already laid out on the bed. Returning, I pull twenty pounds out of my new wallet, handing it to him. "There. That's how much you left me. Good luck getting home."

He slowly rises from the sofa. "So. That is it? You and me, we are finish?"

I peer at him for a moment, chewing my lip. "You decided that for us three months ago. And really, thanks for everything, but … adieu, Marc-Antoine." And good riddance.

CHAPTER 47

"Mrnphh," I groan as I'm bounced awake, cracking open my eyes and studying the peculiar view of the back of a fractured tan leather seat with its dirty mesh bag in which a wrinkled blue-and-white-striped jersey has been shoved on top of a weathered Philips road atlas of the UK. I slowly stretch and straighten, pushing myself upright in the back seat and blink at the low sun blazing through the windshield.

We're en route to Windermere in Nick's beat-up, dusty Range Rover. I peer at Nick, who's driving with a golfing visor shoved into his dreadlocks and wearing dark aviator sunglasses and he looks, well, weirder than hell. Like some whacked-out street bum from LA. Nothing contrived or pretentious about him.

A pop tune I don't recognize squawks faintly from the radio speakers. I swivel my head over and take in Alan, clean-cut and preppy by contrast, speaking softly, something about his thesis advisors at the U of T. It's making Nick laugh so hard it seems he's going to choke, and again I admire his perfect white teeth. It occurs to me these two are close in age and have similar experiences, though Nick, of course, hasn't finished his doctoral studies, and Alan has. In the time I've been sleeping, they seem to have become bosom buddies.

Noting my movement, Nick lifts his head and looks at me in the rearview mirror, though I can't see his eyes. "Morning, princess."

"Mm-humph," I reply, still groggy. I squint at the late-afternoon sun. "How long did I sleep?" My voice croaks.

"An hour and a half, about," replies Alan, twisting around to look at me, grinning. "You zonked out right after lunch. Feeling b-better?"

I stretch and yawn, considering. "I guess so. Jeez, I was exhausted." I shake my head. We left more or less on schedule, about twelve thirty, and I made it as far as Harrowgate for a cup of tea and a sandwich. Then I gave Alan a turn in the front seat and … that's all I remember.

I yank a white pennant out of a gap in the seat back and flatten it out, gazing curiously at a logo with red birds—eagles? —on it. Humph. "Where are we?" I shove the pennant back.

"Past Skipton," answers Nick.

I lean forward, between them, and their combined warm, musky smell fills my nostrils. "We missed Skipton?"

"We skipped Skipton, sleepyhead," Nick says, smiling. "Don't look so downcast. You needed your beauty rest more, and now we have more time for supper before I drop you off."

"I'm sorry, Alan. You wanted to see the castle."

"S'okay, Sophie. We had a little driving t-tour of the t-t-town instead. And Nick's been a t-terrific t-tour guide. He seems to know something about everything! There was hardly t-t-time to do it justice, anyhow. I'll come back someday when I've got more t-t-time, now I know what Yorkshire's like. Maybe I'll come visit you t-t-two."

Huh? I narrow my eyes at him.

Nick clears his throat. "Besides, we've missed you. We'd rather you were conscious during dinner." Nick chuckles.

"Why are you laughing?" I ask, suspicious. "Was I snoring? Drooling?" I rub my face for telltale signs.

Both men snigger and Nick replies, "More like mumbling."

Oh God! "Did I ... What did I say?"

Neither one answers. I glare at Alan, and he turns his eyes back to the view out the windshield, but I can see a dark flush ride up the side of his neck and onto his ears. Nick's shoulders shake silently. Crap! What could I have said in my sleep that's so embarrassing they won't repeat it?

Nick glances back at me. "Nothing much, Canadian. It was rather sweet."

"Oh. That makes me feel much better!"

"Do you want to sit in the front, Sophie?" Alan asks. He's trying to distract me.

It's hard to be embarrassed when you don't know what you've done to warrant it. I pull a tiny pair of Bushnell binoculars out of a side pocket and peer through them at the passing landscape. "It's okay. I'll stay here for now. How long till dinner?"

"We're almost at Settle, then another forty minutes to Kirkby-Lonsdale from there."

I study the countryside silently, and the guys resume their quiet conversation about thesis advisors who made them crazy. But I can hear it in their voices. There's a lot of pride and plea-sure in their reminiscences. I wonder about my own academic future. I've been accepted into the masters of English literature program for September, but to me, it's simply a vehicle for my writing career. I would be smarter studying journalism or busi-ness. Then maybe I could get a real job and support myself. My passion for books overrides, however, and I can always switch later, or become one of those university profs the guys are dissing.

We pass through a small town that seems all tucked in for the night, and before much longer, we approach another. Nick pulls off the highway and winds through the town. I examine the cottages and stone buildings lining the streets.

"There's a little place I remember, on the main street, and I wonder if it's still here." We drive around for a while, Nick peering under the sunshade at the shop fronts. He's ditched the visor and shoved his sunglasses up onto his tangled head, and the setting sun refracts through his green irises, making them catch fire. I sigh. I remember what I was dreaming of. It was another version of the Jorvik Museum dream I had at work the other night. There's something about Nick that's worked its way into my subconscious, and I wonder what I could have said out loud that made them both laugh and blush.

"Aha!" Nick exclaims. "There it is." He finds a vacant parking space and manoeuvres the SUV into it, and we get out. I stop and stretch my arms up to the dusky periwinkle sky. Shafts of setting sun pierce the buildings at the end of the street, laying bands of gold along the pavers.

"This is lovely," I say, looking around at the boxy two-and-a-half-storey buildings lining the street, dormers popping out of the roof at the top, most shops closed for the night, no lights in their windows. I follow Nick and Alan as they cross to the opposite side.

We approach a small inn painted creamy-white with black quoins and trim and white mullioned windows. An elegant burgundy arched sign over the door reads The Snooty Fox in gold letters. "Oooh!" Window boxes dripping with red geranium and blue lobelia dress the upper-storey windows. Up higher is another sign with a picture of a silver fox with his nose way up in the air. I laugh and point.

Nick scowls. "Well. They've fixed the place up. It used to be quite shabby chic. I hope the food's still decent," he says skeptically as we enter.

We pass by an oak-paneled bar with a chunky brown stone wall and dark timbers on the ceiling, into a more refined dining room with a pale green tiled fireplace and gilt-framed pictures and mirrors on the walls. We take our seats on tall dining chairs upholstered in pink gingham. It feels fancy. Hardly shabby chic. In fact, we are all badly underdressed, although the proprietor is friendly and casual and doesn't seem to mind. Not snooty at all.

It turns out to be quite nice, with a great selection of beer and wine, and varied dishes prepared with a lot of fresh local ingredients. The prices are reasonable. Nick and I both choose the lake trout, and Alan has roast pheasant. Nick entertains us with interesting historical anecdotes about the region while we eat.

"So, what's your plan when you get there?" asks Nick. He's forking the remains of his dinner, and it feels like he's avoiding my eye. "Dr. Dean is expecting you, I gather?"

Alan smiles and leans forward. He's obviously so excited about this visit. "Yes, Dr. Davison—the man from the conference—"

Nick nods.

"He actually t-t-t-telephoned him to say we'd be coming. I still can't believe it! And I have the letter. But in any case, our arrival won't be a surprise to Dr. Dean. I suppose if it was inconvenient, Dr. Davison would have said so."

"Hmm. Yes, I imagine. And afterwards?"

"Well, I'll have to get a t-t-train to London tomorrow afternoon. I have the schedule, and I'm hoping, midweek, midday, I can buy a t-t-ticket and get on."

"I hope so. It is peak of summer."

Alan shrugs. "Well. I've got a little flexibility, anyway. My flight's not t-t-till Thursday. But I was hoping to have one day in the city."

"Ask the proprietor of your inn to call and make a reservation in the morning," suggests Nick. He lifts his wine glass and takes a sip, peering at me slyly over the rim. "And you, miss? What is your plan, exactly?"

I purse my lips, suppressing a smile. "I told you. I have to play it by ear. I'm hoping ..." I sigh. The truth is I'm nervous as hell. "I'm hoping that by the time Alan's done talking birds, Dr. Dean will be sufficiently warmed up and familiar with me that it will be easier to ... to say what I came to say."

"Well, I don't envy you," Nick says. "It's a tricky business bringing news like that to an old man. You say he has no idea about Mrs. Roxtoby, or your mom?" When we'd first set out, Nick demanded to hear all the details I'd hinted at the night before, and so I'd filled him in on my growing suspicions that this was my own family, confirmed by my brother. He was suitably astonished.

"Well, I don't know what he knows, or knew, about Mrs. R. I'm pretty certain they've had no contact, though. So, he can't know about Mom."

He shakes his head. "I wonder how I'd feel after fifty-some years?"

"Dr. Davison said he never married, Nick. Think of it!"

"I am thinking of it. He's probably set in his ways and comfortable with his life. You're interpolating, Sophie."

"I know. And I'm good at it." He's right, though. I have to temper my enthusiasm.

"You could be wrong. Dead wrong. Take it slow. You could be turning the poor old gent's life upside down."

"Well, I expect I will." Nick's made his point. I now have a distinctly uncomfortable feeling in my stomach that I'm pretty sure isn't the trout.

"Promise me you'll do what's best for him." Nick rises, smiling kindly and squeezing my shoulder as he speaks, then excuses himself to the loo. I let out a deep breath.

Alan turns to me. "So, pardon me if I'm being nosy, Sophie, but didn't you say you were going home at the start of September?"

"Yes. I am. Now I've got my passport back. Marc-Antoine, of course, spent or lost my money, but I've got some money from my parents."

"But what about Nick? Are you going to leave him? Or are you coming back? What's the plan?"

"Nick? What's he got to do with …? Oh! You think … Nick and I are … Oh, I see. No, no, no." My smile is awkward and I shake my head, feeling a warm, self-conscious flush race up my chest and cheeks. "We're just friends, Alan. You must have misunderstood."

He peers at me with a queer expression. "Yeah. I guess. Does Nick know that?" Alan's fine eyebrows lift in query.

I laugh a little self-consciously. "Uh. Yes, of course." My smile fails me as Nick returns, receipt in hand.

"The bill's paid. Ready to go, then?"

I nod and narrow my eyes at him. Hmm.

CHAPTER 48

Our charming hostess at the bed and breakfast called and booked a train reservation for Alan, and unfortunately, the only time he's able to leave is twelve forty. That means we have about two hours for them to discuss whatever it is they plan to discuss. Alan has been nervous all morning and stuttered terribly through breakfast. I feel so sorry for him. My nerves manifest themselves in a queasy stomach and no appetite whatsoever.

We had to take a ten-minute taxi ride from central Windermere out to this tiny outlying village, which seems to consist of no more than a dozen cottages. Dr. Dean's is at the far end, set apart from all the others. It's a cute one-storey dollhouse with a hipped roof and white stucco walls, minute shuttered windows, and a profusion of pink and white roses climbing the trellised walls. It's all very trim. He either has a gardener or, more likely, is himself an avid one.

When Alan called Professor Dean this morning to arrange our visit, he seemed happy to receive us and asked us to come by around ten o'clock for tea, so here we are. Last night's nerves have amplified and I'm now a wreck as I hover at Alan's side, waiting for Dr. Dean to answer the door. Since Alan has so little time, we've agreed that I will wait in the wings until he leaves, and then have my own conversation with the professor afterwards.

Before Nick dropped us off last night, we arranged to meet tomorrow in Windermere. That will give us both time to do what we need to do. While he never said so, I have a strong suspicion that Nick has gone home to visit his parents in south Yorkshire.

We can hear mumbling and a shuffling gait approaching beyond the screen door, but he seems to be coming from the far end of the house, and it takes a few minutes.

At last, a shadowy image emerges on the other side of the screen, the outline of a moderately tall but slightly stooped man, with broad, rounded shoulders. He's wearing a heather-blue cardigan, despite the warmth of the summer day. Under the overhang of a small porch, we stand in shadow, but he is backlit by strong sunlight angling in through a window in his front room behind him, and the light picks up details: his sparse grey hair, combed neatly over; the bright blues and yellows of his Madras cotton shirt collar, crisply pressed; a glint of metal glasses frame. I have to remember that he's probably about seventy-one. As old as my dad's dad was when he died, although he seems fairly spry. We are in suspension as he pauses at the door, shifts a pair of pruning shears to his left hand, and fumbles with the latch. It takes him a moment, and as far as I can tell, both Alan and I have stopped breathing. The professor is mumbling what must certainly be a curse under his breath.

At last, the door swings open.

"Good morning. My Canadian visitors, I presume." He chuckles softly and amiably, and I relax a little. After we'd intro-duced ourselves, he steps back. "Come in, please."

"Dr. Dean. How k-kind of you t-t-to see us at such short notice," says Alan as he moves into the house. I feel like ducking as I follow Alan into the doll-sized cottage, through the screen door that Dr. Dean holds open, beaming as though we were his favourite grandchildren visiting. I swallow nervously, fist my hands and try to calm my racing pulse. He seems kind. I'm getting warm-fuzzy feelings right away. He certainly doesn't seem to resent our intrusion.

"Apologies for taking so long to answer the door," he says cheerfully as he heads back into the corridor. "I was in the back garden deadheading my roses." His voice is warm as honey, slightly gravelly, and comforting, his accent soft, round and refined, more like Nick's than what I've grown used to in York.

It takes us about the same amount of time to trail Dr. Dean to the back of his shadowy cottage and out the door into his garden as it took him to answer the door, me taking baby steps to avoid treading on Alan's heels. When we emerge, it's clear why he was hanging out back here. It's magical.

Bright sun floods the yard, and his garden is obviously his pride and joy. A small iron table and three mismatched chairs perch on a gravel patio in the dappled shade of two large birch trees whose bark is mottled and ghostly grey. He has already set out a plate of scones in anticipation of our visit. A pair of well-worn garden gloves rests on one of the chair seats. The garden itself is like nothing I've ever seen.

Nearer the house is a stylishly unkempt but cultivated area, with a profusion of flowers, many wild roses hanging with sprays of hips, but also tall, airy flowers like English daisies, cosmos, and bee balm, sunflowers standing sentinel against the side fences, spires of purple foxglove, and nodding columbine in a rainbow of reds, yellows, and violets. The air is alive with the sound of buzzing insects and boisterous birdsong.

I catch a breath in awe. Massive numbers of birds flit in and around a forest of saplings beyond. Fallen tree branches and logs lay scattered, draped with patchwork quilts of moss and lichen. Brownish-tan mottled birds peck industriously for insects among the cavities and cracks in the decaying bark. The air smells moist and fecund, acidic.

The most amazing thing of all is the noise. I have never heard so much birdsong in one place. Long high-pitched whistles, trills, and gurgles, tweets and cheeps and clicking sounds mingle in a constant chorus, as though they are arguing or competing with one another.

"It's so loud!" I feel like I have to shout to be heard.

Alan lets out a belly laugh of delight. "*Luscinia megarhynchos!*" he declares, cryptically. "Look at them all!"

I look but am no further enlightened.

Dr. Dean smiles and cheerfully recites, "'*A poet is a nightingale, who sits in darkness and sings to cheer its own solitude with sweet sounds*' … They are my faithful companions." He rests one large warm hand upon my shoulder and points to the brown and beige birds yanking beetles and bugs from the logs and damp ground.

Nightingales, I guess. Loads of them. What is he saying? That he's lonely? He doesn't seem sad. In fact, he's created his own paradise. How could he be anything but content? Maybe he likes his solitude, his avian companions. Nick's words come back to me—You could be turning the poor old gent's life upside down—and I suffer a flutter of uncertainty about my mission.

Suddenly, one more C-note rises above the symphony, a long, piercing whistle, and Dr. Dean says, "Ah, the tea kettle calls!"

"Can I help you?" I feel compelled to ask.

"No, no. Enjoy the garden. I'll be just a moment." He returns to the house with a sprightly step, and I suppose he'll manage.

I turn to Alan, gawking at the garden like an entranced slave, his mouth ajar and an ecstatic grin stretched across his face. After a moment he realizes I'm looking at him and turns to me, smiling, not saying anything. He blinks.

"How does he get them to stay?" I ask.

"Habitat, f-f-food. He's made it inviting and safe."

Dr. Dean returns with a tea tray and sets it on the little table. We take our seats, I choose the red vinyl and chrome kitchen chair, and he pours and passes milk and sugar. Conversation seems pointless, not futile but superfluous. Despite my anxiety, I know I have to bide my time, and I force myself to sit quietly and soak it up.

Around the edges of the garden are mounds of deep green shrubs, heavy with berries black and blood-red. Hummingbird feeders, with hunks of tropical fruit, and birdhouses of every size and shape perch on fence posts and hang from the eaves of the cottage, even nestle on the ground.

Once we've all had a few sips of tea and munched on sweet little currant scones, the bird guys talk passionately and animatedly for some time. I'm not actually listening to what they are saying, which, partly scientific and partly Latin, is over my head, anyway. But I'm watching Dr. Dean with interest. I can't think of him as my grandfather. Not yet. I could still, I admit, be wildly wrong about all of this.

In my mind's eye is the photo Mrs. R. had, the same one I took from Eleanor's room. I've stared at it so many times it's etched on my brain. Now, I try to compare that memory of a young soldier with the old man seated in front of me. Of course he is animated, and full colour, but I search for similarities in the structure of his face. The vaguely dark-shaded eyes in the old photo could have been this warm brownish colour, flecked with green and gold, I suppose. A bit like my own, in fact. The slicked-back wavy brunet hair could have thinned and greyed just so. His long straight nose and wide mouth seem promising, even though he exhibits the jowls and larger, fleshy, hairy ears and nose that one would expect on a man his age. I can't help wondering if this is what my brother will look like in another forty years.

What I characterized in the photo as the hint of a smile has, if this is he, become a ready one. He smiles easily and often while he and Alan talk, and even though he knows I'm excluded from their conversation, he beams warmly at me in a reassuring way from time to time.

After about twenty minutes, I ask to use the toilet and Dr. Dean gives me directions. I wander alone into his shadowy cottage, through an old-fashioned, tidy kitchen with a massive shiny toaster like a spaceship on the yellow-tiled countertop, into the living room, and down a tight hall to the tiny bathroom.

After I pull the chain on the tank, which is suspended high above my head, and scald my hands with the tap water and curse, I wander slowly back. All the appliances and furnishings seem to date from the sixties or thereabouts. Old and comfy, like Professor Dean himself.

In the sitting room, I pause and absorb the dusky still life. Many books and few pictures populate his home. A cluster of small frames on the fireplace mantel displays the faded mauves and blues of old colour photos. Upon closer inspection, men and women in their forties or fifties, with long pink collar points, plaid pants, and generous, wavy hairstyles from the seventies, some in academic robes, stand side by side, smiling for the camera, the stately college buildings of Cambridge, I presume, in the background. Those were the days. I chuckle to myself. I see no family pictures, so it must be true. No wife, no kids. I sigh.

Before my absence can be noted, I tear my curious eyes away from the interior of the cottage and return to the garden, where it seems Dr. Dean and Alan have hardly noticed I've been gone. They are deep in discussion about Alan's thesis now, and Dr. Dean is frowning and nodding.

I can't listen. I can't follow their conversation, anyway, but my mind won't focus. I'm tense and fidgeting, both anticipating and dreading Alan's departure. The time seems to drag. I stand up, intending to pace around the garden.

Suddenly, there is an eeeee-ohnh-eeeeeee! from the front of the house. The taxi!

"Oh my. The time!" exclaims Dr. Dean. "I wish you could stay longer, my boy. We've barely scratched the surface."

Alan rises. "I do t-t-too, Professor. But I'm so grateful t-t-to have met you in p-p-p-person. You've been so generous with your t-t-time." He thrusts out his hand in farewell.

Dr. Dean lifts himself slowly out of his chair. "This is only the beginning of a long association, Dr. Stapleton. You have my address." He grins at Alan's stunned, delighted expression. "I would like nothing better than to continue a dialogue with one of the leading analysts of the day."

Alan beams, his face quite pink with pride. They shake hands vigorously, and Alan faithfully promises to write with his contact information. He turns towards the house, then recollects himself and turns a chagrinned face to me. "Sophie."

I beam and move towards him. "Alan," I reply and move to embrace him. "I'm so, so glad we met up. And grateful."

"And I," he says as he returns my bear hug. "Good luck with your ventures," he says cryptically. "And I expect t-t-to hear from you when you're back in T-T-Toronto. Hope you and Nick sort everything out," he adds, sotto voce.

Hmm?

He squeezes me once more and releases me, grabs his bags that he left by the front door, and hurries out to the waiting taxi. I left my own bag at the bed and breakfast, since I'll be spending one more night in Windermere. Nick and I are to meet on the bridge in the centre of town late tomorrow morning. Nothing complicated. I wonder what Alan means.

CHAPTER 49

After Alan has gone, Dr. Dean and I return to the garden and sit down again.

"Did you build all of this?" I ask to reopen the conversation.

He smiles. "I guided it gently into its current form."

"How long have you lived here?"

"I've lived here for about seven years, but I acquired the cottage long before and spent many summers in the Lakes."

"It's so beautiful."

"Thank you. Do you like birds, Sophie?"

I hesitate. "Well, I have to say, I never gave them much thought, before this summer." Mrs. Roxtoby's eccentric hotel, her aviary by the pool, flash through my mind, but I say, "I found Alan's paper disturbing."

"Yes. Things have gotten much worse in the last forty years. Since the war. Industry, global travel, and massive consumption have all had their share of negative impact. I don't envy the younger generations their battles."

We are silent a moment.

"Have you any family, Dr. Dean?"

"Ah no. My father and mother died near the end of the war,

unfortunately, while I was away. And my sister long before that."

"You fought in the war?" I say, fishing.

"Well, not in the usual way, though I was looking for adventure. I was trained as a radio operator, and I was stationed in Sweden for a while, at the end."

"Wasn't Sweden supposed to be neutral?"

He chuckles. "Yes, well. Officially. But they helped the Allies more and more as the war progressed, in many ways. The Swedish intercepted German telegraph messages that traversed the country en route to Norway ... occupied territory?" He pauses, uncertain how well I know my World War II history.

I nod. I knew that.

"I was on a secret mission."

"Oh! Oh, really? That sounds intriguing. When did you leave England?"

He falls quiet and pensive, his thumbs tracing back and forth on his knees. Then he says softly, "I remember the day clearly. March eighth, 1945, ironically the day a V2-bomb destroyed the shopping market in New Cross. Not long before V-E Day, but we didn't know it then."

My heart is racing. I've struck gold already, no trace of doubt left in my mind that this is indeed Mrs. Roxtoby's Rupert. My grandfather! I scramble to collect my thoughts. "Um. Were you hurt in the bombing?"

"Not precisely. I was lucky. One hundred and sixty-eight people were killed by that bomb, and I had left the area nearby where I should have been, earlier than I was supposed to. Certainly, that rocket missed me by no more than twenty minutes. I had to leave town immediately, as I'd been given my assignment and was to board a submarine that was leaving port that night."

My pulse careens like a roller coaster as his story unfolds.

"How fortunate that you weren't there as planned, then." I take a moment to process this. This is too much information, too soon. My head spins. I stall. "So, anyway, you have no family left, then? No children?"

"No, no. I never married, regretfully." He pauses. "I would have, if I'd ever met the right girl. Almost did once ..."

I gulp for air.

"... to a graduate student of mine, a lovely Australian lady."

Oh!

"But ... she was too young for me, really. And she would go home to Adelaide."

So. He did fall in love again. Of course. He was prominent, lived a long and satisfying life ...

He continues, as though without pause. "And a good thing too, in retrospect. It would never have done. At the time, I was smitten, but ..." He shakes his head.

"But ...?" I prompt, breathless with anticipation.

He twists his mouth sadly and shrugs. "I had a special girl once, when I was very young. But I lost her, in the war. It wasn't meant to be." His eyes gaze wistfully out at his garden, flicking, following the darting movement of the birds.

I wait, biting my lip, but he offers no more.

"Some fresh tea?" He rises slowly and shuffles into the cottage, adding, "A little snack is in order. It's past noon." He disappears into the kitchen.

I decide to follow. "Can I help?"

"No, no. But stay with me and tell me a little about yourself, and I'll prepare us something to eat. Marmite all right?"

I laugh. "Actually, yes. That would be nice."

He glances at me, a question in his eyes.

"I used to find it ... um ... unappetizing. But this summer I've tried it in a variety of ways, and I've learned to like it."

"Ah, I see. Yes, I suppose it's an acquired taste. During times of deprivation, it was a wonderful treat. But you're a novice."

I smile. "Yes, definitely."

"Well then, I know just the thing." He pulls out a loaf of country bread and carefully cuts perfect thin slices, dropping them into his Art Deco toaster. By the time he's made a fresh pot of tea, the toast is ready and he butters it generously and then spreads a fine gloss of Marmite over the butter. It pools like an oil slick. He hands me mine on a small plate, his eyes twinking in expectation. "Try this then." He nods, knowingly. "Quickly, while it's still hot."

R*ecipe for yummy midafternoon snack:*
   Slice of country bread, toasted
Soaked with melted butter
Very thin spread of Marmite

I sink my teeth into the hot, buttery, salty treat. "Mmmm!" I chew and swallow. "I see what you mean. It's really delicious this way."

He chuckles and takes a bite of his own, then slices a cucumber and offers me some. "Still my favourite. It always reminds me of special family times. I guess you'd call it comfort food. So, Canada. Where from? Tell me about your family."

Cautiously, I do, and we chat and eat for a while, standing at the kitchen counter. Then he clears up our dishes and leads me back into the yard.

"Have you time for a stroll?" he asks.

I nod. "I'm spending tonight in Windermere, and my friend's picking me up at the bridge at eleven tomorrow."

He smiles and turns towards the rear of his wilderness, leading me through it, walking slowly, seeming to place his feet carefully while he watches the ground. I follow, mimicking his care and trying not to tread where he hasn't.

I step forward, transported, into the fantasy landscape he's created on the edge of this tiny village. Farther from the house, his long yard stretches into the Cumbrian wilderness. Thick clumps of young willow and hazel shoots sprout from massive, humped stumps covered with ferns. Primroses, and patches of bluebells decorate a vivid green cloth of moss—like banquets for the gods.

The ground is uneven, with mossy rocks and hollows where water pools, mirroring shards of sunlight and the garden's rainbow of colour. When we get to the coppiced willows, the ground becomes soft and squishy, and moisture seeps into my sandals.

"It's boggy," I observe.

"Yes, in spots. It helps the wood decay and harbours the insects that feed the nightingales and others."

"An ecosystem."

"Yes. A little one, within my sphere of influence. Let's go beyond."

Farther from the house are larger, older trees—oaks, I think —that provide solid shade. Everywhere else the sun is bright and dappled. Beyond the oaks, the outline of the fells stretches into the distance under a clear blue sky. He leads me past the oaks, where several small worn hiking trails branch off, and he heads along one of them. I follow, single file, because it's quite narrow.

"Ah. I'm so enjoying your company I forgot why you came, my dear. Your grandfather, you said? Who was he?"

"Oh, yes." I hesitate. Should I stretch this out or jump right in? My chest squeezes with anxiety, pulse accelerating, now that the moment has arrived. I rub my sweaty palms on my pants and scan the horizon. Either way, it seems really bad. Will he be shocked? Angry? Offended?

He pauses so I can come abreast of him, watching me, blinking.

"Um." A cold sweat breaks out on my face. I squeeze my eyes tightly shut. "Dr. Dean, I'm so sorry. I … uh, my grandfather never knew you. It was an excuse to meet you."

He purses his lips and nods. "I suspected as much, since I never got to know any Canadian soldiers well. I joined late, and then was stationed on a remote island. There sure were no Canadians on Öland with me."

I scowl. "Öland?" I realize I've been caught in my ruse, but I'm so confused, it doesn't quite sink in.

He chuckles. "The Swedish island where I was stationed. We intercepted encoded German messages in '45, trying to second-guess their V-bomb activities. It was really a problem by then. Stressing out the brass."

I continue scowling. Was that his secret assignment?

To my chagrin, his eyebrows lift, and a hint of a smile plays at his lips. "So. Your true reason for visiting me, dear?"

I wet my lips. "Yes. Obviously, I needed to meet you without revealing my purpose. I didn't know how you'd react …" I gaze warily into his warm hazel eyes, my breath frozen in my throat. I still don't, and I'm now petrified with fear. "I didn't even know if you were the right Rupert Dean."

"And I gather that you now believe I am?" I nod, and he continues. "How bad can it be, Sophie? I've lived a long time. It's difficult to shock me."

Skeptical, I swallow. Uh-huh. Well. How do I begin? "It's … Ava," I whisper, watching him closely, unblinking.

His face falls and he stiffens, his eyes glancing away from mine. I guess I managed to shock him, after all. His expression flat, he turns and continues slowly along the path in front of me, saying nothing.

I put one foot in front of the other, following him, my chest tightening. He can't want me here anymore. Perhaps I should turn around and leave. He walks and walks, and I am on the verge of tears by the time he finally halts, hesitates, and turns towards me, his face stricken with evident grief.

"She's gone, then?" His voice is a mere whisper. Then his brows bunch and his lips purse, puzzled. "How did you find out about me?"

"Gone?" Then I realize what he's saying, and gasp. "No! Oh

my God, no, she's alive and well." I shrug. "Well, she's okay. I work for her."

He slumps, visibly relieved, his lower lip trembling slightly. "Did she send you to …?" He shrugs. "To find out if I was still alive?"

"Ah!" I widen my eyes in surprise. "No! She doesn't know anything … anything at all. In fact, I'm afraid she'll be furious when she finds out what I've done."

He frowns. "How did you discover me?"

I sigh, click my tongue, and sigh again, my gaze sliding over the landscape. "I feel so foolish. I was certain this was the right thing to do, and now it seems absurd. I only … I was in, oh! Where do I begin?"

He turns his confused, pained expression away from me and continues along the trail, slowly but steadily up into the hills. "From the beginning, of course."

So, I trek behind him, talking to his hunched back as we plod onward. He's wise. It's easier for me to make sense of it all without looking into his face. I tell him how I found myself at the Aviary Inn, more or less. "It began with a photograph. And I had questions about my mom."

He turns his head to the side. "Speak up, dear. I can't hear so well anymore. In York, you say?"

"Yes."

I watch his fine white hair slide backwards up his skull as his forehead furrows. He speaks softly. "When I returned from Sweden at the end of '45, I'd heard she'd married a Yorkshireman."

"So you just stayed away?"

He nods, his eyes glimmering with pain still remembered, or perhaps fresh, thanks to me. He turns and continues walking.

"It was like a puzzle," I say, loudly, uncomfortably. "A mystery, revealed to me one fragment at a time."

"She calls her hotel the Aviary Inn?" He sounds dumbfounded.

"Yes. Apparently, she's always had a thing for birds. She keeps cages in the garden, and the hotel is full of taxidermy, art, textiles … it's quite famous, I guess."

"It's a wonder I never heard of it, in my line of work."

"Alan had. I suppose through some people at the university in York."

Some minutes pass as we say nothing. He's digesting, I suppose, and me waiting until he's ready for more.

"She did tell me about you, but she didn't say much. She believes you died in that bomb, because she looked for you and never found you then."

He continues putting one foot in front of the other.

I sigh. "And I learned a bit more from Eleanor. Her cousin?"

He nods and grunts.

"She's got a bit of dementia, and she talks to me in the middle of the night … I work the late-night shift." I pause, easing into it. "She seems to confuse me with … someone else. Someone named Barbara."

"That was my sister's name," he mumbles.

Ooh. This is hard. I'm such a coward.

We have reached the crest of a hill, and he pauses, panting from the exertion. The sun is high now and I'm sweating. I stand tall and gaze around me. The vista is breathtaking, more fells reaching out beyond this one. We can see Windermere the town and the lake stretching off into the distance, all blues and greens and gold. It's such a beautiful place, picturesque. I can see why the poets were inspired.

A small grove of oak trees grows beyond the lip of the hill. He looks around and spots a stump and a fallen tree a ways off. He hikes towards it with determination, and then turns around and sits heavily on the log, gesturing to the mossy stump without a word. I sit and peer into his face.

"Go on," he says.

"That day, in March 1945. You were going to meet her. Near

the shopping centre at Farringdon Road and Charterhouse Street. What happened?"

He nods slowly. "I got my papers that morning and had to be on the train by noon so I could get up to Tyneside in time to meet the submarine. We had to pull out under cover of darkness. No one could know. Top secret." He shakes his head. "I had no way to tell Ava. The best I could do was go to our rendezvous early. Leave a message and hope she got it. I was still within earshot when the V-2 landed. It came down at eleven hundred hours and a few minutes. We both ought to have been there." He shakes his head. "I believed she was dead."

"But you found out she wasn't?"

He nods slowly. "Much later. I was pretty sure she was killed in the blast, but I couldn't stop to find out. It was agony to leave like that. I was up there in Öland, grieving for months. After VE-day, when I got back to London in the autumn of '45, I looked for her and that's when I heard she'd got married, moved to Yorkshire, had a family. That was worse, somehow, for me."

"Did you believe she … decided not to come? That day?"

His eyes flatten with a deep, dull sadness. I guess he hasn't thought about this, never mind talked about it, for a long time. Maybe ever. "Not at first. We were very much in love. We were going to marry—there was no question. Against the wishes of both our families too." His nose twitches. "Well, hers in particular. I wasn't worthy. I suppose that's why I wasn't terribly surprised in the end. She was so young, easily swayed by them."

"You loved her very much, to let her go."

His shoulders lift almost imperceptibly.

"Afterwards, I had plenty of time to mull it over. Once the heartache dulled, and as I matured, it seemed rather sensible to me. I guess I'd have done the same if I were her. She made her choice. I assumed she was happy."

I remember Mrs. R.'s words to me not so long ago. *So much of what went wrong had to do with my inability to forget him. To accept that, however true our love was, it was not destined to be.* "But what if she did come to meet you and didn't find you there?"

"But my message …"

"After the explosion. What was left?"

He scowls at me, shakes his head. "After? What was left?"

"A dented birdcage. Two dead doves." I shrug. "That's all."

The sense of it dawns on him. "Perplexing for her."

I nod.

"She didn't find my letter?"

I shake my head. "Not to my knowledge. She didn't mention it. And she certainly didn't know what happened to you, except she thought it likely you were killed in the blast. So many others were. I'm pretty certain you and Ava were separated by sheer chance. Although it seems if you had both made your rendezvous as scheduled, none of us would be here now." Realizing what I've admitted, I hedge. "I mean … I would never have met either of you."

Everything is shifting for him. His face crumples and twitches as he scans the altered landscape of his past. "Why didn't she wait? Or look for me?"

"She did, frantically, as long as she could."

His eyes narrow. "Meaning?"

"She had to get married. She didn't have much time."

"I believed her parents forced her—"

"Well, I suppose they did. But she wasn't able to put up much of a fight … in her … condition."

I watch his face transform, his eyes flashing. Understanding and emotion flit across his features one by one. Mostly, I see a deep pain, a hopeless regret at what he lost. His eyes gaze unseeing, shining with tears; a tremor begins in his bottom lip.

I feel my own eyes burning with tears of sympathy. I inhale deeply through tight ribs, trying to calm my breathing, and force the words out through a convulsing throat. "What would you say if I told you that you have a family … a daughter and two grandchildren?"

"A daughter? But how?"

I lift a brow. "You've forgotten?"

A puff of laughter escapes. "No. No, I haven't forgotten." His smile falls.

He is puzzled and quiet for a long time. "So. You said Eleanor confuses you with someone named Barbara."

"Mm-hmm." I nod, giving him time.

He frowns and pulls a stiff, trembling hand over glassy eyes. "I'm overwhelmed. And getting confused."

I nibble my lip, my nerves taut and humming. I pray I've done him no harm.

"She named her daughter Barbara, after my sister?"

"Yes. I guess so."

"And you resemble her."

I wait, breath suspended.

"Are you her daughter? Is that why you've come to look for me?" He peers closely at my face then, scanning my features as I've studied his.

I smile tentatively. "I … believe so. My mom is named Barbara and was born in York. But Ava doesn't know about me, or you either," I add before he assumes she sent me on this mission.

I shrug and peer into his eyes. "It's something I had to do, Professor." I offer a tentative smile and take one of his hands between mine. "For all I know, any or all of you might slam the door in my face."

"You said neither of them know I'm here?"

"Mm-hmm. Mrs. Roxtoby … Ava seems as though she'd be willing to reconcile with … Oh!" I wince and shake my head. "You don't know about that either."

He peers a question at me.

"It's so complicated. And I shouldn't be the one to explain it to you. But basically, Ava and Mom have been estranged for almost thirty years, and … they … I think they want to reconcile. I think they might."

"Thanks to you?"

I bite my lower lip and glance at the view across the valley. "We'll see about that. I could be making a huge mess of things. It's just all so ..." I sigh heavily.

"Estranged for thirty years?" He scowls. "Why?"

I blow air through my lips. "Family stuff. I'd rather Ava told you herself."

He huffs. "I'm sure she has no interest in seeing me again. She's had a family, a long life. There's no place for me there. Not now, Sophie, despite your sentimental notions."

"You might be mistaken, Professor. I know she's never forgotten you. Did you know she was widowed years ago? She had a son, too, but he also died. And without Mom all these years, she's been so lonely. I know that in my bones."

He shakes his head sadly, placing a hand over his heart. "Aah. It's too late, Sophie, my dear. I thank you for caring, and for going out of your way to meet me and tell me this, and I'm quite delighted to meet you, dear, truly. But ... too much time has gone by. I don't want to interfere in her life."

Tears well in my eyes. "It doesn't have to be that way. Maybe you could be company for each other ... now. If you choose it." I smile hopefully. "And don't forget about Mom and your grand-children." My watery grin is full of optimism.

His expression is pained. I see a glimmer of hope, or yearn-ing, in his face, but he seems afraid. I guess he's keeping a tight rein on his heart.

"You need time," I declare, standing up. "Don't worry. I won't say anything to Ava. Unless I hear from you. Then, if you like, I can break the news to her." I turn and shuffle my foot in the dirt and dry leaves. "If ... if you want me to. Whatever. However I can help, I will."

He slowly rises, shaking his head. "Sophie, little sprite. I ... I don't know. I don't think so."

"Well ..." I swallow my tears and disappointment, and try for a bright tone, but my voice quavers tellingly. "I'll be around until early September, at the hotel, if you change your mind. And I can give you our address in Canada." I shrug.

I can't force him to want what I want. At least I found him. At least he wasn't married with another family. I guess I should have prepared myself for this, but my throat feels tight, my chest aches, and I turn and head back down the trail without another word. I've done what I can, what I came for. The rest is up to him.

On the way back down the trail to his cottage, we talk of other things: his experiences in the war, nature, my career aspirations, my family. He calls for a taxi and we loiter by his front porch waiting for it.

At last, it pulls up. It's the same driver who picked up Alan two hours ago. He opens his door and half steps out. "Ready, lass?"

Impulsively, I hug Dr. Dean, and he rubs my back with a stiff hand. "Goodbye." I daren't call him Grandfather. Not if he doesn't want us.

"Thank you, Sophie. You're a special young lady."

"Thank you, Professor Dean, for listening. For …" I shrug, breaking eye contact. "For accepting my meddling. And for tea," I add with a smile, fighting back tears of frustration and disappointment. "I hope I haven't"—I tilt my head down, frown and examine my toes—"upset you, too much, or …" I make a face, a fill-in-the-blank face, for whatever evil I might have inadvertently unleashed with my hopes and naive good intentions.

As I climb into the taxi and roll down the window to wave, he smiles, kindly but sadly, and raises one hand in salute, like a benediction. "Goodbye, my dear."

CHAPTER 50

*A*ugust 4, 1997, Windermere

*D*ear Mom and Dad,
   I'm in Windermere, in the Lake District. I really am! No faking this time. I've come on a short trip with a couple of new friends. It's so beautiful here. Marc-Antoine is gone. We've split up. You were right. Again, long story. But I'm fine. Better than ever. Please don't worry. I'll phone soon with news.
   Love,
   Sophie

CHAPTER 51

The bridge over the river in the centre of Windermere is jammed with tourists jostling to and fro. Nick and I agreed to meet at eleven at the stone bridge in the middle of town, but I had some time to kill. From my seat by the window of the Jam Tart Café, while I sip coffee and jot a postcard home and doodle in my journal, mulling over all that's happened, I think I see Nick out of the corner of my eye, but then it isn't him. There's a tall, handsome, sandy-haired guy who stands at the centre of the crossing for several minutes, searching the crowd, and I wonder if Nick couldn't make it on time for some reason and sent someone with a message for me. But then he leaves.

The crowd thins a bit. It's now noon and still no sign of Nick. It occurs to me that he may be sitting somewhere else, watching for me on the bridge. I'd better get out there. I flag down the waitress, pay my bill, pick up my bag, and scoot outside and onto the old stone bridge, where I stand in the middle for several minutes, listening to the rumbling rush of water below. Still no Nick.

Then the cute guy I saw earlier returns. He walks part way onto the bridge, gazing at the riverbank, then turns and stares back the way he came, peering intently into the crowd for a long time. He looks at his watch, then back at the crowd. I guess he's waiting for someone too. It's a popular meeting spot, smack in the middle of the biggest town in the most popular summer tourist region in England.

He's hot. Kind of a blend of all the things I like best in a guy. I remember to watch for Nick, but my eyes are drawn back to the stranger again and again. His hair is a shiny, wavy golden-brown that licks the collar of his nicely creased blue Oxford shirt. My gaze slides down past his broad shoulders and lingers. I love the way his dark jeans hug his trim backside. Casual, comfortable, preppy. Umm. Perfection.

Then he turns around and looks directly at me. I flinch and look away quickly, but he caught me staring. My breath catches and I feel myself blushing furiously. Then I sense him approach, and reluctantly look up, cringing inside, an excuse already on my lips.

"I… I wasn't—"

He doesn't let me finish. With a grin, he says, "Yes. Yes, you were. I saw you checking me out." He has a lovely BBC accent, just like …

Flustered, I blabber, "No. No I wasn't, honest. I'm looking for a friend. We're supposed to meet—"

He laughs, a soft familiar bleat, and says, "Hey, Can-adian." His smile is Nick's, his teasing green eyes the same, but devastating in a chiseled, angular clean-shaven face that I haven't quite seen before. Half familiar, half strange. "It's me."

My heart stops. "Nick?"

His unforgettable green eyes sparkle and laugh at me. "You were checking me out. Admit it."

"Nick!" I leap towards him, hands outstretched, just catching myself before I throw my arms around his neck.

His dreadlocks are gone, replaced with dark straw-coloured silky hair that's quite short, and the sun catches and glints off his shining waves. He's wearing one earring—a simple thick silver ring, on which is threaded a single jade bead.

"Holy crap, Nick! Your hair! What the hell happened to you?"

He chuckles softly, shrugging. "I was ambushed."

"What?"

He shakes his head sadly. "Ah, well. Let me tell you the tale."

We sit on the stone parapet flanking the walkway and I gawk at him while he talks. I'm fascinated with the way his jaw moves, and he has a tiny cleft in his chin I didn't know about.

"I actually slept in my car Monday night. Then I got home …" He hesitates. "That's where I went, in case you didn't know."

I smile. I had a feeling.

"So, when I got home yesterday morning, my aunt and uncle and cousins were visiting, everyone sitting at breakfast." He laughs. "They didn't know me at first, with the beard and all. I haven't … um, seen them in a while. Then … Dad and I had a long chat and worked out our differences." Nick's eyes slide away, gazing down at the rushing river, and I realize, despite his making light of it, how difficult this must have been for him.

He smiles and his eyes return to mine. "And then we all had a few Pimm's and lemonade and a quick round of cricket on the lawn, and then we had a few more." He grins. "And we drank a couple of bottles of wine with dinner, and were all sitting around after dinner drinking cognac, talking about my brother Philip, telling stories about all the crazy things he used to do … Anyway, long story short, I … I guess I passed out on the sofa last night." After the slow build-up, he delivers the punch line abruptly.

"You've been known to do that." I shake my head, meeting the comical twinkle in his gaze.

He rolls his eyes. "I don't know if I was set up or if it was the inspiration of the moment. All I know is when I woke up this morning, half my beard and half my dreads were … hacked off!" He gestures to his face, slicing it vertically down the line of his straight nose.

"What? Half? I don't believe it! Who—?"

"There wasn't much I could do at that point but finish the job. Mum says they saved as much of my hair as possible ..." He runs his hand through what's left of it, a mere inch and a half at most, ruffling it in the breeze. "But I don't know if I believe her. The others laughed and laughed." He shakes his head. "They were all in on it, I'm sure. Maybe Mum even put them up to it." His grin is lopsided and reflective of all the affection he feels for his family, and I can't help grinning back. I'm happy for him.

"Well!" I stand up and appraise him. "I really like it. I was getting used to you—liking the way you looked, although I didn't when we first met. But this ..." I nod with approval. "This I like a lot." I reach up and run my fingers through the soft waves that graze his collar. It feels nice. There's no trace of the tangled, woolly dreadlocks.

Telltale pink rises to his cheeks. "Yes, well ... I'll have to wear an itchy wig to work at the Jorvik Centre now."

His smile falters and he stares up at me with heat in his gaze and the ghost of an earnest smile that makes me respond with a blush. I drop my eyes as tingles race over my skin. Wow! This is Nick!

He stands and we walk and talk a little about my visit to Professor Dean, his disappointing reaction to the news about Mrs. Roxtoby, my mom, the fact that he has grandchildren.

"So will he agree to meet with her?" Nick asks.

I shrug. "It didn't look very promising when I left. He was quite shocked, of course. And Mrs. R. doesn't know anything about it yet. As far as she knows, he's dead. I suppose he could reconsider, but ..."

He nods, smiles enigmatically, and shakes his head all at once. "Well, you've done your best, love."

I laugh. "So have you," I reply. Ugh. I just batted my eyelashes at him. This is so weird. My body is hot and restless and wants to wrap itself around his. "With far better results."

"So ..." His mouth twists and his eyes slide to the side. "I can't believe I cut off my hair and shaved when you were finally getting to like my grunge look."

"Um. That's not exactly what I said. I meant … that I've grown fond of you despite your ugly hair."

"Oh! Very nice backhanded compliment, madam!" he exclaims in mock outrage. We laugh together and I stare and stare at him like I'm crushing on a new movie star.

"Stop looking at me that way!" He's blushing now. It's funny, the tops of his smooth, hollow cheeks flood with pink exactly the way they did when half his face was covered with a beard. Now he looks more boyish.

"I can't help it." I can't resist touching his hair again, it's so soft and silky, with gentle waves the colour of fox fur, gold highlights in rusty brown. "I can't believe what you were hiding under all that shaggy hair. You're gorgeous!" I cup his smooth cheeks in my hands and rub, feeling the soft, bare skin of his angular jaw. He really is gorgeous. I gape at his handsome face, at once familiar and strange, like bits of a jigsaw puzzle filled in. Then, embarassed at pawing him, I drop my hands.

His gaze on mine is intense, and it falls for a second to my mouth. He swallows, and his Adam's apple, newly visible, bobs up and down his lean neck. For a moment, I'm convinced he's going to kiss me, and a shiver of anticipation cascades over me.

"Well, my mother thinks so." He laughs and looks away, glancing down, his long brown lashes brushing his pinking cheeks.

"Your family sounds fun. They sound like they were really happy to have you back."

"Yeh. They were," he murmurs softly. "My mum cried. Hell, I cried." He glances away.

My throat clenches, and I swallow. I want to take him in my arms, he is so brave. "Well, even though I had a huge fight with my mum and dad before I left this spring, I'm glad I stayed in touch with them. In retrospect, they were right about Marc-

Antoine. It's a lot easier to go home when you haven't been too righteous."

"Well. You were right about me too. I have you to thank, you know, for straightening me out."

"Me? What did I say to you? I didn't know anything about you."

"Maybe not, but the things you said about Mrs. Roxtoby and her family, they seemed to apply pretty well to my situation too." He stands and picks up my bag. I follow him off the bridge.

"I realized that, with time, my grief and anger over Phil's death had mellowed, and my resentment towards my parents had as well. I figured, the same was probably true for them. We had both overreacted and were increasing our suffering by being apart."

As we stroll along Windermere's main street, looking in shop windows, cafés, and galleries, we are drawn into bakeries and cheese shops and buy yummy things, Bakewell tarts and country loafs and soft goat's cheese.

"And I also hoped that, maybe my father's position about my future had shifted with a little time and perspective."

"What did he want you to do?"

"Well, he wanted me to drop out of archeology for one thing, which I wasn't … I'm still not prepared to do. I'm going to finish my D. Phil. In his opinion, I'd had more than enough history and preferred that I change to business."

We stand in a shop, waiting to pay for some bits of chocolate.

"His principal concern has always been the family assets. It's quite a burden, these days, to manage large estates. But he's so proud of it. He doesn't want to lose it." He seems to be talking to himself. "But it's not just the assets. It's the business he's worried about."

I wonder what he means, but I don't want to interrupt the flow of his story. Seems they have a ton of money. "So … what did you agree on?"

Nick shrugs. "Well, I guess you could say we came to a

compromise. I promised to balance my career in archeology with an interest in the family business. I can do both, there's plenty of time, and Dad's agreed that I might do an executive MBA later on, if necessary. It's not like my old man is going to kick the bucket anytime soon. He's only sixty-three, and he's healthy."

"So, he doesn't really need your help yet."

"Right. Anyway, I accepted my responsibility, and he finally accepted that I have to do it my own way. That he can rely on me. I'm not Philip, and in some ways, it's a good thing I'm not. Dad despaired of him ever settling down. I guess Phil was even more afraid of the responsibility than I am. So, I guess we both accepted that, when it's my turn, I'll do whatever the hell I please, regardless.

More questions flood my mind. "What responsibility? Your turn at what?" Company president? Asset manager? Or maybe they're an old family with a giant trust fund. I don't get why it's such a big deal.

Nick ducks into another shop, effectively ignoring my questions.

The afternoon is mild and beautiful, and we decide to buy more food and make a picnic and get sidetracked choosing things that we can take away to stop somewhere on the route home.

We add wine, smoked Scottish salmon, pears and oranges, and sparkling water to our menu. I buy a tiny book of Wordsworth poems, and Nick spontaneously buys a lovely yellow silk hair band for me. I try it on.

"That looks smashing against your dark hair," he says, adjusting it slightly. The touch of his fingertips on my forehead sends a spark of electricity through me. It's so strange thinking about Nick this way. Precisely what "this way" means causes me to blush.

Finally, we drive off in his beat-up Range Rover, searching the map until we find a hiking trail that snakes along one of the lesser lakes and up over some gentle hills. We agree we're in search of a spot with moss-covered rocks, sunshine, and a spectacular view across the countryside. When we find the perfect place, Nick grabs an old blanket from the boot and we hike out for a half hour or so before settling down with our picnic. We eat and drink and talk away the afternoon. Nick feels like an old friend, but more than that. Someone special. My favourite person.

CHAPTER 52

We tell anecdotes from our childhoods, talk about our brothers, our schools. I'm not surprised to find that Nick went to a private, or public, as he calls it, boarding school called Shrewsbury, but he seems strangely reticent, as though he's leaving out important details. We discuss our passions and the inspiration for our respective careers. We enumerate our best friends from school. And now there's Zoë. We talk about movies and books we love.

The afternoon wanes and we hike back, but it's dusk before we get to the car. We stayed way too long. Nick drives a ways, but by the time we get back to the main road, it's late. We realize we'll never get to York tonight. "We can't do this. We'll fall asleep before we're halfway there, Nick. I wonder if we need to find a bed and breakfast."

"Do you have tomorrow off work? Can you spend another night?

"I'm okay. Mrs. Roxtoby said to take a few days." Once I concur, we stop at the next small village, but there's no place there we can stay, and carry on another while as it grows fully dark.

"I have an idea," Nick says. "I know a place we can stay for free and it's less than an hour's drive."

"I'm game."

We drive on, the headlights cutting swaths in the night. At a bend in the highway, he stops to read road signs, makes a couple wrong turns, has to double back, and finally finds the turnoff he's searching for. We drive down a dark rough lane and I wonder and worry. "Who does the property belong to? Are you sure it's okay? No big guard dogs?" I laugh nervously.

His chuckle is reassuring. "Don't worry. It's unoccupied. It belongs to my family, but I've been here only a couple of times before. It's a shooting lodge my father acquired a few years ago."

"Shooting! How quaintly British upper class."

His tone is dry as he says, "You have no idea."

We arrive at a locked iron gate behind a wall of tall grass and weeds. Nick takes a flashlight from the car and goes outside, fumbles around in the gloom, swearing. The feeble beam of light blinks and goes out.

"Bloody torch is dead."

Finally, he unlocks the gate, and we drive through, the long grass scraping the underside of his chassis. Then we get to a black, hulking building in the trees, which are silhouettes against the inky-blue sky. Seems rather large for a cottage, but then, this is England, not northern Ontario.

Nick gets out again and tells me to wait in the car. I'm trembling and stiff with tension and getting cold. It's creepy and I fret about staying all night in this strange, abandoned house. I scorn my silliness, but the nervous feeling doesn't subside.

At last Nick returns and says, "I found the key. Come on!" He retrieves my bag and his own from the back, and I follow him through an oddly wide, low doorway into a shadowy cold hall that smells of dust and wet stone. I stand in the pitch dark, waiting, staring at a ghostly mound in the centre of the room. The glint of a mirror on one wall reflects black nothingness.

"The electricity is probably shut off."

He reappears from the opposite side of the hall; I scream and jump. My pulse races.

"Shhh. Sophie. It's only me." He laughs and grasps my arms, rubs me to shake off the fright. "I have no idea where the main breaker is. It would take a while to locate it. Probably the basement, if there's even power now." We both shudder. "I would have to grope around in the dark. It'll be quicker to build a fire in the hearth."

I follow him into a large room adjacent to the hall. It smells of mothballs and oily wood. I can barely make out the hulking shapes of cloth-draped furniture in the shadows.

There is a loud clunk as Nick opens the damper. A gust of cold air and the smell of wet ash floods the room and fills my nostrils. He coughs. "There's some dry wood and kindling, at least." He gets a fire going, and the room is dimly illuminated by the flickering light. For the first time, I get a sense of its scale. It's spacious, the ceiling low and beamed. Heavy, draped furniture populates a wine-red patterned rug on a cold slate floor. I peek under a few dust covers, catching glimpses of solid carved wooden antique tables and chairs.

A horned demon on the wall over the fireplace glowers down at us with fiery eyes. I gasp, my heart in my throat. "Oh my God!" I realize it's the taxidermy head of an elk or large deer, its glass eyes gleaming in the faint firelight. "What is this place?"

"I told you, a hunting lodge," he says, distracted, poking at his fledgling fire, which is threatening to expire.

A real hunting lodge, like in books? "How old is it?"

"Hmm." He ponders a moment. "Not very old. I would guess about three hundred years? Maybe older, I don't know."

"Shite!"

He laughs.

"Older than Canada. How long has your family owned it?"

"Not that long." Nick's gaze is focused on his task, his face suddenly stern. "My father bought it a few years ago but hasn't fixed it up yet. He has dreams of breeding riding and racehorses."

"What? Seriously? Who the hell are you, anyway?"

He chuckles, his familiar dry bleat, and pulls a burning stick out of the fireplace. "I'm going to look around a bit, see what I can find, all right? Stay here." Like I'd wander off into the pitch dark.

A few sparks fly off the end of his torch. He stomps on them.

"Nick, be careful!"

"Don't worry, I'm not going to burn the place down. It's built of stone!"

"Watch the rugs, and … and the antiques! Christ, my mother would have kittens if she saw you."

I can hear his soft laughter grow fainter as his torchlight disappears around the corner and fades to darkness.

This is amazing. Racehorses! His family must be really rich. This place is incredible. And practically abandoned! Full of old furniture. Wouldn't Mom love to go through the place with her reference books and price lists?

He comes back carrying his extinguished torch under one arm, an old brass kerosene lantern, which he's lit, and two lovely old glass wine goblets with chipped, gilt rims. He tosses the stick back into the fireplace and sits down on the rug.

We snack again on leftover bread, cheese, and wine. Nick says there isn't any bedding, but we could go upstairs and find mattresses to sleep on or stay near the warm fire.

"I vote for the fire." I shiver, half from the chill, half from fear of spiders and ghosts.

He nods and goes out, returning in a couple of minutes with the old car blanket we used for our picnic outdoors, and drops it on the rug in front of the fire. Then he grabs the end of a dust cover, lifts, and tugs it. It billows, releasing a plume, revealing an old settee with heavily carved arms and feet, and threadbare velvet upholstery. After, he lays the sheet over the rug, pulling the blanket over it, making our bed for the night. We sit down and he nestles an arm around me and my nerves settle, leaving a low hum of excitement and anticipation. We stare at the fire a while, cozy, silent.

It's surprising how comfortable and safe his closeness feels as I inhale the smell of him, clean and warm. I feel like I'm floating on a cloud, calm but exhilarated.

He bends his face to my neck, below my ear, and whispers, "Has it occurred to you that you are entirely alone in an isolated shooting lodge in the barren Yorkshire Dales with a strange man?" The firelight glows warmly on his face, igniting sparks of green light from his eyes with each flare of the flame.

"Yes," I say, smiling. "That is precisely what I was thinking." His body shakes with silent laughter that I feel through his lean chest, pressed to my side. His face is bare and smooth except for the faintest scrape of bristle from the day, and I can feel his hot breath on my neck. He smells of warm cotton, wine, and musky cologne. No trace of dirt or straw. "Though the man is not so very strange," I murmur.

"Sophie."

"Yes?"

"I have a confession to make." He pulls away, and his piercing stare holds me in thrall. "You might not have found me very attractive until you saw me shorn this afternoon—"

I give a soft laugh. It's a little bit true. But not entirely. Something, many things, have drawn me to Nick from the first time I saw him.

"But I have fancied you since the first time I set eyes on you, outside the museum." He's whispering, his voice compelling and sexy, sending a shiver through me.

"Oh, really?"

"Oh, yes, really." He smiles wolfishly, moves closer, wraps his arms around me, and dips his head to brush his lips gently against mine. It leaves me wanting more, and I arch into him, meeting his darkened gaze.

Oh!

"Mmm. All that I dreamt of and more." He drags his tongue across the corner of my lips, and I shiver. He tastes of wine, sweet and warm, and I melt. I exhale slowly, my chest and throat fluttering at his tentative touch.

Heart thumping, I pull away a couple of inches, and say, "That reminds me, what did I say in the car, when I was asleep, that was so amusing?"

"Oh!" He laughs, and I feel his warm breath on my face. "You said, 'Come back, Nick, kiss me.'"

"No!"

"Mm-hmm. Nearly drove me bleedin' bonkers. Alan teased me mercilessly." He leans closer. "Your mouth makes me daft. It's like a decadent pudding, plump and tasty." He kisses me again, nipping my bottom lip in his teeth. "And sweet."

I can't help it. I throw my head back and laugh, and he steals the opportunity to drop a kiss below my ear.

"And your teeth. I adore your teeth." He grins.

"Nick, really. You're being ridiculous."

"No, truly. Your smile melts my heart. It's warm and gorgeous. You're gorgeous. I'm quite smitten."

I'm warm, all right, and getting warmer by the minute. My face is hot with embarrassment, and something more, snaking through my insides like melted honey.

"Look at those rosy cheeks. You're like Botticelli's Venus, womanly and soft and glowing." He reaches behind me and pulls out my scrunchy, then laces his long fingers through my thick hair, flaring it out over my shoulders, making me sigh, my pulse accelerating. "And your hair is spectacular. The colour of Carnarvon's Reach."

"What?" I gasp.

"My father's racehorse. His coat is a deep chestnut, like yours." In between his words, he reaches with his other hand to trace his fingertips over my shoulder. He's caressing me and planting kisses everywhere. My cheek, my neck, my collarbone. I swallow, panting. He unbuttons my shirt and follows his fingers down, kiss by kiss, button by button, until he's peeling it off my shoulders.

He's stolen the air from my lungs. My heart thumps wild and crazy behind my rib cage, thrashing to escape and take flight.

His hand slips around my ribs, and before I know it, my bra has disappeared. He lifts his head and quirks a smile at me, his green eyes dark and sparkling in the firelight. "You've even got wee freckles here, like a sprinkling of golden sugar," he says, and plants kisses on the rise of my breasts, darting his tongue out to lick them. "Look at them all! One, two, three …" He bends and feathers light kisses over me again and again.

"You can't count them all!"

"Oh, yes. I plan to get to know each and every one of them intimately."

Oh my. My breaths come faster and faster under his relentless onslaught.

"Dear God. The more I see of you, the more I want you." He dips his head, caressing and lifting my heavy breasts in his palms, licking and suckling. I swoon and lean back, and he lowers himself over me. Suddenly, hunger firing inside of me, I need to see him too. I need to feel his skin next to mine. I reach for his shirt, grabbing fistfuls, suddenly desperate.

Nick needs no further hint. He yanks at his buttons, tearing off his shirt. My hands find their way to his lean sculpted chest like magnets. His skin is silken, hot and smooth, with a sprinkling of hairs across his chest. My fingertips slide down his ribs to each side and he shudders.

Somehow, with his mouth again hungrily plundering mine, he pushes me slightly away and rids himself of the rest of his clothing and mine in mere seconds. His hand glides down my soft belly to the apex of my legs. My body trembles, arching, aching for him. A small whimper escapes my lips, muffled by our joined mouths, and he groans in response as he nestles between my legs, closer, exactly where I want him.

He hesitates, his mouth retreating for a moment, and

stretches to grab his jeans, rummaging in his pocket for his wallet and pulling out a condom. "Yes?" he whispers.

"Yes," I reply without hesitation.

He smiles at me, and I watch as he tears open the packet, reaching down to roll it on.

My pulse gallops like a racehorse for the finish line. I know what's coming, but I can't believe it's Nick who's inspiring these waves of hot passion running through my body, Nick who is lying me gently down onto the blanket and touching me intimately, Nick who is kissing and nibbling me everywhere, making me shiver and strain with delight and desire, forgetting myself in his embrace. Nick who fills me, making love to me like no one has ever made love to me before. Not just desired, but adored.

CHAPTER 53

Afterwards, we lie together, wrapped up in the dust cover like a pasty, close together, sharing the same hot, halting breaths. He seems to doze a few minutes and then stirs a little.

"Nick? I whisper.

"Hmm?" He's groggy, blissful.

"Tell me who you really are. What haven't you told me? I'm really wondering what you're keeping secret." I chuckle into his neck, and he squirms and bends to kiss me. "Are you a duke or something?"

After a moment of thoughtful silence, he laughs and pushes himself up onto one elbow. "I'm sorry to disappoint you. Not so high on the social ladder, although we are earnestly trying." There's a note of bitter sarcasm in his quiet voice. His smile falls and I see his Adam's apple slide up and down his stubbled neck. He pauses and I wait for what's coming, my breath stilled.

He draws in air, his chest lifting, sighs, and lifts guilty eyes to mine. "But not especially far down either. My father has been knighted, Sophie. A fact of which he's extraordinarily proud. And he's the owner of one of the largest equestrian supply companies in the UK, and consequently the world. And since my brother Philip died, I became the sole heir to his business and his fortune." He swallows.

My heart kicks into high gear. What is he saying? "His heir? You mean—"

"My father created his company from nothing, starting back in the early sixties. Built it from the ground up. We are its sole owners, all the properties, factories, stores. It's worth millions and millions. No shareholders. When my parents eventually kick the bucket, I alone will own the corporation, along with all the baggage of their splendid, manufactured existence."

I wince. "So, you're expected to run the business? That's not exactly what you want to do with your life, is it?"

"Um. No." He kisses me softly. "I've little interest in it."

"But … Tell me about your family, Nick. What exactly did you run away from?"

Nick sighs deeply, his eyes turning away, burning into the flames of the fire, glinting. "During the war, my grandfather invented a … a kind of widget for horses. A new kind of stirrup. He worked in the metal shop of a factory in Leeds his whole life, the simple life of a poor but happy man. But he was clever and inventive. He saw how things worked, and he fiddled at home and in the shop until he perfected this idea. But he never did anything with it."

Nick glances at me, his eyes flashing emerald, his face set in firm lines, the fire throwing hard shadows across his smooth cheek. "My dad knew about it. It was kind of a family joke, apparently, Granddad's stirrup. Dad took out a patent and, granted, without much support from the family, borrowed money to manufacture it. Who knew it would be such a hit? It sold. They had to expand. Broadened the product line to include all the tack, horse blankets—which my grandmother did sew. The line expanded to equestrian clothing, leatherwork. The money started pouring in." Nick sighs.

"But my parents weren't content with their success. Maybe it was the horsey set they dealt with—always rubbing elbows with the wealthy and aristocratic. Maybe they felt inferior." He shrugs. "They bought a big house they could barely afford in Huddersfield and sent us boys to public boarding schools as soon as they could. They were always stressing how important appearances were. Putting on airs. We had to dress impeccably, wear the right labels, drive fancy cars, employ help, use the proper manners and speech of the upper classes. They chose our friends for us, our subjects at school, the sports we played. It was all orchestrated.

"The company grew, and my parents began to socialize with their clients. Yay, we made it! Expensive holidays abroad. A big manor house. A yacht. A villa in Italy. Parties. Dad invested in other ventures and made even more money, expanded his own company overseas. We were moved to better schools, then universities. Wherever the elite went, that's where we were sent. That was our world."

"Je-sus!" All the air leaves my lungs like a deflating balloon. I sit up, staring into the fire. I glance down at his naked body, confused. I recall the nickname, thrown with some scorn at Nick's face. "And who is Tack?"

I can feel him shake his head and chuckle silently. "Tack was what they called us in school, teasingly derogatory at first, but it was mainly Phillip's nickname, and it still feels like it belongs to him. I've always hated it. I don't want his nickname, or his friends. Or his roles. I felt like everyone was constantly rubbing our noses in the fact that we're such ambitious social climbers. It reminds me how artificial it all is, all the posturing and privilege and prejudice."

"Aha. Tack. As in horse tack. I see. Christ, Nick. How can you keep such a thing a secret?" I pull the blanket up over my bare breasts and turn to look at him. He turns away, staring pensively into the fire.

"Well, I wasn't really trying to keep it a secret," he mutters, chagrinned. "I was trying to make it go away. Negate it somehow."

"But why? Tell me why it's so awful."

"Aah, Sophie. When Philip died ... he was ... different from me. Light-hearted, a popular playboy. Everybody loved him. He loved to jet-set, to party, but he partied too hard. Kind of desperately, like so many of those kids with too much opportunity and too much stuff and no purpose or direction. The lifestyle killed him. Or maybe he escaped because he understood too well. I think he buckled under the pressure to meet our father's expectations. For me, Phil's death was a double blow—I lost my big brother and my freedom in a single day."

I struggle to understand. "It sounds pretty intense. Didn't you have any freedom?"

"How can I explain what it's like to be born with such an albatross around my neck? Even though Philip was the one who was groomed for the job, it was always understood that I was his understudy and would contribute. I still had more freedom to do what I wanted, at least in school. I was always standing in the wings trying to make sense of it." Nick's mouth turns down. "Our father had orchestrated his success and we were part of his plan. I moved like a puppet, bewildered, doing as they expected of me, but it sickened me. I think I was a good student because it was the only way I could be myself. Earn something real." He laughs, a bitter sound, and swallows it.

"But it sounds like your dad worked for what he achieved, Nick. That's real. That's worthy, isn't it?"

"When I was very small, we still visited family and old friends. But as we moved up, we saw them less and less. It never felt right to me." He pondered for a moment. "Once, when I was ... I don't know, ten or eleven, I ran away from home and walked all the way to my grandparents' house. They wouldn't take me to see them anymore."

"Are they—"

He shakes his head. "Granddad's gone." He faces me, his expression earnest. "I can never say I'm not grateful for my opportunities. Especially for my education. I can't repudiate that. It's the snobbery. The elitism. The dishonesty that I hate. And the incarceration."

"But don't you have even more freedom than everyone else? You have money, obviously, and privilege. You can do anything!"

He laughs cynically. "Yes. Except be me. Except be authentic. The pressure to conform to my family's expectations, to the society they've aligned themselves with, to my peers, and to the damned company, is enormous. So many of the people I deal with are pretentious, mostly, insincere and affected, or profoundly dysfunctional. And they don't even know it!" His face is flushed and his voice is louder, more animated than I've ever seen him. "And it's not only that, you know, about being pigeonholed and constrained, it's also what I experience as an individual. My life! How people treat me. How can I be normal? How can I even know what it is to be normal?"

"What's normal, Nick? Do you suppose everyone else's experience is somehow uniform? That you and your kind are set apart? You already are who you are, Nick. You have your interests. Your genuine friends. You wouldn't even have these concerns if you were like those people you despise. Everyone belongs to a group. Many groups! Social class is only one. Religion, culture … people choose to identify with their own groups. Artists, intellectuals, political parties, whatever."

"You make it sound so simple. I think you're wonderfully normal, Sophie."

I give him a wry smile. "Why, thank you. I'll take that as a compliment, under the circumstances."

He laughs a little, his shoulders relaxing. "Now that is what I love about you. You're so grounded. You don't have any self-doubts."

"That is patently untrue. I'm the most insecure person I know."

"You don't seem so. You have no reason to be. You seem comfortable in your skin."

"And you seem comfortable in your skin," I reply. "It's one of the things I've always admired about you."

The fact that we're both sitting in nothing but our skin makes us snigger at the irony.

We're sitting up now, side by side, staring at the glowing coals and hot licks of amber from our fire. Nick gets up to put another couple logs on, and his tall, lean frame is silhouetted against the bright febrile glow. The firelight picks out red highlights on his golden-brown hair, like sparks. He's beautiful naked, and it seems somehow fitting that he's been stripped of all his defences, his disguise, his own pretensions on the same day.

Nick is quiet for a while, and I let him be. Finally, he's satisfied with the fire and sits down beside me, our bare arms brushing.

"I love the way you move. With confidence and power."

"It's the priviledge," he snarks.

"Hah. No. Your body is very beautiful to me." His response is a look so intense and focused, his lips parted, I know what he's thinking, and feel a blush unfurl over my cheeks, neck, breasts. But his gaze drifts inward.

"Last night, my dad admitted, after Philip died, he was suddenly terrified that I didn't understand what that meant, for me. He tried to drive it home by making decisions for me. But afterwards, he realized that he went a little mental over Philip, that he wasn't being rational or fair to me. He was more afraid for me than worried about the company or the estate, or anything else. He simply wanted me to be prepared."

"I can see that."

"Maybe so, but last year, all I could see was that he wanted to control my life. I had to prove he couldn't control me, by running away, by rejecting my family, my future, everything. But gradually, I've come to realize that this is who I am. I have to reconcile this part of myself with the rest. I've at least persuaded Dad to invest some of our wealth back into the community. To give back—to education, the arts, research, the environment, even small business development in Leeds and Huddersfield and Halifax. That's what I would do, and I'd be happier playing a role in the company if we started now. I have to reframe it. I had a vague notion that if I could cast off the privileges, then I could escape the responsibilities as well. But there's no escape."

"What do you dread most? What are you worried about?"

He turns his face towards me and peers deeply into my eyes. He seems grateful for the question. "I suppose it's that all my energy will get drained away being, you know, being who I'm supposed to be. So I won't have the vigour to pursue my own passions." His head tilts. "And the business aspects. Dad wants me to drop out of archeology and study business. I really don't want to spend my life doing that."

"So, hire advisors, an executive. You can still direct all the big decisions. You can be CEO or chairman of the board or whatever," I suggest.

"It's … not been done that way. It's expected that I run the show. It's Dad's baby."

"But why? When you own it, you can do whatever you want, right? Sell it, even."

He smiles weakly. "You're right. I guess I assumed because I didn't want the job, I'd naturally be really bad at it." His laugh is wistful. "But who cares?"

"You will be naturally brilliant at anything you try."

His voice drops to a whisper. "I could if you were there, to believe in me, Sophie. To help me with the big decisions."

My stomach twists into knots at his words, and I feel myself flush from my bare breasts all the way up to my hot ears. His words are both thrilling and terrifying. I laugh nervously. "Now don't be talking like that, Savvy. We've only just met!"

He laughs, his worries apparently forgotten for the moment, and he crawls closer to me on all fours, straddling and slowly pressing me back to the floor with his lean, hard body. That's all the talking we'll be doing tonight.

CHAPTER 54

Nick whispers in my ear. "Hey, Canadian."

I stir from a deep, satisfying sleep, and realize I'm lying on a rather hard surface with my head nestled on Nick's arm and shoulder. Everything that happened yesterday comes back to me in a torrent of rich, sensual, toe-curling memories and fluttering sensations. I turn my head to stare quizzically at him, the new Nick, his reduced hirsuteness and increased baggage, my lover. I sigh. It's an overwhelming amount of information to process in my bleary state.

"Sophie?"

"Mmm?"

"I have to get up. Can you lift your head?"

"Oh! Oh, sorry."

He unwraps himself from the dust cover we're tangled in and jumps up. "Bollocks! It's cold!" He leaps around and quickly yanks on his jeans and T-shirt and dances out of the room hopping on bare feet. While he's gone, I get up too, and it is cold. The stone floor is like a slab of ice. I guess the thick stone walls keep out the warmth of summer as much as the cold of winter. Or maybe only the former. This is England, after all.

Nick comes back and we finish dressing and restore the room

to its original mothballed condition. He takes my face between his hands and kisses me, possessively, smoothing my wild hair back with both hands. "You, my darling, look properly ravished."

I laugh and rake my fingers through my tangled hair, taming it into a braid over my shoulder.

"Shall we go somewhere for a good hot tea and breakfast?" he asks.

"Definitely!"

While Nick loads the car with our things and locks up, I stand in the drive and absorb the vast and melancholy splendour of the Dales. I'd heard about them, but the beauty of the English countryside never fails to awe me. Although the shooting lodge has a few old oaks and pine trees growing around it, the surrounding landscape is austere with grassy meadows as far as the eye can see, dotted with tiny white sheep, with rocky outcroppings and ridges in the distance. The green fields are carved up by swaths of stonewall fences, following no visible pattern, evidence of centuries of habitation. Such a little country, compared to my home, and yet so breathtakingly beautiful, and surprisingly empty.

The lodge itself, Nick has informed me, is clad in indigenous roughcast white Cumbrian stone, and the sills, trims, and porch made of local red sandstone. The roof is shingled in slate. It's a far cry from the stick and shingle houses we Canadians live in, even the brick-clad brownstones of Toronto. No wonder! It's three hundred and forty years old. We found a carved lintel stone that read 1658. Mind-boggling!

We drive all the way to Skipton before we find an inn, where we sit down and order a huge breakfast. Scones and Devonshire cream, poached eggs and toast. Sausages and hot tea.

We stuff ourselves and grin at each other like apes, our newfound intimacy curled like a contented cat between us. So much has changed overnight, and yet, I realize now how special and dear Nick has become. Despite his own troubles, he's the one who's been the most caring, empathetic, and loyal to me. The contrast between his quiet, unassuming friendship and Elliot's lies and posturing is striking. I'm humbled by how easily I was led astray by my perceptions of who each of them were, both their attractions and shortcomings.

"I was thinking …," Nick says lightly, and then his voice tapers off, and he sobers. "Sophie?"

"Yes?"

He squirms in his chair and his eyes dart around the remains of our breakfast. "Sophie."

"Ye-es?"

"Have you thought about Oxford?"

I smile a little. What is he getting at? "Well. It has a rather good reputation," I say, posturing a little, and cock one eyebrow at him.

His eyes close and he sighs. "Okay, I'm being daft." He grabs my hand and squeezes my fingers earnestly, and my heart trips into a higher gear. "I … Sophie, I really want you to stay close to me. I feel like we've only begun, and summer is ending too soon, and we're both going back to school. So …"

"Sooo …"

"Well, you could enrol at Oxford. Or if that didn't work out, you could apply to Brooks University. Or perhaps get a research scholarship to the Bodleian Library."

I frown at him. "My mind is reeling with obstacles, actually."

"Such as?"

"Such as … I hadn't any plans to do so. I'm already enrolled at the U of T for September. I wouldn't have a clue how to go about it. I don't know if they would accept me. I don't know if I could afford it. I don't know how I could stay. Do I have to go on?"

He presses his lips together. "Yes. But. All of those are minor, practical questions that can be easily answered or overcome. Tuition is free for UK citizens, and with your newfound grandparents, well … we'd find a way. What's important is … would you want to do it?"

I sit with my mouth ajar for a few minutes, blinking at the table. I guess I understand what he's asking of me. But I don't know the answer. It seems rather impulsive and overwhelming, though I do understand the impulse. I don't want to lose him, or what we've got, either.

When I lift my eyes to his, I see his fears and insecurities, his hopes, behind the surface.

I smile and reach across to take his other hand, meet his earnest gaze. "It's a really sweet idea, Nick. But awfully sudden. I have to give it consideration."

"Wouldn't it be lovely to go to school together?" he offers.

"It sounds lovely." I nod, nibbling on my lip. "But Nick. Until yesterday, I didn't even know who you were. Now you're asking me to … to change everything about my life? I know you didn't mean any harm, but our whole friendship is based on a lot of false assumptions on my part. How is what you did to me fundamentally different from what Elliot did?"

Nick's brows knit together, and he opens his mouth. "Sophie! It's not the same thing at all. I didn't mean to deceive you. I only kept the details to myself. It wasn't because of you either. I was … not dealing with my reality. I certainly wasn't trying to impress you."

"No. You were trying to un-impress me." I laugh.

His mouth quirks in a reluctant half-smile. "But darling, you're so much more than a friend to me."

Our gazes lock across the table, and heat suffuses my face, neck, and body as I think of all the ways he means.

"Anyway." I clear my throat and continue, "The point is, I need time to get used to you and what knowing you means."

His elegant jaw juts and he gnaws on his lips for a minute or two, gestures that still seem unfamiliar with his face now exposed. "See. That's it right there. Exactly what I despise."

"You're right," I concede. "That's unfair. I wouldn't necessarily place that much importance on a guy's family and future prospects at this point in a relationship. But that's the point exactly. I would think about it before I got too involved, never mind rearranged my whole life. No matter who he was. I need a little time to get used to the idea, okay?"

Nick tilts his head to one side. "You already know me, Sophie. Nothing important has changed."

I laugh through a tight throat. "I've only recently learned to stand on my own two feet. I don't want to be rescued by a prince so soon."

His quiet laugh is a cynical bleat. "Merely an absolutely loaded toff. Anyway. That's rubbish. It's I who needs rescuing."

"No, Nick. It's not only me. You've been through a lot, and you need time to get used to who you are too. You have to spend more time with your family, and I really need to go home and work things out with mine. Then, we'll see."

He is silent, breathing slowly. A little shaky. Then he says, "Sophie, I … I need you near me. I think … I love you. I can't explain how different I feel with you. I can be myself, and I feel as though I can handle anything. I want to be with you."

My heart squeezes tight with emotion in my swelling chest, and I look into his intense, clear green eyes, seeing a man I do know and I do trust. I'm humbled by his tender admission. A tendril of tenderness threads around my heart. Ironically, under his bohemian disguise, Nick was everything I was looking for and more: He's smart and ambitious, he's artistic and articulate, he's honest, loving, and loyal. And he's hot. I can't believe I didn't listen to the signs my body gave me and that I let a superficial impression put me off.

I feel as though I might be falling in love too.

What he's saying is so romantic, and yet … part of me knows it's not realistic. If what we're both feeling is real and lasting, then it can withstand a little common sense. "I understand how you feel, Nick. I feel the same way. I'm not saying no … let's wait and see how we feel in a little while. We have a month, right?"

He's such a gentleman. Such an Englishman. I can see a whole array of emotions flicking past his eyes—hurt, hope, fear, determination—but he maintains perfect composure. "All right. If you leave, I'll persevere without you, Canadian, but on one condition."

My face stretches into a smile, my expression opening in question.

"You must allow me to take you home and introduce you to my family before you go away. They need to know who rescued me from the dark side." His smile is broad and sparkling, teasing and affectionate. "I promise they won't cut off your hair."

I blow a pensive breath out before I smile, wondering if their ambition for their son would leave room for a middle-class Canadian girl.

CHAPTER 55

I look up from sorting a pile of receipts on the side desk back at work the next evening. I'm finally making some progress setting systems in place, so there can be a little better organization after I leave. I'd still love to set up the inn with an online booking system.

"Ava wants you." Teddy leans in over the desk and catches my eye, his own cool blue and unfathomable under wiry white brows pulled down like a visor.

"Pardon?" I say, setting aside my papers, my pulse kicking into high gear. She didn't discover where I went, did she? I glance at the wall clock. Eight forty-five. "Why?"

"Dunno," he says noncommittally, coming round to the office door. "I'm to relieve you so's you can have a chat." He shuffles into the office, avoiding my eye, and plops down onto a stool, flexing his stiff fingers in his habitual way.

I frown. Am I in trouble? Has she found out what mischief I've been up to? "Did she seem … angry?"

Teddy stretches his mouth down into a clownish frown, pensive. "Nay. Not especially."

I stand up slowly. Cripes!

"Go-o!" he barks. "She said right noo."

I flinch, startled by his tone. The muscles in my neck and shoulders tense, and I head out the door and scuttle down the narrow corridor under the stair, my pulse racing, wondering if I'm about to lose my job. Well, I must tell her about my plans to go home soon, anyway. I assume she's at her cottage or perhaps in the garden by the aviary, as usual.

Threading through the fading roses, shades of coral pinks, yellows, and white with curling sepia lips, desperately in need of deadheading, I come out past the aviary to a perennial bed by the pool where tall spires of delphinium are dominant now, their deep violet blooms fading into the shadows in the failing evening light, set off by clumps of white marguerite daisies that glow in the dark, little happy faces nodding encouragement. Yes, go on. That's right, go on. My hands are shaking. What could she want?

She's not by the aviary and not in the pool, and I approach the door of her cottage, which stands ajar. My chest squeezes, and I'm sweating. With no real provocation, I feel anxious about this, mainly because it's so unusual. When she has something to say to me, Mrs. R. often speaks to me casually as she passes by the front desk. Those times I've been invited into her cottage, I've already been back in the garden, by the pool. This summons seems ominous.

Possibly, it's because I know my own considerable confessions are long overdue.

"I'm in here, Sophie." Her raspy voice emerges from an open doorway on the far end of the changing room shed, a long, low pale blond building with a shingle shed roof, the half logs smooth and spotted with dark whorled knots. I always assumed the locked door at this end led to an equipment room for the pool itself.

I poke my head in and scowl in confusion. The space is cramped, filled with an old chest freezer and two refrigerators and shelving with glowing orange lights dangling inside glass cases along another. It's dim, the only additional light coming from a smallish, maybe forty-watt, bare bulb dangling from the ceiling. All this refrigeration, and yet the space is warm and muggy inside, and grimy, with a dense fruity smell. I curl my nose.

The doors of the old fridges hang open, but no light shines from within. On the shelves near the door sit a row of white plastic tubs, like oversized vitamin jars, with words printed in slanted block letters on them in black marker. Instead of chlorine, bromine, algaecides, and pH adjustors, the labels read: wheat bran, wheat germ, Heinz baby meal, glycerin, and honey. This certainly is no pool equipment room, but what the heck is it?

As I stand there blinking, Mrs. R. turns towards me and smiles.

"This is my bug room," she announces proudly. "Did you know that crickets cost more than five pence apiece?"

"Hmm?" I blink.

"Crickets. They're very dear. And there's no sense in purchasing mealworms when they can be bred so easily. I'd be destitute in a month."

Now I realize that on top of the mealy, sweet compost-y odour, there is a peculiar chorus of clicking, shuffling, humming sounds.

A light goes on in my head at last. "Oh. You breed your own bird food," I say. My skin crawls with the dawning realization that I'm in a tiny room crammed with insects. The unplugged fridges are insulated houses for the breeding of crickets and mealworms. I've seen her feeding them to her hardbills, but it never occurred to me that she breeds them herself. Who could have imagined such … my mind boggles, speechless. I shudder. Eugh!

"I'm checking on my eggs and babies," Mrs. R. says nonchalantly, opening one of the warm refrigerator doors and pulling out a shallow plastic box with a screen window in the top. I'm pondering if this is a way of incubating baby birds when she peels back the lid and shoves the interior under my nose, where my first sensation is of writhing sawdust. I feel my mouth pull tight in revulsion, but I make a vague, mewling noise in an effort to show polite interest in her hobby, or whatever this is. More like an obsession. The crawling mass resolves into a mealy, tan-coloured texture with tiny white worms crawling in it. Thousands of them.

She replaces the box, checks a few others, in which I can see worms of various sizes, as well as jars with cubes of green florist foam stuffed into them, and then turns to the chest freezer, lifting the lid. Inside there is another dim orange light, and on a shelf about halfway up are messy stacks of paper egg cartons. She reaches in and lifts one, opening it to reveal a million smallish jumping crickets.

The hairs on my arms and neck lift in response and I shuffle back, tucking my chin, and she laughs softly.

We don't leave the bug room too soon for my liking. Mrs. R. leads me to her cottage, and once inside, she scrubs her hands at the kitchen sink.

"Tea and a snack?" she offers.

I nod and sit when she gestures at the table, the knot in my stomach rolling over. If she's firing me, she's taking her sweet time about it.

While the kettle heats and the tea steeps, she whips up some small, neat sandwiches.

R*ecipe for quite delicious sandwiches:*
Two slices multigrain bread
Spread with soft cream cheese
Dijon mustard
Marmite, of course
Sliced tomato
Fresh cracked black pepper

· · ·

I t's another taste sensation. I pour milk into my teacup and add the tea, and while I'm nibbling and sipping, she's back in the kitchen. She has more of those big white plastic tubs, and she's scooping granular stuff into a bucket.

"Is that for the bugs?" I ask between bites.

"Oh, no. This is actual bird feed. I mix together chicken pellet, chick starter, ground-up almonds and other nuts, poppy seed, wheat bran, wheat germ, and some pollen, if I can get it."

I nod. I've seen her distribute this stuff into the little drawers, but I had no idea she mixed it all up herself, or that it was so complicated. I guess this keeps her busy back here. "You're really devoted to your birds. You dedicate so much time to their care."

She shrugs. "Oh, an hour or two a day. But I love it. My interest and knowledge have grown hand in hand over many years."

I hesitate, wondering if I'll be fanning the fire. "Was it Rupert who got you interested in birds?"

She glances up at me and blinks. "Yes."

I wait, but she doesn't say anymore. She closes all her tubs and pops the lid on the bucket. Then she brings a plate of sliced pound cake over to the table and pours herself tea.

I'm still wondering if this is about my snooping around, talking to Eleanor, or searching for Professor Dean. But I daren't ask. I try a slice of cake.

"I bake that for the birds too." She smiles at my puzzled response as my chewing slows down. "It's a tasty pound cake, but I add some soy protein, and when it's a bit dry, crumble it up and mix it about fifty-fifty with the powder. They eat it first."

"It's tasty."

"I guess you're wondering if I asked you to come so I could teach you about aviculture."

I shrug, but my pulse quickens. No kidding!

She takes a long sip of tea, sets down her cup, and sighs. "I received a surprise phone call from my daughter Barbara while you were away."

Shit! My eyes pop wide and I gasp. Mom phoned her? The cake suddenly sticks in my throat. My fingers fly to cover my mouth. It takes great effort to swallow. I attempt to wash it down with tea, choking a little. I didn't have a chance to warn her.

"You know … everything?" I dip my chin, wary, holding my breath, my gaze leaping to hers.

Mrs. R. refills my teacup, her face reposed. Then her thin lips twitch a little and tug upwards at the corners. "I know you are Barbara's daughter, yes. But then …" Her lips twist with mirth. "I suspected that already."

I sit up, the cake wedged in a hard lump in my chest. "Rose?"

She nods. "If I was shocked, it was then, when she phoned from the office. Out of the blue, suddenly, an outstretched hand from the past." She gives her head a little shake.

"So … all this time …"

She nods, her smile stretching, her grey eyes meeting mine with a mischievous twinkle. Would she have even given me a job if she wasn't interested in who I was?

"At first, I had her send you over out of curiosity. I supposed Rose was mistaken, and it was a strange coincidence. But …" She nods, twisting her mouth to one side, her chin wobbling. "The moment I saw you, dear, there was little doubt in my mind. You could not so closely resemble my daughter by chance."

She's not mad at me! I take a deep breath in relief and attempt a weak smile. My own eyes fill with tears, my chin wobbling. "Oh."

Her familiar rusty laugh rattles the air. "But I didn't know what you knew," she says. "Now, Barbara has told me everything."

I freeze. "Everything?"

She pierces me with her steely gaze. "Yes. Well, as much as she knew. She was a little vague on some points. She mentioned that you'd discovered her letters had gone astray, and how that happened."

"I hope you don't think—"

"That you've been investigating?"

"Uhm …"

She smiles. "Well, perhaps not. You have been quite proactive, though, I must say."

My stomach clenches. If she only knew. I swallow and drop my eyes, taking a long sip of tea.

"I can understand your curiosity, my dear, and am grateful for it. You have a warm, caring heart."

I nod. "My friends have pointed out that I … that I'm a little too ready to get involved in other people's business, but I can't seem to help it."

She reaches across the table and pats my hand. "It's a lovely trait. Don't you change a thing." She stares into her teacup for a few long moments. "You know, one might argue that people, on the whole, take too little interest in the troubles of their fellow men."

I glance up, meeting her eye steadily, and venture a small, grateful smile. Tears well behind my eyes. This is my grandmother! And she likes me.

Kindly, she deflects. "Barbara and I talked for a long while. It's … awkward, of course. So many years have passed." Mrs. R. shakes her head ruefully. "We both have tender wounds after so many years of estrangement, resentment, and mistrust. But we want the same thing. She said she'd like to come to England next summer."

Her elated smile is contagious. I feel my face stretch with joy. Huh. Mom managed to surprise me again.

Mrs. R. takes my hand in hers, squeezing. "I'm ecstatic, of course. Especially about being a grandmother." She wets her thin lips. "Between now and then, we'll talk, exchange letters and photos. Try to catch up a bit. I'm eager to spend more time with you as well before you have to go." She sobers, and her eyes glaze with tears. She presses her knuckles against her lips. "I don't understand how all this happened so suddenly, Sophie, dear, but I thank you very much for your part in it."

Tears sting my eyelids, flood the back of my tongue with salt. My lips wobble as I say, "I'm so happy for you both, Mrs. Roxtoby. This is what I'd hoped could happen. I meant to speak to you when I got back, but I guess Mom couldn't wait."

She pulls in her chin in mock offence. "Mrs. Roxtoby, indeed. I do hope you'll call me Grandmother from now on."

That's it. My control snaps and I'm full-on crying now, and of course she is too. After a few moments of outright blubbering and hand-holding, I say, "I'd love that ... Grandmother."

She pulls herself together and smiles. "So. I have my theories, but I was hoping you could enlighten me about these letters. I'm curious about this egg that's lain dormant for so many years, that you, Sophie, have somehow hatched."

My scalp draws tight. I knew it would come to this, and yet I'm not comfortable outright ratting on Eleanor. Pondering how I might tell Grandmother without being so specific, I drag my lips between my teeth, top then bottom then top, and brood, stalling.

She waits patiently. I'm not getting out of this.

I glance up. "Would you believe by accident?" I grin hopefully.

"No." She snorts.

I shake my head. "Well, it's partly true. Zöe mentioned the returned packages." I sneak a peek at her. "I wasn't certain my suspicions were correct for a long time. So I did nothing until I could somehow confirm it. Then my brother came." I shrug.

She purses her lips and nods. "He was here?"

"Yes, last week. But anyway, before that, one night I was visiting Eleanor in her room. She wanders around, looking for a snack, and sometimes she's a bit ... you know, confused. She calls me Barbara." I wince.

She squints and tilts her head to one side, smiling. "As I've said. Your chin, your nose and hair."

"Mm-hmm. Well," I continue, pushing a stray tendril behind my ear, "one night she was feeling nostalgic about the war years and showed me a box of old photos."

I take a long draft of tea, stalling. My suspicions about Mom and Professor Dean are so intertwined, how do I talk about one and leave the other one sadly buried? "I was distracted by a photo that I saw in her box." I look up, wincing. "Eleanor had a small photo of your, your … of Rupert Dean. The same one you showed me." I drop my eyes to my teacup. "I admit I was curious about him, and I suspected he was Mom's father, though I thought maybe she didn't."

Mrs. Roxtoby sucks in a breath and holds it. She nods for me to continue.

"And I wanted to know more. Of course." I fill my lungs, suck on my tongue. "Anyway, I finally phoned home, and when Mom called back, we had a long talk." I shrug. "I just wanted to understand, about Mom and James, about everything that happened to you. She'd never told us anything."

"And is that it?"

I shake my head. "No."

"Go on." She drinks her own tea, waiting. She is a patient woman. A few minutes can mean nothing to her.

I shake my head. "That's when she said she'd tried to contact you many times. That she'd written several letters, but that you'd never acknowledged them. Never contacted her. She was hurt. She … called you proud and … unforgiving."

Mrs. Roxtoby sits rigidly, but slow tears overflow. "There was so much she didn't understand. But the fault was mine. She was a young woman, and I should have trusted her more with my secrets."

"Well, I thought that was the end of it," I say. "But Eleanor was behaving strangely. She showed a peculiar interest in Mom's letter, and that made me wonder. I'd forgotten—that same night I saw Rupert's photo, somehow, a pile of old letters fell out onto the floor. I picked them up, handed them back … anyway, I didn't register anything at the time. Then, much later, I realized some of them were addressed to you. And belatedly, I put the facts together." I point to my head. "And became suspicious."

She is quiet for several minutes. "So, if I am to understand you, Eleanor has in her possession letters written to me, from Barbara, dated when?"

I shrug. "She said she started writing after Matt—"

A shuffling sound draws both our eyes to the open doorway.

CHAPTER 56

A crackling voice speaks. A hoarse whisper. "Here they are Ava. You can see for yourself when they were written." Eleanor stands holding a bundle in her gnarled old hands. She's wearing that blue bathrobe, her hair wrapped in a blue chiffon scarf, and rivulets of tears trace the furrows of her lined cheeks.

"Ellie!" Grandmother's eyes widen. "Come here, my darling."

Eleanor hesitates, holding out the bundle of letters in her gnarled hands.

"Don't be afraid. Come and sit down. We'll talk." She rises, pulls another chair out, and goes to get a cup for Eleanor.

Eleanor shuffles forward and stands by the offered chair, still uncertain. She glances warily at me, obviously uncomfortable.

I reach out and stroke her thin arm, and she sinks slowly into the chair as Grandmother pours her tea and sets it in front of her.

"Tell me everything."

Eleanor sets down the bundle and slides it towards Grandmother. "I took them. I'm sorry, Ava. I couldn't stop myself. I didn't know how to tell you, afterwards. And then they stopped coming."

Grandmother pulls apart the bundle of letters, glancing at the posted dates, shaking her head. She sighs deeply.

"It was Jamie …" Eleanor sobs silently, her rounded shoulders hunching further in her remorse. "I wasn't myself."

"I remember," Grandmother whispers. "We all grieved his loss, Ellie, but you most of all. No one can fully understand a mother's grief."

What? My heart, so recently soothed by my honest conversation with my grandmother, leaps in my chest like a startled bird, fluttering. Did grandmother just imply that Eleanor was Jamie's actual mother? Stunned, I let the implications swirl in my brain. That would, upon reflection, explain … so much.

I squint, baffled, but they are oblivious to my presence now.

"Even I, all these years, I knew Barbara was out there somewhere, living her life, having her own family. It was something I could live with. But you … you lost your baby."

"My baby, my Jamie …" Eleanor weeps openly now, and Grandmother has shifted forward to embrace her and stroke her head while I look on, dumbfounded.

Oh my God! Jamie was Eleanor's son? How did they pull that off? How did I miss it?

"I understand, Ellie. It's all right, darling, shush."

"I'm so so-orry, Ava. So sorry," she sobs. "It was unfair. I at least had William, and Jamie for a while. But you lost Rupert too. Barbara was all you had, and I took her from you." She is wracked by sobs again, resting her head against Ava's strong shoulder.

My breath is frozen in my throat, and a chill rides my flesh. I slowly rise from my chair and slide towards the door silently. Whatever they are talking about, it's not meant for my ears, yet I hover in the open doorway, mesmerized by the far-reaching implications of what I've heard.

"No, no. You forget. It was I who drove her away in the first place, my dear. That was my fault. I wouldn't tell her our secrets, and I should have. I should have."

"Will you tell her now?"

Grandmother nods, her chin rubbing up and down against Eleanor's headscarf. "Yes. What does it matter anymore? We're a couple of pathetic, foolish old women, Ellie. We were too cowed by our families, by convention. If we'd had the nerve to weather a little scandal, we all could have been happy."

"Perhaps. But you still lost your Rupert, dear," sniffs Eleanor, calming somewhat at Grandmother's words.

"Yes. But now we'll have our Barbara back, and her children too. Won't that be lovely?"

I sigh. What a week I've had. Life sure doesn't always give you what you expect. One lesson I have learned in my twenty-three years is that things—and people—are not always as they first appear. It often pays to wait awhile, or to dig a little deeper, to discover the truth.

I quietly slip away, wondering if I'll ever hear the details of their story. I doubt I could have invented so many twists and turns. Even with all that I'd uncovered, who could have foreseen that Eleanor and Mr. Roxtoby had a son together, and that Ava would have gone to such lengths to claim little James as her own? Wait until Nick hears all the latest developments. When he said I was fancying a romantic Gothic tragedy, he had no idea.

CHAPTER 57

Nick is hanging out after walking me to work, as reluctant to leave as I am to part from him. Teddy has long since ceased his glaring and loud sighing when he walks by, and now acknowledges Nick as part of the family around the Aviary Inn. Cook has thoroughly adopted him, bringing him tea and snacks.

Grandma Ava never protests, only smiling indulgently when she strolls by with kitchen scraps or stopping to chat, curious to get to know my new beau. I think they like each other.

Since we got back from Windermere ten days ago, we've been together every moment one or the other of us hasn't been at work. I meet him when he finishes at the Viking Centre, we eat together, walk in parks or along the river, and he walks me to work and lingers until he has to go home to sleep. I join him at his place when I get off in the wee hours and gently wake him. The welcome is always warm.

This has been an endless source of fascination and amusement for both Zoë and the guys in the band. Zoe, for her part, has given notice and moved all her stuff over to Oliver's, and together they're preparing for the big move to London in a few weeks.

"Did the management have any idea this was coming?" I ask Nick now.

"I've never kept my family a secret from them, so I presume it's always been a possibility in Alastair's mind." He's the director of Jorvik Centre, I've learned, and Nick's ultimate boss as well as mentor. "And he's the one who wrote the letter of recommendation to support my application for the Randall MacIver Studentship in Archeology from Queen's College, which he knows I won. So, he knew I'd be going back, eventually."

"Can you keep the scholarship?"

"Well, I'll have to tell them that I no longer have financial need, but the scholarship is primarily merit based, so I'll hold the title for two years, even if they cut back the funds. Or I can donate them back. I would have applied for it even if, you know, things had been different with the family."

He shifts his weight from one elbow to the other, leaning back against the desk at the Aviary Inn, squeezed inside the office despite my initial protests. Whenever a guest comes by, he turns around and shuffles papers on the side table, pretending to be working.

"They'll miss you at the museum."

He shrugs. "I suppose. But I told Al I'd like to come back afterwards, for a while. And my thesis will be based on research done here in York, so I'll be in touch."

"Are there other places you could work after you graduate?"

Nick leans towards me with a broad grin. "I could go to L'Anse aux Meadows in Newfoundland. Then you'd be closer to home while we raise our children."

"Savvy!" I uncross my legs and drop my feet, which I've been resting against his thigh, to the floor with a slap.

"Halfway between the grandparents. Who could argue?" He

laughs. He's been teasing me, carrying on as though we're always going to be together, despite what I said to him about needing time. He's almost got me convinced he'll follow me to Toronto, if necessary, though I know that can never be.

"Seriously, though, that would be cool. For a while."

Now, locking eyes with me, Nick pushes his lanky frame away from the desk and takes my hands, tugging me up out of the chair in which I'm lounging. He draws me towards him until our bodies are pressed against each other and leans his forehead against mine, and my core melts with molten heat. I shudder with instant desire. We are in that euphoric honeymoon stage of new lovers, when a glance sets blood boiling. I take a deep breath, inhaling the familiar musk of his skin, both thoroughly enjoying and trying to tamp down the hot and cold shivers, the melting, tingling feelings that his needy embrace, his sizzling gaze, spark in me. At this moment, it feels as if I'll never get enough of him, his touch, his attention and devotion. I know we shouldn't, but it's late enough that there's no one around other than Teddy, and we are tucked into a corner of the office, partly concealed.

Our mouths are fused, sucking, tongues grappling, and my legs are quivering jelly as Nick's hands caress my back, when I realize someone is standing at the desk looking at us.

"Ahem," I hear for the second time.

I suck air as I tear myself out of Nick's arms, eyes wide, my face burning with another kind of heat. Spinning towards the voice, I let out a yelp and slap my hand over my mouth. A whirl-wind of nerves dances and twirls from my stomach to my throat, and my hand slides down to press there, calming the sensation that my insides are about to take flight.

Professor Dean is standing at the desk.

"Professor!" I gasp, twisting to grab Nick's arm in delight. Spikes of adrenaline tingle through my body.

"Professor?" echoes Nick, not yet realizing why we've been interrupted. He turns his head to follow my gaze and jerks upright, stiffening and pushing me away when he sees the professor.

"Hello, Sophie," says Professor Dean.

A ridiculous giggle bubbles up out of me, and again I cover my mouth with a hand.

"Oh my God! Nick, this is Dr. Dean. From Windermere!"

"From Windermere?"

His brain is apparently being adversely affected by excess blood flow to his nether regions. I meet his dazed countenance, sending silent urgent signals with my eyes. He blinks.

I turn back to the professor. "I ... I ... you didn't call?"

"No." Dr. Dean chuckles. "I made a rather rash decision this afternoon ... called a friend to drive me to York. We've been out for dinner. If I'd thought about it too much, I'm sure I would have changed my mind."

As if he's had anything else on his mind since I left. "Well ..." I draw a deep breath, and it comes out shaky as I press my praying hands against my mouth, fighting the urge to either cry or laugh. "I haven't said anything to Grandma Ava about my visit. Because ... I didn't expect ..."

"I can't imagine why you would, my dear. After what I said." He laughs, and I sense both tension and excitement in the shaky tremors that emerge. "I've taken the bull by the horns. Life is too short. Carpe diem and all that." His face sobers, his eyes darting around the lobby. I realize he's nervous and unsure. "I hope I'm not too late."

I nod, my mind shooting through scenarios. "I'll have to go and break the news to her somehow. Can you wait? Um ..." I turn to Nick again, now standing at attention trying to look both innocent and invisible. I take his hand. "Dr. Dean, I'd like to introduce you to my friend, Nick Savile. Maybe Nick can show you around the main floor of the hotel while I'm gone. I don't know how long ..." I meet Nick's eyes, trying to convey both please and thank you with my searching gaze.

He snaps to attention, his face focusing on the professor's

with a swift warm smile. "Dr. Dean. It's my pleasure. Sophie has told me so much about you." He offers his hand, and the professor grips it and shakes.

"How do you do, Nick."

I place the Back in 10 Minutes sign on the desk, and Nick and I step out of the office and join him in the lobby. I smile nervously and slip through the bar to the garden as I hear their low voices make pleasant small talk.

"I imagine you'll find the avian motif at the hotel quite interesting …" I hear Nick say as I take a deep breath and slip outside. "I understand you recently—" I'm out of earshot. It's about nine o'clock. I know Grandma likely will be wishing good night to her birds at this hour, if she hasn't already gone to bed.

Sure enough, I see her silhouetted against the shimmering aqua lights of the pool and hear her soft murmuring words of affection.

As I approach, she's standing before the dove cage, watching the pair. She's introduced the new male, but he's perched far from Kythereia on a separate lower rung. She's fluffing her feathers, grooming and, it looks like, ignoring his existence.

"How's it going with the new guy?" I ask softly, not wishing to startle her.

She rotates her head towards me. "Oh, Sophie, dear." She turns back to the doves. "Well, it's hard to say. She hasn't attacked him at least." She chuckles.

"What did you call him?"

"Hmm. Well, I'm feeling optimistic, despite the stalemate, so … Ares again. Ares III."

"Sounds … hopeful," I say, fidgeting and glancing over my shoulder. My stomach clenches. It's time. "Um. Grandmother?"

She picks up the tension in my voice and turns towards me, a question in her eyes.

I inhale haltingly through a throat constricted with fear. My breath rattles reluctantly. "You know, I never meant any harm." I swallow thickly.

Her steely eyebrows jump up in surprise.

"I mean, you seemed so lonely. I only wanted to help, to fix everything. Maybe it was my own problems and needing to have some control over something besides my screwed-up life. You've done so much for me ..."

She places one hand on my arm. "What is it, Sophie? Out with it."

I try to meet her eyes, but mine cower and flinch. "Are you happy that I contacted Mom?"

"How could I not be happy? You've returned my daughter to me and given me a family to love." She takes my hand. "No matter what happens now, we get another chance." A promising sentiment. Her face is pink with pleasure, and it seems true that I've accomplished something worthwhile and good.

My eyes slide over to Kythereia and Ares III, still miles apart though they share a cage, and I'm filled with a mix of hope and foreboding. "Maybe I should have left ..."

"You're not responsible for our differences and difficulties, dear. I'm terribly grateful to you for your help. We needed the catharsis that you provided. You have a kind and generous heart. And you're so courageous. You have nothing to feel badly about." She places one hand on my cheek and then wraps her arms around me and gives me a comforting squeeze, but panic rises in me, closing my throat.

"But..." I grimace, struggling for the words as I draw away. Dizziness threatens to swamp me, and I am drenched with sweat, tingling and hot as a furnace. "I also found ... I went ..." What if Nick is right? Professor Dean may have come around, been willing to take a risk, but this could end in disaster, and it will all be my fault.

"Do you mean Eleanor? She'll be all right. Better now that—"

I push her gently away. "No. It's the professor, I mean ... Rupert." My voice breaks, barely above a whisper. As though this news could be any less shocking at low volume.

Her face arrests in confusion, and her grey eyes penetrate my fumbling. Her gravelly voice is barely audible. "Rupert?"

I bite my quivering lip, tears burning at my eyes, which I blink away. I watch intently for her reaction, my stomach churning. What have I done? "He's … he's in the lobby."

She reels, stiffening and throwing her head back, and I lurch forward and grab her arms, afraid she's going to faint. Then she laughs harshly, barking like a crow. "Oh-oh m-my, what did you say? I thought I heard …"

I nod, my face tight with dread. "You heard correctly. I found him. He's here at the Aviary Inn. Now." I swallow through my tears. "He's waiting to see you?"

She scowls, her head shaking back and forth in denial. "But he's …"

I shake my head. "No. He's alive. I went to see him last week, in Windermere."

"You went?" She takes a step back, then another. "Oh, no, no, no. That's not amusing. You're teasing me. You must be." She giggles, a most unnatural sound, and raises a hand to her trembling lips.

The tears I've been trying to suppress are spilling down my cheeks. I shake my head, pleading. "I'm sorry. I didn't know he'd come like this. I thought he wouldn't. I had no chance to warn you."

"But why?"

"To find you. To see you, of course."

Her mouth moves as if to speak, but either she can't form words or decide what to say.

"And," I say, "he knows about Mom and me and Matt. Maybe … I don't know."

"Yes, yes. I understand." She seems to be pulling herself together, though she's pale, as one might expect. She tugs back her shoulders and lifts her trembling chin, smoothing and patting herself, straightening her clothing, her hair. She seems to be processing that she's an old woman. "My goodness, my goodness, yes."

"I never meant to hurt you. I only wanted to help. Please forgive me if it was the wrong thing."

She turns a resolute face towards me, her thin mouth in a determined smile—though a little bemused, incredulous. "How could it be the wrong thing, my love?" Then she draws a deep, rattling breath and heads towards the French doors leading to the pub, stately as a queen.

My God, she's a courageous woman. I follow, full of trepidation, but also admiration. I walk as though my feet are not quite touching the earth, propelled forward as through a tunnel, uncertain what will happen next.

We emerge from the pub into the lobby, but Nick and the professor aren't there. Then I hear murmuring voices from the dining room, getting louder. My chest swells to bursting, my heart thudding against my ribs, pounding in my throat, and I can't draw a breath. As they come through the door, Nick in the lead, he looks up with a start, tensing, and I catch his eye.

Professor Dean steps forward, then freezes when he notices us.

Nick moves towards me, and we slide to one side silently, waiting. I catch a glimpse of Teddy hovering in the doorway of the pub, curious, in my peripheral vision. My breath comes fast and shallow, and my eyes sting, darting back and forth between them, forgetting to blink.

At first, nothing happens. We all stand immobile in the foyer, as though someone has snapped a still photo of the scene. There is no sound but the hushed hum of evening traffic outside on the Mount.

They stare at each other, wide-eyed, leaning forward a little. Gazing and gazing. I can't believe how pale Mrs. R. is. Like a ghost. Like she's seeing a ghost. "Ava," the professor says quietly, and forgets to close his mouth. I see the professor's eyes scanning Grandma, searching, I suppose, for the seventeen-year-old girl he knew. He lifts a stiff, veined hand and runs it through his thin hair, smoothing along his scalp. Suddenly self-conscious, I suppose, of his own advanced age. Trying to imagine himself through her eyes. Then their eyes lock, and after an eternity, his mouth twitches into a tiny smile.

"Rupert," whispers Grandma at my side, taking a small step forward.

Rupert rips his gaze from hers and steps towards the battered birdcage that's been resting on the credenza for over fifty years, as if someone pushed a button, and the film began again, moving at its proper speed. Lifting one hand, he rests it on the cage tenderly. "Kythereia and Ares died in the blast?"

She nods.

His bushy grey eyebrows lift as he turns his gaze back to her face. "Amazingly, we did not."

Her cracking laugh breaks the tension like shattering glass. "Indeed."

He smiles and says, awkwardly, "This is quite a place you've got."

She smiles enigmatically. "Let me show you the aviary in the garden. I have a new pair of doves I'm sure you'd like to meet."

He moves towards her, and she leads the way through the pub out the back door, her hand hooking lightly through his arm, like old friends.

I'm shattered.

Teddy emerges from the pub, through the passage where Grandma and Rupert walked, his eyes bugging out as he looks at me. "What the devil, lass?"

I smile and throw my arms around him in a spontaneous hug. I feel a torrent of laughter pushing up from deep inside, like a bubble of air rising to the surface of a previously calm pool, ready to burst.

The three of us stand there helplessly, then all of a sudden, I know what I have to do. It's as though an explosion of light has gone off in my head, and I'm filled with certainty and confidence. I run to the gilt birdcage and grab it off the credenza, heavier than I expected, racing after Grandma Ava and Grandpa Rupert yelling, "Wait!"

I hear Nick on my heels, cursing, "For God's sake, Sophie, what now? They need their privacy."

"You don't understand, Nick! Come!"

We exit into the garden to find the pair by the dove cage, Grandma explaining how her attempts to introduce the new male have been unacceptable to the female, that they refuse to mate.

I step forward, bringing the cage. "Move them into here. Maybe they'll like it better."

Grandma looks puzzled and peers at me.

My grandfather chuckles, takes the old cage from me, and hands it to Grandma to hold. I back away, standing next to Nick, still holding my breath.

He opens the tiny gate; it whines a little on its rusting, neglected hinges. Then he opens the larger dove cage and slowly moves his hand inside, cooing and coaxing the birds out onto his extended finger, first Kythereia, then Ares III, setting them gently into the old cage one at a time, saying, "There you go, love." As he hands the male in after the female, he says quietly, "Go on, mate, have another go at it. Last chance."

Kythereia sidesteps, shifting her tiny, clawed feet across the old wooden bar, making room for Ares III in their tight quarters as he settles on the perch and fluffs his feathers into place with quiet dignity. He purrs softly, and she swivels her soft, buff head to examine him with glossy, golden eyes.

Grandfather smiles wryly and glances at Ava, who closes her eyes. An expression of joy steals over her weathered features, softening them.

I feel my face stretch into a broad grin and glance at Nick. He grins back and slips his hand into mine, strong and long-fingered, familiar and good. My heart expands in my chest, filling my whole body with a warm flood tide, and all feels right in the world at this moment.

Nick breathes. "Huh. I never would have believed it possible." His hand squeezes mine. "I owe you an apology, darling Sophie."

I squeeze back.

His eyes dart my way, and when I meet them, mine flood with tears. I press my quivering lips together in a tremulous smile, then press my face to his chest as his arms wrap around me.

This was a gift. I knew I had no business feeling smug. I felt only relief and immense joy. This could have gone so horribly wrong. It almost did. But if I'd learned one thing, it was to have faith. Faith in the universe. Faith in people. And faith in myself.

You have to take risks. And you have to hope. And you have to believe anything is possible.

EPILOGUE

D*ecember 17, 1998, York*

Nick pulls into an empty parking spot in the small front lot of the Aviary Inn, and we lurch out of his old Range Rover and meet at the boot. He pulls out as many bags as we can carry between us in one load.

"I'll come out for the rest later," he says, and pauses. Our gazes lock and he smiles. "Ready, love?"

I nod quickly and sigh. "Unbelievably, yes."

He leans forward to kiss me quickly. Then again, more slowly, with a quiet hum.

It's been a long day. We left our flat in Oxford as early as we could manage, despite a last-minute meeting between Nick and his advisor, then stopping for petrol and snacks for the road before heading north. Still, it would have been only a three-and-a-half-hour drive without the unavoidable detour to see his parents, which added another three hours altogether. They'd never have forgiven us if we'd come to Yorkshire and failed to visit them, despite the fact one or the other of his parents pop in to see us at least once a month. Mrs. Savile loves to check up on us.

And driving conditions were less than easy. Though thankfully there was no rain today, it was a dreary grey day with strong wind gusts. I can see the fatigue around Nick's eyes, and I want to tuck him in as soon as possible. It's going to be a busy week, with both a wedding and Christmas celebrations, and so many people to catch up with.

We trudge across the wet asphalt, careful not to slip. It would be tragic to drop any of our load, which includes wrapped gifts and garment bags for our fancy clothes.

Under the familiar turquoise awning, Nick pauses on the stoop to free up one hand, and yards open the heavy wooden door with its fresh coat of pale blue paint, holding it for me to pass through. I smile at the new restaurant sign painted on the awning to the right. Avante Restaurant is very popular now, with guests and locals, and Mrs. D. has a new apprentice cook and waitstaff.

We manoeuvre ourselves into the lobby, releasing steamy breaths of relief into the warm, spiced air.

But before we can rest, of course, we'll have to greet everyone who's gathered. This is the first time my entire family has been together in one place since, well, since the summer it all changed.

Despite Nick's pleading, I did in fact go home to start my semester at the University of Toronto last year. And of course spent time at home with Mom, with Dad, and with Matt. Our respective busy schedules meant we couldn't sit down together until last Christmas. And for that reason, because each of our families had so much to work through, Nick didn't join us. It was hard to be apart for eight months, but we emailed every day and spoke on the phone every week, and our friendship only grew stronger with absence.

Until the spring. The moment both of us were free for the summer, he landed in Toronto, and it was my turn to introduce him to my family and friends, my campus, and hometown. I confess I preened a little, escorting my tall, hip, handsome British boyfriend everywhere. That was our honeymoon summer, when I worked only part time helping Auntie Em with the businesses, so Nick and I had all the time together we wanted and could finally lose ourselves in romance and passion.

It was also a kind of testing ground, to see whether our relationship could withstand the daily intimacy of cohabiting, family, and time. A lot of paperwork was done as well, too, since we were soon certain of what we wanted to do.

Nick helped a lot with the UK bureaucracy, but I was able to apply to Oxford on the strength of my University of Toronto credentials and my pending British citizenship. He might have expedited my admissions just a bit. I needed a student visa to tide me over since I won't get my citizenship until sometime in the new year. Sadly, this is the first year tuition is no longer free in the UK, but still, a thousand pounds is still far less than tuition at home would have been. It was all surprisingly easy.

Nick has been delightfully free of stress and anxiety since he's worked things out with his family. They've reached a compromise that Nick can live with, so he can finish his education and work in his chosen career, as long as he devotes a certain amount of time to learning the intricacies of the family businesses, alongside a new COO hiree. As Mr. Savile says, the secret to his success is hiring smart people you can trust, not holding tightly to the reins every moment. Eventually, it will all be Nick's, but barring a tragedy, not for a long, long time yet.

Now, we set our bags on and over the new lobby chairs and venture into the lounge, where voices and laughter clue us in to where everyone has gathered. As I pass, I cast my gaze back at the reception desk and office, my old haunt, where an unfamiliar dapper man in a maroon vest and black tie clicks away at a keyboard under the glow of golden light. He seems unbothered by our arrival. I sigh and smile.

Inside the lounge, my eyes adjust to the dark, woodsy interior, where sconces and candlelight flicker and illuminate the gleaming woodwork, decorated with holiday greenery, berries, and twinkling fairy lights, as well as the smiles that turn our way.

My face stretches happily as Mom bustles over, her ease and air of propriety still a little amusing to me, while mostly making my heart swell and my eyes tear up a little. She scoops me into a warm perfumed embrace, kissing my cheeks. Her lips are warm on my cold skin.

"Sophie, sweetheart." She sets me back, glowing with contentment, and turns to take Nick's cheeks between her palms, smiling and kissing him too. "Hello, Nick. Thanks for bringing our girl safely."

We've seen Mom a few times this fall, though she's been here in York since February of this year, leaving her businesses at home under Aunt Em's care. At first, she just came for an extended visit, to spend time with Grandma Ava, and to get to know her father. But soon she was drawn into the Aviary Inn and its workings, unable to resist her desire to fix and improve everything she saw and lighten Grandmother's load so she has time to hang out with Grandpa Rupert.

In Mom's vision, the inn would be all it had been in the fifties, and more, new and improved for the coming turn of the millennium. That computer booking system is now installed and running, and the inn is busier than it's ever been.

I scan the faces crowded into the cozy lounge, and it appears we're the last ones to arrive. My first target is Dad, and I descend on him as he rises from his leather barrel chair, setting down his drink, and we embrace and kiss each other. We haven't seen each other since mid-August, when Nick and I left Canada together. He looks happy, almost a little teary. I think being here with Mom is a big deal for him, and having me and Matt here might just be pushing him over the edge into blubbering.

Despite Mom's extended stay here, she and Dad are well on their way to reconciliation, but this is only his second visit. It turns out the separation had more to do with her general discontent, made worse by perimenopausal misery, than any true marital difficulties. She's happy now. Happier than I remember ever seeing her.

Nobody is quite sure how it's all going to work going forward. Dad's got years till he retires, so, presumably Mom will eventually return home to Port Hope and her own bed and breakfasts and antiques once she's satisfied everything here is running smoothly, and Grandma has permanent, well-trained management help.

At her age, Grandma really doesn't want to, nor should she have to, work anymore. Besides, though Grandpa Rupert basically lives here with her now, they escape to his cottage in Windermere frequently for a week at a time. I think maybe they'd like to stay longer. All the birds are an issue, since someone has to care for them all no matter where they live, and sorting that out takes time.

But those are details for after the wedding.

I move around the room, hugging and kissing my grandparents, who sit side by side on the settee, holding hands. They grip my hands too tightly, matching broad grins on their faces. They look a little drunk.

My brother Matt, and Alan, who flew over together, now hang out at the bar with Teddy, drinking smoky, peaty whiskies and listening to his stories, laughing.

"Ah, lass. You've come," says Teddy.

I circle the bar to give him a big hug and kiss, and he pours drinks for us. There's only one empty club chair, so Nick sinks into it and pulls me down onto his lap, wrapping his arms around me snugly. We fit together like a hand in a glove, moving as one, familiar and comfortable. The tingling warmth builds between us, and I think the sooner we retire for the night, the better. There are far too many layers of clothing between us. We might just have enough energy left to peel it all off.

Apparently, there are still a few registered guests at the hotel, but in a few more days, it will be closed to the public. Then, as we pitch in to tidy up, move furniture around to prepare, and help Mrs. Delicata in the kitchen, new guests will trickle in.

Wedding guests who will also be joining us for the holidays. Grandma Ava's younger brother Harry, who moved to Australia after the war and she didn't stay very close with, and his wife Bernie, along with one of their adult children. This is a cousin named Marvy, a few years younger than Mom, who she apparently knew existed but has never met. And Eileen, from London, the widow of Grandma's youngest brother Stuart, who died in his forties. Their son Pip will fly up last minute for the wedding but is apparently an important banking dude in the city. Divorced, no kids. Sounds kind of awful. I had no idea about these great-uncles and -aunts and cousins and have yet to meet any of them.

A few close friends of Grandpa Rupert's are flying in from all over the world, as well as a couple of his own cousins. Those who are still alive and can fly, that is. But that's academia for you. A very jet-setty crowd.

Why are all these people making the trek to the Aviary Inn to join my family for Christmas? Well, it's because of the wedding that will take place on Christmas Eve. The marriage of Ava and Rupert, of course. A winter wedding, in more ways than one. That was Grandma Ava's idea, and we all thought it was gorgeous and have thrown ourselves into the planning. Mom especially is in her element. It's perfect.

"Where's Eleanor?" I ask, suddenly aware that she's missing.

"Oh, she's about somewhere," Grandma replies with a smirk. "Probably napping." That's the other change that Mom has brought about. Eleanor is getting more care, a little medication to help with her memory, and goes out to socialize at an elder day care centre every day. She has a boyfriend, apparently. Maybe she'll even bring him to the wedding as her plus-one.

It's after eleven. The exhaustion of the day has caught up with me, and I feel a pinch and burn erupt from my heart to my neck, my quivering lips, my moist eyes. I sniffle and blink back tears.

Ever attuned to my feelings, Nick's arms tighten around me, and he turns his face into my neck, kissing the overheated skin and murmuring beneath my ear. "Had enough, love? Shall I take you to bed?"

I nod, and he heaves me up and stands, keeping his hands on my waist. "Well, folks. We've had a long day and shall retire. We'll see you all at breakfast," he announces on our behalf, and his caring grace and warmth fill me with a swell of pride and love. I'm so lucky to call him mine.

We slip out amid calls and murmurs of Good night, darlings, and Love you. I retrieve the key to our assigned room from Kent, the new clerk, while Nick heaves most of our luggage up the red-carpeted staircase and I grab the rest and follow.

Once we dump all our stuff in our room, we take it in and then stand face-to-face, gazes locked in amusement, not a little relieved to be alone together at last. We're surrounded by peacock feather–covered wallpaper, dark wood framed prints of exotic birds, and the antique four-poster bed covered in a luxurious rose-coloured velvet spread and embroidered shams. This is one of the rooms Mom has embellished, and it feels like we've entered a Victorian bordello. A slow, mischievous smile spreads across Nick's face, and I feel myself aping him. "We can get the rest from the car tomorrow, right?" he says.

"Mm-hmm." I nod, sidling closer, until my front is smooshed up against his, and his arms snake around me, his palms coasting up and down my spine and over my hips the way I love. Our lips are almost touching, our sweet, spiced rum–scented breath mingling, when I whisper, "If you have any energy left, I want it all for myself," sliding my hands up and around his neck.

He replies by kissing me, softly at first, then, with a satisfied, rumbling sound deep in his throat, firmer, one hand skating up to cup my nape, his long fingers digging into my hair, the other down low, pulling me in tight. I never get enough of him, and I deepen our kiss, tasting him, soaking up his clean earthy scent that I adore.

The long tiring day is forgotten as we scramble to remove each other's clothing, flinging it around the small room, our kisses heated.

Suddenly, we tangle our feet in the clothes tossed to the floor and stumble, tumbling together, until Nick catches us with a hand outstretched against the window frame. We stand together, naked, panting and laughing when the lights along the garden pathway and shimmering in the blue water of the pool flicker and catch my attention.

I sigh, turning to look outside, thinking wistfully of last summer, filled with anxiety, fear, hope, and discovery. So much has changed since then, in my family, in my life, and inside myself too. Now I'm calm, settled, happy. I'm no longer grasping to make sense of things or turning myself inside out to please others.

Nor do I need to fight to assert my own will or voice my opinion. I'm content to feel myself unfolding every day, learning, expanding, and accepting what comes. My curiosity, about people, the world, and my place in it, have only grown stronger, fueling my creative desire to tell stories. But now I don't apologize for it. This is who I am. There's no one else like me, and I like myself just fine.

I turn back to tighten my embrace around Nick, who makes every day so much better, when he pulls away. "Look." He gestures with his chin outside the window, and I turn back, peering out.

Standing in the open doorway of Grandma's cottage at the back of the garden, I spy Grandma and Grandpa both, who have also turned in for the night. But they've paused at the threshold, and Grandpa has swept Grandma Ava into a passionate embrace. They are kissing too, until his kisses drift down to her neck, and she tilts her head back, eyes closed, rapturous.

I draw away from Nick to slap a hand over my mouth, to stop myself from exploding with delighted laughter. "Oh my God!" I whisper, giggling and dipping my forehead to touch Nick's in shared delight.

"There you go," Nick says, chuckling, "That's how it's done," and mimicking Grandpa by burying his head in the crook of my neck, kissing and nibbling, while gripping me tightly and lifting me from the floor.

I squeal with surprise, and laughter rips from my throat as he steps away from the window and falls with me onto our bed, covering my body with his, his kisses roaming over me. Then we forget all about the romance happening out the window as we immerse ourselves into our own perfect love scene.

THE END

Thank you for reading Secrets at the Aviary Inn. If you enjoyed it, and would like to learn more about books by MaryAnn Clarke read on! Turn the page for an excerpt from the award-winning The Art of Enchantment.

Subscribe & Follow MAC!

You can get exclusive excerpts and inside scoops, and ideas that strike her fancy as well as a free novel by subscribing to her newsletters at:

https://www.subscribepage.com/maryann-clarke-author_book

AN EXCERPT FROM

THE ART OF ENCHANTMENT

A Life is a Journey Novel

CHAPTER FOUR

No sooner had Guillermo entered the salon than his brother-in-law, Paulo, approached him with an indecipherable expression on his face and handed him a glass of vivid garnet-hued wine.

Guillermo lifted the glass to his nose. "Eh? What's up, Paulo?" They had insisted he come for dinner this weekend, and after Bianca's oddly distressed phone call, he was anxious to know what was going on.

Paulo sipped his wine, dipping his long aristocratic nose into his glass, and peering at Guillermo over the rim with a twinkle in his dark eyes. "First tell me what you think. Then tell me what you're up to, *fratello*."

Guillermo shrugged and sipped. The intense flavors of wild dried cherry, plums, and forest fruit rolled over his tongue. Hints of spice, tobacco and warm earth. He swallowed and took a breath, letting the powerful tannins grab his palate. "Nice. Brunello ?"

"*Si.* I'm playing with the oak, and the aging. This is just out of oak. It's a little experiment of mine."

Guillermo nodded and took another sip, swishing and letting the bright ripe fruit flavors explode in his mouth. Paulo had real talent. He really would succeed in rebuilding the Cittadini

Brunello di Montalcino family winery. Guillermo wished his own elder brother showed some interest in restoring the home farm and vineyard, but his political career precluded all of that.

"*Bene*. Good work, *fratello*." This was a little joke between them, brothers by marriage. There had been a little rough patch, at the beginning, when Paulo and Pia first married. They were very different in temperament, Paulo staid and quiet to Guillermo's reckless and adventurous spirit. But now, they understood each other very well. They were two sides of the same coin, and tolerated… no, loved each other. Pia had chosen well. Guillermo was more comfortable with Paulo than with his own elder brother, Jacopo, who was more like Father, and not in a good way. Guillermo moved into the comfortable green salon and chose an arm chair, easing back.

"Well?" said Paulo.

"Well, what?"

"Tell me the truth about this woman you brought. It's a spectacular ruse to bring a friend for the weekend, but you know it's not necessary. Your…eh, *inamorata* are always welcome, despite Pia's…" Paulo gestured vaguely, and they both understood what this meant. Pia's pinched faces, rolling eyes, earnest lectures about his love life, his choice of women, his future.

Guillermo choked on a swallow, coughing. "Did you see her? You have to be kidding me."

Paulo waited, eyebrows lifted, clearly convinced there was more to the story.

"No, no. This is really just as I told you. I don't even know this woman. Besides she's too old, I think, and priggish. I'm not sure what she is, but certainly no *inamorata* of mine." He laughed softly. "You should know better, Paulo. I have high standards."

Although none were known to stick around very long, Guillermo always had a glamorous, beautiful woman at his side. Women seemed to like him very much, so that had never been a challenge.

Paulo laughed, "I do know, but seriously. You just rescued her? This doesn't seem like you."

"Certainly it does, *caro*." Pia entered the room with a plate of antipasti in her hand, bending to offer it to Guillermo. He helped himself to some prosciutto and olives. She met his eye with a smile. "My little brother is most selfless and benevolent. A *buon Samaritano*." She brushed his long hair from his forehead as she had when he was small, carried the tray to her husband, and bent to kiss his mouth. Then she set it on a small table and left the room. "You don't know him if you think he would leave a stranded lady on the roadside."

"Were you listening in?" Paulo asked, but she didn't reply, tossing a smile over her shoulder.

Both men burst into laughter as she walked away.

"It's true," said Guillermo, lifting his brows and giving his head a little shake, "I'm a saint," and they laughed again.

Just then the object of their conversation entered the room, and their laughter died in their throats. Guillermo glanced up into the most astonishing wide-set blue-green eyes, the color of the Ligurian sea, set in a lovely oval face, surrounded by a thick mane of stunning auburn hair loosely tied back. A Pre-Raphaelite painting. Such a plump mouth, wide and ripe for kissing. She was so much younger than he had thought.

He shot to his feet, nearly upsetting his wine. He set it down and strode toward her.

"Signorina! *Bella*. How well you look." He would have thought she was an entirely different person, but he knew there was no one else here but the housekeeper-cook. Clio had made a dramatic transformation into an exquisitely beautiful woman.

A pink flush rose into her alabaster cheeks. Delightful. "Thank you." Her gaze dropped shyly to the rug. "I…uh. Your sister was kind enough to lend me some clothes until mine are laundered."

Ochre freckles dusted her nose. An angry red lump swelled on her forehead. Her forearms were patched with bandages. He reached out to take her hand, bringing it quickly to his lips, so soft, she smelled like lavender and ointment. "They suit you very well."

The sound of Paulo clearing his throat brought him to his senses. He stepped back. "Ah. How rude of me. My sister's husband, Paulo Cittadini. Please meet Signorina Clio...em. '*Scusi*. I have forgotten again." His eyes met Paulo's, in which he saw the suppressed laughter and teasing that he kept from his face.

"Clio Sinclair McBeal." She narrowed her eyes and snatched her hand away from Guillermo, reaching for Paulo's, now standing beside them.

"You are not badly injured, I hope?"

"Not at all, *grazie*."

They shook hands, and Guillermo ruefully reviewed their playful conversation from a moment ago. This beautiful young woman he would gladly take to his bed. It seems his body knew better than his mind, even in the dark.

"*La ringrazio molto per avermi fatto benvenuto nella vostra casa,* Signor Cittadini," she thanked him. "I find I am at your mercy this evening."

Again Guillermo marveled at her excellent Italian. But for a slight accent, she could have been a native. Paulo said, "You are American, Signorina?"

"Please, call me Clio. Yes American and Canadian, both."

While her attention was focused on Paulo, Guillermo let his eyes roam over her. She was tall, as he had already observed. But in the dark, under the mud and wet shapeless clothing, the rest had escaped his notice completely–except for her breasts, of course. His body betrayed him with a hot spasm in the groin. Not only young, but beautiful. Pale and soft, with vivid eyes and hair, long limbs and luscious curves that had been hidden under her utilitarian trousers and shirt, and were now only hinted at under her sister's long silky skirt and sheer, flounced blouse.

Guillermo felt himself flood with warmth and stir in his trousers. What a surprise.

"A glass of wine, Clio?" Paulo offered, and she consented.

When Paulo had stepped out of the room, Guillermo recovered his manners and turned to her with a welcoming smile. "I am so happy to see you dry and comfortable, Clio. I hope you will not mind recovering here for the weekend. I am very happy to have the opportunity to get to know such a beautiful woman much better."

"For the weekend?" she squeaked. "Are we not returning to Florence tonight?"

Guillermo froze. *Eh?* "Tonight? Of course not. It will be much too late after dinner. And I came for the weekend. My visit here is long overdue, and my sister is expecting me to stay."

"That was before–"

"Not at all. You are as welcome as I am. You must stay also."

"But I have–"

Paulo returned with her wine. "Yes, I insist also. It is no imposition, I assure you. We have plenty of room."

"Oh no." She bit her lip, drawing Guillermo's attention to it's fullness and rich ruby color once again. "I don't mean to be ungrateful, but I have an appointment. It's very important."

"In Firenze? Tonight?" Paulo asked.

"Yes. I must–"

"It's much too late now, Clio. It would take us more than two hours in the dark," Guillermo said.

"But… did the police call about my car?"

"*Si.* They called. I'm afraid your car will not be transported to Montecchiello until tomorrow. And that's only if they can find the fellow with the truck on a Sunday. I told them you would contact them on Monday, and I can take you there on the way back to Firenze, as long as we leave early. I have a meeting in the city."

She seemed to deflate, and her aquatic eyes swam with tears. A long-fingered delicate hand rose to her brow. She had a red welt above her eye, and she flinched as she inadvertently touched it. "I'll be kicked out now. I have to call him. I have to…" She turned to Paulo. "May I use your telephone, please?"

Kicked out? Of where?

"Of course," Paulo said.

"Here. Use my cellular," said Guillermo, handing it to her. His chest squeezed with compassion. She was so overcome with some inexplicable grief. He felt a powerful urge to comfort her and protect her from whatever dire consequences seemed to await her late return to the city.

She took his phone and excused herself, retreating to the far side of the room, and slipped into an armchair facing the dark windows. He watched her anxious reflection in the glass as she dialed. He was quite overcome by her beauty and frailty, all the more so because it took him by surprise. He sensed a kind of stubborn strength in her, despite her having been overwhelmed by her traumatic experience.

"Hello? Dr. Jovi? It's me Clio."

Guillermo tried not to eavesdrop, but he was compelled by his curiosity. A doctor's appointment on Saturday night? He glanced up to find Paulo silently observing him, an expression of amused pity animating his face.

"…and so he brought me here, to a country estate. I won't be able to…"

"Uh. What's for dinner?" Guillermo asked half-heartedly, trying to tear his attention away from Clio. Whatever Pia served would be delicious, he knew.

"You'll find out." Paulo laughed, picked up the weekend newspaper and shook it out. He obviously knew Guillermo wasn't really listening.

"…so sorry, Dr. Jovi. I know I'm behind. I know I promised. I couldn't help…"

Surely no one could blame her for the accident. Guillermo stood up. He could help.

"*Scusi*, Clio. Please allow me, to vouch for, uh…"

Clio looked up at him, her distress apparent. She said nothing as he gently took the phone from her hand. "*Buonasera,* Dr. Jovi?"

The nasal, gravelly voice of an old man replied, "What? Who is this?"

"This is Guillermo Gabriel d'Aldobrandin."

"D'Aldobrandin…of the uh, *il Ministro dei MIT?*"

"*Si.* My brother Jacopo. It is I who came upon Signorina Sinclair this evening, after the automobile crash. It is very lucky for her that I arrived on the scene."

"Indeed?"

"*Si.* I believe she would have suffered hypothermia if she had stayed out any longer, although her injuries, thankfully, are not serious. I assure you the young lady was not to blame in any way. It was a terrible accident caused by some delinquents. She is very distressed that she cannot keep her appointment this evening. She has tried to persuade me in every way that it is essential, however, I cannot return her to *la citte* until Monday, perhaps midday. Once we have investigated the condition of her wrecked vehicle in Montecchiello."

"Oh? Is that so?"

"*Si.* It is. I trust you will be able to reschedule this important engagement with Signorina Sinclair? I would feel personally responsible if she were penalized on my account."

A gruff noise emanated from the phone. Guillermo did not know what to make of this taciturn old man. "Please put Clio on the phone, *Signor.*"

"Of course. *Buonasera Dottore.*" Guillermo handed the phone back to Clio with a reassuring smile, though he was no further enlightened as to the nature of Clio's emergency, or the identity of the old man, and could by no means assure her that disaster had been averted.

Clio listened as the old man apparently found plenty of words for her ears, and Guillermo backed away, returning to his chair and his glass of wine. Again he met Paulo's eye, and between them they silently agreed the whole business was strange. "Way to name-drop, *fratello*." Paulo's newspaper came up again, and Guillermo sighed.

"But I have." Clio exclaimed. "Everything became clear today, Dr. Jovi. I was going to write it up before our meeting. I see it now."

Guillermo's ears pricked up again.

"Yes, of course, I have photographed it and made sketches. Mm-hmm."

Her voice had altered, growing impassioned and musical. "The painting of Saint Clare of the Cross at the Franciscan Monastery was a revelation. It was so like Bernini's Saint Theresa, and yet not. The situation was different, not so public. There was a unique quality to her ecstatic state.The artist is unknown, but yet very talented. Her swoon is most exquisite. One can only assume the artist knew his subject very intimately. And it pre-dates Bernini. Yes. And if you have not seen the blissful expression on the upturned face of the little saint, Dr. Jovi, then you must make the pilgrimage one day to see it in person."

Guillermo leaned forward and peered at the glowing reflection of Clio in the window glass. Her posture had changed. She sat upright, and her face was open and animated. Instead of folded inward and contained, her body moved energetically and expressively, her hands drawing languid arcs in the air. The scene caused a stirring in his loins, yes; how could it not given the subject matter and the messenger, but also a pressure in his chest. An acute tension. Her passion for her subject moved him, as it transformed her. And if he thought she was beautiful before, now he could see that there was much more to this enigmatic woman who had fallen into his lap.

"Dinner is ready, everyone," announced Pia as she strode into the salon. "Please come to the table. Oh. I'm sorry, Clio, I didn't realize you were on the phone."

"No. I'm finished. It's alright." Clio stood up, once again

reserved and polite, but a rosy flush remained on her cheeks, and her eyes were dark and bright with remembered excitement. Guillermo was smitten.

End of sample

Get your copy of The Art of Enchantment here:
The Art of Enchantment
Books2Read.com / AOE

ACKNOWLEDGMENTS

I have many people to thank for helping me bring this book, in particular, to all of you—not least of which are my family and friends for their continued love, encouragement, and support.

This manuscript has been a part of my life for many years. The original idea popped into my head during a long sleepless night of jet lag at a charming little inn in York, England—which provided the seed of inspiration for this story. Yes, it's a real place, though I've made it my own. That was in 2007!

The manuscript took shape, and was workshopped and made better, by colleagues at the 'Halloween Writers' group for years, as well as by cherished alpha reader Kyla Larson, while I figured out the story. Subsequently it was subjected to intense feedback from colleagues at a Banff Centre summer intensive on the novel under the wise tutelage of celebrated Canadian novelist and short story writer Audrey Thomas.

Later, just after winning a CIBA Chatelaine prize, a generous development edit by another notable CanLit author and mentor, Gail Anderson-Dargatz, helped me see further potential and outline improvements I might make. Yet it took years before I saw my way to making the necessary changes to create the story as it stands today.

Finally, I owe thanks to beta readers Diana Stevan, Gail Halverson, KT Litwin, all accomplished authors in their own right, as well as my most devoted reader-at-home, John Scott. And last, but certainly not least, thank you to my brilliant editor

Jennifer Sommersby for providing insightful review and advice to bring the story to its optimal form, and helping me to overcome the most stubborn of my quirks and shortcomings. Whatever faults remain, fall to me alone.

ABOUT THE AUTHOR

USA Today Best Selling author MaryAnn Clarke has been called 'an artist with words' and lauded for expertly drawn and lyrical prose that transports, descriptions that leap off the page, realistic, relatable four-dimensional characters, complicated relationships, and complex stories that grip your heart.

She is a Chatelaine Grand Prize winner and Next Generation Indie Book Award finalist for The Art of Enchantment, first in the Life is a Journey series about young women on journeys abroad who discover themselves and fall in love while getting embroiled in someone else's problems. Her Having it All series is about professional women struggling to balance the challenge and fulfillment of their careers with their search for identity, love, family and home. Her newest series include The Most UNLIKELY series and the Off the Grid Christmas Trilogy. The Reporter's UNLIKELY Reunion was first runner up for the Indie Author Project Contest Romance Prize. Secrets at the Aviary Inn is a Finalist for the CIBA Somerset Award for Literary Fiction.

Always eager to fill blank pages and empty canvases with

ideas swirling in her head, MaryAnn set out to write emotionally engaging stories that walk a tightrope between intelligent Women's Fiction and heart-warming Romance.

A polymath who studied Fine Arts, Urbanism, Architecture and Gerontology at university on both coasts of Canada, she turned to her first love, writing stories, when she realized she could have more fun with fewer rules to follow as an author, than working as an architect, or a university researcher. When not writing, she meditates while hiking wooded mountain trails, does yoga and Pilates to fend off decrepitude, reads eclectically, contemplates wormholes, experiments with painting abstract expressionism, kills plants and tries not to burn dinner while solving her next plot problem. Now that her chick has flown the coop, Clarke lives on beautiful Vancouver Island, Canada with her husband and cats. Although she knows she lives in Paradise, she still loves traveling the world in search of romance, art, good food and new story ideas.

Subscribe & Follow MACS!

Fans can get exclusive excerpts and inside scoops, and ideas that strike her fancy as well as a free novel by subscribing to her newsletters at:

https://www.subscribepage.com/maryann-clarke-author_book

WANT TO CONNECT WITH ME?

You can read more about MaryAnn and her books, or get in touch at:

www.maryannclarkescott.com
maryann@maryannclarkescott.com

www.ingramcontent.com/pod-product-compliance
Lightning Source LLC
Chambersburg PA
CBHW030919120726
47906CB00002B/395